VEE
AND THE BATTLE WITHIN

VEE
AND THE BATTLE WITHIN

JAG SHOKER

Copyright © 2024 by Jag Shoker

The right of Jag Shoker to be identified as the author of this work has been asserted by him in accordance with the Copyright, Design and Patents Act 1998.

All rights reserved.

No part of this publication may be reproduced, distributed, or transmitted in any form or by any means, including photocopying, recording, or other electronic or mechanical methods, without the prior written permission of the publisher, except in the case of brief quotations embodied in critical reviews and certain other uses permitted by copyright law.

This novel is entirely a work of fiction. All characters in this publication are fictitious and are the work of the author's imagination. Any resemblance to real persons, living or dead, is purely coincidental.

Cover illustration by Hannah Victoria Gregory.

ISBN: 9798328213356

1st edition | 2024

Non-fiction books by Jag Shoker:

Playing The Beautiful Game

The Seven Masters Moves of Success

You Will Thrive

For Dhyan, so you never forget what Viryam means.

Jag Shoker is a leading mind coach to a range of high-profile clients, working within business, professional sport and entertainment. He is also the author of the non-fiction books *Playing The Beautiful Game*, *The Seven Masters Moves of Success* and *You Will Thrive*.

Vee & The Battle Within is Jag's debut fiction novel.

www.jagshoker.com
@the_mind_coach

PART ONE

Manifestation

1

Breaking free

Come on, Vee. Just do it.

Everything hinged on this decision. Was it the right call? Was it the right thing to do? What might others think?

I got up from my desk but hesitated.

Don't back out now.

Nervously, I gathered my belongings, shrugged on my coat and headed where I needed to go. My colleagues looked up. They tracked my steps. They were supposed to be on their phones, blitzing sales calls, but all eyes were on me.

I reached the glass enclosure of the boss's office. She was on a call. I looked down at the ground and put my hands in my pockets. Her conversation went on for a while but I waited there, awkwardly, my pulse rate rising. Finally, she hung up. I lightly tapped the glass door. She looked up with obvious irritation but gestured impatiently for me to enter.

"What do you need?" she asked, making no attempt to disguise her annoyance.

"Um…"

I was still second-guessing how I should say what needed to be said.

"In your own time, Vee," she said, sarcastically tapping her watch.

Am I sweating?

I felt like I was sweating.

I bit my lip. "The thing is –"

"Yes."

"I can't work here anymore."

"What?" she replied, her face contorted with surprise.

"This job…it just isn't me."

I felt relieved I'd got my words out.

She jerked her chair back away from the desk and glared at me.

Well, this is awkward.

I tried not to flinch. I knew she was going to make this as painful as possible.

"What the hell, Vee? You've only been here for *one… bloody…week*!" she screamed, holding one finger in the air. "How do you know this job isn't for you?"

"I… just know."

I felt blood rush to my face.

"Do you know how hard I had to push to get you this job? You've got no sales experience, no track record. But stupidly I saw something in you."

"I'm sorry."

What else could I say?

She shook her head.

"I stuck my neck out for you. Now I'm going to look like a right twat."

It was probably the truth but I couldn't let her think that.

"No one will think you're a twat," I tried to assure her.

"Oh, be quiet. I should have listened to Matt." Matt was her boss. "He said you looked flighty."

Flighty? Ouch!

"Tell him it's my fault," I replied, feeling cut by her last remark.

Others had accused me of that in the past.

"Oh God, I intend to. It's not my fault you've turned out to be a complete time waster."

Neither of us said anything next. An uncomfortable silence settled between us like a thick blanket of air. I looked over my shoulder. The whole office was staring back at me.

I just want to get the hell out of here.

It was a shit place to work; Suffocating and stifling. How could anyone hope to succeed in an environment like this?

I stood there, unmoving, unsure of what to do or say next.

"Obviously, you don't need to pay me," I offered up apologetically, breaking the silence.

I felt bad for letting her down. Really, I did. So the last thing I wanted was payment for services not rendered. An honourable gesture, I thought. But evidently, it was the last straw. She jumped up out of her chair and sent it flying backwards.

"Just *fuck off!*" she screamed, pointing to the door.

Wow. I must have caught her at the wrong time.

I tried to apologise again, but she was seething so I decided it was best to remove myself from the situation. I left her office and briskly made my way through the sea of stunned faces.

For a second, I did loiter by one of the desks: Lisa's. She was cute. Very cute. Discreetly, she lifted her hand off her keyboard and waved goodbye.

"Call me," she whispered, more mouthing the words than saying them.

Out of politeness, I was about to say I would but, a further volley of insults from my now ex-boss sent me swiftly on my way.

Hastily, I made my way out of the small ground-floor office and down a short flight of steps which led onto a busy London street.

My heart was beating rapidly. I had no idea where I was going as I walked through the crowds of people jostling past me.

Then, it hit me – the full implication of what I'd just done.

Shit! I've just walked out on a job…again.

I stood there, my face between my hands. Twelve months ago, I was not the kind of guy who'd do something *so* impulsive. And yet, this was the *third* occupation I'd walked away from in just under a year.

Two conflicting feelings began vying for prime real estate in my mind. The first was embarrassment.

What are people going to think?

I'd only lasted in this job a week. A new record. Why did I keep hopping from one job to the next? Why couldn't I settle down? See anything through?

The way things were looking – despite all the advantages afforded to me from youth – it was unlikely I'd become even half the man my father was. A man who had overcome struggle after struggle.

Dad's going to blow his top.

I knew there would be consequences this time around. Dad was not going to tolerate my whimsicalness any longer. He'd already dropped that hint before.

I looked up towards the grey, overcast sky and grimaced. But, as a ray of sunshine broke through a small opening in the clouds – just on cue, as these things tend to happen – I discerned a second more positive feeling stir within me. Optimism.

At the tender age of twenty-five, great possibilities were still mine to pursue. I was sure in my heart that destiny had something special lined up for me. I'd felt that way since I was a kid.

I strode forward again down that crowded London street, this time with more zeal. Just ahead of me, a set of traffic lights turned red as a brand-new Porsche 911 pulled up at the lights, its metallic black paint gleaming.

I love that car.

Despite the clouds, the driver still wore a pair of aviator sunglasses. They looked good on him. The car looked good on him. The music playing from the Porsche's perfectly calibrated speakers hit all the right notes.

I stared at the car, then back at the man. He looked like he was writing his own rules. Like he had all the answers. The kind of man who was living *the* life.

I want to live that life.

Now, maybe I could. I was free once more to chase my own destiny. But what destiny was that? It was all a mystery to me back then.

If some fortune teller had told me then how I would arrive where I am now, I'd have called them crazy.

If I'd been told about the people I'd meet, the places I'd go, the celebrity circles I'd break into, I would've laughed in their face.

If that very same predictor of the future had told me about the reality-shifting spiritual phenomena I'd experience, I'd have politely asked them what, exactly, were they smoking.

And yet I narrate this story as a forty-five-year-old man who can look back on the past twenty years with a spectacular sense of wonder and, thankfully, with the veritable eye of wisdom that only hindsight can bring.

I started out, two decades ago, in search of two very conventional prizes: *fame and fortune*. But what I found was infinitely more rewarding, more worthy than all the external recognition in the world, and more valuable than all the trappings of success.

This book recounts that journey. It's an ego-bruising voyage. An unexpected struggle. A coming-of-age adventure. A battle within, between my ego and my soul. I hope it's a story that might just change your life. Perhaps the next one, too.

At times, the words I narrate may seem unbelievable to you; the path this story takes may stretch your idea of reality and its inherent possibilities. In fact, there is so much to tell you, I may not be able to confine the story to one singular book. But, this book will carry us a good distance along the way through tales of rising ambitions and thwarted desires; false dawns and inner struggles; fuck ups and surprising moments of spiritual awakening.

This is a story I feel compelled to write. It's one I nearly wrote twenty years ago. But, I was not ready to tell it then. I am now.

I assure you, every meaningful occurrence in the pages that follow is true.

Make of that what you will.

2

"*She's* better than a shrink."

Two days had passed by.

I was sat on the rooftop terrace of the small apartment I rented. Tell a lie, dad paid the rent. But not for long. It had been an ongoing arrangement. 'A little incentive', as he called it, for me to stand on my own two feet. But all that had changed now, after he'd just left my apartment, in anger.

Walking out on that shitty sales job had felt euphoric. Like a scene from a movie, with a pumped-up soundtrack playing in the background, firing up the motivational juices.

It had felt like a bold move. A demonstration of my self-belief. An act of faith in myself, my spirituality and the Universe's promise of abundance – reserved for all those courageous souls prepared to chase their destiny.

That's what I told dad.

He took a slightly different view on things.

"You're not a kid anymore," he said.

"*I know.*"

"So, when are you going to grow up?"

"Dad, I'm a man now, not a boy," I hit back.

"Then act like one."

I shook my head.

"Vee, when are you going to take responsibility for your own life? When are you actually going to see something through?"

It felt like he was wagging his finger in my face and I was an eight-year-old boy again.

I tutted back some incoherent reply.

"I didn't pay all that money for your education for you to waste your potential," Dad reminded me, *again*. "I did it so you might become someone one day."

There it was again. The pressure to be someone. Something exceptional. 'A man of influence' as dad liked to call it. He wanted me to be one of life's front runners leading the pack. A leading light others would look up to.

"You don't need to worry about me anymore, dad," I said, through clenched teeth. "The Universe has got my back."

Dad tutted. "You and your *bloody* spiritual clichés! It's not the Universe that has had your back all these years. It's me and your mother."

I shook my head.

Dad looked up at the ceiling, then back at me again with utter exasperation.

"We struggled, so you would never have to," he sighed. "But maybe that's the problem."

"What is?" I asked.

I had a bad feeling where this was going.

"You've never had to struggle. Perhaps that's what you need to do…work things out on your own for a while. See whether the Universe really has got your back."

I fell silent, but then the anger took hold.

"I'm not scared to go it alone," I said, outwardly defiant but inwardly afraid.

"Good," dad replied, with a steely look in his eyes, "because I'm turning off the money tap."

"Sorry, what?"

"The bank of mum and dad is closed," he said, making his point clear. "And it's not going to reopen until you get your act together. Until you prove you can make something of your life."

"Huh. Fine by me."

"Yeah, we'll see."

That's how we left things.

Dad had thrown down the gauntlet. I had fiercely accepted the challenge. But now, after he'd left in anger, I felt less bolshy. Less fearless. More concerned about how I was going to cover the cost of my extortionate rent. *And* everything else.

Just to point out the obvious, the rent never felt extortionate when dad was paying it. It did now, knowing payment would have to come from my own shallow pockets.

Dejectedly, I looked up to the sky and then back out at the view before me. There was an expanse of green trees. Beyond that, a panoramic view of London in the distance.

I loved that view. I loved what it represented – one of the greatest cities in the world, replete with no end of opportunity. Even for the most ambitious. Usually, that thought, and this view, never failed to uplift me. Not today.

With dad's words still ringing in my ears, I looked out over the wide vista before me.

What am I here to do?

I had no real answer. I felt vexed. I wanted to make my mark on the world. But how? I had no idea. Not because I lacked imagination. Quite the reverse. I had no end of ideas. But I was hopelessly caught between them all. I wanted to become someone.

But who?

I wanted to be something.

But what?

I scanned the London skyline. I looked for inspiration in the impressive landmarks that punctuated the horizon before me. But no joy.

Just then, a familiar thought popped into my head. I looked back into my apartment at the bookshelf below the wall-mounted TV. It contained a decent spread of books. Self-help, popular psychology and spiritual stuff.

I walked back inside and picked up a book without thinking. I flicked it open at random. It was something I liked to do every now and then. Invariably my eyes would land on some life-changing advice – on some words I needed to hear. Not this time. Only frustration came from these words I read:

When there is conviction in what you do, you will attract everything you need your way.

I tossed the book to one side.

How can I attract what I need when I don't know what I want to become?

How could I pay my own way when I didn't know what job to do? Just then my phone buzzed. A text message, from my mate Trev:

A few of the lads are going out for a drink. You coming?

I didn't need a second invitation.

It was 8pm. We met at a wine bar in Covent Garden. It was a charming place with exposed brick walls and arches.

One of the lads got the first round in. Trev got in the second. With the banter free-flowing, I held court for a while, telling the others how I'd just walked out on my job. I should say, this tendency to take centre stage was not unique to me. I was born into an extended family of showmen – something else I felt the pressure to live up to.

"Damn! I'd love to tell my boss where to stick his job," said Trev.

"Do it then!" I replied.

"Are you gonna pay my bills, big shot?"

I laughed.

"Didn't think so."

Trev reminded me, not everyone had a dad to bankroll their future.

I tutted back. My nostrils flared. Irritation took hold for a split second.

But Trev was just being Trev. It was just banter. I didn't rise to his comment. Besides, he didn't know the truth: dad was not bankrolling me anymore.

As Trev gassed away, my eyes caught sight of an attractive brunette sat at the bar. She was flanked on either side by a couple of lady friends. She looked over my way. I smiled. She smiled. That was my cue. This game of flirtation had become familiar territory to me. A welcome distraction from life's more serious preoccupations.

"I'll get the next round in, boys," I said.

Seizing the moment, I walked straight towards the brunette with well-rehearsed confidence and said: "So, I saw you looking at me, looking at you, and I wondered who looked at who first?"

She laughed. "I think we both know the answer to that."

"So... we agree, it was you."

She laughed again.

A good sign.

"Hi, I'm Vee," I said, extending out my hand.

"Rose."

"That's a nice name."

"Thank you."

"It's a beautiful symbol too."

"Really?"

I nodded. "The rose that transforms the air with its scent, is like a heart that radiates out its love."

"I see there's more to you than cheesy chat-up lines."

I laughed, bowing low before her.

"So, what do you do?" she asked.

"I'm kind of in between stuff."

That was about as honest an answer as I could give.

"What is it that you want to do?"

I shook my head. "I haven't got a fucking clue."

She giggled.

The conversation was progressing well, so I gave her a quick rundown of my recent life story:

How I'd walked out on that dead-end sales job.

How twelve months before I walked away from my first grad role.

How at the time, I thought I knew exactly what I wanted to become – an actor.

How I enrolled on a six-month drama course and loved every minute.

But how I became unsure of my next step when the course ended.

"So, what did you do?" she asked.

"I walked away from acting."

"But *why*, if you loved it so much?"

"I'm not sure."

The truth was I began doubting myself. I know others thought I had all the confidence in the world. Outwardly, I did. Inwardly, it was another matter. I questioned if I had what it took. What if I wasn't good enough? And acting was a competitive industry. What if I wasted my life chasing a dream, spending my most valuable years in some unproductive pursuit?

Some of my friends were already well up the career ladder. I didn't want to fall behind in the mad dash to get ahead. Back then, life felt like a race. And I wanted to be the front-runner.

"What is it that you *really* want to do?" Rose asked, with genuine interest.

"Right now, all I want to do is … talk to you."

"Aww. I'm flattered. But seriously. What's your dream?"

I shrugged my shoulders. "Depends."

"On?"

"What day you catch me. Sometimes, it's to be an actor. Some days it's making it big in business. Other days, I'm convinced I'm going to write a bestseller. One with a riveting plot line that might change the world in some beautiful way."

I studied her face to see if she was impressed. But her expression gave little away. She was rather reserved, but not in any way unfriendly.

She was just about to say something when someone grabbed me.

"There you are," said Trev. "I thought you were getting a round in? Trust you to go missing in a bar full of women."

Rose laughed and shook her head.

"I'm Trev," he said, reaching over me, and holding out his hand. "I'm Vee's more attractive sidekick."

Rose raised an eyebrow in good humour.

"Ok, maybe I'm not," Trev smiled. "But I'm way funnier, which reminds me, do any of your mates like average-looking guys with a killer sense of humour?"

Rose laughed. "I can only ask."

"Sorry," I interjected. "Normally, I'd just tell him to eff off. But I better get that round in."

"No problem," she replied. "But after, come and find me. I've got something for you."

Rose smiled and turned back towards her friends.

"You're *such* a lucky fucker," said Trev, as we turned away and faced the bar. "Life comes so easy to you."

Trev thought I lived a charmed life. But there was something he'd conveniently forgotten. When we were kids, Trev was better than me at everything. It seemed everyone was. I was *that* kid. The one who was always overlooked. The one who was always last in line.

My mind darted back to a painful memory:

1985 – a P.E lesson. I am the last kid waiting to get picked. Two team captains argue over why I *shouldn't* be in their team.

"You have him!" says the one.

"No, *you* have him!" says the other.

The rest of the class laugh, compounding my embarrassment. My lower lip quivers. I am close to tears. I am unable to hold them back. But the humiliation spurs me on. I get angry. I silently declare to myself: one day others will sit up and take notice of me. The vow rages within me. Like a burning fire, somewhere deep inside my soul.

"So, are you going to get her number?" Trev asked, breaking into my thoughts.

Trev assumed securing Rose's number was just a formality. But Rose seemed a tough nut to crack.

"Maybe," I replied.

"*Maybe?* If you don't want it, give it to me!"

We both laughed as the bartender came across and took our order. Once I'd got my round in I went back in search of Rose.

She was sat at the back of the bar chatting away with her friends. Their conversation hushed as I walked over. Knowing smiles spread across their faces as I drew close.

"So, what have you got for me then?" I asked her.

"It's not what you think," came the reply.

"Oh really? What is it?"

"I think I know someone who can help you?"

"He better be a good shrink," I laughed.

"*She's* better than a shrink."

Rose took a pen out of her handbag. She scribbled down a name and number on a napkin. She pushed it across the table towards me.

I glanced down at it.

"Who's Sophia?" I asked, reading out the name.

"Someone I know. Someone you should meet. Someone who can help you figure things out."

"What does she do?"

"She'll explain," she said, giving nothing more away.

I looked down at the napkin and then pushed it back in Rose's direction. "I'd rather have your number."

"Sadly, I'm taken," she replied, apologetically. "But take Sophia's number. It will be more valuable to you than mine."

I looked back down at the napkin. I was about to decline the offer when Rose interrupted me.

"*Take* the number. Call her. It might be the most important thing you do this week."

She picked up the napkin and held it out to me.

How bizarre.

Who the hell was this Sophia?

I was about to back away. But something made me take her number.

3

"We need to meet."

It was the next day.

Call her? Don't call her?

I kept toing and froing. I looked down at the napkin with Sophia's number scribbled on it.

I knew nothing about her. I'd got her number from someone I hardly knew.

Why on earth would I call her?

But I felt compelled to do just that. I needed to sort my life out.

Maybe she can help.

For the record, sorting out my future wasn't my only concern. The past too was a problem. Specifically, an unpleasant memory. It was of a strange – almost supernatural – experience I had on the night of my twenty-first birthday. It had scared me *shitless*. The months that followed it were dark and depressing. From time to time, it still cast a dark shadow over my thoughts. But I won't tell you about it yet.

I continued to stare down at the napkin, thinking back as I did to the events of earlier that week. I winced.

How nonchalant was I?

I began chastising myself for walking out on that job. And the one before. And for walking away from acting too. I couldn't go on like this. Just hopping from one thing to the next, being afraid to commit. Dad was right. I needed to grow up. No more being a kid. It was time to be a man. Time to prove to dad – to the world – that I could make something of myself, *by myself.*

I reached down, picked up the napkin and then my phone. Tentatively my fingers dialled the number. The line rang out a few times. I felt partly relieved there was no answer. I was just about to end the call when a voice spoke.

"Hello."

"Is… that Sophia?" I asked hesitantly.

"Yes, that's me. How can I help?"

Her tone was melodiously upbeat.

"Ok, this is going to sound stupid but someone I met in a bar gave me your number."

"Can I ask who?"

"Rose."

"Ah yes. Are you Vee?"

"Yeah. Look, this is all a bit weird, for me at least, but Rose insisted we should meet."

I winced again. The whole conversation felt absurd.

A thought suddenly crossed my mind: Rose and Sophia might be having a laugh at my expense. Or maybe it was a dare or a bet. I decided to proceed with caution.

"Well Vee, Rose doesn't give out my number willy-nilly. She must have had a strong hunch about you. I think we need to meet."

Need to meet?

A tad presumptuous, I thought.

But I was curious. I wanted to know who this Sophia was and how she might be able to help.

We agreed to meet.

The first of our many encounters was intriguing, to say the least.

4

Sophia

I was running late.

I ran full pelt to the café where we'd arranged to meet. I stopped yards just short of the entrance.

Right, come on, Vee. Compose yourself.

I tried to catch hold of my breath as I pushed open the café door.

Oh, man!

There was not a spare table in sight. I glanced down at my watch. I was fifteen minutes late and was now standing behind a long queue of people waiting to be seated.

That was when I *felt* her stare.

I looked across a little distance to my left. I saw a woman sat there, very upright on the edge of her chair. She had a Mediterranean complexion. Her hair was dark brown and tied back in a bun. She was casually dressed in blue jeans and a white jumper. She was staring right at me. Intensely.

"I take it you're Vee?" she called out.

She motioned for me to come and join her.

Awkwardly, I jostled past the queue and made my way across. Her light brown eyes met with mine. I was struck by the strength of her gaze. I felt uneasy. Exposed. Like she could see right through me. Right into my messy interior and jumbled up thoughts.

I sat down opposite her and crossed my arms.

"How did you know it was me?" I asked.

"Oh, I just knew," she replied casually, as though it was self-evident.

"Oh, ok."

"Although, I did wonder whether you were going to show up," she said, tapping her watch.

I squirmed. "So sorry I'm late."

"I'm just teasing," she said playfully, with a degree of familiarity which belied the fact we'd only just met.

"Let me get the drinks by way of an apology," I said getting to my feet. "What would you like?"

As I hurried off to order a latte for me and a decaf cappuccino for Sophia, I could still feel the weight of her stare. I glanced back over my shoulder. Our gazes met. She smiled. I smiled. Feeling uncomfortable, I turned the other way.

Seconds later, I looked back.

She's still staring.

We both smiled. Again, I was the first to flinch and look away.

Is she trying to psych me out?

If she was, it was working. I was feeling weirded out by it all. Furtively, I glanced back again, pretending to look at anything but her.

I wondered how old she might be.

Early thirties?

But she seemed older. More mature. But I couldn't put my finger on why. It was not down to the way she looked.

I ordered the drinks. The barista told me he'd bring them across, so I headed back to the table and sat back down. I readjusted my chair so it was not facing Sophia quite so directly. As I did, she brought the palms of her hands together and gently rested her chin on her fingertips.

"I know exactly why you are here," she said, smiling.

"*You do?*"

"I do," she replied confidently. "But why do *you* think you are here?"

The directness of her question surprised me.

"Like I told you, Rose suggested it. She said you might be able to help."

"With what?"

Not knowing where to begin, I hesitated.

"Take your time," Sophia said warmly.

I leaned my head back against the chair and started at the most obvious place – how I'd walked out of my job one week earlier.

I began narrating my tale, speaking rapidly and breathlessly as was my custom back then. Soon, I'd told Sophia everything about the last year of my life. The drama course. My desire to become an actor. The self-help books I'd read. The ideas they'd inspired. Like writing a book myself. Starting a business. Working in TV. All that stuff.

The minutes raced by. I continued to ramble on, giving in to my habit of circumlocution. Sophia for her part just listened intently without saying a word. She simply smiled. Nodded here and there, gesturing to me that she was following all that I was saying.

It was strange sitting there with her in this packed café. There were people having business meetings. Young students noisily chatting away. Mothers swapping stories with each other, as little toddlers sat on their laps or lay asleep in strollers that blocked the space between tables. I was aware of all that happening in my peripheral vision. And yet, as I told my tale, it felt like everything else was tuned out. Like it was only Sophia and I sat there in this coffee shop.

She waited patiently for me to finish. She was about to speak when the barista arrived with our drinks. He carefully placed them down on the table.

She waited for him to leave and then looked up to the ceiling, evidently weighing something up in her mind.

"Remind me, why exactly did you quit your job?"

"I didn't enjoy it. It's not what I wanted to do."

"I see. And what do you want to do?"

I shuffled uneasily in my seat. This felt like the beginning of a cross-examination. Her opening questions felt tough.

Hang on.

Something dawned on me. I knew nothing about this woman and I was telling her everything about me.

"Sorry Sophia, can I ask you a question first?"

She nodded and smiled.

"What exactly do you do for a living?"

"I wondered when you'd ask that," she replied unfazed by the question. "Let's just say I'm many things to many people."

"Ok."

"But think of me as a kind of acting coach for now."

"Oh right. So, you think you can help me make it? As an actor?" I asked shifting back in my chair.

"I want to help you become what you're destined to be. But being an actor may not be it."

What?

"So… how exactly do you propose to help me then?"

She calmly took a sip of her cappuccino. "Imagine life is a drama."

"Ok," I replied, unsure where she was going with this.

"In this drama, I want to help you play a certain role more effectively."

"Which role?"

"Being yourself."

"*Myself?*"

She nodded. "You're about to embark on a journey of self-discovery. It won't be easy."

I looked back at her sceptically. "Am I?"

She nodded again, as if absolutely sure. "There's a lot you don't know about yourself yet. You've got some major blind spots."

"Have I?"

"Yes. That's why you get so confused at times."

I tried to hide my defensiveness. But Sophia's confidence and challenging demeanour had put me on the back foot. It was not something I was used to.

She must have sensed my discomfort. In a softer tone, she said, "Can I ask you a question?"

"Sure."

"If your success was never in doubt, what would you choose to do?"

I shook my head.

"That's just it. I don't know!" I replied, surprised by the emotion my answer conveyed.

"You said you could be an actor."

I nodded.

"Or a TV presenter."

I nodded again.

"Or an author."

"Yes."

"What's the common theme here, Vee?"

I thought for a second. "They're not your typical 9-5 careers."

"What else?" she asked, trying to coax a deeper response.

"They're exciting careers."

My answer was part truth. Here's the whole truth: these careers could make me *famous*. Like so many hopeful wannabes, I'd glibly equated fame with success. I thought if I shot to fame, I could finally say: *I'd made it.*

Sophia considered my answer. "And what excites you about these careers?"

"They're a chance to do something inspiring. Something entertaining."

Something that would make me stand out. But I omitted that part, not wanting to come across as too obvious.

"Ok," Sophia continued, "so just pick a career and go for it?"

I started drumming my fingers on the coffee table. She was pushing me hard.

I stopped drumming. My head dropped.

"What if I fail?"

Sophia smiled.

"There you go," she replied, her tone encouraging. "*Now* we're getting somewhere."

Evidently, we'd made a breakthrough.

5

Observations

"Do you believe in yourself?"

Sophia was direct and to the point.

"Yes," I said instinctively, but not convincingly. "It's just the pressure that gets to me sometimes."

"What pressure?"

"To succeed. Or at least, not to fail."

Sophia nodded. "Belief so often is the defining line between success and failure."

"I know. But it comes and goes with me."

"How?" she asked, taking another sip of her cappuccino.

"I doubt myself. A lot. But then there are moments when I feel I can do anything."

"Like when?"

"When I believe in more than just me. When I believe in…"

I hesitated.

"In?"

"…God."

"Do you believe in God?"

I nodded back.

"I mean like *really* believe?"

She looked me straight in the eyes. I tried not to flinch.

"I do," I replied, as if sure of it in my soul. "I've always believed, ever since I was a kid, even when…."

I paused, checking back on myself.

"Even when?"

My mind flashed back to that time I didn't like thinking about. For a second darkness descended on my thoughts. I shrugged it off as best as I could.

"It doesn't matter," I said, not wanting to open up any line of discussion that would take me back there.

Thankfully, Sophia didn't push the issue. She sat for a moment looking into the distance, thinking intently about something.

"Can I share some observations with you, Vee?"

"Of course."

"They might be a little hard for you to hear."

Really? But you hardly know me, I thought.

Still, I wanted to hear what she had to say. Although I feared it too.

"I'm sharing this stuff because I feel you can handle it. Ok?"

I nodded.

Sophia leaned back and got more settled in her chair.

"Observation number one: you lack courage. Observation number two: you've got no conviction," she said, making a clenched fist with her right hand.

I was taken aback. It felt like she was calling me out.

"You've had it easy all your life. It's why you're always looking for the path of least resistance."

"Uh, ok," I mumbled back.

But, what do you even know about my life? I thought.

"You like the idea of following your dreams but not when things get hard. That's when you quit. You hardly ever see anything through."

I squirmed in my seat.

"But you don't have to see anything through do you?" she added, bringing her drink to her lips but keeping her eyes fastened on me.

"What do you mean?"

"You know your family is always there to support you, financially. But even with this great safety net, you still lack the courage to go it alone. You've never had the balls to follow your own path."

No balls?

But I couldn't deny it. Sophia had got me down to a tee. But how?

I tried to recall what I had and hadn't said to her. I'm sure I mentioned nothing about my family. I certainly hadn't said anything about dad pulling away my safety net – and my need now to make it on my own.

"Random question, is Vee short for anything?" she asked interrupting my thoughts.

"Viryam."

"That's a strong-sounding name. What does it mean?"

"It's Sanskrit. It means courageous, or something like that."

"Funny that," she said flashing a knowing smile in my direction. "Your name means courageous and the one thing you're lacking is… *courage*."

She paused to observe my reaction. "Shall I go on?"

I nodded back without saying a word.

"It's time to start practising what you preach, Vee. It's the only way you'll understand the difference between knowing *about* something and knowing *of* something."

I looked back at her with a blank expression.

"Knowing things in theory is very different to knowing them through hard-earned experience. You certainly talk a good game but have you really lived life?"

Sophia paused again as I sat there silently. Uncomfortably.

"Now this is particularly important," she said leaning in towards me. "Stop using your titbits of wisdom to dazzle others."

I smiled sheepishly. I did do that back then. I tried to cram as many quotes and aphorisms into my head as I could, for that reason. Sometimes it stressed me out. The limits of my head space, unable to keep up with my voracious need to know ever more and to be the smartest person in any room.

But, in defence of my younger self, I did like inspiring others with my spiritual soundbites too. I did like sharing beautifully packaged nuggets of wisdom with people which might shift their perspective to a better place – one more powerful and free.

"Share what you know to help, not impress others," Sophia continued. "It's vital you remember that."

She paused once again. I used the opportunity to gather my thoughts.

"How do you know all this about me?"

"Some things I've worked out from what you've said. Others, I just sense."

I felt exposed. But curious too.

"Just going back to what you said, about my lack of conviction," I remarked, shuffling in my seat, "how do I fix that?"

I purposely didn't mention anything about my so-called lack of courage. I didn't like the thought that I was somehow not brave enough.

"Do these three things," Sophia replied, as if already expecting the question. "One – learn to focus. Two – listen to your intuition. Three – have faith in your spiritual side but be patient with how it unfolds."

She paused there, giving me a chance to process her suggestions.

"Do these three things and you'll stop being so swayed by the opinions of others, Vee. Start looking *within* yourself now for the answers you need."

"But how?"

It all sounded easier said than done.

"A little more meditation, silence and self-observation will do you wonders."

Sophia glanced up at the large clock on the wall behind me. I looked back at it too.

"Wow," I said, noting the time. "The minutes have really ticked by."

"They have. I'm sorry to end it here but I've got to go."

We got up from our chairs.

"Thank you for today. I needed it."

"Yes, you really did."

"Can we keep in touch?" I asked as we made our way out of the busy café.

"Sure. Reach out when you need to."

We said our goodbyes and headed in opposite directions when Sophia suddenly called out: "I forgot to say, buy yourself a journal, Vee."

"A journal?"

"Yes, start documenting your experiences. Note anything significant, no matter how strange or trivial it might seem. Things are about to get quite interesting for you," she said, prophetically.

She smiled mysteriously and left.

I took note of her suggestion. I'm glad I did. If I hadn't, I might now be looking back into hazy recollections of the past asking myself - did all that really happen?

But everything that follows really did.

6

Heads, yes. Tails, no.

Focus.

Listen to your intuition.

Have faith in your spiritual side.

I reflected on Sophia's three suggestions as I queued up for my morning caffeine hit. I was stood outside a chic little coffee shop near Marble Arch; a favourite hangout of mine. Its coffee was that good there was always a queue winding out of its urban-styled interior.

Today was no different.

The wait in line gave me time to think. Two weeks had passed since Sophia and I had met. Her suggestions were clear enough. But I'd become more fixated on the shortcomings in character she'd pointed out in me:

A lack of courage.

A lack of conviction.

A tendency to quit when things got hard.

As I shuffled along the queue – finally making it inside the café – these flaws in my psychological make-up began to niggle away at me.

Am I that flaky?

But before my negative musings ran any deeper, I got distracted by a man further up the queue.

"Hey come on, man!" he shouted at the barista behind the counter. He spoke with an irate American accent – New York if I had to guess. "Speed up the show already!"

It suddenly occurred to me the queue was shuffling along much slower than usual. There was only one barista on duty. Not the usual three.

The barista was a young guy, about my age. I felt sorry for him. He worked tirelessly. Made each speciality coffee requested with no fuss, diligently wiping down his espresso machine, steam pitcher and frothing spoon for every new order. All this whilst taking more abuse from the tetchy American.

What an arsehole.

He spoke to the barista like he was beneath him. Like he was nothing. I felt like giving the American a piece of my mind but I didn't want to make an awkward situation worse. Thankfully, after ten excruciating minutes, he left with his grande, triple, soy, no-foam latte in hand.

Finally, it was my turn to be served.

"What can I get you?" asked the barista, rubbing his forehead with the side of his arm.

An extra hot hazelnut latte.

That was what I wanted but I couldn't put him through the ordeal of making one.

"Just a bottle of water, mate," I said.

He looked relieved by my simple request.

"Tough day at the office?" I asked him, as he pulled the water out of the fridge behind him.

"You could say that," he nodded. "That'll be one pound fifty, thank you."

"I would have told that American guy exactly where to shove his soy-no-foam-latte," I said, as I paid for the water.

The barista smiled, tiredly. "Believe me. Nothing would have given me more pleasure. But I can't afford to lose this job. I've got a young sister to look after and a sick mum who can't work."

"Oh," I replied.

The barista's admission felt more like a steely reminder to himself rather than any attempt to seek sympathy for his difficult plight. I was about to say something in reply but he was already serving the next customer.

I walked out of the café feeling guilty. Here was a young guy working his guts out to provide for his family. And here was me – whimsical me. Flighty. Flaky. Nonchalant. Walking out on jobs left, right and centre because they weren't quite my cup of tea.

The barista had a powerful motivation: *necessity*.

But what was mine?

I considered the question as I found myself aimlessly strolling through Hyde Park on what was a cold winter's day. The answer hit me quickly enough. I had a point to prove. I wanted to show dad I could take care of myself. Show him I had the guts to see something through.

I thought back to Sophia's three suggestions and shook my head. I hadn't even been able to see them through. In fact, I'd actually followed the exact opposite of her advice.

In the last two weeks:

I exhibited no mental focus. My mind just hopped from one thing to the next: signing up with a talent agency; sketching outline book ideas on random bits of paper; talking to friends about start-up business ideas.

I didn't listen to my intuition. I just talked incessantly to others about my future. I asked them what they would do in my position. Some said: be bold, follow your dreams. Others said: play it safe. All the different opinions just left me more confused.

I showed no faith in my 'spiritual side'. Uncertainty just got the better of me.

As I walked through the park, kicking wet leaves off the ground, I took a fifty pence coin out of my pocket to play heads or tails with my future.

Write a book? Heads yes, tails no.

I flipped the coin.

Tails.

I didn't like the answer. I flipped it again.

Should I become an actor? Heads no, tails yes.

Heads.

I didn't like that answer either. But I couldn't be bothered to flip the coin another time.

Tired of my mental deliberations, I sat down on an empty park bench and buttoned up my coat. The barren leafless trees around me summed up my mood.

I reached into the thin leather briefcase I was holding and pulled out my journal.

I read the last thing I'd written:

Act with courage to bring your dream to life :)

I felt agitated re-reading it. I needed to act but I didn't know what to do. Even if I did, the fear of failure was holding me back. If only I could admit it, my lack of courage was crippling my dreams before they'd even had a chance to see the light of day.

Old fears began taking root again:

What if I never amount to anything?

What if I waste my potential?

What if I have blown my parents hard earned money on a wasted education?

So much pressure.

I felt like there was now a ticking clock in my mind. I had to prove myself and fast. The longer I didn't succeed in making something of myself the more others would doubt me. The more I would doubt myself.

Huh.

I looked off into the distance, staring at nothing in particular. My mind drifted back in time. To my childhood:

1990 – I find myself in a new position. I've gone from being the unfancied kid at school to one of the leading lights. I'm sitting with my headmaster in his office.

"I must say, we're all rather surprised you've won the academic scholarship," he says clapping his hands together.

"How come, sir?"

"Well, quite frankly, Vee, when you first arrived at the school, we all thought you were rather thick!"

He laughs. I smile.

I know in the past I've been a slow starter. But not now. Things are going really well. Across the board, I'm excelling. But the expectations of me have gone from nothing to sky-high. *Too high*. I feel a change taking place within me: I'm scared now to fail.

Unbeknown to me at the time, this was a turning point in my life. With a growing reputation, came growing pressure. From that moment on, part of me started playing it safe. Only doing what I knew I could do well. But not pushing my limits beyond this. Or trying anything new or risqué. Not now, fearing I had *an image* to protect.

But I didn't want to live like this. I didn't want to sit around twiddling my thumbs, holding myself back. I wanted to be more. Do more. Prove to myself and the world I could amount to something. Something that would command respect, where no one would ever have the temerity to talk down to me like the American had done with that poor barista. I wanted people to look up to me. Cast admiring glances in my direction.

I need to do something that will set me apart. But what?

How could I prove myself, if I didn't know what I wanted to do?

My mind felt dull. I felt defeated. I slumped back into the park bench. I took a deep breath in and sighed, releasing a small cloud of misty air which floated up and away from me.

I closed my eyes. Rolled my neck from side to side. An unexpected dose of microsleep assailed me. My head dropped forward and then jerked back violently.

Ouch.

Instinctively I grabbed hold of the newly formed crick in my neck. I rolled my neck again from side to side. It was racked with tension. It always was back then.

I really need a massage.

On cue, my mind drifted back to a quaint spa I'd walked past the other day. Near Marylebone station. I'd taken note of its number. I called to see if they had any appointments. To my surprise, one was available almost immediately.

"We've just had a cancellation. Can you get across here in thirty minutes?" said the voice at the other end of the line.

"Yes, yes, I can," I replied, rising quickly from the bench.

"Great, you'll be with Lauren. Can I take your name?"

"It's Vee."

I decided to walk rather than catch the tube. I thought the fresh air would do me good. But I got caught up on the way. I noticed an elderly couple trying to cross a busy street where there were no traffic lights. No one was paying any attention to them. I knew I might be late but I couldn't just leave them there. I ran across to their aid.

"Do you need a hand getting across?" I said, when in touching distance of them.

"Oh, that is so very kind of you," they both replied.

When I saw an opening, I stepped into the road and ushered them across, holding up my hand to halt the traffic on either side. A couple of cars honked impatiently. I did my best to ignore them.

"God bless you," they both said, after safely reaching the other side.

Their faces were lit up with gratitude.

On account of my love for my grandad, I always had a genuine affection for the elderly. And concern.

We chatted briefly. I waited for a natural break in our conversation, said my goodbyes and then made a mad dash to the spa.

It was located on a quiet side street, set within a row of Georgian terraces. I arrived five minutes late. I wiped away the beads of sweat running down my forehead as I walked in.

A young blonde-haired woman with a neatly braided French plait looked up from behind the front desk. We were the only two people there.

"Vee?" she asked in a mild accent which I couldn't quite place.

"Yes. Lauren?"

She smiled and nodded. "It's good to meet you. If you'd like to follow me, it's this way."

What followed next, caught me by complete surprise.

7

The clairvoyant

I was lying face down on a heated massage bed.

The room was dimly lit with candles. Soft meditation music played in the background. Scented incense infused the air. Lauren began gently soothing my aching muscles.

Oh. She's good.

She worked silently without saying a word. Then, she said something completely unexpected.

"I'm not just a masseuse," she whispered, close to my right ear.

Hello.

What kind of an establishment was this?

I lifted my head to one side and looked up at her.

She smiled back. Was this a Candid Camera moment?

I was about to jump up off the bed with nothing but the towel to hide my modesty. Seedy rub-downs or whatever else I thought she was about to offer were not my style. Thankfully she quickly clarified her meaning.

"I'm also a clairvoyant," she said. "And I'm picking up *a lot* of information about you."

What?

"Seriously?" I replied, raising an eyebrow.

Lauren nodded. "Would you like a reading? There's no extra charge."

She'd caught me by complete surprise. I wasn't expecting that. We had a couple of very amateur palmists in the family. Ones that would tell you about your lifeline and love line but couldn't remember which way around was which. But I'd never had my future told. I'm not sure if I wanted to either. What if she revealed something I didn't want to hear? Or she told me I was destined for failure, not success? What if she confirmed my deepest fear? That I might not amount to anything special. That I might not become what I felt the need to be: a cut above the rest.

But the temptation was too much. My curiosity was aroused.

"So," she said. "Shall I begin the reading?"

"Um. Yeah. Why not," I replied, making up my mind.

Keep your cards close to your chest, Vee.

I decided to not give her any information of my own accord. Nor would I confirm or deny anything she said.

Never once stopping the massage, Lauren began the reading.

"Your energy levels are low," she said speaking in a hushed but more definite tone of voice. "It's due to mental indecision. You're at a crossroad. You don't know which way to go."

True.

But it could be true of anyone.

"You're surrounded by opportunities," she continued. "But the fear of commitment and failure is holding you back."

There was silence for a minute.

"You're a free spirit who keeps hopping from one thing to the next. And yet on another level, you are very mentally focused. You're poetic and creative too. It's a side of you that others don't yet see. At the moment, you're perceived as being a rather complex character."

I had to admit, her words were close to the truth.

"I'm being told you need to take *action*," she continued, placing particular emphasis on that last word. "By not acting with a definite desire, you're not allowing the Universe to give you what you want."

My mind began racing. Everything appeared to be pointing this way. Life's message seemed clear: *Act. Make something happen, Vee.*

After another pause, Lauren continued the reading.

"Just do something. Whatever you do, whatever you attempt, ultimately you will not fail. One thing will keep leading to another. The right doors will keep opening. The right opportunities will keep coming. People too will be drawn to you. But they may not know why."

Another pause.

"And stop doubting yourself," she began again. "You *will* be successful. By the age of thirty-five, you will have found your calling. That thing you are here to do."

Thirty-five!

That was a lifetime away.

"But what *is* my calling?" I asked.

I needed to know now. Not in ten years.

"You'll find out," she replied, firmly. "Stop being in such a rush. Patience is one of your weakest attributes. But…"

She paused.

"But what?" I asked, eagerly.

"Something *will* happen in the next three weeks. A major development on the job front. It will help you settle and focus."

There was silence for several minutes as she continued only with the massage.

I lay there spellbound. I was about to ask another question when she spoke again.

"Your grandad…"

Grandad?

"What about him?"

"I'm being shown how spiritual he is. Much more than he lets on. He's guiding you. He wants you to fulfil your potential."

This last point was true. He took a real interest in my life.

Nothing more was said in relation to my future. Instead, Lauren began revealing things about herself. How she'd spent the last twelve months of her life under the guidance of a spiritual teacher. How before that she was a bit wild and off the cuff. How now she'd settled down and dedicated herself to the spiritual path. She told me she had developed her psychic abilities through dreams which turned out to be accurate premonitions.

"At first I was scared by it all," she said, massaging my scalp. "But now I'm comfortable with my gift."

God, I had so many questions I wanted to ask but just then she gently struck a small brass gong. The massage was over. The reading had ended.

"Please don't mention any of this when you come back out to reception," she whispered, leaning in close again. "The other therapists don't know I'm clairvoyant."

"I won't," I replied, reassuring her.

She left me to get dressed. I sat up and puffed out my cheeks.

Did that really just happen?

This was my first ever encounter with a psychic. It felt awesome. Surreal. Otherworldly. It would not be the last time a psychic crossed my path. Others would come out of the blue, to give me faith when needed.

I got to my feet, buzzing with a newfound excitement. Whether any of the reading proved true or not, one thing was clear. It was time to do something – *anything*.

The Universe it seemed would take care of the rest.

8

More courageous

I headed home on the Underground. My mind churning over with thoughts.

I watched the hordes of passengers come on and off the packed carriage I was squeezed up in. Did any of them know their future like I now knew mine?

I mentally replayed everything the clairvoyant had said. I felt upbeat. Uplifted. I wanted to book in for another reading. But I told myself to not be so over-eager. Besides, at fifty pounds a massage, I couldn't just book in again. I had to be more responsible now with my pecuniary affairs after dad had cut off my line of credit.

Sophia's name then crossed my mind. She'd said things were going to get interesting. They had indeed.

Shall I call her?

Would I be imposing? Was it too soon to call again?

When I jumped off the Tube at my stop, I stepped to one side of the busy platform and took out my fifty pence coin.

Heads, I'll call her. Tails, I won't.

I flicked up the coin.

Heads!

Perfect.

I was happy with what 'destiny' had decided. Although, I'd just have flipped the coin again if it had landed on tails.

I called Sophia. We arranged to meet for a second time.

It was two days later.

We were face to face once more in the same packed coffee shop where we'd first met. The hustle and bustle around us meant no one would overhear our conversation. That suited me perfectly.

After exchanging pleasantries Sophia cut to the chase.

"So, what's on your mind?"

"You were right."

"About?"

"Things getting interesting. I had this bizarre experience the other day."

Sophia cocked her head to one side. "Did you, now?"

I nodded. "Listen to this…"

I told her everything I could remember about my psychic encounter. But instead of playing out what Lauren had said in the order it happened, my mind hopelessly hopped around in the back-to-front way it remembered the conversation.

I was in full flow when I became conscious of how Sophia was looking at me. At the space *around* me, as if I had an aura and she could see it.

I paused.

"Don't stop," she said. "I am listening."

"Um. I forgot what I was saying."

I'd lost my train of thought.

"You were about to reveal Lauren's two predictions."

"Oh yeah," I replied, becoming animated again. "She said by the age of thirty-five I'll have found my calling and that something *major* is going to happen in the next three weeks."

Sophia raised an eyebrow but was otherwise unmoved.

"How crazy is that?" I said, wide-eyed.

Sophia rolled her eyes and smiled.

"Oh, Vee. I could have told you all of that."

What?

Was she implying Lauren's clairvoyance was nothing to get excited about? Or that she herself was psychic? Or, that Lauren's reading was nothing more than clever conjecture?

Sophia interrupted my mental speculations.

"Well, you've always been a doubting Thomas. Maybe if her predictions come true your faith might grow."

Always been a doubting Thomas?

She'd casually reeled off the sentence like we'd known each other forever. She acted that way too.

"Do you think there's truth in what she said?" I asked, pressing on with the conversation.

"Maybe. Maybe not. Time will tell. Nothing about the future is ever set in stone. Much will depend on you."

"On me?"

"Yes. On the decisions you make."

"Can you see the future?"

I felt childish asking the question.

Sophia didn't answer.

Bizarrely, she reached over and pinched my bicep. "Have you got a pain here?"

"Yeah, how did you know?"

"Oh, it just flashed up at me," she said casually.

My jaw dropped. I looked back at her in disbelief. "It flashed up at you? How?"

"Like a little light. It's just a slight blockage in one of your meridian channels. Nothing to worry about."

Sophia's eccentricity caught me by surprise.

"Are you clairvoyant too?" I asked.

"Not really," she replied, evasively. "But if there's something I need to know life has a way of revealing it to me."

Suddenly, my mind was caught between two different speculations. Did Sophia have extra sensory powers? If so, what more might she be able to reveal about my future?

"Do you think I will find my calling by the age of thirty-five?"

Sophia was about to reply but hesitated.

She looked up to the left and then to the right as though playing out some inner conversation that I wasn't party to.

"No. No. No. That can wait for another day," she said quietly to herself. "Let me start with this. Stop thinking so much about the future. Slow down, Vee. Focus on where you are right now."

"Uh, ok."

I felt annoyed. She'd totally disregarded my question.

"And speaking of slowing down," she continued, "don't even get me started on the way you talk."

"What's wrong with it?" I asked, screwing up my face.

"You talk so fast, Vee, your words carry so little effect. Learn to wait…pause…*think*… before you clothe your thoughts in speech."

My jaw tightened.

"And stop starting one sentence before you've finished another."

"Do I do that?"

"*Yes,* and it makes you so hard to follow. If you really want to make your mark on the world one day, master the art of speaking with more power."

She let those words hang in the air for effect. They reminded me of being that *man of influence* dad always spoke about; of being the front runner in my family. A thought that had been powerfully engrained into my mind.

"As for your mind," Sophia continued, shaking her head. "It's full of static."

"Static?"

"Yes, electrical fuzz. All haphazard and noisy."

She was right there. Thoughts were forever whirring around in my head.

"Is it really possible to quieten the mind?" I asked.

She nodded.

"But how?"

"*Meditate*. You already know all this," she said, as though I was a seasoned monk. "It's only through a quiet mind you'll hear your soul. It's your soul that will guide you to your calling."

I looked back at her doubtfully. "Am I ever going to find out my calling?"

"As I said before," she spoke firmly, "trust your spiritual side but be patient too. The answers you need *will* come."

I tutted. I didn't mean to but I did.

"But I need answers now," I moaned.

"That right there is the crux of your problem. Everything you know is straight out of a book. You have knowledge but no faith. Concepts but no courage. Passion but no patience."

I rubbed the back of my neck. "Ok. I get that. But can't you tell me anything right now that will point me in the right direction?"

Sophia weighed up the question.

"Vee, if I just give you the answers I'll deprive you of the joy of discovering them for yourself."

I looked back at her pleadingly.

"Ok. Maybe I can ask you a few questions."

"Yes, anything," I replied, shuffling forward in my seat.

"Last time we met, you mentioned the thought of writing a book"

"Yep."

"If you had to stake your whole future on writing that book and it being a success, could you?"

I hesitated. "Um, no."

"And the business ideas you have been entertaining. Would you invest a hundred thousand pounds of your own money in any of them?"

I thought long and hard about it.

"No."

Sophia's questions were cutting through my whimsical fancies with ruthless ease.

God, what is she going to ask me next?

But just then, there was a loud shriek.

"Thief!" a woman cried out. "He's stolen my bag!"

I turned around. A young kid in a hoody was running right towards us, clutching a handbag.

What happened next, happened rapidly.

I froze but Sophia stuck out her foot. She tripped up the teenage delinquent and leapt onto his back when he was flat out on the floor. In the blink of an eye, she had his arm behind his back and her knee between his shoulders.

I, like everyone else watching, gasped.

The young kid spat out a few choice words. I had to hand it to him, together they formed an interesting combination of expletives.

Sophia leant down and whispered something into his ear. He was surprisingly attentive. Immediately, he let go of the handbag. Sophia set him free and he scarpered out of the café, falling over a stroller as he went.

Sophia picked up the handbag and calmly walked over to the elderly lady who it belonged to. She handed it back to her with a kind smile and some comforting words. The lady looked overcome with shock and gratitude.

"Bloody hell! That was impressive," I said when Sophia returned.

Sophia waved away my compliment, as onlookers cast admiring glances in her direction. I was surprised there wasn't a ripple of applause.

"What did you say to the little shit?" I asked.

Sophia smiled. "I told him, 'You've just got taken down by a woman half your size who's old enough to be your mum. If you don't want your mates to know about it, *let go* of the bag!'"

I laughed. "Next question, where did you learn those moves?"

Sophia laughed. "Let's just say, I've been quite the martial artist in a past life or two."

Past life?

I looked back at her as if to say: *are you serious?*

But Sophia quickly moved the conversation on. "So, where were we?"

"I just told you I couldn't invest a hundred thousand pounds of my own money in any of my business ideas."

"Ah, yes. So, moving onto the whole acting thing, what about it do you like?"

I looked up into the air. "Umm, playing different characters."

"Which characters?"

"Never really thought about it."

"I know. That's why I am asking you. Ok, out of choice would you choose to play a hero or a villain?"

I pursed my lips.

"…probably the hero," I replied, feeling shallow. I'd definitely watched one too many Bollywood movies growing up.

"But if life gave you a choice between playing a hero in Hollywood or being a hero in real life, what would you choose?"

I felt split.

"I'd choose to be a real-life hero," I replied, saying what I thought she wanted to hear. Especially, after witnessing her heroics moments earlier.

"So, be *that*. Do what all real heroes do – start acting with more courage in your own life."

Sophia's words instantly resonated. They lit a spark within me. I sat up straighter in my seat.

Just then, her phone vibrated.

"I'm sorry. Got to go, Vee."

I glanced down at my watch. I couldn't believe an hour and a half had passed so soon.

"Thank you for today," I said, getting to my feet. "I feel a lot clearer."

"Good."

"What do I owe you for this session?"

"Nothing."

"*Nothing?*"

"It doesn't feel right charging you."

"But why?"

"I'll tell you another time. But for now, promise me one thing."

"Sure, what is it?"

"One day, someone will come to you seeking help like you have come to me. When they do, pay it forward. Help them. Ok?"

I assured her I would.

As she walked away a surge of conviction coursed through me.

Now we're getting somewhere.

Sophia may have flattened that mugger, but she left me feeling all uplifted.

It was time – to be the hero of my own story.

9

Grandad

Be more courageous. But how?

I had to land a job and keep it. Show dad and everyone else I could see something through and make a success of myself.

But time was my biggest foe. I needed more patience and a stronger belief that everything would come together in time. Perhaps time then was also a gift. Like Sophia had said, I needed to think, speak and act with more power. That was going to take time. I sensed no easy fixes on that score.

But where should I begin?

Somewhere. Anywhere, Vee.

That was Lauren's advice.

A few days later, an intriguing next step emerged. I wrote it down in my journal:

> **Visualise what you want**
>
> **until you manifest what you desire.**

I'd read the line in some New Age book on manifestation. Instantly, I liked the idea. I went to work on it straight away. Every day, at the same time in the same place, I sat down cross-legged with my eyes closed. I relaxed my whole body, one muscle at a time and imagined with unshakeable belief (as directed by the book) that the universe was bringing the ideal job my way. I tried to feel this belief pulsating in every cell of my body. I promised myself: *when* life opened the right door, I'd walk right through it. Decisively. Courageously. Fearlessly.

The stage was set. I just needed that door to open.

I honestly thought some miraculous lead would come my way. Surely the significant development on the job front that Lauren had predicted would manifest in some glorious fashion.

But nothing happened.

No inner guidance flowed. No external signs pointed the way. No earth-shattering moments of destiny appeared. I grew restless. Patience was not my forte back then. It wasn't a mental muscle I'd developed yet with any degree of power.

As the days rolled on, I was assailed by a whole army of nagging doubts. What was I doing? Was the power of attraction even real? Could I just let go and trust the universe to bring my way what I desired? Was I just abdicating responsibility for my future to some higher power I had no proof actually existed?

On the ninth day, my mind rebelled.

"Arggghh. This is not working," I shouted out in frustration.

The meditative pose I was sat in was clearly not infusing me with any sense of calm. I felt pissed off. The last nine days – a long span of time when you're impatient – felt like a complete waste.

How ironic.

All that effort to feel unshakeable belief coursing through every cell of my body just saddled me with a whole heap of doubt.

Just then, my phone began vibrating. It was on the floor next to me. I glanced down. It was grandad:

"Hello, Papa."

"Viryam!" he replied in his characteristically strong tone.

I smiled. No one except him called me by my full name.

"I haven't seen you for a few days. Why don't you come and see me?"

I told him I'd come straight over. I had nothing better to do.

An hour later, I arrived at my parent's home in the leafy suburb of Hampstead. I still retained a set of keys to the house so I let myself in and shut the door behind me.

My mum appeared in the hallway. "Ah, Vee, it's you."

She hugged me tightly and playfully refused to let go. I bent low and embraced her affectionately.

"Hi, mum."

"What a lovely surprise. I wasn't expecting you. Is everything ok? You're not poorly, are you?"

She frowned suddenly and put her hand on my cheek to check my temperature. Now, two things defined mum. A heart that had no end of love and a mind that had no end of worry.

"Mum, I'm fine," I smiled, reassuring her.

"No, something's wrong. You wouldn't be here otherwise."

"Nothing's wrong mum. Papa just asked me to come and see him."

"Oh. I see. Well, he's upstairs in his room."

I kissed her on the cheek and was about to make my way to grandad when mum stopped me.

"Vee, do you need any money?"

I shook my head. I felt a tad annoyed. Did mum think I was incapable of earning my own money?

"I won't tell your dad if you do need some," she added.

"*Mum*, don't worry. I can take care of myself. But thank you anyway."

After making further attempts to reassure her, I made my way up to grandad's bedroom. I walked in on him doing some light squats. Impressive, for a man touching a hundred. Grandad always had this philosophy of working hard but never too much. My mind shot back to the first time he told me this:

1992 – I'm fifteen and flushed with testosterone. I'm in my bedroom doing weights. Grandad passes by my door. He pauses.

"Check this out, Papa."

I point to all the weight racked up on my barbell. It is the most weight I've ever lifted.

Grandad watches with amusement and pride as I squeeze out as many reps as I can. My face is all contorted with tension. My veins are about to pop. I push out one final rep before violently dropping the barbell on the floor.

Grandad walks up to me. He puts his hand on my shoulder and says: "Remember: in all things, never too little, never too much."

It was sage advice. What scientists refer to as the Goldilocks Zone. Or, *'eighty percent is perfect'* as the zen saying goes.

Grandad finished the last of his squats.

"Viryam! How are you?"

He walked over, upright and regal as he greeted me.

"I'm ok," I replied, sitting down on the edge of his bed.

Grandad adjusted his turban, smoothed out his flowing white beard and sat down next to me.

"Do you know, God came and met me today," he said, taking hold of my hand.

"Really? What did God say?" I asked, playing along.

"Nothing," he smiled. "He just came and sat in my lap."

"*God sat in your lap?*"

"Yes. I was in the temple praying, when a little child came and sat in my lap. He looked up at me and smiled. It was like God himself was smiling at me through those happy innocent eyes."

Grandad's eyes welled up. They always did when something pulled on his heartstrings. A single solitary tear fell down his cheek. Then another. With no sense of rush, he wiped them away.

"Anyway, tell me. Have you found another job?"

"Not yet."

Grandad nodded thoughtfully. "You know your father is concerned about you."

"Yeah, he is," I replied, feeling my jaw clench. "That's why he's cut me off."

Grandad smiled, his eyes full of compassion and wisdom. "He hasn't cut you off. You know that. He's just placed a challenge at your door. I once did the same with him."

"I don't mind being challenged. I just don't know which way to go. I don't know what to do."

"Don't you want to follow your dad into the family business?"

"No," I replied, firmly. "I want to do my *own* thing."

That was the truth. I'd got sick of people asking me when I was going to take over *daddy's business*. I'd had enough of people telling me how easy I'd got it. I wanted to achieve my own success. I needed to be my own man and step out of dad's shadow.

"Good," grandad replied, patting me gently on the back. "You'll find your way. When you do, you *will* be a success."

"How can you be so sure?"

Grandad smiled. "You know why."

India.

Grandad reminded me of my first visit there. I was only nine years old at the time, when the local village holy man blessed me and prophesied that one day, I would be a man who would realise his full potential.

Grandad never forgot the prophecy. Nor did he ever let me forget.

Coincidence or not, that India trip had a definite effect on me. Before going, my body was weak. My mind, passive. When I returned, my body grew strong. My mind grew sharp.

A little turning point from the past flashed before my eyes:

1987 – A race. Against my cousins. My dad and uncles are pitting us against each other, again. Before India, I would come last every time in these contests. That was standard. But this time, something is different. *I* feel different.

"On your marks… get set…GO …." Dad shouts out.

I'm off the pace.

But I start to gain ground.

I begin overtaking the other stragglers, then cutting through the leading pack.

I glide past them with ease. They look my way, stupefied.

I feel *so* fast. Like a cheetah eating up the Serengeti.

I can't believe it – I win!

I can still remember that moment clearly. The shock and surprise on everyone's faces. The attention I got. The admiration I received. I felt like I'd arrived. It was the first time I'd come first at anything. Up until then, I'd been living in the background. In the shadows. Now, I was front and centre. And I *loved* it.

After that race, I began excelling. I surprised others with my sudden progress. My life suddenly shifted onto a whole new trajectory.

Something else happened – I began believing in the holy man's prophecy. Perhaps it was self-fulfilling. I don't know. But I felt stronger, better, more able for it.

I never told grandad this, but years later that same prophecy also saved my life. It pulled me through those dark melancholy months when I didn't want to live.

But that was all past me now. Now I wanted to live the greatest life possible. I just needed a push in the right direction.

"Papa, how will I know where my future lies?" I asked, my mind returning to the present.

"Ask God."

I smiled. With grandad, everything came back to God.

"How?"

"When you pray, ask him to reveal the way."

I shook my head. "I have been praying *and* visualising. But nothing has happened. Not one thing."

So much for 'Ask and it shall be given. Seek and ye shall find'.

Grandad looked at me thoughtfully. "And what else have you done?"

The challenge in his tone of voice surprised me.

What else?

"Nothing. What more can I do?"

Grandad smiled at my naivety.

"Viryam, first *you* must do all you can. Only then can you leave the rest to God."

"Yeah, I know all that stuff. Pray as though everything depends on God but act as though everything depends on you. But I don't know what I'm here to do."

"Listen closely. God will point the way. But you must be brave and seize that moment when it comes."

My head dropped. An outward sign of my lack of courage.

"Being brave is never easy at first," grandad said, sensing my struggle. "But it gets easier when you push through your fears. It's just a little uncomfortable at first, that's all."

But that was just it. I hated feeling uncomfortable. It was like Sophia said: I'd always had it easy. I'd always followed the line of least resistance.

Her words had annoyed me, at first. But there was truth in them. I always looked for the easy way out. Take the past nine days. I sat cross-legged on the floor for a few minutes each day, hoping for some extraordinary opportunity to fall into my lap like manna from heaven.

But it was as clear as day to me now - praying and visualising wasn't enough. If I wanted something to happen, *I* needed to make it happen.

I got to my feet, more determined. Playfully, I beat my chest for added motivation.

Grandad laughed.

"It's time to be a bit braver," I said.

Grandad nodded.

"Yes, but don't dismiss the power of prayer," he replied, slowly getting to his feet too. "Just remember, pray with belief and act with faith."

Back then, I might have doubted myself. But not grandad. He had lived through his fair share of challenges and heartaches. But he never lost his faith in God. It only grew stronger with time. Despite being born into poverty he became his own man.

My dad too had become self-made, against the odds. Working in bakeries, foundries and factories. Doing whatever it took to get by until he saw his chance to do his own thing.

That's what I wanted too. To be my own man, doing my own thing. It was no easy task. But now, galvanised by grandad's words, I was up for the fight. I was ready to battle. I was going to act with more courage, more faith, more determination.

I'm going to seize the next opportunity that comes my way.

It came, unexpectedly – in a taxi queue of all places.

10

The taxi queue

I wasted no time.

Immediately I began searching for jobs. I checked the internet. I trawled the appointments sections in all the broadsheets. I called friends to enquire about any openings where they worked.

Hedging my bets, I also applied for a couple of jobs that would keep me ticking over financially until I found *that* dream job. By shaking a few trees, I hoped something might drop my way, even if it wasn't quite manna from heaven.

Now, this is where it gets interesting again.

A little more eccentric than my conventional job-seeking methods, I speculatively ventured into central London twice in some vain hope that something unexpected might happen. You know, in the same way I fortuitously connected with Sophia and then ran into Lauren, the clairvoyant.

So, here's the thing. The second time around something *did* happen.

I was walking through Soho when I randomly stopped outside some office window. I looked up at the company logo. It said ELEVATE in bright orange letters. I'd never heard of the firm before, but peering into its office I got the strangest impression.

I am going to work there one day, I thought.

But immediately the whole notion seemed absurd, so I dismissed it and went on my way.

A week later, my short burst of effort yielded a reward. I was offered an interview with some firm in Canary Wharf. It was only for a job that would keep me ticking over until something more desirable came my way. But it was a start. I agreed to meet them the next day.

It was the following morning.

Suited and booted I headed to London Euston. When I arrived, the concourse was packed with irate commuters. There was lots of huffing and puffing. But no trains coming or going. A signal failure on a key underground line had caused some severe travel disruption. I glanced down at my watch.

Shit.

I was already running late. There was no chance now of getting to Canary Wharf on time using the Underground. I sprinted down a flight of stairs which led to the taxi rank. I only made it halfway down.

Are you kidding me?

I was stuck behind a long queue of people. I lightly tapped the elderly man ahead of me on the shoulder. His head was buried in a newspaper.

"Excuse me," I said, causing him to look up. "Is this the taxi queue?"

He looked me up and down with disdain, like I'd asked him the most obvious thing in the world, which clearly, I had.

"Yes," he tutted, rolling his eyes. "I think it's safe to assume this is the taxi queue."

His sarcasm wasn't lost on me but I had other things on my mind.

I'm never going to make this interview.

I glanced down again at my watch and then up at the queue. It was impossible to say how long it would take to secure the taxi I needed. I looked behind me. The queue there was as big as the one in front.

I undid the top button of my shirt, loosened my tie and rolled my neck from side to side. That's when I noticed the smartly dressed woman behind me crouching down on the floor. She was rummaging through a small suitcase, from which she pulled out a neatly bound presentation.

No way.

I noticed the bright orange logo on the cover of the presentation deck:

ELEVATE

That was the company in Soho whose office I was standing outside the other day. What were the chances? Immediately I began to speculate. Maybe there was something behind that feeling I'd had.

Maybe I am going to work there one day.

The more I thought about it the more I was convinced.

It's a sign.

It had to be. I watched with interest as the woman called a number off a business card stapled to the front cover of the presentation.

"Hey Simon, it's Jo," she said to the person on the other end of the line. "I'm going to be late."

Not wanting to come across as prying, I looked the other way. But my ears tuned in. I heard an irate voice speak back.

"Yes, I know he's a big deal for our firm," she whispered back in reply. "But it can't be helped. There are hardly any services running from Euston. I'm just waiting for a cab. I'll call you when I'm close. Please pass on my apologies."

Who's this 'big deal' she's on about?

I turned her way a couple of times. I tried to catch her eye but she was now scrolling through some messages on her phone.

I felt a strong urge to talk to her.

But should I?

I was going to get out my fifty-pence coin and flip it discreetly. But suddenly doing that felt childish.

Come on, Vee. Think, think, think.

Suddenly, I knew what to do.

"Excuse me," I said turning back towards her. She looked up from her phone. "I couldn't help hearing the tail end of your conversation. If you're in a rush, why don't you jump ahead of me in the queue?"

The lady smiled back.

"That's very kind. But I'm going to be late regardless. Besides, you look in a hurry too."

"Just a job interview," I replied, shrugging my shoulders.

"What's the role?"

"Just some admin post."

"Nothing to write home about then?" she smiled.

"Not really."

I looked back up the long queue ahead of me.

"I'm Vee by the way," I said, turning back around.

"Hi. I'm Jo," she smiled back.

We shook hands.

"I hope you don't mind me asking Jo, but what do you do?"

The question worked like a treat. A flowing conversation opened up between us as we slowly shuffled along the queue.

Jo explained that she worked for Elevate, a talent management agency looking after top celebrities in sports and entertainment.

In turn, I told her about the past year of my life. Interestingly, I found myself talking with more charm and charisma than usual. Perhaps it was Sophia's suggestion to slow down my speech and finish off my sentences. Whatever it was, I spoke with a certain eloquence that surprised even me.

The extra confidence I exuded was not lost on Jo. "Do you know what?" she said, interrupting me mid-flow. "You should come and work for us. I think you'd love it."

"Really? Is there a job going there?"

"Possibly. But even if there isn't, I just know Sebastian would love you."

"Sebastian?"

"Sorry, he's our managing director. He's always looking for fresh talent."

I tried to conceal my excitement. The conversation had flowed exactly where I'd hoped.

Without realising the time, we found ourselves nearing the front of the taxi queue.

"Vee, send me your CV. I'll pass it on to Sebastian," she said, handing me her business card.

"Thanks, Jo. Hey, look, why don't you take my cab," I insisted, as we finally arrived at the front of the taxi queue.

"But what about your interview?"

"Something better has just come up!"

"Now you know I can't promise you anything," Jo laughed. "But send across your CV. I'll see what I can do."

After Jo left, I loitered there for a few seconds. A taxi pulled up in front of me. I stepped forward but then stepped back. I decided I didn't need a cab anymore. Without a second thought, I walked away from the long line of disgruntled commuters behind me.

I glanced down at my watch. It was unlikely I could have made the interview on time anyhow. Besides, my mind was now elsewhere. I had a strong feeling within me. One of imminence. Like I'd caught hold of a golden thread which was running back from the future I desired.

In that moment, I was utterly convinced. Jo and I had met for a *reason*. The impromptu conversation we'd struck up felt significant. It couldn't just be a coincidence.

That's what I told myself as I walked out of Euston station into a cold morning breeze.

For the record, meeting Jo *was* significant – a genuine sliding doors moment that changed my life.

11

A major development

I was on a high.

Everything was unfolding perfectly. It felt like days earlier I was meant to stand outside that Elevate office; I was meant to be late this morning; I was meant to be in that taxi queue; I was meant to meet Jo at precisely the time life had so brilliantly orchestrated.

As I walked away from Euston Station I called ahead and cancelled my interview.

"Something has come up," I smiled, as I told them.

But as the cold morning air assaulted my senses, the second-guessing began:

Have I done the right thing?
What if the conversation with Jo leads to nothing?
What if this isn't some kind of big sign?

Just then my phone rang. It was my father.
"Hi, dad."
"How was your interview son?"

Shit!

I'd forgotten I'd mentioned it to him last night when he called to have another father-son talk about my future.

"I decided not to go," I said screwing up my face, expecting to be grilled.

There was an excruciating moment of silence.

"Why didn't you go?" he asked sternly.

"I was going dad but the trains from Euston have been delayed. But I have just met a lady in the taxi queue. She said there might be a job going at her firm. Sounds really interesting. Just want to see where that leads before…"

"A *taxi* queue?" my father interrupted. "That's where you think you'll find a job?"

I suddenly realised how absurd it sounded.

"Dad, I've got a good feeling about this one."

"You and your good feelings! How can you still be so blasé about everything?"

Dad took it upon himself to remind me of *every* whimsical choice I'd made in the past twelve months. There were a few.

"*Ok*, dad. I get it."

He tutted. "When are you just going to grow up, Vee?"

"*Dad*, why are you even worried about me?" I snapped back. "You made it quite clear, it's my struggle and mine alone. Leave it with me. I'll be alright. I'll make it big one day. You'll see."

My words were passionate. More out of defensiveness than self-belief.

There was silence at the other end of the line. Was dad feeling guilty now? Unsure whether this parental experiment of his was a good idea after all?

"Son, I only have your best interests at heart. I just don't want to see you waste your potential."

"I *won't*, dad."

"Well, you better work hard then, to make something of your life. It's not all going to fall into your lap."

Dad's time-honoured lecture then followed. How being the son of an immigrant family, I couldn't afford to just be as good as everyone else. I had to be better. I had to be the best – if I was going to overcome the racial barriers others may put in my way. The barriers others *did* put in his way. Dad worked hard to overcome them. In fact, dad worked hard full stop. The thought of him giving his blood, sweat and tears to help the family cause aroused a feeling of admiration within me. But guilt, also. Up until now, I had whimsically floated through life whilst he had no choice but to knuckle down and work.

"Vee, did you hear me?" he said, snapping me out of my thoughts.

"Yes, dad. I did."

"I hope so. I hope one day you become someone we can all be proud of."

I tutted under my breath. Did all this pressure to be someone do more harm than good?

And I still had no idea what the fuck I even wanted to be.

I hung up the phone and rolled my head from side to side. Minutes earlier, I'd felt brave walking away from that taxi queue. I thought I was acting with faith. Trusting my intuition. Reading the signs. Following my gut.

But now, doubt and belief went to war with each other on the inner battleground of my mind.

When am I going to get some bloody conviction?

In the blink of an eye, I went from feeling gloriously up to despairingly down. Without a fight, my courage had given way to despondency.

Challenging days followed.

I sent my C.V. off to Jo but heard nothing back. Now, meeting her didn't seem like destiny at all. Just coincidence, pure and simple. The type life randomly throws up from time to time.

She was probably just being polite when asking for my C.V.

Impatiently, I looked up to the heavens. I asked for closure one way or the other. Quite arbitrarily, I decided: if I heard nothing back from Jo by the end of the week, I would dismiss the opportunity and start actively looking again for a job with more tangible prospects.

A few days later the matter was decided.

A colleague of Jo's got in touch. She invited me to an interview. For a Talent Assistant role at the firm. God knows what that was but I was excited. It appeared as though one of Lauren's predictions had come true. That something major would happen in *the next three weeks*.

I grabbed my journal and checked the date. Lauren and I had met just under three weeks ago. The timing of events and how they coincided with Lauren's prediction all added to the sense of destiny I was suddenly feeling again. My mind instantly rebounded back.

It's fate, I told myself. *The Universe has got my back.*

The interview was to take place in five weeks, coinciding with the start of a new year. It gave me time to sharpen up my act. I got fitter. More mentally prepared. Each day I found out what I could about Elevate, its competitors, its clients and the industry.

Each night, I rounded off the day with some visualisation. The details were always the same. I saw myself striding confidently into Elevate's offices, making a winning impression on everyone I met and getting offered the job.

With only days left to the interview, I felt ready. Gone were all the usual doubts and frustrations. My mind had stopped hopping from one idea to the next. For now, I was all in with the Elevate opportunity. Every cell in my body told me it was the way to go.

If a further confidence boost (and test) was needed it came from an unexpected source. A day before the interview, I was about to walk into a tailors just off Oxford Circus when I felt a heavy hand grab my shoulder.

"Vee!" a voice boomed out.

I turned around.

There stood a man dressed in combat boots, black army pants and an obscenely tight black t-shirt which was threatening to rip open any second. I hadn't seen this guy in over a year. Not since I'd left my first grad job to do my acting thing. He was the burly security guard who used to man the reception there.

"Hey, how are you?" I said, struggling to recall his name.

"Great, thanks," he replied, gruffly.

"Cool."

"I've got to hand it to you. You look in really good shape, Vee," he said playfully punching my arm, harder than necessary. "You been working out?"

"No more than usual."

"Well, you look a lot better than when I last saw you."

"Oh, thanks… Mo."

I finally remembered his name.

"So, are you an actor now?" he asked, cutting to the chase.

I shook my head.

"But that's what everyone said you'd left to do. Are you struggling to make it or something?" he asked, with the affectation of care.

I saw a sardonic smile flash across his face. Spotting fleeting micro expressions had always been a natural gift of mine.

"No, Mo. I'm not struggling to make it. Just decided acting wasn't my thing."

If I didn't have the interview with Elevate tomorrow, Mo's comment about me struggling might have hit a raw nerve.

"I'm surprised you left in the first place. Everyone liked you there. I wouldn't have thrown away an opportunity like that."

"Yeah, look Mo, I've got to go."

I edged away from him, hoping to bring our impromptu meeting to a close. Mo had a real penchant for never-ending conversations.

"Before you go, there's something I want to know."

"What's that?"

"A few girls in the office had a thing about you," he said, abruptly shifting the topic of conversation. "How come? It's not like you were the best-looking guy in the building."

I had to laugh. Mo's insults were more amusing than offensive.

"I'm not sure Mo. Ask one of the girls."

Mo gathered up some saliva and spat it out on the pavement. We both looked down at it. Mo with pride, me with disgust. Staring back at us was a hearty-sized portion of yellow and green phlegm.

When Mo looked back up, he was about to say something else but I cut him short.

"Good seeing you mate but I've *really* got to go," I said, stepping into the tailors.

"Don't let me hold you back," he replied.

As a parting gift, he playfully whacked my arm one last time and left.

Finally, I was in the tailors.

Running into Mo got me thinking about my days at the firm where I used to work. It's true – I'd managed to make a winning impression on people there. Not just the girls.

As the tailor handed me the suit jacket I'd come to collect, I remembered something Lauren had said: "People will be drawn to you but they won't know why."

I tried on the jacket. It was an old one that just needed taking in a little. I decided against a new one. My shrinking bank balance just wouldn't allow it. But no matter. The old one, thanks to the tailor, now fitted perfectly.

I surveyed myself in a mirror as my thoughts raced ahead to my upcoming interview.

You've got to walk in there tomorrow and own it, Vee.

Normally the thought of having to perform would make me nervous. But strangely, I felt no pressure at all. Only excitement at the possibilities that lay ahead.

Tomorrow would be a day of destiny.

I was ready to seize my chance.

12

The interview

It was one of those perfect starts to the day.

I awoke before my alarm. I was out the door sooner than expected. The Underground train arrived the moment I set foot on the platform. I reached Elevate's office with time to spare.

I smoothed out the creases in my jacket. I straightened my tie, strode confidently into the building and walked up to the receptionist.

"Hi, I'm Vee. I'm here for an interview."

"Hey, Vee," he replied. "Take a seat behind you. Someone will be with you shortly."

I turned around. Two young guys were sat on one leather sofa. An older lady on another.

"Hey," I said, walking over to them. "You all here for the interview?"

They nodded back but no one spoke. They all did their best to avoid eye contact but from the stealthy glances they exchanged, the temptation to size up the competition seemed too hard to resist.

I turned my attention elsewhere. To a series of framed photographs displayed on an exposed brick wall. It was a roll call of Elevate's top clients: award-winning actors, sports stars and best-selling authors.

Impressive.

I leaned in to take a closer look. Instantly, my mind was transported to the future. I imagined my own photograph hanging there one day after I'd made it.

"You could be managing stars like that soon," a voice suddenly whispered from behind.

It was Jo.

"Hey, Jo! How are you?"

"Really well, Vee. How are you feeling? Not too nervous I hope?"

"No, I'm all good thank you."

I straightened up my posture to prove it.

"Good. Now we don't want anyone to think you're getting any preferential treatment," she said in a low voice, "but I just wanted to say, good luck."

"Aww, thank you."

"That and don't let me down," she joked.

I laughed.

"No pressure but I've been talking you up a bit."

Jo pulled a face of mock apology.

"I won't let you down. I promise."

And do you know what? I really didn't.

Before the interview, I had speed-read a book on body language tricks ('hacks' I guess they'd now be called) to create a great first impression: matching and mirroring (but not mimicking the interviewer), strong eye contact (but not a psychopathic stare), a strong handshake (but not a bone cruncher), standing up straight (but not too stiff like you've got a carrot stuck up you know where).

I think I got all that down to a tee. But it was more than that. From the first interview on, something came over me. Not in the conventional sense of that term. Quite the reverse. I felt like some higher–self had taken over. I spoke with more power. Exuded more confidence. My presence became more commanding.

I didn't strain to find the right words. I didn't succumb to doubt. I didn't try to impress anyone with clever-sounding answers. Everything flowed naturally. Effortlessly. Maybe this is what the Taoists referred to as *Wei Wu Wei*: effortless effort.

I'd had moments like this before: operating at the height of my powers but feeling as though *I* was doing nothing at all. Nothing except witnessing the flow of life working through me with ease and grace.

It was definitely deeper than any surface-level confidence. From wherever it flowed, it had the desired effect. At times, my interviewers spoke to me as though I'd already got the job.

The final interview that day was with Rick, one of Elevate's talent agents. I waited in one of the company's sleek meeting rooms for him to arrive. He sauntered in ten minutes late.

"So, *you're* the guy Jo met in a taxi queue," he said, slamming down his pad on the circular table which separated us. "You're quite the story in the office."

We shook hands and Rick sat down.

He leaned back in his chair imperiously with his hands clasped behind his head. For a second, I thought he was about to put his feet up on the table. But he kept them on the ground. His short legs spread widely in front of him – manspreading, I think they call it.

He kicked things off by asking a few cursory interview questions. Run-of-the-mill stuff. Then, he changed tack.

"Look, I've read your C.V., you're obviously a bright guy. But what do you know about the talent management industry?"

"Not that much," I conceded honestly.

"I like that, Vee," said Rick, sounding pleased with himself. "That question was a test. To see if you're a bullshitter or not. There's a few of them in this industry but it gets you nowhere fast."

I got the impression that Rick was prone to speaking the odd bit of bullshit himself.

"Well, since you know nothing about the industry," he said, emphasising the word nothing, "let me tell you about it."

I sat back and listened to Rick, amused by the fact that I was the one being interviewed but he was the one doing all the talking –all about himself.

"So, the thing is Vee, if you're prepared to work hard and learn from the right people, maybe, if you play your cards right, ten or fifteen years from now you might be sitting where I am today," he said, concluding his monologue.

"That would be something," I replied.

But ten or fifteen years!

I promised myself if I did get the job, I would get there in half the time.

"Well, I've seen what I want to see. I've heard what I want to hear," Rick said, getting up with a touch of drama. "Good luck with the rest of the process."

With that Rick cut the interview short and sauntered out of the meeting room the way he'd sauntered in.

I leaned back in my chair, reflecting on how the interviews had gone. Ten minutes later Jo popped her head around the door.

"*So*, how do you think you've done today?" she asked, walking in.

She pulled up a chair close to me.

"Alright, I hope."

"Hmmm," she replied, her face becoming graver. "I'm afraid after giving it much consideration we've decided *not* to give you the job."

What the f…? I thought but thankfully did not say.

"Oh, ok," I replied with fake composure.

"Yes, we all agree we're not going to put you forward for that job…"

Jo paused, adding further suspense to the moment.

"…because we think you're better than that."

Phew!

I breathed a sigh of relief. "You had me there."

Jo laughed and mimicked the serious look that had evidently appeared on my face.

"On a serious note, we're going to invite you back for another interview. This one will be with Sebastian."

"The managing director?"

She nodded. "He is looking for someone to work directly with him. We all think you might be a great fit."

Yes! Yes! Yes! Come on!

"Oh wow, that's great," I replied, keeping a lid on my excitement.

We continued chatting for a few minutes. She spoke in glowing terms about Sebastian.

"The best boss I've ever worked for," she beamed.

She assured me the two of us would click.

But just before I was about to leave, she said, "…just don't be intimidated by him. Be yourself. Ok. That should be enough."

13

"Do you get bored easily?"

It was two weeks later.

I was back at Elevate, sat outside the managing director's office. Voices from inside edged closer to the door. I sat up straighter as it swung open.

Here we go.

Two men walked out engaged in lively conversation. I recognised one immediately. He was a well-known British actor but for the life of me, I couldn't remember his name. Seeing a celebrity up close for the first time threw me. I was gripped by nervous excitement. I was being given a glimpse of a glamourous new world and I wanted to be part of it.

As the actor and, who I assumed was, Sebastian were about to head towards reception, Sebastian turned to me.

"Sorry to keep you waiting, Vee. I'm just going to see this rather distinguished gentleman out of the building," he said, turning towards the actor who smiled warmly in my direction.

"Sure, no problem," I replied, trying to play it cool.

As they walked away, I tried to remember the actor's name. But without success.

Al…Alfred? …No…Albert…yes…Albert something or other…

In no time at all I heard footsteps coming towards me. Sebastian was back already. I got up and shook his hand. He was a good four inches taller than me. He cut an imposing figure.

"Come in," he said, ushering me into his office.

It was luxuriously appointed. There were photographs displayed all over the room. Black and white images of Sebastian with a host of A-list celebrities. You couldn't fail to be impressed by the company this man kept.

Be cool, Vee.

I took a seat on a low-slung sofa, as directed. I tried to be calm. But my heart was racing.

"You're not going to believe this, Vee," he said, taking a seat on the adjacent sofa. "I ran into your old boss last night."

My heart pounded faster.

Uh oh! Which boss?

If it was from my last job I was screwed. Thankfully it was the boss from the job before. The one where I'd left with more credit to my name.

"He said you're a bright kid who works hard."

Here comes the 'but'…

"But he said you get bored easily."

I shuffled nervously on the sofa. "Oh, right."

Sebastian locked his hawk-like eyes on mine. "Do you get bored easily?"

As his penetrating gaze bore through me, I responded honestly to the question.

"I have in the past. I have been whimsical at times. But I think your mind focuses when you know what you want."

I was pleased with my answer. I tried not to show it.

"And what do you want?" challenged Sebastian, unmoved.

"This opportunity."

I felt more belief surge through me. Or was it adrenaline?

"But what about that last sales job you took? Jo said you lasted there a week. Didn't you want that opportunity too?"

"I did. But I quickly realised it wasn't for me."

"Why?"

"I didn't like the company's values."

"What was wrong with them?"

"I think they lacked integrity."

"And what does integrity mean to you?" he asked, keeping his eyes firmly locked on me.

"Not misleading others by saying one thing and doing another."

"What else?"

"Um, acting true to your principles."

"And what are your principles?"

Bloody hell.

He looked at me sternly.

"Honesty and transparency are important to me," I replied, thinking about it.

A further onslaught of tough questions followed. Their intensity surprised me. I responded sharply to everything he asked. The interview felt like a fast-flowing tennis rally. Back and forth. Back and forth.

Finally, the questions stopped.

"Ok, Vee. Let me tell you what the job involves..."

He said he was looking for an executive assistant. "A bag carrier."

"I need someone capable, shadowing my every move. Someone sharp and fast on their feet. Sound interesting?"

"Yes, definitely."

Sebastian smiled for the first in the interview. I permitted myself to do likewise.

"Ok. I'll get back to you. Just so you know, I'm casting my eyes over a couple of internal candidates too."

We both got to our feet.

"Thank you for the opportunity," I said, as he walked me to the door.

"Thank you for coming. You did well today…" he said, patting me on the back. "…for someone we've scouted in a taxi queue."

I smiled and walked away with one thing on my mind.

I want this job.

14

Another reading

A week passed by.

I was in Paris for a long weekend with a group of friends. Sounds more glamorous than it was. Frugally, we were staying in a budget hotel outside the city; somewhere everyone could afford. That suited me fine. My finances were getting stretched already. Just one extortionate rent payment saw to that.

Anyway, I digress. Back to Paris. A lovely city – but my mind wasn't there. My heart wasn't in it. I paid cursory attention to my surroundings. The stormy weather didn't help. Spending time indoors meant I was constantly checking my phone.

There had been no word from Sebastian or Jo. I felt as wretched as the weather. To everyone's relief, a blue sky prevailed on the final day of the trip. It revived me. Sitting on the steps of the Sacre Coeur I felt more optimistic.

Have faith. You met Jo for a reason. You'll get the job.

Was that me or my intuition speaking? Who knows? Either way, I felt better. More uplifted.

For a week after my return from Paris, I managed to valiantly keep the optimism going. But just as water finds its way through any available cracks, doubts weaved their way back into my thoughts. I became less sure of what lay ahead.

The stakes had also risen in my mind. After the interview with Sebastian, I couldn't resist telling dad that I was sure I was going to get the job. I'd feel like a fool now if my confidence had been misplaced.

With doubts now winning the balance of power in my mind, I finally relented and did something I was holding off from doing. I called Lauren, the clairvoyant, for another reading. I hoped the princely sum of fifty pounds it would cost me would be money well spent. After Paris, it was money I could ill afford to spend.

Two days later I arrived in Marylebone in good time for my next treatment.

As I waited in the spa's reception for Lauren to arrive, I noticed the curious behaviour of the other two therapists. They talked in hushed tones and glanced twice in my direction. It made me feel uncomfortable.

Perhaps it was nothing but it sparked off an uneasy train of thought. Was it right to see a clairvoyant? To know your future? To know what would happen in time, ahead of time?

Maybe the future is something we should not be told.

As I wrestled with this thought Lauren appeared.

"Are you ready, Vee?" she asked, not acknowledging the other two therapists in any way.

I nodded and followed her to a treatment room. As I entered, I could still hear the whispering voices of the other two therapists but I couldn't make out what they were saying.

Lauren left me to get undressed. A minute later she returned. She gently placed her warm hands on my shoulders. Silently, she began kneading my muscles.

Do I need to ask for a reading?

I wondered what I should do. Lauren, however, remained silent, forcing my hand.

"Are you able to do another reading?" I asked awkwardly.

I felt weak-minded as I posed the question.

"Yes, of course," she replied, as though expecting it.

For a short while she remained silent. Then, her words began to flow.

"Don't worry about the job," she began, with a tone of conviction. "You'll hear about it by Friday. Things will go well for you there. You will get a pay rise by the end of this year and another pay rise and promotion next year."

I was astounded. She was so definite with her predictions. I listened eagerly for more revelations. To my disappointment, nothing further was said on the career front.

She was silent again as she began working on my lower back. Minutes ticked by.

"I sense real excitement in the spiritual journey that lies ahead of you," she then continued. "By the end of the year, you'll be amazed by how far you've come and by what you've experienced."

There was another long pause.

"By the age of forty…"

"Yes…"

"…you'll know amazing things. You'll have an incredible amount of knowledge but…

"But what?"

"You won't be able to share it with most people… it may even be harmful to do so."

I was captivated by the spiritual direction the reading was taking.

"Remember, your grandad is here to guide you," she began again. "He can answer your questions. Spiritually, he knows more than he is letting on."

Another prolonged pause. Long enough for doubt to surface in my questioning mind.

Is she making this up?

I began speculating: was she really receiving messages transmitted to her from beyond the physical world?

Several minutes passed by. Lauren said nothing further.

In the silence that enveloped the room, my mind vacillated between two thoughts. Was Lauren a genuine clairvoyant or just a charlatan? One that might be filling my head with intriguing possibilities that had no basis in reality.

Finally, she spoke again.

"*A lot* will happen this year. Stay present. Trust that life will lead you where you need to go. But if you get lost …"

She paused midsentence as though she was about to reveal something really important, "…ask for the truth to be revealed, so you may see reality for what it is and know which path to take."

Nothing else of significance was said. It gave me an opportunity to reflect on why I'd come: to know if I'd get the job. There was no doubt in her mind that I would get it. She seemed absolutely convinced.

Could she really be telling the truth?

Four days later, on *Friday,* I got my answer.

15

You couldn't make it up.

I was about to step into a restaurant with some friends when I received a call from an unknown number.

I answered as my friends walked on ahead of me.

"Hello."

"Vee, it's Sebastian."

My heart began to race. Finally, I would know my fate.

"Hi Sebastian, it's good to hear from you."

"I'm going to make this quick," he said firmly.

I bit my lip, expecting the worst.

"The job is yours, if you want it."

What?

The news didn't register. I stood there motionless.

"Vee? Do you want the job?"

My face erupted into a smile. "Absolutely!"

I clenched my fist, waving it triumphantly.

"Great. Just one minor point. I'm going to put you on a three-month probation."

"Yeah, sure."

"Just standard practise, so we can get a feel for each other."

"No problem."

Now I'd got my foot through the door I was confident I would find a way to stay there and progress.

Sebastian ended the call by saying his personal assistant would be in touch with the contract and paperwork.

"Yes, yes, yes!" I screamed.

Hearing my ecstatic outburst, one of my friends came back out of the restaurant. "What's happened, mate?"

"I got that job!"

"Which one?"

"The one I told you about, where I met that woman in a taxi queue."

My friend shook his head. "For real?"

I nodded back, wide-eyed.

"You couldn't make it up," said my friend.

"Honestly, it's surreal," I replied.

I stood there motionless, savouring the moment.

"Are you coming in?" he asked, holding open the door to the restaurant.

"Just got one more call to make."

"Ok. I'll go back and tell the others we've got something to celebrate."

As he left me to it, I dialled the number I'd been hoping to call all day.

"Hello, is Lauren free by any chance?"

I wanted to tell her she'd got it right. I did hear back by Friday!

On Friday!

"I'm sorry. She doesn't work here anymore," the woman on the line replied, coldly.

What?

I was stunned. I'd only seen her there four days ago.

"Do you know where she's moved on to?"

"No, I don't," came the reply. Her tone suggested she didn't care either.

I hung up.

Shit.

Maybe Lauren had been asked to leave because the other therapists found out she was offering psychic readings to her clients. Admittedly, it wasn't the best spa etiquette.

It's probably for the best.

That's what I convinced myself.

After visiting her again, I couldn't shake the feeling that I shouldn't make a habit of seeing psychics. The danger of becoming dependent upon them was a real one.

But still, I was in awe. Her predictions had come true:

There was a major development on the job front within three weeks.

I did hear back about it by Friday.

I did get the job.

Lauren's predictions had given me faith. I felt I was on the right path. But I'd heard enough for the time being about the future. There was no reason, for now, to hear anything more of what might lie ahead. No matter how strong that temptation might be.

Now, permit me a little digression.

I'm sure it will interest you to know that in time *all* of Lauren's predictions came true. I did find my calling by the age of thirty-five. At forty, I did possess a great deal of esoteric knowledge I couldn't widely share.

But there is so much to tell you between where the story is now and where it leads. Like I said before, it's unlikely I can cover it all in one book. Maybe not even two. So many other people, possibilities and challenges were yet to come my way. So many links in the chain were yet to be made.

But for now, Lauren had given me a glimpse of the future I couldn't yet see. One which destiny was urging me to grasp.

16

Forget everything

Two days to go.

That's all that remained until I started at Elevate. The journey here had galvanised my mind. Bolstered my belief. Given me the courage to act when moments of opportunity came my way and the confidence to seize them, so they didn't pass me by.

An exciting future was opening up.

The glamour of the celebrity world and the mystery of the spiritual path now beckoned. Unexpectedly, these two diverse worlds were converging. With the hand of providence guiding my steps, everything felt like it was happening for a reason.

What that ultimate reason was, I didn't yet know. The link between the celebrity and the spiritual world was not clear to me. But life appeared to have a plan. I became even surer of this when I visited grandad that day. I went to tell him about my new job. But he had interesting news of his own.

"Viryam, I want to tell you something," he said, holding my hand firmly and drawing me closer to him. "It's important."

"What is it, Papa?"

"I have been asking God for a gift."

He gripped my hand tighter, ensuring he had my full attention.

"What gift?"

"A spiritual gift."

"For who?"

"You," he replied. "A gift I can leave you with before I die."

Die?

I looked back at grandad, not knowing what to say.

"And then the other day God answered my prayer," he said, with tears characteristically welling up in his eyes.

"He did?"

"Yes, I was told that at the age of forty your spirituality will unfold. That's when you'll walk the path in earnest. This is the gift that lies in wait."

Hold on.

My mind shot back to what Lauren had said: by the age of *forty*, I would know amazing things and have incredible knowledge, much of which I wouldn't be able to share.

"Why at forty?" I asked grandad.

"That's what I was told."

"By who?"

"A teacher."

"Which teacher?"

"One that appeared before me, when I was meditating."

"Appeared? *How?*" I asked, not wanting to sound as sceptical as I did.

"That doesn't matter," he replied, wiping away more tears. "Just remember what I've said. One day you'll know it's true."

I smiled and squeezed grandad's hand. I hoped this affectionate gesture would mask my scepticism, that as nice as his words were, they were nothing more than sentimental speculation.

But then again: *forty?*

Was it just coincidence Lauren and Papa had mentioned the same age?

To be honest though, either way, I didn't plan on waiting until forty for things to get going. For me, my spiritual journey had already begun. What happened the next evening made me believe this even more.

I was back in my apartment, getting various accoutrements ready for my first day at work. I was riding high with positive expectancy about the job and my future.

But an insidious little thought squirmed its way into my mind:

What if you fail to live up to expectations?

I started to contemplate the worst. For the first time in a long time, negative thoughts threatened to drag me down. Just like they had blighted my way at crucial moments in the past.

In my younger years, I'd been a capable sportsman. In another life, my destiny may have lay in this field. But as a young kid whenever I found myself excelling at levels beyond what I thought possible, my doubts screwed me over. They held me back when it should have been time to push on. I was determined to not let this happen again. Not now, when my future seemed most bright.

As the evening wore on, these anxious thoughts were having a field day in the back of my mind. The weight of expectation steadily building within.

I needed a distraction.

Perfect.

I noticed a DVD a friend had given me – a film about a man who had lost his short-term memory and was desperately trying to piece his life back together.

I played the movie. From the first moment to the last, it enthralled me. I kept thinking: *what would it be like to forget everything?*

The question utterly captivated my mind. Unusually so. Long after the film had finished, I couldn't stop thinking this one thought, about forgetting everything. Ironically, it triggered the release of a whole series of memories:

Beautiful moments I'd cherished.

Things I'd learned.

Great experiences I'd had.

Places I'd visited.

People I'd come to know and love.

My mind was a repository of valuable items I was determined to hold on to. Memories and knowledge that I held dear. Things I always wanted to remember.

Suddenly, I became gripped by fear.

What if I do forget everything?

The thought unnerved me. I could think of nothing else. It was like a koan, from the Zen Buddhist tradition – a riddle given to a student to sit quietly with and reflect upon. One that may for a time perplex the mind, but then bring a sudden moment of enlightenment or spiritual clarity.

A koan that always stuck in my mind was: what is the sound of one hand clapping?

To be honest, the question just bamboozled me. And now, my own mental riddle had me flummoxed.

What would it be like to forget everything?

What *would* it be like to forget everything?

What would it be like to forget *everything*?

The more I asked the question, the more the answer eluded me. The more I asked it, the quicker the thought began spinning in my mind.

Literally spinning. Like a powerful vortex of energy.

I suddenly realised it was a force I couldn't control. The thought spun ever faster in my mind. Relentlessly picking up more speed. It showed no sign of stopping. Round and round it went. Faster and faster, it spun.

I'm losing my mind.

It was a real fear. But then, something remarkable happened.

Suddenly, out of nowhere, there was complete stillness. Absolute silence. In that still serenity, I heard a voice speak within: "The power of negativity works by sowing the seeds of doubt in your mind."

The voice was emphatic. But I couldn't tell you if it was my own or that of another. But it spoke with certainty and power. The words were said with such conviction that they made the deepest imprint on my mind. I've never ever forgotten them.

Once again, there was silence.

Everything was so still.

Then, a sudden rush of energy surged through me, from my feet to my head. It felt *so* good. Orgasmic even. The most blissful feeling you can imagine that showed no sign of relenting. I felt as though my consciousness was rising. Higher and higher. Freeing itself of every limitation that had ever held it back.

One by one, every past doubt, worry or fear my mind had ever entertained fell away, as though I had let go of everything negative that had ever blighted or conditioned my mind.

I felt liberated. Free. Like nothing could hold me back. Like I could be anything I wanted to be. I felt limitless. This was the truth of who I was. Not those fears and doubts that had weighed heavy on my mind.

In this orgasmic moment of spiritual release, I felt like laughing out loud. I felt deliriously mad with happiness. I felt so alive, like I had infinite energy. Like I was this unbounded energy.

For several minutes, I resided in this state of exhilaration. I hoped the experience would never end. But slowly, its intenseness wore off.

But the afterglow remained.

As I lay there taking it all in, I realised that all my life I had longed for a moment such as this: of spiritual release and bliss. Finally, gloriously, such a moment was mine to savour.

Somehow, I'd managed to go beyond my everyday mind. I let go of everything I *thought* I was. But, no feeling of emptiness or nothingness ensued. Instead in that deep silence, I touched something infinitely greater than I could have imagined. A divine essence within.

Now, on the eve of starting my new job, I felt anything was possible. As I stood on the cusp of a glamourous new world of work, a door to a greater spiritual dimension had unexpectedly swung open within.

For the next few months, excitement would be the keynote of my life. Spiritual experiences and worldly progression would be mine to enjoy.

However, permanently letting go of everything negative that had conditioned my mind would prove more challenging. The everyday concerns of life would once again dominate my thoughts. The as-yet-unknown and rogue elements of my own ego would take time to tame. They would take strength to overcome.

In the distance, darker clouds were forming on the horizon. Unforeseen challenges were heading my way. I would have to fight my way back to this higher state of mind and all-consuming feeling of bliss.

But we are not there yet in the story.

From where I stood right now, everything was on the up. I was riding high. The ticking clock of pressure in my mind had gone. The loss of my parental safety blanket was no longer a concern.

I was ready to walk into the exciting new world I had manifested and seize every good thing coming my way.

17

The keys to the kingdom

It was the next morning.

I floated into the Elevate office with the highest expectations. The intensity of the spiritual experience the night before had subsided, but the thought that anything was possible was more alive than ever in my mind.

Nothing's going to hold me back.

As I stood in reception waiting to be greeted, I thought back to that expansive experience of bliss. What if I hadn't watched that DVD? Would I ever have had that spiritual experience?

There was no way of knowing. But it all added to my growing sense of excitement. Life was proceeding in an almost magical way. I was following my very own yellow brick road.

I glanced around the reception area. The wall showcasing Elevate's most recognisable clients again caught my eye.

I'll be on there one day.

That's what I promised myself. Perhaps it was strange that on the first day of my job in talent management, I was thinking more about being the talent than managing it. But this was the hope I secretly harboured. This was the ambition I inwardly entertained.

This job was a step in the right direction. I felt sure of it.

Just then, I felt a light touch on my shoulder which snapped me out of my reverie.

"Sorry, I didn't mean to make you jump," smiled an attractive lady with dark hair, cut neatly into a short bob. "I'm Sonia."

It was Sebastian's PA. We'd spoken on the phone a couple of times.

"Hey. It's so good to finally meet you," I replied.

"Likewise. Heard a lot about you. Can't wait to get acquainted but Sebastian's waiting for you."

She took me straight to his office.

When I arrived, I was pleased to see Jo there. She was having an animated discussion with Sebastian.

"We were just talking about you," he said, firmly shaking my hand. "Jo's put together a two-week induction for you. But …I've just had a better idea."

"You have?" Jo asked, raising an eyebrow. She turned to me and shrugged.

"Yes," Sebastian replied, putting his hand on my shoulder. "I'm just going to give Vee the keys to the kingdom instead."

Jo looked perplexed but not more than me.

What keys to the kingdom?

Sebastian looked my way with his hawk-like eyes. "For the next month, go where you want to go. Meet who you want to meet. Learn as much as you can about the business."

"And then?" I asked, tentatively.

"Then, present back and tell me everything you know about what we do. Agreed?"

I nodded. Jo shook her head. Sonia scribbled something down and Sebastian clapped his hands, evidently pleased with his own suggestion.

"Your time starts now," he smiled, tapping his watch. "Don't waste it."

He signalled we were free to leave.

I followed Jo out of the office, excitement and fear both welling up within me.

"That's just Sebastian all over," said Jo. "Always putting people on the spot."

I tried not to look flustered as she threw her hands up in the air and shook her head.

"He likes to give you an opportunity to prove yourself. But you know what they say about too much rope…"

I did and it made me feel nervous.

Sebastian may have given me an access-all-areas pass but my mind was racing away with itself: *what should I do next? Who should I meet first?*

Just then, Sonia emerged from Sebastian's office.

"Follow me," she whispered.

She led Jo and I to her desk.

"I've got a tip for you, Vee," Sonia said, in a soft low voice.

Jo and I both leaned in closer.

"The first person you should meet for a coffee is," she paused, adding extra suspense to the proceedings, "…me."

"Brilliant idea!" said Jo. "You can give Vee the low down on where to go and who to speak to."

"And who not to waste his time with," replied Sonia, giving me a wink.

I liked her already. I smiled back gratefully.

For the next hour, Sonia gave me all the valuable insights I needed. What Sebastian liked and disliked. Who he rated and who he didn't. Who to speak to and who to avoid.

It seemed nothing escaped Sonia's attention. She was sharp and observant. But with a wonderful easy-goingness. I felt indebted to her for giving me the inside track.

Right then!

Armed with what I needed I wasted no time. Over the next month, I spoke to everyone Sonia suggested. I gathered all the insights I could. As I did, I kept up a real charm offensive. I tried to make a favourable impression wherever I went. On the whole, it worked. Except for this one guy. He took real exception to my happy disposition.

"I'm sorry," he said, when he followed me out of the office one time. "But no one can be that fucking happy all the time."

I smiled back apologetically, held out my hands and shrugged. It turned out he was one of the internal candidates Sebastian had overlooked for my role.

I was about to tell him that I'd had a bad time of it once. That depression had dragged me down, just like it had with others. But I got the impression that nothing I might say or do would make the slightest difference. He clearly despised me, despite all my efforts to bring him onside. Perhaps he'd picked up on one of my weaknesses back then – the need to be liked.

Anyway, one month later, I presented my findings back to Sebastian. He drilled me hard on everything I had learned. Harder than I expected. But I was up to the mark. I responded well to every question that came my way. But then, he said something that threw me.

"I've been keeping tabs on something," he said.

"On what?" I asked.

"The company you've been keeping in the office."

I was surprised by the comment. And the level of scrutiny it implied. Big Brother came to mind.

"I hear you've been talking to that young apprentice no one can get a word out of."

"Adam?" I asked.

Sebastian nodded.

"He's a good guy," I replied. "Just a little shy. But he's coming out of his shell."

"So I've noticed," Sebastian said, with the faintest hint of a smile. "And what about the cleaners?"

"*The cleaners*?" I asked.

"Yes. I've been told you always talk to them too. How come?"

How come?

I began chewing my bottom lip. "Because I see them every day. I know they're agency staff but to me they're a part of this firm, like everybody else."

Sebastian stared back at me, poker-faced.

I felt a little aggrieved. "Can I ask, who told you I talk to them?"

Sebastian smiled. "They did. I talk to them too."

I smiled back. Underneath his stern persona, he was definitely one of life's good guys.

"Speaking of talking to anyone and everyone, Stines is in the office tomorrow morning. Can you meet and greet him and take care of anything he needs?"

"No problem," I replied, holding back my excitement.

Albert Stines was the British actor, who was in Sebastian's office on the day of my interview. I'd met him a couple of times since then. He was one of the firm's top clients. A genuine A-lister and one of Sebastian's inner circle – a cadre of influential individuals that would be the envy of little black books everywhere.

Meeting Stines the next day was memorable for other reasons. It was also the day I received my first ever Elevate pay cheque. A financial shot in the arm. But also, a declaration of my self-dependence. I was becoming my own man. I was moving under my own steam. The pain of losing dad's line of credit, no longer a concern.

With my bank balance rebuilding, my confidence rising, I felt like there were no limits. I was flying! If my professional life was taking off so too was my spiritual life.

Literally.

Things started happening I never even imagined were possible.

18

Lucid

Something had definitely shifted within me.

Ever since that whole 'what would it be like to forget everything' experience, my real life started to feel like a dream. My dream life, more real.

Each morning, I woke up with greater dream recall than ever before. I remembered multiple dreams in vivid detail. Then one night, something happened. Something extraordinary, in an ordinary dream:

I was taking a leisurely drive in a black Mercedes with two people I'd never met before. The three of us happily chatted away like the dearest of friends. That's when it happened. I 'awoke' in my dream. For the first time in my life, I was lucid dreaming – aware that I was dreaming *whilst* I was dreaming.

Immediately, I sensed I could take control of the dream. That I could make things happen that were not possible in physical reality. But I didn't. I simply enjoyed the drive and chatted away with these 'familiar strangers' fully aware I was dreaming.

A few nights later, I was lucid again.

This time I took control. Through the power of thought alone, I transformed the dream scene before me. One moment I created rolling green fields as far as the eye could see. The next, I transformed it all into a sprawling city.

I was astounded by what I could do. Excited by the possibilities lucid dreaming presented. I began researching the phenomenon. I wanted to become even more lucid.

I found success with one particular technique. When going to bed at night I would repeat out loud: "I'm going to sleep now. I will be dreaming. When I'm dreaming, I know I will be dreaming."

Once or twice a week, the technique worked. I would lucid dream in an uplifting way. Literally. Whatever dream my consciousness was caught up in (no matter how normal, weird or wonderful) I would spontaneously find myself floating up and levitating off the ground. Given this was physically impossible, I knew I must be dreaming.

But what started happening next surprised me most.

When I found myself levitating an incredibly powerful force would take hold of me. It would propel me at tremendous speed, in some definite direction. I never knew where. But the projecting force did.

It was a force I was unable to resist. Sometimes being propelled into the sky, past the clouds and towards the stars. At other times, across oceans or stunning landscapes.

Eventually, the projecting force would ease and I would arrive in a place of unspeakable beauty like the heart of a sun, a mountain top, a lake or a field full of wildflowers.

Every time I awoke from these lucid experiences I felt tremendously energised.

It felt like I was living two lives. One unfolding in the day at work. The other at night in my dreams. But they felt more than just dreams. They felt so *real*. One lucid dream in particular felt more significant than the rest. It happened one night, a few months after I'd started at Elevate:

I was in some disused warehouse. Suddenly, men appeared from all sides. They seemed intent on causing me harm. I jumped up in the air as one man came towards me with a concealed weapon. I suddenly found myself levitating. I realised I was dreaming. I realised I could fly. I shot out of the warehouse through an open window.

As I floated in the sky, I suddenly felt the projecting force take hold. It propelled me at breakneck speed across a verdant landscape. Past streams, rivers and cities. I felt like I knew the terrain below. Like I'd been there before.

Finally, the projecting force eased off and I found myself in a field facing a wooden gate that sealed its perimeter.

I walked towards the gate. As I did, the ground beneath me turned to mud. Every step forward plunged my feet deeper into the mire. I heard a voice speak. As is the way with a dream, I knew whose voice it was without needing to be told: the gatekeeper's.

"Go back!" he warned.

Desperately, instinctively, I knew I needed to get through the gate to see what was on the other side. But the gatekeeper used scare tactics to halt my progress. As I waded through the mud, he filled my mind with fear. He told me to stop where I was or bad things would happen.

Still, I pushed forward, not knowing if I was sinking in the mud or making progress towards the gate; every step taking tremendous courage and determination.

Finally, after an eternity of effort, I made it past the gate. Or so I thought, for the gate and gatekeeper disappeared. Before me stood a grand manor house set in the most beautiful grounds. I walked through them to the main house.

There was a party taking place. It was in full sway. The guests were dressed in the finest clothes. They spoke in the finest accents. They were eating the most exquisite foods. I overheard many of the conversations taking place. They were full of pride and arrogance –conceited guests congratulating themselves for being in such lavish surroundings.

Everything about the party felt false. Fake.

I wanted to break free. I *needed* to break free. But I couldn't find the way out. The inside of the manor house felt like a huge complex maze with many passages and doors. As I searched for the exit, I suddenly realised I could pass right through the walls like a ghost. But every wall I went through led me to another room, then another. Finally, I found myself in the centre of the house.

I looked up and saw a large glass dome above me. Without so much as a thought, I flew up right at it. I thought it might break but I passed right through. But then, another glass dome appeared above me and then another and another. No matter how high I flew, I couldn't break through the glass ceiling.

Undeterred, I flew back down into the manor house. I had to find another way to escape. As I roamed through its opulent halls that threatened to imprison me, I came across a small passageway. At its far end was a stained-glass window.

I knew what I needed to do.

I took a moment to compose myself. I crouched down towards the ground and then flew at the window with terrific speed. I hit it with real force. It shattered into a thousand pieces.

Finally, I broke free.

I shot up into the sky and then back down towards the earth. Once again, the projecting force that had become so familiar to me now took hold. It propelled me forward. I raced across green rolling hills until I came to a place of unspeakable beauty.

I slowed down to take in all the glorious details. The colours I saw transfixed my eyes. They were more luminous and vivid than anything I had seen in my waking life in the 'real world'.

In this place of beauty were majestic elephants, zebras and exotic birds. Beautiful lakes, waterfalls and fountains. As I flew through this lush heavenly paradise, I saw an expanse of sea ahead of me. Over it, the sun was setting in an iridescent sky.

Still lucid through the whole experience, I decided I'd gone far enough. I willed myself to wake up, to document the dream in my journal. This was an experience I never wanted to forget.

I woke up feeling elevated. I glanced across at my alarm clock. 4.30am.

I sat up and smiled. What I was seeing in my dreams appeared more real than reality itself. Spiritually speaking I seemed to be waking up.

As I sat there in the stillness before dawn, I felt a sudden urge arise within me. I wanted to share these experiences with someone who might understand them. Someone who wouldn't think they were strange.

I knew it was time to call her again.

19

A load of bollocks

I called Sophia.

We arranged another meeting. Once again, she was accommodating with her time. She suggested we meet in a couple of days.

Before then, I had what on the face of it appeared to be a dull meeting with two lawyers, Katie and Rishi. Sebastian asked me to meet with them to tie up some loose ends on a contract. As we settled down in an exorbitantly furnished meeting room, Katie politely kicked off proceedings with some customary small talk.

"Have you been at Elevate long?" she asked.

"Just a couple of months."

"Sebastian doesn't take on people lightly," Rishi said, his tone colder and more formal than his colleague's. "I assume you have a background in talent management?"

"Not quite," I smiled back. "I actually met one of Sebastian's colleagues in a taxi queue. We got talking. One thing led to another and here I am."

"Gosh!" exclaimed Katie, locking eyes with mine. "I love that."

Nice eyes.

I noticed for the first time how pretty she was. Long blonde hair. Sparkling hazel eyes. Soft delicate features. The perfect girl next door.

"So, what *is* your background?" asked Rishi, rather rudely I thought, given I was his client.

"It's kind of hard to say."

I gave them both a quick potted history. You know the one. My first graduate job. The acting thing. My week-long job in sales. My first few months at Elevate. My story had become a well-rehearsed elevator pitch.

Rishi looked unimpressed. But Katie flashed another pearly white smile in my direction.

Nice smile.

"Well, clearly fortune favours the brave," she said, gesturing towards me with her hand.

"I really believe it does," I smiled back.

"Where do you get your courage from, Vee?" she asked.

"Shouldn't we get back to the contract?" Rishi interrupted. He slid a copy of it across the table to me.

"We've got time," said Katie, pulling rank.

Rishi sat back in his chair and fiddled with the rim of his glasses to disguise his annoyance, whilst Katie looked expectantly in my direction, waiting for an answer to her question.

Courage?

"I think it comes from a spiritual place. I've always had this belief that everything will work out if your heart is in the right place."

Rishi rolled his eyes but Katie responded enthusiastically.

"That's such a nice thought," she replied, bright-eyed.

And that was it. For the next fifteen minutes, all Katie and I discussed was spirituality. Whilst Rishi looked on sceptically, the conversation flowed from clairvoyants to coincidences, to destiny. We were about to discuss energy fields and auras, but Rishi had clearly had enough.

"I think what you're talking about is a load of bollocks."

"Rishi! Don't be so rude," said Katie, embarrassed.

"But it *is* a load of bollocks. Isn't it?" replied Rishi, staring confrontationally in my direction.

He looked pleased with his attempt to unsettle me. For a second, he had.

Come on, Vee. Think of a clever response.

"What specifically is a load of bollocks?" I asked him, buying myself time.

"All this talk about energies and auras," he replied, mockingly waving his hands in the air as though imitating a ghost. "No one can sense these things. It's just speculation."

"Ok. I've got a question for you Rishi," I said, as the perfect riposte came to mind.

"Go on," he replied, smugly.

"How do you feel when you're ill?"

"Like shit."

"Like you've got no energy?"

"Yes."

"So, you're willing to admit there is a state in which you have no energy?"

"Yes," Rishi replied, struggling to see the relevance of my questions.

"But, you're not willing to admit there is an equal and opposite state in which you have an abundance of energy? An energy that you can feel? Or that somebody else might be able to sense?"

Rishi fiddled around again with the rim of his glasses. "Well, I've never thought about it like that before."

Katie did her best to conceal her amusement. I decided that was a good point to turn our attention back to dotting the i's and crossing the t's on the contract.

Thirty minutes later we were done. Rishi got up and excused himself from proceedings with a cold and clammy handshake. I got the impression he expected Katie to follow his lead. But she told him she'd be up in a minute or two. Rishi muttered something to himself and left.

Katie and I were now alone.

"Now, is it just me or does Rishi not like me very much?"

Katie laughed. "Just ignore him. He can be like that sometimes. He's a good lawyer though."

"Well, thank God he has at least one redeeming feature."

Katie laughed.

"Vee, it's so refreshing to meet someone who isn't so bloody corporate," she said, propping her elbows up on the table and resting her face between her hands. "I really wish I was as brave as you. My life is so predictably dull."

"There's nothing stopping you being brave. Courage resides within us all."

"Do you think so?"

I nodded. "It's there in that feeling we have that life can change for the better. That we ourselves can become something more."

"I can't remember the last time I felt that way, if ever."

Katie's head dropped.

"I know you have the courage you need," I replied, trying to uplift her.

Katie looked back up at me, her face a mixture of doubt and hope. "I wish that was true. But I find it hard to believe…in my case at least."

A trace of dejection flashed across her face before she smiled and it disappeared.

I wondered how I could help her. Get her to see things differently. Then, it came to me.

I shuffled forward in my seat. "Let me tell you about this experience I had…"

I told her about the *what it would be like to forget everything* experience. About the silence. The stillness. The bliss. About how my consciousness expanded. About the conviction I felt, that I – *we* – could be anything we wanted to be.

Katie looked spellbound.

"Why doesn't something like that happen to me?" she asked, ruefully.

"It can," I said emphatically, as if sure of it.

I told her next about the lucid dreams. How they appeared more real than life itself.

The captivated look on Katie's face spurred me on to greater lyrical heights.

"Have you ever heard that poem by Coleridge?" I asked her with an extra air of mysteriousness. "About dreams?"

She shook her head. "I'd love to hear it."

I cleared my throat. I wanted to do the poem justice. I recited it with all the poetic flair I could muster:

"What if you slept,

And what if in your sleep you dreamed

And what if in your dream you went to heaven

And there plucked a strange and beautiful flower

And what if when you awoke, you had that flower in your hand

Ah, what then?"

"That's beautiful," replied Katie.

Our eyes met once more, sharing silent words of their own.

"Vee, you're wasted in talent management."

I awkwardly waved away her compliment. It's ironic. Like most people, I loved receiving praise. But I didn't actually know what to do with it when it arrived.

"Seriously, you could be an inspiration to so many," Katie mused.

"Do you think so?"

She nodded, with the sweetest smile.

"Well, if I ever find my calling…"

"Do you know what it might be?"

I puffed out my cheeks. "Who knows?"

"I'm sure you'll find out. The world needs more uplifting souls like you. Not the kind who always knock you down."

"Sounds like you're talking from experience."

She nodded. "I've got horrendously competitive siblings. The kind who'd rather pull you back, than push you forward."

I shook my head. "Katie, you've got so much going for you. Don't let anyone hold you back."

"I try," she said. Her voice quivered. "It's just hard when all your life you've been told you're not good enough. That you shouldn't set your sights so high."

Our eyes met again but only briefly. Katie looked away. Her eyes welled up. My heart melted. I reached across the table and lightly touched her hand.

"God, I can't believe I'm actually crying," she said, wiping away her tears before they had chance to escape, "in front of a client too."

I thought my own eyes were going to well up.

"It's ok," I reassured her.

"It's just so hard when you've been told so many times that you'll never amount to anything."

"Katie, don't let anyone tell you what you can and can't do," I replied, defiantly.

The words came out with more passion than I expected.

"That's ok for you to say. You have got so much going for you," Katie smiled, dejectedly.

"Well, this might surprise you then…" I said, leaning forward. "When I was a kid, no one thought much of me either."

"Really?" she said, cocking her head to one side and wiping away the last of her tears.

I nodded back. "That's why I always cheer on the underdog. Or believe in that person no one else believes in. That was me once."

Our gazes met once more. There was so much softness and kindness in her eyes. I felt drawn towards her.

Just then, her phone vibrated with a text. She glanced down to read the message.

"It's Rishi," she said.

"Is he insisting you come up right this minute?" I laughed.

"Something like that. But, if I had it my way I'd sit and talk to you all day."

Me too, I thought.

There was something about this softly-spoken lawyer that made me feel warm inside. Like lying on the grass on a summer's day, holding hands with the one you love.

"I better get this contract all tied up," Katie sighed, as we both got up.

"Yeah, I should get back to it too."

"But," she said, scribbling down her number on a piece of paper. "Perhaps we could meet up again sometime, away from work?"

"I'd love that," I replied, as our eyes locked one last time.

We stood there for a second.

I didn't know whether to kiss her on the cheek and hug her goodbye. That was what I wanted to do. But I shook her hand gently instead. Her skin, like her nature was soft and delicate.

I don't know if it was something about Katie or that everything in my life was clicking into place, but I floated out of the meeting room that day with my head in the clouds.

What a journey life was turning out to be.

As I headed back to the office, I thought ahead to tomorrow's meeting with Sophia.

There was so much to tell.

20

For real

We were sat in the same coffee shop again.

It felt like no time at all had passed. Yet, so much had happened since we'd last met.

"So, what's been going on?" Sophia asked, flicking a stray strand of hair behind her ear.

The question was just the invitation I needed.

Careful not to leave out any detail that might be significant, I launched into the sequence of events that led to my job at Elevate. I told her how well I was doing and about the famous people I was regularly rubbing shoulders with.

Sophia, however, was unmoved by the household names I dropped into the conversation. Although, she did raise an eyebrow when I mentioned Albert Stines. The silver fox was clearly a favourite with the ladies.

"And away from work?" she asked. "What's been going on?"

My face lit up.

"This is where it all gets very interesting," I replied putting my cappuccino down. "I know you said to be patient with my spiritual side but listen to this..."

I gave her an animated account of my spiritual experiences and lucid dreams. How I felt like I could do anything. How real my dreams appeared. The amazing voyages they took me on. The exhilaration of flying over oceans and mountains and of seeing beautiful places of natural beauty, so vivid in colour.

I told her about the gatekeeper, the manor house and the glass ceiling I was unable to break through. I told her what happened when I finally did escape and of the paradise I saw.

Eventually, I stopped speaking. I looked towards her expectantly. I wondered what she might say. Her response surprised me.

"There's a reason why all these places in your dreams look so real. They are."

"*What? Really?*"

Sophia nodded. "They exist on higher planes of consciousness. Your ability to see them is a reward."

"For what?" I asked, intrigued.

"Your spiritual endeavour."

"*Really?*"

She nodded again.

I'd read somewhere previously about different planes of consciousness. Like the astral and mental planes. I never once thought they were real.

"I have seen those places too on the other side," Sophia added.

"Other side?"

"Beyond the veil of this physical world," she clarified.

"Really?"

I really was saying *really* a lot.

"Yes, really," she smiled as though it was the most natural thing in the world and certainly no big deal. "I saw a grand house just like you. But my challenge wasn't to break through a glass ceiling."

"What was yours?" I asked, leaning forward towards her.

"I had to jump over a very high boundary wall. Every time I jumped another would appear. Then another, until finally, I cleared them all."

I didn't know what to think. The common elements in our respective experiences suggested there was something more to them. But I still couldn't wrap my head around what.

"What are these experiences?" I asked.

"They're tests."

"Tests?"

"Yes, spiritual tests."

"Of?"

"Your character. Your heart, desire, bravery, willpower."

I felt a sudden rush of satisfaction. Pleased I'd overcome these tests – *if* what Sophia was saying was true.

Sophia broke into my thoughts as if sensing what I was thinking.

"I should warn you, however," she said, her expression more serious this time. "Your spiritual journey has only just begun. You're not always going to be flying over oceans or floating away on pink fluffy clouds."

I felt like she'd burst my bubble.

"Life may get more difficult for a while," she added, solemnly.

"Difficult?"

I didn't expect that.

"You're stronger now, Vee. That means the challenges you'll be called upon to face will be bigger too."

My eyebrows knotted.

What bigger challenges?

Inadvertently, I thought back to my battle with suicidal thoughts. It was all in the past now. But I still didn't want to think about that time, when I was in danger of losing my mind and grip on reality.

Shall I tell her about it?

I contemplated whether I should. But I resisted. I'd never spoken a word to anyone about it. Not one soul.

"But don't worry, Vee," Sophia said, intruding once more into my thoughts. "No matter how hard you're tested, have faith you will always find the strength you need to do what needs to be done."

After a nervous intake of breath, I did my best to shrug off the dark thoughts that had momentarily resurfaced. I reminded myself: my life was on an upward trend now.

Sophia studied me closely. "You look pensive."

"No, I'm ok."

"Are you sure?"

I nodded.

"I hope you're not deflated by what I just said."

"Of course not," I lied.

"That's good, because you've made great progress these past few weeks. That's why I really need you to listen to what I'm about to say next."

It sounded like more warnings coming my way.

They were.

21

A light worker

Sophia brought the palms of her hands together and rested her chin on her fingertips. "You need to be careful now, Vee."

"Of what?" I asked, mystified.

"You're shining brighter than before."

"I don't understand."

"People will be more drawn towards you now. They'll more easily come under your spell. Don't manipulate them with your charm or dominate them with your presence."

What?

I stared back at her indignantly. Sophia smiled to soften the mood. But her comments felt unfounded and unfair.

Manipulative? Domineering?

"I'm not that kind of person," I replied. But as I did, my mind raced back to the meeting with the two lawyers, Katie and Rishi:

Did I manipulate Katie with my charm?

Did I dominate Rishi with my presence?

Sophia interrupted my thoughts. "I'm only saying this pre-emptively."

"Pre-emptively? In case of what?"

Sophia looked thoughtful, as though working out the best way to proceed. "In case your ego takes over."

"*My ego?*"

She nodded. "There's a danger it might get out of hand."

"How?"

I felt put out by her comment.

"The more spiritual progress you make the more others will find you attractive," she replied.

"What's wrong with that?" I shrugged.

"You'll have greater influence over others. But you must not misuse this power.*"*

She spoke like I'd already been guilty of this in the past.

"I wouldn't do that," I replied, sure of it. "I'd never take advantage of anyone."

"Not intentionally, no. But …"

"But what?"

Sophia hesitated. "Just remember one thing, Vee. Your charm, charisma and good looks are *not* the reason why others – especially the fairer sex – find you attractive..."

She paused to get my full attention.

"…Your spiritual energy is. You're a light worker, Vee, and light workers are always attractive to others."

"*A light worker?*"

I'd never heard the term before.

"You're a channel for divine light. You're one of those spiritual souls that are here to help others."

I recoiled back in my chair.

Is that all I'm here to do?

I wanted to entertain people. Inspire them. Wow them. That's what pulled me towards acting. That's why I liked the thought of writing a book. That's why I pushed myself when playing sports in my youth. That's why I spoke about spirituality every chance I'd get.

But if I could admit the truth to myself – I can now, I couldn't then – I loved to inspire *and* impress in equal measure.

That's why the thought of just helping others didn't sit well with me. It didn't appeal to me one bit, no matter how I tried to frame it.

"What makes you think I'm a light worker?" I asked, frowning.

"Many reasons."

"Like?"

"You may not see it yet but you have a wonderful sense of humanity. You care about people. You have that special gift."

"What gift?"

"Of uplifting others. Making them feel like they can reach up and touch the sky. It's just your ego…"

"What about it?"

"It's in danger of getting inflated."

I shook my head indignantly, as if to say: *you really don't know me, do you?*

"Vee, all I'm trying to say is your ego *could* lead you astray. I'm not saying it will."

"I think you're misjudging me. That's not the kind of guy I am," I replied, my ego reeling.

I looked away from Sophia, disgruntledly. As I did, I saw a man in a pinstripe suit arrogantly click his fingers to summon a waiter in the café.

Now there's a man with an ego.

I was nothing like that. I looked back at Sophia, with pursed lips, contemplating how to respond, if at all.

"Look, all I'm saying is be careful, Vee. Just don't misuse the spiritual gifts at your disposal. It's happened before…"

What?... Before?

Sophia was about to say something else but quickly checked back on herself.

"No – that can wait for another time," she said holding back whatever was on the tip of her tongue.

"What can?"

"Doesn't matter," she replied, waving away my question.

"No, go on," I asked, intrigued. "What were you going to say?"

"Really, it was nothing, Vee."

"It didn't sound like nothing."

Sophia just shook her head, like it was no big deal.

I paused. What was she withholding from me?

"So, what do light workers actually do?" I asked, changing tack.

"Vee, it's not what they – *we* – do that matters," she replied. "For light workers, it's *the being in the doing* that is important."

It sounded like she'd said something profound but it was lost on me. My mind was preoccupied.

What was she about to say before but didn't? What was that all about?

"Sorry, I didn't catch that last thing you said," I replied, with a slight shake of the head.

"I was talking about the being in the doing," she repeated.

It sounded like some arcane Zen saying. I tried to decipher its meaning, without success. That annoyed me. Normally, *I* was the one dispensing wisdom. I was the one rattling off philosophical sound bites. Like always, Sophia seemed to have the edge on me, spiritually. It was something I was having a hard time accepting.

"So, what's the being in the doing?" I asked, sullenly.

"I'll explain. In this world, everyone is so preoccupied by what they *do*," she said, putting particular emphasis on that last word. "For a living, I mean. Don't you agree?"

I nodded.

"Especially in the world of glamour where you now work. Whether it's celebs or corporate execs, it's the one question everyone asks – *so, what do you do?*"

I nodded again.

"But spiritually speaking, it's *who you are* that matters," she said, placing her hands over her heart. "It's who you choose to *be* that defines you. Not what you do."

I nodded again but I was only feigning to understand.

I was one of those people who were preoccupied with what they did for a living and what that implied to others. I liked the fact that I worked for Elevate. That I worked directly for the managing director. That I was rubbing shoulders with celebrities. All of that made me feel good about myself.

It made me feel special.

And what's wrong with that? I thought, thinking back to her warnings about my ego.

I looked off into the distance, trying to process what she'd said.

I didn't quite know what to make of it all. Our conversation today had so many ups and downs. I liked the thought that I'd progressed spiritually. That I'd been rewarded for that growth with the experiences I'd had. That bit I liked.

But the prospect of things now getting harder dampened my mood. The thought of having to rein in my personality bothered me. The thought I could potentially have an out-of-control ego depressed me. The thought that I was some kind of light worker – here just to serve others – burdened me.

Sophia sensed my apprehensions.

"Look, I didn't mean to weigh you down, Vee. I'm happy you have made such great progress. Really, I am."

She stressed that last point like I needed convincing.

"But it would be remiss of me, as someone who is here to help you, who wants nothing but the best for you, if I didn't point out some of the warning signs which may spell danger ahead."

"Thanks," I replied flatly.

I forced a strained smile from my lips.

Sophia smiled back. She then did that strange thing again, of looking at my aura. This time, she kept her gaze firmly locked on the space above my head. She held it there for an uncomfortably long moment.

"What is it?" I asked.

"Your crown chakra. It's very active."

"Isn't that a good thing?"

"Not when it's vibrating as haphazardly as it is."

My eyebrows furrowed. "I don't understand."

"It's like your mind is bopping along to a bad pop song rather than flowing with a beautiful symphony."

At the time, I knew very little about chakras but I knew there were seven of them. Now I can reel off the Sanskrit name for each chakra if you asked. On occasion, I can even sense their energy. But I have never (yet) been able to see them. I've only met three people who claimed they could. Sophia was one of them and according to her, my crown chakra was a cause for concern.

"Maybe just slow things down, Vee. Ease off a little on all fronts," she suggested.

"Why?" I asked, concerned.

"There's a danger you might be burning the candle at both ends. Give yourself a little rest."

That was where we left that conversation. It left me feeling flat. My past meetings with Sophia had always ended on an uplifting note. Not today.

"Thank you," I said getting to my feet.

I told her I was appreciative of her time. Again, despite my remonstrations, she refused to take any payment for her services.

So, we said our goodbyes.

I had walked into that meeting with Sophia on a high. All light and free. Now, I felt weighed down by the danger warnings she had saddled me with – about the bigger challenges ahead, about my ego getting out of hand, about my crown chakra vibrating the wrong way!

But, as I walked away from the coffee shop, a soothing thought reconciled the conflict brewing in my mind.

You don't have to believe everything she says, it said.

It was true. I didn't.

But, time would tell that Sophia spoke the truth. Things would get hard. My ego would get inflated.

Unfortunately, I had little appreciation then that 'pride goeth before the fall'.

22

Choking

Three days passed by.

I was off my game. It became outwardly visible when Sebastian unexpectedly caught me off guard in a meeting.

"Vee, why don't you share some insights from your acting days with us," he said, completely off the cuff, as his senior management team looked on expectantly.

Acting days?

I could hardly call them that.

I stood up, cleared my throat and rambled off a few incoherent words. I looked for some reassuring glances from my audience. None came.

I felt lost. Sebastian's impromptu request had thrown me. I tried to come across as though I knew what I was talking about. I tried to find some clever parallels between acting and business.

"Pitching for business is just like acting…" I said at one point.

But then, I thought: *that makes the whole process sound inauthentic.*

And Sebastian was all about being real. Not fake.

I tried to recover my line of thought but I was just talking shit. The vacant stares looking back at me told me as much. It was obvious I'd lost my audience, along with my train of thought. I got the distinct impression a few of the onlookers were enjoying watching me crash and burn.

Soldiering on, I struggled to piece together the right words. I had no idea where I was going with it all.

How long have I been up here?

It felt like I'd been hung out to dry, for days. My mind felt scrambled. I looked across at Sebastian. He knew I was struggling. His eyes narrowed as he looked at me, floundering helplessly. But in this awkward, agonising moment there was nothing I could do to salvage the situation – the weight of expectation was too much. I was crumbling.

Stop screwing this up, Vee!

But the longer I spoke, the more my cheeks flushed with embarrassment, the more my voice quivered with fear, and the more I struggled to hide the discomfort of being put on the spot.

Fuck.

I couldn't deny it. I was choking under pressure and everyone in the room knew it. I felt like I had done as a young kid –vulnerable, weak, not good enough.

As far as career-defining moments go, it was nothing more than a blip. But at the time, it felt devastating. Up until then everything at Elevate had progressed smoothly. Better than expected. But now I felt like I'd lost ground. Lost respect. My star was not shining as bright. Would others think less of me? Would Sebastian rate me less? I felt like I was tainted in his eyes.

"Let's move on," was all he said when I brought my rambling talk to a limp and unsatisfactory close.

That night before surrendering to sleep, I was assailed by a stream of negative thoughts. Each one screaming out the same message:

You're not as good as you think you are.

These mocking thoughts depleted me. My body felt weak and shivery. As I fell asleep, my dreams took on a desperate air. At one point, I realised I was lucid dreaming but when I jumped upwards to fly as normal, I couldn't. I just span round and round uncontrollably in the air.

In another dream, I found myself driving a speeding car which veered haphazardly all over the road. Then, the dream shifted. I was presenting on stage, but standing there naked and exposed before a sniggering audience.

I awoke the next day disgruntled.

I ventured into the kitchen, hoping a strong sugary cup of coffee might revive me. Walking in, a book I'd left lying around caught my eye: *The Tao Te Ching*.

I flicked it open at random:

'Fill your bowl to the brim and it will spill.

Keep sharpening your knife and it will blunt.

Chase after money and security and your heart will never unclench.

Care about other people's approval and you will be their prisoner.

Do your work, then step back. This is the only path to serenity.'

I smiled, tiredly. These were words I needed to hear.

Serenity.

That's what I needed.

I had been pushing hard on all fronts. I was progressing fast at work. Building strong relationships. Attending every networking event going. But in all that busyness, my mind was preoccupied with something else: Sophia's warning that bigger challenges were coming my way.

What could they be?

Not being able to see them looking forward, Sophia's warning about the future triggered the unwanted release of difficult memories from harder times gone by.

Five years.

That's how long it had been since battling past that spell of suicidal depression. I say 'spell' but it felt more like a life sentence. Thinking back, the darkness of that time had descended surreptitiously. Like a huge dark cloud that appears from nowhere but casts its ominous gloom everywhere. One moment it was light, then all went dark. One moment I was riding high, the next I'd plunged head-first into what felt like an inescapable ditch.

If I was more discerning back then, perhaps I would have noticed that the signs of my impending fall from grace were there in advance.

The first came on the night of my twenty-first birthday. It was a strange *supernatural* encounter. I do not use that word in italics lightly. What happened on that macabre night started off as a dream:

1998 – I am running a business. I sense I'm very successful but arrogant too. I can feel my inflated pride overflowing with every step I take as I survey my corporate empire.

That's when it happens.

As I am walking, full of conceit and puffed up on my own ego, I fall down a huge hole that opens up before me. I keep falling and falling and falling. Dropping deeper and deeper.

Then, I hear laughter. Evil mocking laughter emanating from demonic faces that suddenly appear all around me. The laughter is unending. The fall is unending. This torturous moment is unending.

Will it ever stop?

Then, I hit rock bottom and see the vilest face you can imagine. Its evil laughter is greater and more penetrating than all that has gone before. The terrifying sound and sight of this hideous entity is too much to bear.

I wake up, drenched in sweat lying on my back. I am breathing heavily and anxiously. But I am grateful the dream has ended. Unfortunately, the torment has not.

I look up and see two greenish ghouls hovering above me; their faces every bit as evil as the ones I'd seen in my dream. They snarl. They try to suck the very life out of my body (I have no other way of describing this).

I try to scream. I try to move. But my body is paralysed with fear and my mouth forcibly closed shut through some invisible means.

I silently plead with my eyes for them to stop. But they do not let up. I feel myself being pulled upwards towards them and then violently dropped and then pulled up once again.

I try to scream once more. Still, no sound comes out.

Then, one single word appears in my mind: *God*.

The invisible force that is holding my mouth shut is suddenly unable to restrain my voice.

"God! God!" I shout, in desperation.

The divine word has power within it. Both creatures vanish before my eyes.

I am sweating even more profusely now. My breathing is erratic and my heart, racing. It's the strangest most terrifying experience I can recall.

Was it a dream?

I know that's what you must be thinking. That's what I would think if someone narrated this nightmare tale to me. Perhaps it was? But to this day, I'm adamant. *I was awake.*

Either way, it doesn't matter. It was a prophetic sign. One I missed. It was a warning of the impending danger my pride and arrogance posed.

But all that registered at the time was the fear and strangeness of the experience. Not the message it was trying to convey.

I wish I had taken heed of it. It would have saved me *a lot* of pain and mental anguish I didn't need to suffer. Or did I?

I think it's time to tell you what happened.

23

Five years ago

Let's go five years back.

1998 – 2 months after my twenty-first birthday:

I don't like thinking about that terrifying supernatural ordeal on the night of my twenty-first.

My mind is working in another direction now.

I've become religious. I've stopped drinking. I've become vegetarian. I feel deeply spiritual. Elevated.

But my friends tell me I've changed. They say I'm different but not 'good different'.

They tell me: "Stop being so glib and sanctimonious."

I tell them, *they* need to change. They need to become more serious about life and their purpose.

"Don't squander this life," I warn them. "It's too precious to waste."

They accuse me of being sententious: "Walking and talking like God himself."

I pay no attention to them.

Next, they tell me: "You've got some kind of messiah complex."

I do feel like *I am* destined to be some kind of guru. That feels like my destiny. But I don't tell them that.

Dad wants me to join the family business. But I don't feel like I'm here to follow in his footsteps. They are too big to follow anyway. I don't think I can match dad's success commercially.

But no matter. Spirituality is *my thing*. It's my forte. My strength. My passion. It used to be sport. But I feel like I've missed the boat now on any major sporting triumph. Spirituality now is my only path.

1998 – 4 months after:

I'm in a debate with a man I hardly know. We're discussing God.

"Stop speaking like you've got all the answers," he accuses me.

"I'm not. But there is an answer for every question," I reply back calmly.

He shakes his head. "Ok. So, why do bad things happen?"

"What do you mean?" I ask back, totally flummoxed.

"If there *is* a God, why do bad things happen? Why do people get murdered? Why do women get raped? Why do children get abused?"

Um.

I have no answer. I have no idea. I have never thought of such things. The depravity of mankind has never even entered my mind. Until now.

I feel unsettled. Ungrounded. Like someone has just pulled the metaphorical rug from underneath me and I am falling.

1998 – 5 months after:

I'm still falling. Just like I had in my dream. That had ended in minutes. But I keep falling and falling, for real. A fall from grace to the depths of utter despair.

The further I fall the more my thoughts torture me. The more my inner world frightens me. I'm desperately struggling to figure out why bad things happen. I *need* to know. I feel like my whole sanity depends on it.

But I am lost. I've taken a terrible detour. I am a man tormented by his own thoughts.

I keep thinking: What if *I* am bad? If I am evil? If we all are? *What then?*

These thoughts are screwing me over. All I see around me are the countless bad things happening in the world. The world is closing in on me. Like a dark oppressive shadow. I can't lift my head. When I look forward it feels as though I can't see anything in my peripheral vision, only darkness.

1998 – 6 months after:

I've started hearing voices in my head.

Despicable voices urging me to do despicable things. I feel disgusted. I am ashamed of the evil thoughts running riot within my mind. I'm so scared of my own thoughts.

Why has my mind become so wretched? Where has its purity, innocence and goodness gone? How can I seal this Pandora's Box of evil?

I dare not listen to the news or of any bad tidings. I can't bear to hear about the horrors of this world in case they exert some malicious influence on my mind and lure me into doing something terrible.

I am sick of hearing the malignant voices in my head.

Leave me alone, I keep telling them. But they won't.

It's too much.

I've decided: if this is the way life is going to be, I don't want to live this life. I don't want to hear these voices. I don't want to do anything bad. I don't want to hurt anyone. I would just rather *die.*

For these six suicidal months after my twenty-first birthday, I wrestled with these thoughts daily. Hour by hour. Hardly anyone sensed my desperate inner struggle. Outwardly, all seemed ok. Inwardly, I was barely functioning.

Wherever possible I avoided talking to people. Or if I had to, I avoided eye contact. I didn't want them to glimpse in my eyes these tormenting thoughts that had hijacked my mind. Thoughts that felt hideous and alien to me. Thoughts that were not my own but I was now somehow in possession of and unable to offload.

Each passing day became more of a struggle. How long could I live like this?

At the time, only one thought kept me going. The prophecy. The one grandad never let me forget. The one the holy man in India had revealed. That one day, I would realise my full potential. This thought gave me a glimmer of hope. That there was still something good and decent within me. Something I could salvage.

It was when things were at their worst, that relief finally came. As I contemplated how I might kill myself, a clear-cut thought shone brightly in my mind. It brought with it the life-affirming clarity I so desperately needed.

That thought was this:

If you have resisted this force of evil so much, you can't be bad. You must be good.

How true.

This one thought saved my life.

It put me back on the right path. It gave me faith once more in myself – in my innate goodness. I rebuilt my life from here, brick by brick, one positive thought at a time.

Five years on from that hellish experience, things had changed massively. I was stronger. Much stronger. My fight back to sanity had ensured that. It was a hard slog but it had toughened me up.

But what about those big challenges Sophia mentioned?

I'm sure she hadn't intended it. I'm sure she believed in that old maxim: forewarned is forearmed. But her words had cast a shadow of doubt on the future.

Everything was going so well, but now I kept thinking of everything that might go wrong. I feared the darkness of the past may return; that other inner demons were still lurking in the shadows.

Anyway, let's get back to the story.

As I was sat in the kitchen, sipping that sugary coffee, looking with tired eyes at the beautiful Zen-like cover of *The Tao Te Ching* I knew I needed to snap out of all this negativity. Let go of this mental heaviness. Simplify things in my head.

I got up and put the coffee down. I decided to do what I always did when I needed uplifting: visit grandad.

He was sat cross-legged on the back lawn of the family home. A lightness spread over me as I observed his radiant disposition. His face was calm and serene. He was meditating with his eyes closed. No doubt enjoying some inner bliss. As the sun triumphantly emerged from behind a cloud, I'm sure I saw a glow around his head.

I stepped forward towards him. He half opened his eyes and smiled sweetly. He stretched his arms high above his head before they fell gracefully into his lap.

He then spoke these wise words:

"Sometimes Viryam the best thing you can do is just enjoy where you are."

He smiled.

I smiled back. "Papa, that's just what I needed to hear."

He nodded back as though to say: *I know.*

So, that's what I decided to do.

Let go of all thoughts of the past and future. Totally forget about clairvoyants, predictions and destiny.

I was simply going to enjoy my life, right here, right now.

It's ironic then: by letting go, my mind took hold of a compelling new direction.

24

A very lucky face

Let go. Enjoy where you are.

This became my mantra. The simplicity of grandad's words cut through all my mental complexity. The more I repeated the mantra, the more I realised how much I was holding on to. Fears. Worries. Doubts. Expectations.

I'd forgotten about the simple mindfulness practices grandad and Sophia had suggested in the past. I had become too preoccupied with my thoughts. I was too much in my own head. I hadn't been in the moment at all.

But now, I was enjoying letting go of the past, the future and of thinking too much. This inner shift felt like such a release that I even thought about writing a book: *The Art of Letting Go*.

I let go of that thought too. There was just too much letting go to master.

But the deeper I practised the art of letting go, the more I discerned a change within me. Something worth noting. My mind rebelled. It panicked. It didn't want to let go. It feared being in the moment. It felt uneasy at ceding control to caprice, chance or fate.

I sensed its underlying fear; that I was dispensing with it.

I assured my mind I wasn't.

I wrote in my journal:

I'm freeing you up not pushing you away. Unlocking your potential, not wasting your power.

Partially reassured my mind went along for the ride. As I learned to let go and live more in the moment my energy rebounded. I felt stronger. More alive. I was living spiritually again.

As my energy radiated out, people responded favourably. I connected with others easily. Spontaneous conversations flowed freely.

Whether it was a chat with a stranger I'd just met or an impromptu meeting with someone in the office, the conversation nearly always flowed to one place – the subject of spirituality.

Whenever I got the opportunity, I waxed lyrical about it. In my exuberance, I can see now (but could not then) that my spiritual theories sometimes ran well ahead of my experience.

But others didn't seem to mind or care. They *seemed* to be moved by my words. This spurred me on even more. If I touched on a topic like the power of attraction, they looked engaged. If I told them about the serendipitous chain of events that led me to Elevate, they looked inspired. Like they too wished to set sail on their own life-affirming journey.

The more I conversed with others spiritually, the more my mind yearned to make a bigger impact. To reach more people. To make a real difference. I know we all talk about making a difference in our highest moments of altruistic aspiration, but I really wanted to do something.

Something *big*. I just didn't know what.

Then, three separate incidents occurred which gave me a fantastically enticing idea.

The first incident:

I was travelling on a train. I struck up a lively conversation with the young woman sat opposite me. I can't even recall how it started. I was actually hungover. I'd attended an awards ceremony the night before that went on until the earlier hours of the morning.

Whatever did spark the conversation into life, words (surprisingly) flowed with ease from my lips. Maybe I was still a little drunk from the night before. That was very possible. But whatever it was, I spoke with eloquence about life. I spoke emotively about my journey.

The young lady on the train was moved by the conversation. Sometimes she laughed out loud. Other times she sat silently, seriously, listening to my every word. Occasionally, she leaned back to reflect. Then, she'd lean in to share a story or two of her own. When it was time to go our separate ways, she said: "Thank you. That was the most memorable conversation I've had with someone I've just met."

I smiled back. "It's a conversation I won't forget either."

She was about to leave when she turned back. "You should write a book about all this stuff."

"Do you think so?" I asked.

Immediately, I *loved* the idea.

She nodded back.

"Well, maybe I will."

"Well, if you do, let me know. I, for one, would love to read it."

She scrambled around in her handbag for her business card and handed it to me before she left. That was the exact moment I first thought of writing *this* book. Or at least some version of it.

The second incident:

It took place a few days later. I was checking into a hotel for a work event. The receptionist was tapping away on her computer when I casually glanced to my right and happened to see Lauren, the clairvoyant. She was heading out of the hotel. I hadn't seen or spoken to her since my last reading, months earlier.

"Lauren!" I called out, dashing across the hotel lobby to catch her before she left.

She turned around and looked at me intently. Evidently, she was struggling to place my face.

"It's me, Vee," I said, surprised that she couldn't remember me.

"Vee?"

"You did a reading for me at the Marylebone Spa."

Lauren looked up to the left as if shifting through her memory banks. Then suddenly, as recollections so often occur, she instantly remembered who I was and hugged me affectionately as though we were old friends.

"So, have things started turning out as I suggested they would?"

"Oh gosh, yes!"

I was about to launch into an enthusiastic rendition of everything that had happened since we'd last met. But we were interrupted by the hotel receptionist. She needed my credit card to complete the check-in procedure.

As I fumbled around for my wallet, I noticed Lauren looked in a rush.

"Sorry, I hope I'm not holding you up," I said, apologetically.

"I've got a minute but only a minute," she replied.

Finally, I found the wallet. I pulled out my credit card and handed it to the receptionist.

I thought quickly of how best to use the time life had serendipitously afforded Lauren and I.

"I'm thinking of writing a book," I blurted out. "About my spiritual experiences."

I looked at her expectantly. I hoped her powers of clairvoyance would tell me whether it was a worthwhile undertaking.

"That's a fantastic idea. I get the impression you'll be well-known somehow. It's just as well. You do love the limelight."

She laughed after making that last remark.

Her first comment excited me. Her last troubled me. I know I liked the attention I got. But was it that obvious? I hardly basked in the spotlight. The thought of it made me feel shallow and ego-driven. But I brushed off her comment.

As when I first met her, a hundred and one questions assailed my mind. There was so much I wanted to ask. But now was clearly not the time.

A car horn sounded outside the hotel.

"That'll be my taxi," Lauren said apologetically. "I hope our paths cross again one day."

With that, she was gone.

But the thought of writing the book remained. My conviction to do so, even stronger than before.

The third incident:

This was stranger than the other two. It took place later that day after meeting Lauren.

A bearded man with an orange turban came right up to me on a busy street.

Without any preamble, he made the most bizarre statement.

"You my friend have a very lucky face," he said triumphantly, in a deeply sonorous voice. He spoke with a marked Indian accent.

I didn't know what to say in reply. What a strange compliment. What the hell constituted a lucky face in any case?

"I want nothing from you," the turbaned man reassured me, holding his palms out.

"Ok," I replied, unsure where this was all going.

"It's just that when I saw your face in this crowded street, I felt compelled to tell you something," he then said, speaking louder than necessary.

"Tell me what?" I asked.

A smile spread across the man's face.

"That success will be yours to enjoy. Life will favour your progress," he said, holding his arms aloft to make the point even more emphatically. "All will work out for you, whatever road you choose."

"Um, thank you," I replied, glancing around to see if anyone was witnessing this peculiar scene in which I had unwittingly taken centre stage.

I noticed a group of school girls standing nearby staring in my direction. They were giggling away and clearly enjoying the spectacle. I smiled back with embarrassment.

My gaze then returned to this stranger standing right up in my personal space. I wondered if he was mad. If he was, he was certainly a well-dressed madman. He wore a smart suit with a shirt but no tie.

"Would you like me to reveal more?" he then asked. "There is more your face is telling me."

"No. No, thank you," I replied, holding my hand up to him.

Maybe he genuinely was some kind of physiognomist, if there is such a thing. But I really didn't want to prolong the conversation any longer, in case it took an even weirder turn.

So, I quickly stepped aside from the man and briskly walked away.

Seconds later, I looked back over my shoulder. He was still looking my way, smiling mysteriously.

But when I glanced back a second time, he'd disappeared into the busy throng.

I did question this stranger's sanity. Nevertheless, I did take what he said as a good sign. For at the very moment he had approached me, my mind was busily engaged with thoughts of writing a book.

The idea was gaining real traction in my mind.

I imagined how many people I could reach. How many copies it might sell. How much money I might make. How the book might be my ticket to a bigger and better future. One that would see me take my place on Elevate's famed wall of talent – or another wall like it. The kind of success that would prove to others (dad especially) that I'd made it.

With these thoughts happily swimming around in my mind, I walked onward through that busy street with renewed vigour.

I had a book to write. A future to create.

For the first time, I thought I knew what I *really* wanted to do.

25

That's brave

Here's a quote I once read:

"When you are inspired by some great purpose, some extraordinary project, all of your thoughts break their bonds. Your mind transcends limitations; your consciousness expands in every direction; and you find yourself in a new, great and wonderful world. Dormant forces, faculties and talents become alive and you discover yourself to be a greater person than you ever dreamed yourself to be."

The words belong to Patanjali. I have the utmost respect for them. I have found that it's true: when your intention to do something is strong, great possibilities come about. Great capabilities awaken within you. Your inner and outer worlds burst into life with exciting new connections, both thrilling and unexpected.

All sorts of favourable developments occur that assist you in fulfilling the good purpose you have enshrined in your heart and envisioned in your mind.

In this state, the power of intention and attraction, seem like certainties. Universal laws upon which we can rely and build out our future dreams. This is the kind of conviction

I have now, but as a young man of twenty-five, I could only speculate on the veracity of Patanjali's words.

But the moment I got serious about writing the book, they began to feel true. Unexpectedly, all sorts of weird and wonderful things began happening; the very stuff I hoped would fill the pages of a bestseller.

Just a side note: to the more spiritually au fait amongst you, the experiences that follow in the coming chapters may seem run-of-the-mill stuff. To others, I fear they may sound far-fetched. But that's fine. I'm not here to convince you of anything. Besides, this story is not about the experiences themselves but the journey they inspired.

So, let's get back to it. It all began, as it so often does, unexpectedly. Understatedly.

On account of a tight hamstring, I'd booked in for a consultation with a physio. As she checked my range of mobility and began pinpointing the cause of the problem, she suddenly stopped what she was doing.

"Can I ask you what you do for a living?"

I told her about my job at Elevate.

"That surprises me," she said.

"How come?"

"I thought you might be doing something with a little more…oh how can I put it?" she replied, searching for the right word. "Gravitas."

"Really, why?"

I tried hard not to feel slighted by her comment.

"It's your aura."

"*My aura?*"

"Yes, when you walked through the door, I was kind of taken aback by it."

"How come?"

"You've got a very solid, confident aura. Sorry, forgive me, this must all sound very strange coming from a physiotherapist," she said, stretching out my hamstring.

"Not really," I smiled back. "It's the kind of conversation I tend to have with people I've just met."

"Really?"

I nodded back. "I had a massage recently where the masseuse turned out to be a clairvoyant."

"Oh, wow."

I told the physio I also knew someone who could allegedly see auras. Not to mention chakras and meridian channels.

"God, that's *so* interesting," she replied, prodding the area in the back of my leg that felt tender.

Ouch.

I grimaced as she worked her way deeper into the offending muscle.

"Sorry," she said. "Just tell me if the pain is too much."

I nodded.

"So, can you see auras?" I asked, getting back to our conversation.

"No. Although I do notice a faint transparent glow around people."

I told her I'd observed that too. A subtle white glow around one inch thick around a person's outline.

"I think it's just a trick of the eyes," I said.

The physio shook her head and looked at me.

"I think it's more than that," she replied. "I think that outline glow is the energy field around the body. I feel it more than I see it."

"Like how?"

"I get very strong feelings about people straight away. Like good or bad vibes."

"What did you sense about me?"

"Like I said," she replied. "Solid and confident. Strong and yet gentle too."

I felt pleased that my invisible aura allegedly reflected back well on me.

"This is so surreal. I came here for some physio and here we are talking about auras."

"I know, it's amazing."

I nodded. "I'm going to write a book about this stuff."

"Really? Fiction or non-fiction?" she asked, now massaging the muscles around my hamstring.

"Non-fiction."

"Have you checked out any scientific literature on it?" she probed.

"No."

She looked surprised.

"The book will be autobiographical."

"Wow. That's brave," she replied, flashing a raised eyebrow at me.

"Really, *why*?" I asked, unsure what bravery had to do with it.

"I couldn't put my whole life story out there."

"Why?"

"You know what most people are like … critical … sceptical … cynical."

I have to confess in my youthful naivety, I'd only really thought about how thrilling a read the book might be. I never once thought about how people might discredit or question it.

"Hopefully they won't rip it to shreds," I joked.

She laughed and crossed her fingers. "I do think a little background research might do it good. Just for context and credibility."

She reeled off some books she felt I should read.

"But it might get a little dry with too much science and theory," I replied back, as if that were the case.

But this was the truth: I couldn't be bothered with any time-consuming research. I was in a rush. I wanted to get my book out there. Strike while the iron was hot. In my mind, it was an instant bestseller already and I was its best-selling author.

The physio stopped what she was doing and cocked her head to one side.

"Maybe it's worth writing as fiction…" she then offered up. "Might give you a little more creative licence."

I looked back at her doubtfully. "No. I don't think so."

I want it to be a true story…my story, I thought.

"Ok. But just do this one thing then," she said fixing her gaze on mine.

"Go on," I replied.

Her suggestion was intriguing.

26

Out of body

"Read this book..."

The physio mentioned the name of a very well-known children's book of old. Now, a timeless classic.

"I know it's for kids, but there's so much latent spirituality infused in its pages. I'm reading it right now. I think you should too, before you write your own book."

My eyes widened.

"You're not going to believe this," I said, shaking my head.

"What?"

"You're the *third* person *this* week to recommend *that* book."

It's true. Three people independently of each other (without any prompting from me) had suggested it.

The physio stared back at me with childlike wonder.

"If the Universe was ever going to give you a bona fide sign," she said, holding her hands up to the heavens, "this is it."

I didn't need any further convincing.

A day later, I purchased the book.

I decided to read one chapter a night, slowly, in the hope any hidden symbolism would reveal itself. The fact that three people had randomly suggested the same book made me feel as though there was something written within it that I needed to hear.

With these thoughts in mind, I began working my way through it. One night – not too long after – the book had a very peculiar effect on me.

I was lying in bed, turning its pages, when the strangest sensation came over me. My body began to feel lighter and lighter. A sensation I'd never felt before. So light, in fact, I imagined I could just *float* away.

How strange.

If you have a rational mind, firmly grounded in scientific rigour, this floating sensation I describe may sound a touch bizarre. I know that, because my own mind, despite its spiritual inclination, tends to always think on scientific lines.

But whether it was this children's book, or a sentence, word or mantra from it that made me feel this way, I cannot say. Perhaps it was the way I was reading the book? Or maybe, it had nothing to do with the book at all. I don't know.

What I do know is, I couldn't deny what I was experiencing. I felt as though I could literally float right out of my body.

Days later *I did*.

Here's what happened.

It was early one weekend morning. I was lying in bed listening to a progressive relaxation CD. As instructed by the soothing voice narrating the exercise, I tensed and relaxed my muscles in turn.

Starting with my feet I worked my way up through the legs, the core and the upper section of my body. As I did, I felt myself sinking into the mattress. A real heaviness overcame me, especially my face.

That's when the strangest thing happened.

I felt my legs kick up into the air. But weirdly I couldn't see them. But there they were (or at least appeared to be) invisibly floating in mid-air.

Instinctively, I jerked up and down and felt myself kick out of my body. Surreal as this is to narrate, I found myself floating up towards the ceiling.

I was having an out-of-body experience!

Excitedly and nervously, I willed myself to float up and touch the ceiling. Then, I floated down to the ground before willing myself up again.

Suddenly, a voice called out.

"Vee, Vee," I thought I heard it say.

I tried to make out whose voice it was and from where it had emanated. But I was propelled back into my physical body, like a stretched rubber band that had been let go.

For a few seconds, I just lay there, contemplating the awesomeness of the experience. And the realisation: my consciousness could exist *outside* of my physical form. What a mind-bending shift in reality.

I laughed out loud.

But the strange series of sensations were not over. If I felt light before, I felt its complete reversal now. As I tried to get up off my bed, my body felt extremely heavy. Cumbersome. Like I was wearing a two-tonne suit of armour.

I can't move.

Actually, I could but each step forward felt like a massive test of will. But slowly and surely, my body recalibrated and took up its usual weight and feel.

I felt euphoric. Like I'd somehow defied the physical laws of the universe. I felt limitless. What else might be possible?

I wanted to tell someone about the experience. I needed to. It was too epic not to share. Instinctively, Sophia's name came to mind.

She *had* said things would get harder for me. But if anything, life was becoming more magical. I had to tell her this.

I called her right there and then.

She answered the phone.

Her response was not what I expected.

27

Stop rushing

Ten minutes non-stop.

That's how long I spoke to Sophia about my out-of-body experience.

She listened patiently at the other end of the line, whilst I made sure I disclosed every detail I could about every sensation I'd experienced.

The conversation was one-sided. I spoke rapturously. She said nothing.

"Can you believe it, Sophia? I was actually *outside* my body," I said, finishing up my buoyant account of what had happened.

I waited eagerly for her response. It was underwhelming when it came.

"You just experienced a split in consciousness," she said with a distinct lack of emotion.

"Sorry, what?"

"Temporarily, your consciousness may have separated from your physical form."

"I know. It was amazing. Like I was levitating or something. Do you think it will happen again?"

"Maybe," Sophia said, uninterestedly. "You might experience it regularly now or not again for a while."

Her tone was so indifferent. It bothered me. It was like I'd called to tell her I'd just put out the trash. Or had tomato pasta for dinner. But this was no plain vanilla quotidian happening – I'd just had an out-of-body experience!

Why was she so matter-of-fact about it all?

Perhaps she's envious?

But I immediately dismissed the thought.

"Can you travel when out the body?" I asked.

"Travel?"

"I mean can you consciously choose to visit some place or meet someone?"

I hoped the question might excite some passion in her for the conversation.

"Yes," she replied. "But you need to develop continuity of consciousness first?"

"Sorry, what?"

This was beginning to sound like a lesson in metaphysics.

"You need to be conscious when you leave, return or are outside the physical body. That takes mastery, Vee."

"Have you mastered it?"

My tone was more challenging than I intended.

There was silence at the other end of the line.

"Vee, I'm not going to say whether I have or I haven't," she replied, her voice firm and non-committal.

"Oh, ok."

"But what I will say is…"

"What?"

"Stop rushing this stuff."

"*I'm not*," I hit back defensively. "Everything is happening of its own accord."

"Vee, just be careful what you wish for, ok."

I was silent for a second or two.

"So, what should I do?" I asked, flatly.

"Just don't chase these kinds of experiences."

"And if I have another out-of-body experience?"

"Be relaxed. Just see where it takes you."

"Oh, right."

"Just a word of warning though…"

More warnings?

Sophia had dished out a good helping of them the last time we met.

"Just be careful you don't get lost down a rabbit hole."

We ended the conversation there.

I scratched my head. Why had Sophia been so indifferent? Like my OBE was no big deal.

How many people can say they've ever had one?

Not many. Otherwise, we'd all be talking about them.

And what was with all these warnings?

She'd dampened my enthusiasm the last time we spoke too. Like she was purposely reining me in. Telling me not to manipulate others. Or dominate them. Or whatever else.

Now I was being told not to rush things and to be careful what I wished for. All this, whilst my spiritual life was actually taking off.

I don't get it.

But I decided something there and then: Sophia was not going to hold me back.

I wanted to explore the possibilities that were opening up, not shut them down. Share them with the world, not hide them away. I wanted to write my book, not shelve my experiences.

I felt defiant in the face of her advice.

I'm going to find out more about OBEs.

So, I decided to pay a visit to a little spiritual book shop, not far from where I lived. I loved going there. Even when I had no reason to. It had become a favourite hangout of mine. A little sanctuary away from the hustle and bustle of London life.

I'm glad I did go.

Another unexpected conversation lay in wait. A reality-shifting one.

28

"Ever had one of those?"

I walked through the front door.

The wind chimes hanging in the entrance played out their melodious notes. I took in the scent of incense wafting through the air. My eyes savoured all this quaint little shop had to sell. Spiritual books. Natural candles. Gemstones. Incense sticks. Yoga mats. Tarot cards. Rustic wooden furniture. And of course, the customary range of Buddhas to suit all tastes.

I made my way over to the books. I knew exactly what I was looking for. I was in luck. I found a book on astral projection and another on OBEs. I began leafing through them. Instantly, I was absorbed. So much so that I didn't realise there was someone standing next to me.

"Ever had one of those?" said a softly spoken voice.

I looked to my right. A petite middle-aged lady with dark, cropped hair was looking back at me through thick-rimmed spectacles. A yoga mat was tucked under her arm.

"Sorry. Have I ever had…?"

"One of *those*," she replied, tapping the front cover of one of the books I was holding.

"An out-of-body experience?"

"Yes," she nodded back.

I wondered how best to respond.

"Have you ever had one?" I asked.

"Oh gosh, yes. Many times!"

What?

"Really?"

"Yes, I still remember the first time it happened," she replied, gleefully. "I must have been ten or so. I was standing next to my mother when I fainted. The next thing I know, I was floating above the scene and could see my mother below, cradling me in her arms."

"Fascinating. I had…"

I hesitated.

"You had what?" she enquired.

"…my first-ever experience this morning," I replied, finding the courage to share my truth.

"Really? Do tell me more."

I told her everything I'd told Sophia earlier.

"Oh, how wonderful. Isn't being out the body such a delight?" she said playfully.

"It was liberating."

There was a moment's pause.

"Can I ask you a question?" I then asked.

"Sure."

"Do you have continuity of consciousness when it happens?"

"Sorry? Continuity of ….?"

"Consciousness."

The friendly spectacled lady stared back at me, blankly. Evidently, she'd never heard the term before. To be fair, neither had I until Sophia had mentioned it this morning.

"I don't know what you mean, unfortunately," she replied.

"Sorry, what I mean to say is, are you always completely conscious when leaving, returning or being out of your body."

"Oh, I see. No, I can't say I am."

"Oh."

"But I do float out quite regularly."

"Really?"

She nodded. "And when it happens, do you know what I love to do?"

I shrugged my shoulders and smiled at her childlike wonder.

"I float up onto the roof of my house and sit there in the middle of the night, enjoying the silence."

"Sounds very pleasant," I replied, trying not to look too incredulous.

"Oh, it is," she replied, as if describing a mere walk in the park.

"And what do you do then?" I asked, in a hushed voice. "After sitting on your roof?"

I glanced around to see if anyone was eavesdropping. But we were safe. There was no one in earshot.

"Well, if the mood takes me, I fly up into the night sky, past the moon and towards the stars."

As you do, I thought.

I looked at her in disbelief as she emulated a fast-moving rocket with her free hand.

"Can you really do that? Fly towards the stars?"

"Of course. But I don't always do that. Sometimes I visit places here."

"Here?"

"Earth," she clarified.

"Yes. Of course, Earth" I replied as if we were having the most normal conversation.

"Or if not a place," she added, "I visit someone I want to see."

"How do you get there?"

"I just will myself there."

I shook my head. "But *how*?"

"Don't know how but I know it's possible. They call it remote viewing. Apparently, you can travel anywhere in space and time."

"*And time?* As in the past or future?"

"Allegedly," she nodded back.

It's strange. Despite my own spiritual experiences (that many would find hard to believe), I was having a hard time believing in hers.

"But let me just say," she continued, "I've never time travelled. But I know for sure remote viewing is a thing."

I didn't know what to make of this all. Yes, I'd had an OBE that very morning. But the thought of travelling anywhere in the world just by willing it, was a bridge too far for me.

"Sometimes all this stuff doesn't seem real," I said, looking at the books I was holding and then back at her.

"I know," she replied, cheerily. "But I've learned to trust in my own experiences and honour my own truth."

She glanced down at her watch, almost dropping her yoga mat in the process. "It's been such a pleasure chatting to you."

"Yes, thank you for the most intriguing conversation."

She smiled back.

"Before I go, can I make a suggestion?" she said.

"Sure."

"Don't force any of this," she said, tapping one of the books I was holding. "Let it flow naturally."

I nodded back.

"Because I know what you, young folk are like," she said, pointing a playful finger at me. "Always in a hurry."

I blushed.

With that, she smiled warmly and left.

I stood there, in a bit of a daze.

Did I really just have that conversation?

Whether what she'd said was true or not, I was intrigued. If these were the kind of possibilities on offer, I wanted to explore them. See if they were real. Experience them, *if* they were. Then write about them, so the whole world could know of them too.

And know of me, I imagine my ego whispered, not loud enough for me to hear.

29

The tree

Ok.

Time to hold my hands up.

I know Sophia said to stop rushing and the spectacled lady in the bookshop told me not to force things, but I was a little too pumped up on the possibilities before me.

I reasoned:

If I am going to write this book and this book is going to be a riveting read, I need to be more adventurous. Push the boundaries of possibility.

This was all I could think about. So, when I was at work, overseeing a glitzy PR campaign for a client or compiling a strategy deck for Sebastian, all I could really think about was: *how can I float out my body again?*

Every evening, I tried my best to relax. I listened repeatedly to the guided relaxation CD that had triggered my first OBE. But frustratingly nothing happened, at first. But then, finally, some encouragement.

One night, when semi-awake in the early hours of the morning, I felt my arms and legs lifting away from the bed. Like I was about to float out. But nothing else happened.

Two weeks later, something did.

It was the middle of the night. I was half awake. Half asleep. I suddenly got the feeling I was going to float out. Lying on the bed, I felt my physical body get heavier but a subtle body within me get lighter. As the two separated I floated up off the bed.

Yes!

I was having another out-of-body experience.

At once, I looked down to see if my physical body was lying there. But I got distracted by a thought. A possibility. Could I float through my bedroom wall to the garden outside?

It was a queer thought. But it felt entirely possible. To my utter amazement, I managed the feat effortlessly.

Woah!

I couldn't believe it. I'd just experienced the sensation of passing right through a solid brick wall. As if by osmosis.

I was hovering above the garden now. I looked up at the night sky. It was dark with beautiful hints of pink and red.

Suddenly, a thought occurred to me. I could go anywhere in the world. A thousand and one destinations flashed before my eyes. Each one vying for attention. But the excitement was too much. Before I could even say "OBE", I was back in my bed, fully awake in my physical body.

Instantly, the scientist in me took over. I ran to the bedroom window and pulled back the curtain. I couldn't believe it.

The sky!

It was dark with beautiful hints of pink and red. The exact same sky I'd seen when out of my body. This couldn't just be coincidence. Could it?

The next morning, I had a catch-up coffee with Katie, the lawyer. We'd become close. Professionally and personally. We talked about all sorts of stuff – big and small, profound and light-hearted. She knew all about my book idea and was already its biggest fan.

When we met up that morning in a quiet corner of a little Soho coffee shop, I told her about my OBEs.

Her eyes widened. Wonder and intrigue etched all over her face.

"I'm not doubting you but are you sure you weren't dreaming?" she asked.

"I was completely lucid."

"And you hadn't been smoking any questionable substances?"

I laughed. "Come on, what do you take me for? I *really* had an out-of-body experience."

"Well, then that's bloody amazing, Vee!" she said, leaning into me as we sat side by side. "You've got even more magical material for your book."

"I know. It's really mind-blowing how stuff keeps happening."

"But why doesn't anything like this happen to me?" she asked, playfully banging her fist on the petite coffee table next to us.

"Wait, there's more," I said, swaying towards her. Our shoulders touched ever so slightly as if guided by some magnetic force of attraction.

I told her about the lady in the bookshop and our chat about sitting on rooftops in the dead of the night.

Katie laughed out loud and shook her head with unexpected delight and amazement.

"Do you think that stuff is possible?" she asked.

I shrugged. "The way I'm feeling right now, anything seems possible."

"For you maybe."

"No, I think for all of us. You, me, the lady in the bookshop…everyone."

Katie shook her head. "I think you're special, Vee. That's why this stuff happens in your world, not mine."

I waved away her praise. But deep down I couldn't deny it – I did feel special. Katie especially, made me feel this way.

"I love our conversations," she said, placing her hand on mine.

"I do too."

"You're such a breath of fresh air, Vee."

Our eyes locked, like they had done so many times before. But this time was different. Katie leaned in towards me. I moved towards her. Her lips touched mine. It was the sweetest kiss.

"Sorry," she said. "Was that too forward of me?"

"No," I smiled.

"I just thought it might be nice to get to know each other a little more intimately," she said, softly.

I gazed affectionately into her hazel eyes. I really liked her. She was kind, intelligent and so easy to be around. She was exactly the kind of woman any man would want to settle down with. But that was the problem. I didn't want to settle down. Not yet.

"Katie, I really like you but I just need you to know, I don't want to get into a serious relationship right now."

She pulled away from me, ever so slightly. I saw a look of something flash across her face. Relief? Surprise? Disappointment? It was hard to tell.

"Well, maybe I'm not looking for anything serious either," she said, playfully dropping her head to one side.

She leaned in and kissed me again, more passionately this time.

Oh, right.

I wasn't expecting that.

"Hey, you should come to Barbados!" she said, when our lips parted.

"Barbados?"

"I'm heading out there with some friends in a couple of weeks. They're a nice group of guys and girls. You should come."

"Won't I be imposing?"

"You'll be the opposite of imposing," she said, leaning in towards me again.

"What if there are no rooms available in the resort?"

"We're renting a villa. You can stay with me," she said, our eyes meeting and communicating our secret desires once more.

That sold it for me. I didn't need any more convincing.

"Well, in that case, count me in," I replied.

"Perfect," she smiled back.

We chatted and cosied up until we had sipped the last of our coffee. As we got up, ready to leave, Katie made a throwaway remark: "Hey, imagine if you could astral project to where we are staying in Barbados."

"What an idea," I replied, as we laughed and walked away, arm in arm. "I could save on the airfare!"

So, here's the funny thing.

After our conversation that morning, my mind started thinking a crazy thought – what if I *could* see where we'd be staying in Barbados? What then?

For the next two weeks – just by way of experiment – I made that my intention. If I floated out of my body, Barbados would be my destination. I'd will myself there. That was the plan. But that didn't happen. But something else did. Another lucid dream:

I was hovering five hundred yards away from a beautiful tropical island. Its white sandy beach and idyllic backdrop of palm trees beckoned me towards it.

Realising I was dreaming, I consciously decided to fly towards the island. Floating effortlessly just above the sea's azure surface, I glided towards the beach. As I did, the softest breeze caressed my face. The sound of the waves moving gently beneath me soothed my soul.

When I reached the shoreline, I felt myself being guided, past the palm trees to one tree in particular. It was set a little further back and towered over the others.

Strangely, as I circled around it, it felt like I was being shown this tree for a reason. Like its size and shape and the unique configuration of its branches were being indelibly imprinted on my mind.

That's when I awoke.

My body was teaming with energy. I glanced down at my alarm clock: 4.10am.

As pleasant as it was, I thought nothing more of this experience. Until I was in Barbados.

After we'd arrived at the villa, straight from the airport, Katie and I headed towards our private beach area feeling all footloose and fancy-free. Unlike Paris, this trip was way more lavish. We'd paid way over the odds for this stunning slice of heaven. But we were all young twenty-somethings after all. Light on responsibility, with disposable income to burn (how quickly things change).

Anyway, as we strolled along on the beach's white powdered surface, I suddenly stopped dead in my tracks.

"Hang on," I said.

"What is it?" Katie asked.

I didn't reply. I looked out to sea and got the strangest feeling.

I've been here before.

Slowly, I turned around and glanced back behind me. "No way."

"What is it?" Katie asked, tugging my arm.

"It's the tree. The one I saw in my dream."

I'd told Katie about it on the flight over from London.

Katie looked back at me with wonder. "Are you kidding?"

I shook my head.

"This is unreal," I said. "No one would believe me if I wrote about this in my book."

"Are you sure it's that tree?"

"*One hundred percent.*"

Katie shook her head with amazement.

"You've *got* to write this book, Vee," she said, her hazel eyes sparkling in the sun. "Even if it's pure escapism, people will lap it up."

I fell back and lay on the soft white sand. Katie kneeled beside me and began playing with my hair. As I looked up at the white clouds leisurely moving across the bluest of skies, my mind raced ahead of itself:

How big might this book be?

This was just before the days of social media, Instagram, TikTok and podcasts. Before the time of followers, influencers and global audiences. Before the time when people would do anything – strange, provocative, dangerous, humorous or outlandish – to gain attention.

Before the time, when it became easy to become well-known for doing very little. When what people did on a reality TV show or a social media post seemed more important than how they really lived their lives. When giving off the impression of success seemed more important than doing the hard yards that actually merited well-earned fame and recognition.

Yes, it felt a lot harder to succeed or get noticed back then. But that didn't faze me. Not one bit. I dreamt of instant success. In my eyes the book could (would) rapidly become a worldwide sensation.

I imagined how thrilling it would be to read. How many copies it would sell. How many languages it would be translated into. How amazing it would be to travel the world, living the life of a best-selling author.

I felt like I was already there. Living that life.

Living *the* life.

Lying on this private beach with Katie by my side, I felt anything was possible.

Looking back, I'd experienced nothing of significance. What was I actually going to write about? But none of that registered back then. I was too caught up with the idea of writing a book that might make me famous.

My ego was all in.

What I needed now was a brilliant title. Something captivating that would get the world's attention.

30

"I know what I'm going to call it!"

I didn't waste a moment.

When the others were soaking up the Bajan sun, I was sat cross-legged on my sunbed, furiously making notes. When they asked what I was doing, I took great delight in saying: "I'm writing a book!"

A best-seller.

I felt inspired. Like for the first time in my life, I was actually pursuing my purpose, doing what I was meant to do in this world.

But two or three days in, I had to put my notebook down. I needed a break. My brain was frazzled. I decided to play a little beach volleyball with the others. We were only ten minutes in when a brilliant thought struck me just as the ball was smashed in my direction.

Without thinking, I caught it mid-air.

"What the hell, Vee?" said one of the guys. "You just killed a really good rally."

Holding up a hand of apology I quickly turned to Katie who was on my side of the net. "I know what I'm going to call it!"

"Call what?" she asked.

"The book," I replied.

"Oh, Vee," she smiled. "Couldn't this have waited?"

I shook my head.

"Well, go on then," she said, amused. "What is it?"

I whispered the title in her ear.

Katie's eyes danced with delight.

"Oooh, I love that," she said, giving me her seal of approval – a peck on the lips that served as a little pat on the back.

"Ahem," said one of the others. "Are we playing volleyball or what?"

"Just one second," I replied, handing off the ball to one of the guys.

To the sound of groans, I ran back towards my sunbed, picked up my tattered make-shift notebook and scribbled down the title, so I wouldn't forget:

Dreaming Reality

For the rest of my time in Barbados, *Dreaming Reality* captivated my thoughts. My notebook was packed with ideas. Even on the flight home, when Katie's gang of friends either drank or slept away the hours and minutes, I continued to scribble away. Whenever anyone looked in my direction, and saw me grafting hard, it gave me an extra push. Like what I was doing was really important. Like it really mattered.

At one point on the flight back, Katie lifted her head off my shoulder and told me to rest.

"Yeah, yeah. I will," I replied, with no such intention. "I'm just thinking about the front cover?"

"What about it?" asked Katie, yawning.

"I need something artistic. Something that captures the intersection between dreams and reality. Something which suggests our dreams could be more real than reality itself."

"Just keep it simple, Vee. Your face on the front cover will do just fine."

Her suggestion found fertile soil in my mind. I imagined myself walking into a huge bookstore and seeing my book paraded on the bestseller's shelf. I could see the front cover clearly. An airbrushed photo. A perfect smile. Shining eyes. Immaculate hair.

I was lost in thought and Katie had fallen back to sleep when an air stewardess appeared by my seat. She'd caught my eye earlier when I'd boarded the plane. She had an attractive face and a bubbly disposition.

"What can I get you?" she asked.

"Get me?" I replied, confused.

I suddenly noticed the little red light above my seat. "Oh, sorry. I think I must have hit the Call Button by mistake."

"No bother," she said, leaning across me to reset the button. "It gave me an opportunity to stretch my legs. I think you must be the only passenger still awake on the plane."

I looked around the cabin. She was right. "I'm just working on something. I'm writing a book."

I shamelessly reeled off that last sentence like an elevator pitch.

But she looked impressed. She asked me what the book was about. I told her. She looked even more impressed.

"I'd like to write a book one day," she said, shifting her weight from one foot to the other, causing her arm to lightly brush against mine.

"Why one day? Why not, today?" I replied in a tone of voice which screamed *carpe diem*.

She smiled. "Yeah, you're right. I might just make a few scribbles of my own," she said, looking down at my notepad. "They say everyone has got at least one book in them."

I smiled. "They do."

A look passed between us. One I knew well – that if we were in a different time, place and situation we'd be open to getting more intimate with one another. It was just the sort of fleeting flirtatious glance my ego craved –a little drug. A shot of dopamine to light up the reward centre in my brain.

Now, I don't know if it was the high altitude or this little exchange with the flight attendant, but as she walked away, I really started getting ahead of myself. After publishing the book, I imagined modelling contracts, product endorsements, and maybe even a small film role coming my way. Maybe the book itself might become a movie? And who better to play the lead role, than *me*?

Nothing seemed off limits.

As the future possibilities ticked up in my mind, I remembered how one newspaper had described a best-selling author in this niche:

The new rock-star of spirituality

That could be me.

I got drunk on the thought of all the rock and roll possibilities that would be mine to seize.

Upon returning to London, I spent every spare moment writing. The first chapters of *Dreaming Reality* came together effortlessly. I'd penned ten thousand words before I knew it.

I can't describe the pride I felt when I hit *print* for the first time and collated the first fifty pages of my manuscript.

I was in the office at the time. It was late. No one else was there. I held the manuscript in my hands before looking around me. Elevate was the perfect place to launch my journey to stardom. It couldn't just be coincidence that I worked in talent management. But I wasn't there to manage the talent. I was going to be the talent that others managed. That's what I told myself as I printed off two more copies of the manuscript. One was for Trev. He was an avid reader. And a philosophically minded chap too. His take on the book would be valuable.

The other copy was for Sophia. She'd already played a big role in the story. I wondered what she'd think of it.

I called her there and then to arrange a time to meet. She was suffering from a heavy cold.

"What is it, Vee?" she asked, cutting to the point, her voice raspy and hoarse.

I didn't know if I should continue the conversation. She sounded heavily congested. But I couldn't resist.

"I'm writing a book," I blurted out.

"About what?" came the reply, after a notable pause.

"My spiritual experiences."

Silence again.

"Vee, I thought I told you not to rush things."

"I'm not, it's just all these crazy things keep happening. I really want to write about them."

There was no response from Sophia.

"I also want to write about you and our conversations in the book."

Sophia breathed heavily. Or was it a sigh?

"Vee –"

"Yes?"

"Don't mention my name directly in the book. Or if you do, use an alias."

"Ok," I replied, taken aback.

I thought she'd jump at the chance of being in my book.

I didn't know what to say next. But Sophia cut the conversation short in any case. "I really don't feel well, Vee. Call me next week. Ok?"

A week later, I called her back.

She seemed more herself this time. She told me she'd be really interested to read the book. Once again, she told me not to make any direct reference to her within its pages.

I promised I wouldn't. Although, I still couldn't understand why.

I also promised I'd buy her lunch – a thank you, for all she'd done. I told her I'd unveil the manuscript then.

A week later we met in an American diner. It was only a short drive away from my apartment. It was largely empty when I got there. It was only 11am on a Monday morning.

I felt a rush of anticipation as we sat down.

I hope she loves the book.

But the meeting didn't start well.

Not well at all.

What happened felt like a punch in the stomach. A real bruising affair.

31

One big ego statement

I proudly pulled out my manuscript.

It had a little yellow post-it note on the front cover with *Sophia* marked on it. I placed it carefully on the table, smoothing out the front page. I'd printed it on luxury A4 paper, for that extra little touch.

But Sophia didn't look down at it.

Rather mundanely, she asked: "So, how are things going at work?"

"Yeah fine."

As we engaged in a little small talk, I noticed an attractive waitress over Sophia's shoulder.

Hello.

She was busy cleaning one of the tables. Perhaps she felt the weight of my stare because she looked my way. We exchanged glances. She smiled. I repaid the compliment.

Then…BANG!

Sophia thumped the table between us with the palm of her hand. The unexpected thud disorientated me like a rude awakening.

"I'm *here,* Vee!" she said sternly. "Not over there."

Sophia turned around to see what I was looking at. As quick as lightning, the waitress looked the other way.

"I might have known. Do you know how often you do that?"

"Do what?" I replied, sheepishly.

"Flirt with other women when you're sat here with me."

"I don't. *Do I?*"

Sophia sneered. "You don't even realise you're doing it."

She was right. My eyes were always roaming. Hoping there would be some beautiful woman in the vicinity who'd catch my eye and return my amorous glances.

But, here's the stupid thing. I never for one second thought anyone would catch me in the act. Let alone Sophia, with those hawk-like eyes. Katie had mentioned once or twice that I was an incorrigible flirt. I just took it as light-hearted banter. But here I was, being told off for it.

"Sorry," I replied, feeling red-faced and shallow.

"You do it *a lot,* Vee. It's almost like a compulsive need with you."

I had no response. My face was riddled with embarrassment.

"Seriously, Vee. Become more self–aware. You've got so many blind spots."

She said I should pay more attention to my personality self. What was it doing? Feeling? Thinking? What did it need? What did it desire?

"Observe it. Otherwise, you'll become a slave to it," she said.

I felt like I was back at school, being chastised by my Headmistress. But things were about to go from bad to worse. After the attractive waitress had come across and awkwardly taken our order, Sophia and I sat in silence.

As per usual, she observed me intently. I flinched and looked away.

"That's another thing you do," she then said.

What now?

She was going for it with the nit-picking. What was up with her today?

She pointed out that I was tapping my fingers on the table. She said I fidgeted a lot.

"You need to work on that," she said, drilling the point home. "Be more graceful, Vee. More reposed. More dignified. It's more important than you think."

Feeling scrutinised, I took both hands off the table and placed them on my lap. But that felt weird. So, I crossed my arms, only to uncross them again. In the end, I just clasped both my hands under the table. They couldn't move that way.

"Is that it?" Sophia then asked.

She was pointing to the manuscript.

"Yep."

"May I take a look?" she asked, picking it up.

"Of course. That's your copy."

Sophia flicked through it, reading no more than a sentence here or there. She then did something rather odd. She held the manuscript between both her hands and closed her eyes.

She can be so weird sometimes.

I looked around the diner uncomfortably. Thankfully, no one was watching.

With her right hand on the front cover and her left on the back, it looked like she was weighing it up, *telepathically*. But I had no idea really what she was doing. It made me feel uneasy.

Twenty or thirty seconds later, she opened her eyes and smiled.

"Well," she said. "What can I say about your book?"

You could tell me how good it is?

"This book –"

"Yes –"

"…is the biggest pile of egotistical crap I've ever had the misfortune of reading."

*Say **what**?*

How could she possibly have deduced that from just holding it? I stared back at her. Thunderstruck.

"This book is just one big ego statement, Vee. It's self-obsessed, self-indulgent and self-absorbed."

I gulped.

"Can I ask you a question?" she continued.

I nodded back, almost in fear of what was coming next.

"Why do you even want to write a book?"

I thought long and hard.

"To enrich the world," I replied, tentatively.

She laughed. "Oh my God, that's exactly my point. You're so caught up in yourself. You can't even see how self-obsessed you've become."

My face went the deepest shade of red.

"And what are you writing about anyway?"

"My spiritual experiences."

She laughed again. "You've hardly had any. Tell me what true spiritual realisations you've had?"

I was silent.

She shook her head. "Exactly. So how do you hope to *enrich the world* with what you've written?"

I sat there. Stunned. Like a victim of some unprovoked attack.

"Can I ask you another question?" she then said.

She didn't wait for me to reply.

"If I had a choice, between reading your book or that of …" At this point, she mentioned one of the most famous sportsmen on the planet, "…. whose book would I choose to read?"

I was getting cut to shreds.

"His," I replied.

My tail was now firmly lodged between my legs. Maybe permanently so!

"Exactly," she said, holding her arms aloft, as though it was bloody obvious. "I'd want to know about his life because he's actually done something worth writing about."

Ouch.

That coup de grâce hurt like hell.

But Sophia cracked on. She pointed out that up until then, my own life had been "a largely uneventful, easy-going affair. With no real adversity. No hardship. No hard-earned experience."

Are you just going to take this, Vee?

I felt like hitting back. I was going to tell her I'd once been suicidal and I'd bounced back from that. But I just kept my mouth shut.

Just then Sophia's phone rang.

As I watched her move away from the table to take the call, I felt angry and embarrassed. Angry by the brutal comments she'd made. Embarrassed by how much of an ego-maniac I was being portrayed to be.

Feeling bruised, my ego went back on the offensive:

How does she know the book is self-obsessed? She hasn't even read it.

Is she really all she's cracked up to be? She seems more scathing than spiritual.

With these thoughts stewing in my mind, she returned to the table.

"Right, where were we?" she asked, smiling as she sat back down.

You were just annihilating my character.

That's what I felt like saying. But I just sat there and said nothing. I actually felt like I could cry. Why did I feel so upset? So wounded?

Never in my life had I been so wide of the mark. Could my book really be *that* bad? Was I really *that* self-obsessed? No one had ever been so brutal with me before. Not even my dad.

"Ah yes, I remember," Sophia said, gathering her thoughts. "We were talking about your book."

I slumped back in my seat. Feeling like half the man.

What the hell was she going to say next?

32

Cut off at the knees

"You don't like me very much right now, do you?"

Sophia watched intently for my response.

My face hardened. "I'm just surprised."

"By what?"

"The harshness of your comments."

Sophia smiled softly.

"I can see why. Sometimes you're so unaware of how you come across."

"Am I though?"

That's it, Vee. Stand your ground.

She nodded back as if there was no disputing it. "All I've done today is hold up a mirror, so you can see yourself as you are."

"It seems I'm rather self-obsessed," I replied, feeling hard done by.

Self-pity was coming really easy to me right now.

"Oh, come on, Vee. Don't take it so personally. I'm here to help you, not slate you."

"Well, I'm feeling pretty slated at the moment."

Her character assassination had felt brutal.

"Vee, you're an intelligent, caring guy with real humanity. I've told you that before, haven't I?"

I shrugged.

"And you're making real progress, spiritually."

I gave the slightest of nods.

"You've just got a big ego, that's all. It just needs a little taming."

Sophia smiled again to lighten the mood, but I wasn't having any of it.

"So, shall I just scrap the whole book idea then?"

I leaned back in my chair and crossed my arms.

I was feeling sorry for myself. Like my dream had been cruelly wrenched away from me.

Sophia paused and did that thing again of outwardly conversing with her inner guide.

After mulling it over, she said: "What I'm allowed to tell you is…"

Allowed?

It was like she was a high priestess with a line into God; some modern-day Oracle of Delphi.

I cut her off mid-sentence. "Who exactly were you talking to just then? A spirit guide?"

"That's one for another day, Vee. Let's stick with you and your book."

It felt like she was evading my question. But I couldn't be bothered to push it.

"Writing this book is a challenge for you," she continued. "To focus and sharpen your mind. You need to develop it like a muscle. You with me?"

I nodded.

"Imagine you're writing a thesis. You need a framework, a structure, a clear-cut premise. Something that will enable you to flesh out your central ideas."

"Ok," I replied. "Go on."

"When writing remember, truth has a beautiful simplicity to it. Your book must capture that."

I nodded again but I was feeling patronised.

Have you ever written a book? I wanted to fire back at her. But I kept a lid on that angry thought.

"If you are going to write this book, for God's sake write about real issues."

"Like what?" I asked like a stroppy teenager.

"Stuff that people are really interested in. Like suffering, death, the ego, relationships, money, sex, marriage, religion, the mind..."

Sophia looked like she could have gone on and on with her enunciation of pithy subjects to write about. But she paused and looked thoughtfully in my direction.

"These are all great and germane things to write about. But, at the moment, you're too caught up in yourself to write clearly. This," she said, placing her right hand on my manuscript, "is just about you and nothing else."

"You picked all that up by just holding it?"

She nodded back.

I reached for the manuscript, to put it back in my bag where it could hide away in shame. Sophia stopped me.

"Wait. There's more."

"Like what?" I huffed.

"Your style of writing."

"What's wrong with it?"

"You'll write a good book one day. One with substance. But you're not there yet."

"No?"

"Not even close. Your thinking needs to mature for your writing to become –"

"Become what?"

"What's the phrase…well rounded."

"And how do I do that?"

I wish I hadn't asked.

"Don't make unsubstantiated comments. Don't presuppose that everyone knows what you're talking about. Don't use crappy new age language and don't intimate what you know, just say it."

"Uh, ok."

I felt like a boxer who had been jabbed a few times in the face.

"And please don't kid yourself that you know more than you do."

She paused before continuing. "Don't think you're more evolved than you are. Don't be condescending. Don't be judgemental. Don't be self-indulgent. Don't be opinionated and for God's sake Vee, don't ramble."

I tried to take it all in. Soak up all the punches. But all I heard was: don't do this and don't do that.

My head dropped. I felt utterly demoralised. If Sophia wanted to cut me off at the knees, she'd succeeded.

"I know all this has been hard for you to hear. But I genuinely have your best interests at heart."

I didn't reply.

"But if I don't tell you how it is, you might not overcome the big life challenge you're here to face."

"And what's that?"

"To conquer your ego. This is your battle within."

She said everyone had one major life challenge to overcome. One major life lesson to learn. For some, it was living with more courage, determination or love. For others, harmony, selflessness or self-reliance might be the main themes.

Mine it seems was my ego.

She said I needed to appreciate how formidable an opponent it really was. My spiritual progress depended on it.

She looked at me again. More tenderly this time. "How are you feeling?"

"Like a fool."

"Well, don't. You're no fool."

I shook my head. "I'm not so sure."

"Vee, it's the sage that battles his own ego. The fool just battles everyone else's."

"I've heard that before somewhere."

"It's a Sufi proverb."

I nodded.

There was a long pause. Sophia eventually broke the silence.

"Do you know, we've had this very same…"

She suddenly stopped abruptly, mid-sentence.

"Actually, no. Let's leave it there," she said. "You've already got lots to think about."

I didn't push back. My mind felt overwhelmed. My ego, fragile.

"But before you go," she said. "It's only fair that I share something with you. About me. About my challenges."

I sat back in my seat, intrigued.

This I've got to hear.

She hardly ever spoke about herself. What she revealed surprised me deeply. I'm not going to disclose what that was. I never have done, to anyone.

But it was clear. Sophia had her own imperfections, flaws and conflicts. An inner battle raging within her, different to mine. *Very* different. But equally intense.

"It seems we all have our issues," I said.

She sighed and nodded back. "Yes, we do."

My ego still felt bruised. But Sophia had momentarily softened the blow.

It was only a moment's respite though.

My battle within had only just begun. Soon, I would realise how formidable an opponent my ego really was.

33

"Do you think I've got an ego?"

There was no denying it.

I was rattled.

I walked away from my meeting with Sophia with a fiery conflict brewing within. Part of me was determined to change if Sophia's criticism of me was true. But another part, prepared to fight back – challenge whether her words had any validity at all.

I got into my car and sat there for a few seconds. My right hand on the steering wheel, my left on the leather-bound gear stick. A plan formed in my mind. I needed to make three stops on the way home.

The first was Trev.

I'd handed him a copy of my manuscript a few days ago. Given Sophia's brutal assessment of it, I wanted to get Trev's take on it. A second opinion. Thankfully, he was in when I dropped by.

"Hey, did you get a chance to read my book?" I asked, crashing down on his sofa. I noticed my manuscript lying there on one of its well-worn leather cushions.

"Only a couple of pages. Might take a little time to get through it, mate."

Why? I wondered.

It was only fifty pages. It wouldn't take that long to read.

"Oh, how come?" I remarked.

I casually picked up the manuscript and leafed through it, pretending not to be all that bothered.

"Mate, first things first, I want to do it justice and take my time to really absorb what you've written."

"And second?"

"Second, I'm going to need a dictionary to get through it."

Trev started laughing.

His comment surprised me. He was articulate and well-read.

"You're a voracious reader Trev. What words didn't you know?"

"Voracious? What does that mean?" he said, grinning at his own joke.

"Ha-ha. Come on, seriously Trev. What words didn't you know?"

"Let me think," he replied, scratching his beard. "Oh, yeah that's it…meretricious."

Meretricious.

I recalled the word instantly. I'd plucked it from a thesaurus. It's ironic. My book was beginning to feel more than a touch that way.

Unsure of the manuscript now, I was glad Trev hadn't got his teeth stuck into it yet. I dread to think what he might have said. Knowing Trev, he would have found all manner of ways to poke fun at it. All good-natured banter, I'm sure. But no doubt it would have proved too much for my bruised ego.

"If it's ok with you mate, I'm going to take the manuscript back," I said, folding it into the inside pocket of my coat. "Got some new ideas I'd like to weave in."

Naturally, Trev had no objections.

Shortly afterwards, I left him to it, thankful he hadn't read more of "the crap" I'd written.

Next stop was grandad.

I caught him just before his afternoon walk.

"Let's walk and talk," he suggested.

I walked alongside him. But I didn't say too much. Grandad, as was his habit, began pointing stuff out to me. The birds, the insects, the trees – "life's little wonders." But I wasn't really paying attention.

I waited for him to pause.

"Papa, do you think I've got an ego?"

He stopped in his tracks, turned towards me, placed his hand on my shoulder and laughed. Heartily.

"What's so funny?"

I'd asked him a serious question.

"Viryam, of course you have an ego. What's wrong with that?"

I shrugged. "What if I think too much of myself?"

Grandad shook his head as we started walking again. "I thought a lot of myself when I was a young buck like you. But it gave me an edge."

He told me how competitive he was back then.

"I hated losing, at anything," he smiled. "I'd be miserable for days if things didn't go my way."

"What changed?"

Grandad chuckled to himself as though remembering some humorous turning point in his life. "I just realised, there is more to the world than me and my ego."

Just then, he stopped outside a neighbour's garden.

"Look at this flower," he said. "I noticed it yesterday. What do you make of it?"

"It's pink," I replied, stating the obvious.

"What else, Viryam?"

"It looks a bit top-heavy."

"Yes, that's it," he said, patting me on the back. "It's very top-heavy. The stem can hardly support its weight. It's buckling under the pressure."

I looked back at grandad, unsure where he was going with this.

"The ego is like that flower," he said.

"How?"

"When our head gets too big for our shoulders, we buckle under the weight of carrying it around."

I liked the analogy. But was *I* like that flower?

Grandad motioned with his hand that we should continue our walk.

"Don't worry about your ego," he said, touching my arm. "It will fall away as your spirituality grows."

That was sage advice. But I was too preoccupied with myself right then to benefit from its wisdom.

We continued on our way. Grandad walked lightly by my side. I felt weighed down with every step.

There was, however, one moment of light relief. Towards the end of our walk, we had to make way for two elderly ladies who were walking towards us on the same side of the pavement.

As they walked past, one of the ladies raised her hand and gave grandad a little finger wave and smile. Grandad playfully wiggled his fingers back.

Hello. What's going on here then?

"Papa, were you just flirting with that lady?" I asked grandad, when both women were out of earshot.

"Oh, that's just Maggie," he said.

Maggie?

"You know her?"

Grandad nodded.

I shook my head. "So, what was that little smile all about?"

Grandad laughed. "Viryam, when I see Maggie, she smiles. I smile. She wants nothing. I want nothing. It's a happy state of affairs. I think you youngsters don't know how much happiness can be conveyed in a smile, a wave, or a friendly word."

"Hmmm," I replied.

Grandad was almost a centenarian, but he was still full of surprises.

Normally, I would have probed a little further. Pushed for more details, like just how often did he and Maggie finger wave at each other? You know, just for the fun of it. But I was too caught up in my own concerns. Looking back, I wish now I had asked the question!

Anyway, the final stop was Katie.

She was surprised when she opened her door. "I didn't expect to see you today."

"Just thought I'd pop by and surprise you."

"Aww," she replied with outstretched arms, giving me a hug.

Later, after two glasses of Sauvignon Blanc, I summoned up the courage to address my real reason for being there.

"Katie?"

"Yes."

"Do you think… I'm self-absorbed?"

"Where the hell did that come from?"

She looked surprised by the sudden deviation in the conversation.

"Just wondered, is there a danger I come across that way?"

Katie shook her head. "Not at all. How can *you* be self-absorbed when you're always trying to inspire everybody else?"

She reeled off a few examples to support her point.

"Thanks," I replied.

I should have felt better for hearing these words. They should have acted like a soothing balm for my bruised ego. But deep down, I knew Katie was too nice to say anything negative.

My mind still felt troubled. Sophia's words were still ringing in my ears: *self-obsessed and self-absorbed.*

They were on repeat in my head.

"So, anyway," Katie said, clapping her hands. "When do I get to read your book?"

Oh fuck, the book!

The last thing I wanted was for Katie to read it.

"Still working on it," I lied. "I'll tell you when it's ready."

But I had no intention of doing that. Not yet. I needed to read it again. I needed to know if it really was as self-indulgent as Sophia had suggested.

I mean, could it really be that bad?

34

Serendipity

It was worse.

For several days the manuscript lay on my coffee table, staring back at me. Tormenting me. I was too afraid to pick it up. But when I did, one morning before work, I wished I hadn't.

It wasn't just bad, it was cringe-worthy.

It sounded every bit as pompous and self-absorbed as Sophia had made out. I could see that now. I threw it away from me in disgust.

What utter crap.

How could I have written something so diabolical? I never wanted to see the manuscript again. I wanted to banish every trace of *Dreaming Reality* from my mind.

I sat there for a while with my eyes closed. My hands covering my face.

What must Sophia think of me?

I was about to get lost deeper in my despair and embarrassment when I remembered: Sebastian. I had a meeting with him later. I quickly got my things together and headed to the office.

Braving the morning rush hour, I reflected back on the past couple of weeks. Work had just become a secondary consideration. I did everything asked of me easily enough on auto-pilot. But my mind had been elsewhere. Always completely absorbed with the book. I wrote every chance I got. A fat lot of good that did.

I had such high hopes for the future. Such grandiose plans. They turned out to be nothing more than sand castles in the sky. Egotistically floating on nothing but hot air.

I had imagined becoming an overnight success. A New York Times best-selling author. My book, translated into forty languages.

It was all pie in the sky though. The fall back down to earth was as quick as the non-existent rise. Everything felt so mundane, now that my pipe dream had vanished.

When I got to work, I grabbed a coffee. I needed to compose myself. Get prepped. I didn't want to walk into Sebastian's office out of sorts and ill-prepared.

Minutes later I was sat opposite him, waiting for him to finish up on a call. He glanced across at me as he wrapped up the conversation. What was that look in his eyes?

He hung up and turned to me. "So, how's the book going?"

What?

How did he know about it? I turned a deep shade of red.

"Umm. How did you know I was writing one?"

"Vee, you must have realised by now that people in this office talk. Besides, you've hardly kept it a secret."

That's true. In my exuberance, I had mentioned it to a few people. Just not Sebastian.

I didn't know what to say.

"Look, what you do in your spare time is your concern. Ok."

I nodded.

"But when you're here, I need you one hundred percent on the job. Got it?"

I nodded again.

"You've got a lot going for you, Vee, but you're a little too whimsical at times. Don't end up like those creative types who dream all day long but never see anything through."

I turned an even deeper shade of red.

First Sophia and now Sebastian. I was getting it from all angles.

Sebastian looked thoughtful. "You actually remind me of someone?"

"Who?"

"*Me.*"

I looked back, surprised.

Sebastian put his silver fountain pen down and pushed his leather-bound notebook away from him. His expression softened. His hawk-like gaze became less intense.

"I was a lot like you in my twenties. Felt like I could do anything. But all I did was hop from one job to the next."

"What changed?"

Sebastian laughed. "The jobs dried up, along with my bank balance."

Sebastian had dropped his usual corporate veneer. He felt more human. Someone I could connect with.

"So, what did you do?" I asked.

The focused intensity returned to his eyes. "I knuckled down, Vee. That's what I did. It's got me where I am."

I bit my lip. I was about to respond but didn't. I had a sinking feeling inside. A fear that I might not have what it takes to succeed.

"I get the same feeling about you."

"You do?"

He nodded. "You can do anything *if* you put your mind to it, Vee."

Hope stirred within me. Instantly, I felt uplifted. All that pressure to be someone would go away if I could put my faith in what Sebastian had just said.

"But you've got to know what you want," he continued. "Then, be relentlessly determined to get there. Otherwise, you'll be all potential and no end product."

That last thought scared me. It was one of my biggest fears: not realising my promise. Not measuring up to that person I felt the need to be.

I walked out of Sebastian's office more inspired than when I'd walked in. It was one of his rules for life: people should always walk away feeling better for having seen you.

But as I returned to my desk a certain frustration registered too.

My book project was in tatters. I was back at square one. I had no idea again what I *really* wanted to do. I thought the book was it. But writing a good one now felt beyond me.

With this pipe dream gone, others vied for its place. Once again, I thought about becoming an actor. Or maybe a presenter. Once again, my mind entertained all sorts of whimsical fancies. At one stage I even convinced myself I could still carve out a career in professional sport – at the age of twenty-six!

Ridiculous.

Deep down I knew. Each dream was nothing more than a chimaera.

For the next few weeks, I was on a real low ebb. So, I just kept my head down. Got on with whatever I was asked to do. I didn't think about writing books or acting or anything else.

Normally, I would have called Sophia by now. To give me some painful but needed life-changing advice. But I didn't. I wasn't ready. My ego still felt tender. Bruised like a peach.

I didn't want to see anyone else either. Katie included. I avoided her as much as I could. I knew she'd only ask about the book.

But the more I kept myself away, the more separate I started to feel from the flow of life. That flow that had carried me here and brought unexpected opportunities my way. But everything now felt flat. I needed a spark. I needed to reconnect with life. So, I did what I usually did in my lowest moments. I turned to God.

Some help please, I asked, looking up to the heavens.

I asked for a little inspiration. Some spiritual uplift. It came serendipitously. Literally.

By chance, when I was flicking through a book, my eyes fell upon this word I hadn't seen before: *serendipity*.

I looked it up. I liked its meaning. I wrote it down in my journal:

'The fact of finding interesting or valuable things <u>by chance</u>'

Anyway, that very evening when I was flicking through the TV channels for something to watch, what should I come across? A film called *Serendipity*.

I knew it was a sign.

My excitement rose. I watched the film with interest. It was all about acting on chance coincidences. Following your intuition. I realised right there. That was what I'd done this past year. That was what I needed to do now. But what was my intuition now telling me to do?

For days, I kept asking that question.

The answer became clear.

It wanted me to do something I didn't want to do: meet Sophia again.

35

We've met before.

We were face to face once more.

It had been four weeks since we last met. Four weeks since her brutal assessment of my book – and me.

"How have you been?" Sophia asked.

"Ok."

"Are you sure?"

My shoulders slumped. "No, not really."

"What's up?"

"I'm confused."

"What about?"

"I feel like I'm always at a crossroads. Never sure which way to go."

"There's a good reason for that."

"There is?"

She nodded. "You find it hard making decisions."

She was right. That's why I used to flip that fifty-pence coin so much. Let fate decide so I didn't have to.

"Just be honest with yourself, Vee. What do you really want to do?"

I shook my head and sighed. "I *still* don't know."

"Forgive the cliché question, but what if you couldn't fail? What would you do then?"

"Not what I'm doing now."

"Is it really that bad?"

"No, it's ok," I replied, rubbing one side of my face. "But the prospect of working in corporate for the rest of my life depresses me."

"What wouldn't depress you?" she asked, changing her line of questioning.

She took a sip of her coffee but kept her eyes firmly planted on me.

I looked up at the ceiling as if the answer lay there.

"Something creative. Expressive. Different. I don't know. Like I said, I'm confused."

"But do you know *why* you're confused?"

I shook my head.

Sophia smiled. "I've given you one reason before."

"My self-absorption?"

She nodded back. "If we get too caught up in ourselves, we don't see the way ahead clearly."

"Speaking of self-absorption, I did go back and read my manuscript."

"And?"

"And you were wrong. It's not that bad."

"Really?" she replied, surprised.

I nodded. "It's worse."

We both chuckled.

"It's good you can laugh about it now," she said, momentarily resting her hand on my arm. "A sense of humour is a handy quality to possess on the spiritual path."

I nodded. "So, are there other reasons? For my confusion."

"Yes."

"Like?" I asked leaning in.

"The fact that you don't know what is driving you."

"Is it fear?"

I'd read somewhere that all our behaviours flowed from two principal emotions: love or fear.

"Yes," said Sophia, sipping her coffee. "But alongside your fear is a need you have that sits behind everything you do."

"What need?"

Sophia looked me in the eyes. "The need for constant external validation."

"I don't understand. How?"

"Vee, you're always seeking attention, admiration and approval from others."

Am I? I asked myself.

I tried to process what she'd said but it was a lot to take in.

But Sophia pressed on. "It's why you're *so* preoccupied with the way you look."

"What?"

"You know you're an attractive guy, Vee. But you play on it. Admit it."

I screwed up my face. Was I that obvious?

"Have you ever thought, Vee, if you weren't born with such a handsome face what would you be like?"

What a strange question.

"I don't get what you mean?"

Sophia shifted back on her chair. "Would you be as charming and debonair as you fancy yourself to be? Would you flirt as much as you do?"

"I'm just being friendly when I flirt," I replied, acting all innocent. "It's just banter."

"But is it? What do you gain from it? Apart from having your ego stroked."

She paused, letting the question work its way into my mind.

For some reason, I thought about the PAs in the office. I did flirt with them, a lot. And I did get a lot of preferential treatment in return.

My documents were the first to be typed. I always got the best meeting rooms. I got coffee without ever having to ask for it.

"Ok, maybe, I get a little extra special treatment. But I'm just being nice, that's all."

"Have you ever asked yourself *why* you are so nice?"

Of course I hadn't.

"It's nice to be nice," I replied, as if it was self-evident.

"It is, but what's your motive for being nice?"

I shrugged and crossed my arms.

Another bloody interrogation.

"Don't be lazy, Vee. Think about it. What do you gain by being nice?"

I tried to get my mind into gear. Sophia's questions were taxing my brain.

"What do I get by being nice…umm…people like you more, I guess."

"Hallelujah! There we go," she replied, throwing her arms up into the air.

Sophia explained that my tendency to be nice came from my need to be liked. My tendency to impress came from my need to be admired.

The cogs started turning in my brain.

"It's because you're so bothered about what everyone thinks of you," she continued, "…that you don't have the courage to be who you really want to be."

Sophia's observations were uncomfortable. And true.

"It's a shame really," she said.

"What is?"

"You have so much to give. You have real spiritual gifts at your disposal, Vee. But..."

"But what?" I interjected.

"All this need to be liked and admired poses a danger."

"It does?"

She nodded as though it was self-evident.

"What danger?"

"You might misuse your gifts for your own selfish gain. And we really don't want that to happen. Not again."

"*Again*?"

"I've seen you do it too many times before. In too many of your past lives."

"Wait a second. *What*?"

"This is not the first time we've had this conversation."

"*What*?"

"We've met before, Vee. In other lives."

She paused to let me grasp the enormity of what she was saying. I thought she was joking. But she was deadly serious.

"That's how I know you at the deepest possible level. Quite possibly, at the moment, I'm the only person that does."

That was a big claim. I'd known her less than twelve months.

"You really think we've met before?"

"Absolutely," she nodded back.

"In other lives?"

She nodded again. "That's why I don't accept any payment for our sessions. Doesn't seem right charging an old friend."

I really thought she was playing with me but she wasn't.

"So, go on then. Tell me about one of our last lives together," I said, putting her on the spot. "What happened?"

"Are you sure you want to know?"

"Of course."

This, I just had to hear.

36

Poisoned

Greece.

That's where we'd allegedly met in a previous life together.

"I was a hetaira and you, a statesman," Sophia said.

"A hetaira?"

I'd never come across the term before.

"Like a Geisha. A courtesan for men of wealth and power."

Oh, right.

"So, what was I like back then, in Greece?" I asked, playing along.

"You had it all, Vee."

"Really?"

I smiled at the thought.

"Yes. But you were young, impulsive and immature."

"Oh."

"And you indulged a little too much in your love of power, wine, and women."

"Sounds like fun," I joked.

"It wasn't. Your self-indulgence cost you dear."

"How?"

"You were poisoned by someone you'd wronged."

"*Oh*," I replied, gravely. I felt a chill go up my spine. "Then what happened?"

"You died."

"What? *Really*?"

I wasn't expecting that.

Sophia nodded. "If it's any consolation, you had it coming."

"Well, that makes me feel better. So long as I wasn't killed off for a mere peccadillo or two."

Sophia smiled. "You do make me laugh, Vee."

"Why?"

"*Peccadillo*? Really? Which other guy your age would use such a word?"

I shrugged.

I'd plucked the word from a movie I'd watched recently. I was itching to casually drop it into a conversation.

"Don't take this the wrong way…" I said.

"I won't" Sophia replied, pre-emptively.

"But how do I know if this Greek tragedy is even true?" I asked. "Can I do some kind of past life regression?"

"No need," she replied. "You will know about a past life when you're ready to know, *if* it's something you need to know. But quite often it's best not to know."

"Why?"

"Because we haven't always covered ourselves with glory in the past. Hence, why you were poisoned."

We both laughed.

I have to confess, as spiritually open-minded as I was, I found this alleged past life story hard to believe. And yet, I didn't want to dismiss it either. There was a possibility it could be true.

But Sophia, a hetaira? Me, a Greek statesman? One who met with an untimely and unsavoury death? A touch far-fetched – don't you think?

But I felt unsettled by the whole notion of it. The danger that I might misuse my spiritual gifts worried me. The thought of things going horribly wrong in this lifetime perturbed me.

I shuddered as I remembered that dream on the night of my twenty-first birthday: my ego puffed up with pride; the fall down that dark bottomless hole; seeing those ghastly life-sucking creatures.

"*If* what you're saying is true," I said, really stressing the *if*, "how can I make sure I don't make the same mistakes again?"

Sophia leaned forward, as though she was about to reveal a secret.

"Don't misuse your gifts," she whispered.

"How can I make sure that doesn't happen?"

Sophia shot me a look as if to say: *Come on, Vee, surely you know the answer to your own question.*

But I just stared back at her, blankly.

"Use your talents to serve a greater purpose," she said, spelling it out for me. "Beyond ego gratification."

I rubbed my forehead intently. "But I feel like different parts of me are pulling in different directions."

"This is the battle within we've spoken about," she said locking eyes with mine. "The one you must win."

She told me: the soul wants to pursue the spiritual path of helping others. But the ego is more interested in self-glorification and impressing others.

"You have to decide which path to take," she said, holding out her left and right hand. "You have to decide what you're really here to do."

"But *what am I* here to do?" I asked, vexed.

"Ultimately, I know but I can't tell you."

I tutted.

"Vee, it's something you must discover yourself."

I huffed. "Why does it all have to be so cryptic? Can't you just give me a hint?"

It annoyed me so much that Sophia apparently knew what I was here to do but I, myself, had no idea.

"I've told you before Vee, you're a light worker. But *you've* got to work out how to shine your light, in your own way."

"But why am I finding that so hard?"

"Because at the moment, you're too preoccupied with your self-image and what others think of you."

My head dropped. *Not that again.*

"Stop worrying about the way you look, how much you earn and what your job title says about you. Then, you'll find your calling."

"Ok. So, it's as easy as that?"

Yeah right.

"No. It might take some time. You might need a few bites of the cherry until you find your thing."

I let out a very audible sigh of frustration. Sophia reached across and put her hand on mine.

"Stop fretting about everything, Vee. Stop trying to figure it all out right now. We have all of eternity to get this right. Every lifetime is an evolutionary step forward. Sometimes that step is big. Sometimes it's small. But forever forward we go, with all the wisdom we gain."

"Ok if that's true, who cares what happens in this life?" I asked, testing her theory.

Sophia smiled. "I'm sure your future self does. Do you really want to make bad choices today that make you suffer tomorrow?"

"No."

"Do you really want to make the same mistakes over and over again?"

"No."

"Do you really want your life to get harder because you don't learn your lessons sooner?"

I shook my head.

Ok, I get it.

"Then decide, Vee. Is it time to make that spiritual shift or will your ego cost you everything again?"

"Could that really happen?"

Sophia shrugged. "It all comes down to choice. This life holds great promise for you if you sublimate your ego. If not, I sense problems ahead."

"Like what?"

"You might be sailing your ship into stormy waters."

"Really?" I replied, shuffling uneasily.

She nodded, gravely. "Years from now, I might be sat opposite you in some dingy bar, watching you drown your sorrows."

"Why? What might happen?"

"Just be careful, Vee. That's all I can say."

"You've got to give me more than that," I said, throwing my arms up in the air.

"Just be aware of your ego. Especially in those celebrity circles you're moving in. There's more danger of you sinking in that environment."

That night I had a lucid dream. I knew it was symbolic:

I was walking in a park when I became aware that I was dreaming. I felt the urge as I always did to fly. As I floated up in the air, I felt that projecting force I'd come to know so well, take hold of me. It propelled me at great speed across a beautiful verdant landscape. But I felt topsy-turvy as I flew.

Eventually, I arrived in a narrow valley with perfectly shaped trees and luminous white flowers. Beyond the valley, was a serene-looking meadow with a large ornate tree at its far end. Beyond the tree was a white picketed fence with a gate.

I approached the gate. I longed to go beyond it to the other side which was veiled by thick fog.

But the closer I got to the gate, the more fearful my mind became.

"Don't go any further," it pleaded. "Things will never be the same if you do. *You* won't be the same if you do."

The voice was incessant with its pleas. I sensed a new spiritual world beyond the gate but my mind was desperate for me not to cross. I remained frozen where I was. Unable to go back and unable to go forward.

Soon, I was surrounded by the densest fog. Confusion and fear took hold. I had no idea which way I was now facing. I had no idea which way to go.

Then, I woke up.

I didn't realise right there and then. But a formidable foe had awoken within me.

My ego had been stirred and it was ready to fight back.

37

Highs and lows

Something felt different after last night's lucid dream.

Something had shifted within me.

I awoke with the following thought lodged in my mind:

The middle ground is hell.

What gave rise to it? Being caught between two worlds? Between the spiritual path and my own personal desires. Between being a light worker or the guy who craved the spotlight.

I had the week off work, so I just lay in bed, mulling it over. Inadvertently, my mind journeyed back over the past twelve months.

There had been some real highs. I grabbed a pen and noted them down in my journal:

Walking out on that sales job.

Meeting Sophia and the spiritual conversations we'd had.

Meeting Lauren, the clairvoyant and the predictions she'd made.

Meeting Jo in that taxi queue.

Lauren's initial predictions coming true.

The orgasmic spiritual high I experienced after thinking: 'What would it be like to forget everything?'

The sublime feeling that followed it. That I could do anything.

Getting the job at Elevate. Making my mark there.

Riding high on the feeling that everything was meant to be.

Meeting Katie. The conversations we'd had. How intimately acquainted we had become.

Flying in my lucid dreams. Being projected to beautiful places.

My out-of-body experiences.

Seeing 'that tree' in Barbados, after seeing it first, in my dream.

How I felt when I started writing my book.

How amazing it felt to be 'Dreaming Reality' for real.

The exhilarating thought of sharing my spiritual journey with the world.

Feeling like I was in touching distance of fame and fortune.

My journey in life had really begun to unfold. Lauren, the clairvoyant, had said this would be my first year of real spiritual realisation. That by the end of it, I'd be amazed by how far I'd come.

She hadn't lied. The last year had been extraordinary.

But then looking back, there were also the lows. I made a note of these too:

Sophia telling me (when we first met) that:

When things get hard, I tend to quit.

I hardly ever see anything through.

I need to stop trying to impress others with my spiritual knowledge.

I need more courage and conviction to follow my own path.

Sophia telling me (on the last few occasions we met) that:

Things were going to get harder.

I needed to rein in my personality.

I shouldn't manipulate or dominate others.

I was some kind of light worker who was here to serve.

My book was one big ego statement.

I was self-absorbed and self-indulgent.

I needed to conquer my pride and ego.

There was a danger I could misuse my spiritual gifts.

Things might end badly for me if I did.

That I was allegedly poisoned in a past life **because** *I did.*

That I needed to be careful.

That I might be sailing my ship into stormy waters.

I liked Sophia. Really, I did. And after the first two times we met, I left on both occasions feeling uplifted. Clearer about myself and my future.

But the last few times we met felt so different. It was all too serious. I'm sure she had my best interests at heart. But everything she said of late felt like some kind of warning which subdued my normal jaunty self.

I loved my spiritual side. I had invested so much into it. But lately, all my conversations with her around that subject felt burdensome. I felt stifled. Weighed down. I felt like she was asking me to be someone dull and saintly. Not charismatic and entertaining, like I wanted to be. Like the men in my family all aspired to be.

A showman. That's what I longed to become. The man who was centre stage, not the guy who was helping others anonymously behind the scenes.

But her character assassination of me felt brutal, at times. Even if – on occasion – it was warranted.

As I weighed up the ups and downs, I felt bad for thinking it but I questioned if the spiritual path was for me. Could I really be some kind of light worker? How I was feeling right there and then, I doubted it.

I sat up in bed. A new stream of thought gripped my mind. I wrote it down in my journal:

I want to do something special. Something extraordinary that no one else has done. I want to show people what I'm capable of. Show them what I'm about.

The thought of being a light worker felt incompatible with this new line of thinking. It just didn't appeal to me. The thought that I was here *just* to serve others felt utterly restrictive. Don't get me wrong, helping others felt like a nice thing to do. Noble too. But back then, at that precise moment in time, it was not what *I* wanted to do.

The matter was settled.

I was going to do something special. I was going to be all that I could become. Renewed ambition began coursing through my veins.

I stared ahead at my bedroom wall. It was now a big movie screen in my mind. Images of an exciting future started flowing across it. My eyes narrowed. My heart raced a little faster.

I'm going to do something big.

Just then, my phone rang. It was Sebastian.

"Hey Vee, what are you doing tonight?"

I hesitated.

What should I say?

I didn't want to get roped into some work event on my week off.

"Nothing much really," I replied, deciding honesty was the best policy.

"How do you fancy going to the premiere of…"

He mentioned the name of a blockbuster Hollywood movie that was about to hit the big screen. It was predicted to be one of the highest-grossing films of the year.

"It's Leicester Square. Red carpet. Black Tie. Champagne reception. VIP seats. *The works*," he said.

"Wow. I'd love to go if no one else wants to," I replied with alacrity.

"It's not a case of no one else wanting to go. I want you to go. It's a reward, Vee. You've worked really hard this past year. You and a plus one are already on the guest list."

"Thank you. I really appreciate it."

"You're welcome. I won't be there. But make the most of it."

"I will!"

As soon as Sebastian hung up, I called Katie. I'd seen a little more of her these past few days.

"Katie, my darling," I said, putting on a posh English accent. "Change of plans for this evening. Put on your best frock. We're going somewhere a little special, sweetheart."

"Where?" she asked.

She screamed when I told her.

PART TWO

Realisations

38

"Do you know Albert Stines?"

The camera flashes.

That's what hit me most as we pulled up outside the premiere, just yards from the red carpet. They were incessant. The paparazzi were out in full force. Behind them stood a large crowd of excited fans, raucously calling out to the stars on the red carpet.

Sebastian's driver parked up the luxury BMW we'd travelled there in and jumped out to open the rear door.

Katie stepped out first. She looked stunning in a long black dress that accentuated every curve of her svelte figure; the side slit in the sexy black number exposing almost the entire length of one of her smooth, perfectly shaped legs.

I jumped out next, wearing a tightly fitted black tuxedo. I could hardly move in it. But I felt like a million dollars. Especially with Katie by my side.

We headed towards the red carpet. It was sectioned off by a roped crowd control barrier. An immaculately dressed woman with a clipboard smiled as we approached.

"Can I have your names please?" she asked, with the glitziest of smiles.

"Vee and Katie, from Elevate," I replied, tinkering with my bow tie.

She checked us off her list. A tall security guard, dressed head to toe in black, unclipped the rope as we were ushered onto the red carpet.

"Wow," I whispered into Katie's ear. "This is unbelievable."

She looked distracted.

"Oh my God, Vee, look who it is!" she said, as discretely as she could.

It was the cast of the film. A whole array of Hollywood royalty, just ahead of us on the red carpet; almost in touching distance.

"Just… be… cool," I told Katie.

But my own heart was beating fast. What excitement. What exhilaration; especially with what followed. It was unforgettable. As the cast of the film moved off the red carpet, all the lights, cameras and attention turned to us. Katie and I stood there, stunned and blinded by the flashes of light.

With every flash, I felt more seduced by the moment. My worldly ambitions rising, my ego growing.

"Do they think we're famous?" Katie whispered to me, striking a pose – one hand by her side, the other lightly resting on her hip.

"Play along with it," I laughed, standing tall beside her, shoulders back, chest out.

I cannot tell you how much I loved this moment. It felt like I'd arrived. I was where my ego always wanted to be. In the limelight.

More now than ever I felt the urge to be someone special. To be a star.

Maybe I do love the attention, I thought, soaking it all up. *But what's wrong with that?*

Another lady with a clipboard appeared by our side. She gently encouraged us to move on. Katie did immediately. But I hung there for a few extra seconds, milking the moment.

In those seconds, a new desired future sprawled out of my imagination: the red carpet extended indefinitely before me, taking me to the finest locations, connecting me with the most interesting people, propelling me into A-list inner circles, introducing me to lucrative opportunities and more money and fame than I knew what to do with.

"Vee…Vee!" Katie called out.

I snapped out of that ego-fueled reverie and looked across at her. She signalled as discreetly as she could for me to step off the red carpet. As I traipsed across to her, she shook her head and laughed at my attempt to linger in the spotlight.

The second lady with the clipboard – and an equally glitzy smile – then ushered us into the cinema foyer, housing the champagne reception.

"You can't get enough, can you?" Katie said.

"Of what?" I replied, with an innocent shrug of the shoulders.

"The attention!"

"I think all eyes were on you, not me," I replied, deflecting her comment. "You do look absolutely ravishing."

Katie's eyes gleamed, as she modestly suppressed the smile of satisfaction forming on her lips.

Skilfully, she then swiped two champagne glasses off a waiter's tray. She handed me one. We chinked our glasses and toasted our good fortune.

"Here's to a night with the stars," Katie said, knocking back half a glass of champagne.

"Easy there," I replied, taking the smallest sip from my glass. "The night is young my lady."

"Just need to calm the nerves," she said, looking around with excitement and diffidence. "I still can't believe I'm here."

With heightened anticipation, I surveyed the room from left to right.

Everywhere I looked I saw recognisable faces. Household names. Movie stars. Sporting Icons. Musical legends. It was a glittering array of talent.

The atmosphere was electric.

Already little cliques had begun to form. Small groups of celebrities flashed pearly white smiles at each other. They talked animatedly. Laughed expressively. All the while looking around the room to see who else was worth mingling with.

Yes. There were all these stars. And then, there was Katie and me.

We stood there, slightly away from it all, with our backs to a wall.

Katie looked overwhelmed.

"I *can't* believe Sebastian gave you these VIP tickets," she said, downing more champagne.

"Yeah, it was really nice of him. He's a great guy."

I tried to play it cool. Like coming to these events was all old hat. Like I'd been here many times before. I had got used to seeing celebrities this past year. But this all felt a bit extra special. Not to mention, surreal. I'd only had a few sips of champagne but already the atmosphere was intoxicating.

"Shall we mingle?" I said to Katie, with mock confidence.

"No way. Not yet. I need some more champagne."

She swiped another glass when a waiter waltzed past us, placing her empty glass back on his tray.

"Vee, look over there, it's…"

I didn't hear the end of the sentence. My attention got pulled in another direction.

In the crowd of celebrities, I noticed someone I knew. It was Albert Stines.

I looked his way. He noticed me and held up his hand. I returned the salutation.

"Do you know *Albert Stines*?" Katie gasped.

I nodded back.

"Oh my God, Vee! He's walking this way," Katie shrieked, tugging my arm.

He was and he was being accompanied by a very attractive lady with dark auburn hair. She was wearing a long flowing gown, that was red and revealing.

God, who is she?

I couldn't place her face. Then it dawned on me. It was Rachel Hanson. One of the supporting actresses in the film and one of Hollywood's rising stars.

"Vee, my man!" Albert said, shaking my hand firmly.

"Hey Al," I replied.

I could call him that now. We were on more than first-name terms. He was a good friend of Sebastian's and had become a de facto friend of mine.

Katie looked on mesmerised.

"Rach, this is Vee. He's the guy who can get you on the cover of any magazine."

Am I?

"Are you?" Rachel said, leaning over, kissing me on both cheeks.

I noticed she didn't acknowledge Katie in any way.

"Hey, if that's who Al says I am, who am I to argue?" I replied, trying to sound suave and impressive.

"And who is this beautiful young lady?" Albert said turning to Katie.

"Katie," she replied, offering up her hand. "It's such a pleasure to meet you."

"I was about to say the same thing," Albert replied. "You stole my line!"

Katie laughed. She was clearly star-struck but she managed to get a conversation going with Albert. It gave Rachel and I the opportunity to get acquainted.

"So, what do you do, Vee?" Rachel asked, sipping her champagne but never once losing eye contact with me.

"I work in talent management," I replied, staring into her big brown eyes.

They were captivating. I felt like I was getting lost in them. Drowning in them.

"Oh. So that's why you can get me on any magazine cover."

"That would be it."

I felt like a fraud. I'd never got anyone on the cover of anything.

For the next ten minutes, we conversed on all sorts of subjects, whilst Albert and Katie continued their conversation. Katie looked more at ease now. Albert had a way of making people feel that way.

I too was feeling more relaxed around Rachel. I noticed how she laughed at all my attempts to be funny. How she reached out and touched my arm on several occasions as we spoke.

Good signs.

"There's something deeply mysterious about your eyes," she then said, out of the blue. "There's so much…depth in them."

"Why, thank you."

She fluttered her eyelashes at me. I gazed back at her with a superficial look of sophistication emanating from my eyes.

"So, tell me, Vee, are you a spiritual soul?"

Hell yeah.

That was just the invitation I needed.

I began speaking about the subject I loved most. Soon enough, I'd told her about the book *I was* writing. I left out the part about it being a complete disaster. And the fact I wasn't actually writing it anymore. But I pressed on regardless. She looked impressed.

"What an interesting chap you are," she said, stroking my arm. "And dare I say it, attractive too."

My heart pounded even faster.

Is Rachel Hanson flirting with me?

Just then, a microphone crackled.

"Ladies and gentlemen and distinguished guests, can you please make your way to screen one," a voice said. "You'll be escorted to your seats from there."

As Katie and Albert broke off their conversation, Rachel leaned in closer towards me. I couldn't help but take in her perfumed aroma. Her scent was as captivating as her looks.

"Let's talk some more," she whispered in my ear, as her lips softly caressed my cheek. "I'm staying at The Grosvenor. The Park View Suite. See you there at midnight."

With that she and Albert left, leaving me and Katie alone.

"What did Rachel Hanson just say to you?"

"She said it was nice meeting us," I lied.

"Meeting you, you mean. She didn't even look my way."

"You know what these celebs are like," I laughed, trying to make light of the situation. "Anyway, we'd better get our seats."

As we headed towards screen one, my mind was already elsewhere. *Midnight at The Grosvenor,* it whispered silently, getting ahead of itself.

39

Midnight

My head had been turned.

Literally.

I couldn't stop looking Rachel Hanson's way. I was spellbound. My eyes were captivated by her seductive splendour as she stood at the front of the movie theatre, with the director, producer and other cast members of the film – each sharing their take on the movie.

"You can't keep your eyes off her," said Katie, tracking my gaze, as Rachel made her way to her seat.

"Don't be silly," I replied, laughing off her comment. "So, anyway, what did you and Albert talk about?"

I hoped the change of subject would throw her off the scent.

"Oh, you know, this and that," Katie replied, not giving much away. "He's a bit of a silver fox, isn't he?"

I smiled. It was an obvious attempt to get back at me for the 'rapturous attention' she said I'd shown Rachel. Given the hint of jealousy brewing in the air, I tried to be more discrete when I next looked in Rachel's direction.

I hoped she'd look my way. I desperately wanted our eyes to meet once again. Even for the briefest of seconds. But she was absorbed in the film. She didn't look over once.

But when the film had finished and the audience were getting to their feet, I noticed her casually scanning the theatre. Finally, our eyes met. She smiled and silently mouthed one word to me. I didn't need to be a lip reader to catch her drift.

"Midnight," she said discretely, tapping her watch in case there was any danger of me misunderstanding.

Immediately, I looked across at Katie. Thankfully, she was looking the other way. She hadn't seen this brief exchange between me – a relative nobody – and Rachel, this seductive Hollywood siren, who'd completely bowled me over.

As Rachel departed, Katie reached across and put her arm in mine. I felt a pang of guilt within. We weren't officially 'seeing each other'. But we'd never put a label on our relationship either. At times, we felt like the best of friends. Sometimes, more than friends.

It's ironic. A lot of my couple friends over the years have talked about a *celebrity pass:* the one famous person they could play away with if life miraculously presented the opportunity. Well, Rachel Hanson felt like my pass; the exquisite appeal of this Hollywood actress too hard to refuse.

"Soooo…" Katie said, with a mischievous look in her eyes. "The night is young. Let's live it up!"

I glanced down at my watch: 10.30pm.

I only had ninety minutes to wrap things up with Katie, if I was going to make it to The Grosvenor for midnight.

"Katie, I'd love to party –"

"But?"

"I've got a really early start tomorrow."

"Aren't you on holiday this week?"

Oh yeah. Oh shit.

"Ah, it's Sebastian…he just needs my help with something."

"With what?" Katie asked, quite innocently.

"It's all a bit private and confidential. I'd have to kill you if I told you," I joked. "Or maybe get you to sign a non-disclosure agreement instead. Yeah, that would be easier."

Katie chuckled but her laughter gave way to a smile of resignation.

I hated lying. I *really* did. I've never been the kind of person who lives easily with a guilty conscience. Katie looked disappointed. That made me feel even worse. But there was no way I was giving up a date with Rachel Hanson. Who the hell would?

A man with higher principles, that's who. I know that now. But those principles held less sway over me, at the time. Infatuation had taken hold. I'd taken leave of my senses. My head had been turned. The glamour and temptation of the moment too much to resist.

As we started to shuffle away from our seats back to the foyer, I noticed Albert Stines up ahead. He was talking to a couple of guys I didn't recognise.

I tapped Katie on the shoulder and then pointed in Albert's direction.

"Did you get his autograph?"

Katie shook her head and stuck out her bottom lip.

"Shall we get it?"

Immediately, she perked up. "Do you think he'd mind?"

"Not at all," I replied. "He's the perfect gent."

He really was.

We made our way over to where he was standing. I tapped him on the shoulder.

"Al, we're heading off," I said, as he turned around.

"So soon, Vee? The night is young my friend."

"*That's* what I told him!" Katie interjected.

I held my hands up by way of an apology.

"Working early tomorrow, unfortunately," I said, frowning. *Lying.*

"That's a shame," Albert said.

"But before we go, Katie couldn't possibly get your autograph, could she?"

"It would be my absolute pleasure," he replied.

I handed him a pen and Albert signed one of the event programmes Katie was holding.

Handing it to her, he kissed her on both cheeks. Neither too formal nor too intimate. He then bear-hugged me, almost lifting me clean off the ground.

"She's a keeper, by the way," he whispered in my ear.

As we walked away, Katie nudged me playfully in the ribs.

"What did he just say?"

"Oh my God! You don't miss a trick, do you?"

Katie smiled.

"*So*, what did he say?"

"He said you're a keeper."

Katie's eyes gleamed with the compliment. "Well, maybe I'm not yours to keep."

I placed both hands on my heart, pretending to be mortally wounded. We both laughed and made our way out, arm in arm, to where I'd told Sebastian's driver we'd meet him.

The moment he saw us, he promptly jumped out of the car and opened the driver-side rear door.

"Can we drop Katie off first?" I asked him

"Of course, sir," he replied.

It was 11.30pm when we reached Katie's house.

"Are you sure you don't want to stop over?" Katie said, her eyes seductively meeting mine.

"I'd love to but –"

"…you're working early tomorrow. Yes, I know!"

"Sorry," I replied, feeling the need to look away as she continued to gaze into my eyes.

That guilty feeling had taken hold once more.

"Thank you so much, Vee," she said interlacing her fingers with mine. "Tonight, I lived a life a girl could only imagine in her dreams."

I smiled. It was a line from the movie we'd just watched. A line Rachel Hanson had delivered on screen.

Surprisingly, I remembered the next line of the script:

'I'm glad it was you by my side and no other.'

The line belonged to Rachel's on-screen lover. But I couldn't bring myself to say it. I know Katie was being playful. But saying the line felt deceitful.

"I'm glad…you had a great night."

Katie smiled. "I really did. It's one I'll never forget."

She leaned over and kissed me on the lips.

I felt bad as she made her way out of the car and to her front door. Opening it, she turned around and blew me a kiss.

Our eyes met one last time.

More guilt.

As I waved Katie goodbye, my heart sank at the thought of misleading her. But my excitement rose at the thought of seeing Rachel. It was a heady cocktail of emotions.

Sebastian's driver turned around.

"Home, sir?"

"Umm…no. To the Grosvenor Hotel, please."

For a moment, he looked surprised. But he turned the other way and asked no further questions.

It was 12.01am when we arrived.

I thanked the driver, gave him a tip and told him I'd make my own way home from here. I jumped out the car and half ran into the hotel. The concierge adroitly opened the door and bid me good evening as I rushed by him.

"Good evening," I shouted back, half looking his way.

Quickly, I made my way over to the reception desk.

"Could you tell me where the Park View Suite is?" I asked.

The receptionist behind the long front desk looked me up and down suspiciously.

"And who are you here to see?" he asked, very formally.

"Miss Hanson," I replied, trying to be all nonchalant about the whole affair.

"And you are?" he asked, picking up the phone on the front desk.

"Vee."

He pressed a couple of buttons on the phone and waited for an answer.

"Yes, Miss Hanson. I'm *terribly* sorry to disturb you, but I have a Mr *Vee* in reception for you."

"It's just Vee," I interjected.

He abruptly held his hand up to my face. A firm request not to say another word.

He listened intently to the reply at the other end of the phone and then said, "Yes, of course, Miss Hanson. I'll escort him up, personally."

He put the phone down. "It's this way, sir."

His tone has changed.

I followed him, as he walked briskly towards the elevator. My heart started to beat faster.

Fuck. This was really happening.

40

"You've got the lines, kid."

12.07am.

I was stood outside the Park View Suite.

The receptionist showed me to the door and left me to it. He'd hardly uttered a word, nor made any eye contact. If ever there was a model of perfect discretion, he would be it.

I drew a deep breath in, pulled off my bow tie and undid the top buttons on my shirt.

Ready, Vee?

I knocked on the door.

For some reason, I imagined Rachel would open it wearing a fluffy white bathrobe with her silky auburn hair tied up in a bun. But when the door opened, she was still wearing that long, revealing red dress.

My, oh, my!

She tilted her head seductively to one side. "So, you came?"

"I did."

I felt breathless as our eyes met, using all my willpower to stop my gaze falling to the most revealing parts of her dress.

"Well, now you're here, let's go," she said, walking out of her suite.

"*Go?* Where?"

"Follow me," she said, grabbing my hand. "You'll like this place."

A taxi was already waiting for us outside. It took us to a large three-storey townhouse in Mayfair – a private member's club. There was a queue to get in but we were ushered past it by the concierge on the door. He tipped his hat to Rachel as we walked by.

"Thank you, Ronnie," she said, giving him a little peck on the cheek.

I gave him an appreciative nod, before glancing back at the queue. A long line of partygoers stared back at me, enviously.

"Nice place," I said to Rachel, as we walked into the townhouse's sumptuously appointed hallway.

"It's cool, right?" she replied. "Only good vibes in here."

I joined my thumb and index finger together, to gesture just how perfect this place and this night was turning out to be.

"Good evening, Miss Hanson," said the lady on reception.

"Hey," Rachel replied, casually. "I've got a plus one. Do I need to sign him in?"

The lady looked across at me.

"No, I think it's quite alright," she said, looking me up and down. "If you'd like some privacy, I can check if the anteroom is free upstairs."

"No, we'll head downstairs to the cocktail bar, if that's ok? I get the feeling this one, likes to party," she said, pointing my way.

I flashed my eyebrows back at her.

"Yes, of course," the receptionist replied. "The night is young."

That was the *third* time I'd heard that phrase this evening. I felt guilt-ridden hearing it again. I wondered what Katie would think if she knew where I was and who I was gallivanting around town with.

It turned out, the night was young.

For the next three hours, Rachel and I danced. Talked. Flirted. Mingled. And drank one too many espresso martinis. Rachel ran me through the finer points of how to make the perfect one; the most expensive vodka, the perfect coffee liquor, freshly made espresso. But it went straight over my head. Or should I say to my head. I don't know how many of them I knocked back. It was not like me. I was usually an abstemious drinker. Two or three glasses of wine, every now and then, that was all.

But Rachel was so easy to be around. Light-hearted, spontaneous and playful, she was bringing out a more adventurous side in me. She was pulling me – seducing me – into a world of freedom, fun and frolics. One moment she was sat on the bar, blithely waving her arms in the air as the DJ played her requested track. The next moment, she'd jumped off and pulled me into a quieter spot where we could talk freely at an intimate table for two.

I felt like the luckiest man alive. What a night. I was revelling in it.

Me and Rachel Hanson!

I felt like I was falling in love.

I could stare into her beautiful brown eyes all night long if chance would ever permit. Surely, bumping into her at the premiere was our meet-cute moment.

It was now 3.30am.

The club was about to close. The lady on reception had kindly called us a taxi. We decided to wait outside. Rachel needed a fag. I needed some fresh air.

As I was leaning back against a stone pillar, Rachel stood in front of me. She looked into my eyes, put her arms around my neck and kissed me softly on the lips.

I hoped the kiss would last forever, but we were disturbed. Two flashes of light went off to my right.

Rachel immediately pulled away from me.

"Fucking paps!" she said.

"Who?" I asked, dreamily. Drunkenly.

I was a little slow off the mark. One too many espresso martinis. And now feeling punch drunk from the taste of her lips.

"The paparazzi," she said, covering her face. "They just can't leave you the fuck alone."

Thankfully, just then, our taxi arrived.

We both jumped in. Several further flashes went off. I turned around and saw the outline of a man holding a camera.

Rachel looked back and gave him the finger.

He smiled back, holding his camera triumphantly in the air.

"I hope you don't mind being in the papers," Rachel said, falling back in her seat.

"Wouldn't be the first time," I replied, reclining back with her. "I've really got to stop kissing Hollywood actresses in public."

Rachel laughed.

"Do you know what? This is the most fun I've had in ages," she said, placing her hand on my thigh.

"Such a good night," I replied. "The premiere was epic, this place was epic, the company was…"

"Stop right there," she interrupted. "The premiere was not epic; it was bloody dull."

"Really?"

She nodded back. "I take it you're a premiere virgin."

I laughed at her choice of words.

"I'm not too ashamed to admit tonight was my first time."

"Well, I'm glad I made it special for you."

I felt her hand move higher up my thigh. Her perfectly manicured nails lightly caressing my skin through the thin fabric of my trousers.

"Wait a second," I said, halting her advancing hand with mine. "Are you really Rachel Hanson? Or just some attractive doppelganger that's here to tempt me into a wild night of debauchery?"

"Well, the real Rachel Hanson has a butterfly tattoo on her inner right thigh. Would you like to see it?"

"It would be rude not to," I replied, rather eagerly, as the last few drinks we'd consumed started doing their worst.

Rachel was about to pull the slit in her dress to one side when the Taxi pulled up outside The Grosvenor.

"Sooo…" she said. "Are you coming up to see my tattoo?"

I surprised myself by what I said next.

"I would love to Rachel but…"

I was interrupted. By the *taxi driver*.

"Now this I've just got to hear," he said, looking back at us. "What kind of numpty turns down Rachel Hanson?"

Surprised by the unexpected interruption, we both looked his way and laughed.

"Well, he'd better have a bloody good excuse," Rachel replied, turning towards me and punching me in the arm, but nearly missing with her aim.

"Well, the thing is, I'm pissed as a fart," I began. "I'm hardly going to remember any of this tomorrow morning."

"And, what's your point?" asked Rachel, jabbing her finger into my chest, more than once.

"Yeah, what *is* your point?" asked the taxi driver, clearly enjoying his part in the proceedings.

"My point is," I said, hiccupping and pointing a drunken finger in the air, "if I'm going to spend a night with the stunning Hollywood actress…that is Rachel Hanson…I want it to be a night I never forget. Not one I can't remember."

"Can't argue with that," laughed the taxi driver, taking his hat off to me.

"Aww," said Rachel, squeezing my hand and giving me a drunken kiss on the lips.

"How about seven PM tomorrow?" I said, finding it hard to pull myself away from her. "I'll pick you up. We'll drive out somewhere nice."

"It's a date," she replied, holding out her hand so we could shake on it.

She then grabbed both sides of my face with her hands and gave me one last lingering kiss to seal the deal.

As she left the cab, the taxi driver turned his head towards me.

"I've gotta give it to you. You've got the lines, kid."

I smiled, just as the taxi started to spin a little.

"…and a serious amount of self-restraint too," the taxi driver laughed, scratching his head.

As we pulled away from The Grosvenor, my mind stumbled ahead to tomorrow.

I had some planning to do if the night was going to be half as spectacular as all the drunken extravagant thoughts now sloshing around in my head.

41

I need a new car!

My phone was ringing. It sounded like a fire alarm.

"*Arrrggggh!* Who the fuck is that?"

My head was pounding.

I fumbled around for my phone with eyes closed. I knocked a lampshade and a half-empty pint of water off the bedside cabinet.

"Shit!"

Still, I didn't open my eyes. I couldn't. The light was too bright. When I finally retrieved my phone, I brought it close to my face.

Squinting, I first checked the time: 10.45am.

Then, who the missed call was from: Sebastian.

I dropped the phone on the bed and rubbed my eyes, tiredly. I dared not get up; in case I threw up. But I felt sick lying on my back too.

Slowly, gingerly, I hauled myself up and sat on the edge of the bed. My head instinctively dropped towards my chest like a lead weight. It felt like a herculean task to lift it any higher.

I thought back to all those bloody espresso martinis and shook my head in disgust.

Urgh.

"This is why we don't drink, Vee," I scolded myself.

I'd never been a big drinker – "my body is a temple" and all that. But I'd got carried away last night.

Last night…last night…what happened last night?

I tried to remember.

Rachel Hanson's image drifted happily across my mind. I felt like death, but I couldn't help but smile. I don't think I'd ever had a more memorable night.

As the thought of Rachel eased my headache, I woozily dragged myself into the shower. As the hot water cascaded down from the square rain showerhead above, my energy started to lift.

For several minutes, I just stood there, getting drenched. Feeling more invigorated. Then, suddenly I remembered.

Fuck.

I'd told Rachel I'd take her out that night. Possible plans for the evening ahead started racing through my mind.

I needed to go all out. This was a once-in-a-lifetime opportunity.

I need a new outfit…

New shoes…

A new watch…

What else do I need?...

Bollocks!

I need a new car!

I jumped out the shower.

Shit!

I'd promised Rachel I'd take her out for a drive, somewhere nice.

Now, for the record, there was nothing wrong with my car. It was a decent little two-seater convertible. On a nice sunny day with the hood down it turned the odd head or two.

But I convinced myself: it wasn't special enough.

The engine didn't have the roar needed, the car didn't have the presence required, the badge wasn't prestigious enough, to really impress Rachel Hanson.

As I hurriedly towelled myself dry, my phone rang again. This time it was Katie.

I didn't answer. Seconds later a text message flashed up on the screen:

Had the best night ever. Girls in the office can't believe I met Albert Stines! Anyway, shall we meet up tonight? Dinner at mine? xx

I didn't reply to the text. I didn't have enough time. I needed to go on a spending spree. Fast.

First up was the car.

Obviously, I didn't have the time or money to buy a new one. But I knew I could hire one. We did it all the time at

Elevate, for PR events or for clients who were in town and needed something nice to whizz around in.

After making a few calls I procured exactly what I wanted. A certain black, rear-engine, rear wheel drive German sports car.

A Porsche 911, no less.

It was gleaming when I picked it up. I wanted to stand back and admire it from every angle. But there was no time. Immediately, I drove across to Kensington, which was close by. That was where the designer clothing boutiques were that would help complete my look for the evening.

By 4pm I'd run up quite a hefty bill:

£2,150 – Two weeks hire of the Porsche.

£1,750 – A new watch.

£750 – A suite at a luxurious five-star hotel, on the outskirts of London.

£240 – Two new designer tops.

£225 – A pair of aviator sunglasses.

£155 – A pair of designer jeans.

£105 – A pair of new leather shoes.

£45 – Secure parking for the car whilst I hit the shops.

£25 – A haircut.

I hadn't even been on the date yet and I was already £5,445 down. I'd never spent that much money in one go before. But I had recently got a pay rise (coincidentally, as Lauren, the clairvoyant had predicted) so that helped cover most of the outlay. Not that I was thinking about the cost. One rarely does at the height of extravagance. Besides, there were no other serious demands on my money.

There was only one thought running through my mind now: impressing Rachel Hanson.

And I planned to pull out all the stops.

As I got back into the Porsche, I remembered the two missed calls I hadn't returned from earlier that day.

I called Sebastian first. He answered almost straight away, unusually for him.

"Hey Vee, how was last night?"

"Unbelievable," I replied.

"I bet. I heard you made quite an impression on a certain actress."

I paused. How did he know?

Then it clicked.

"Have you been speaking to Al?"

"I have. He was very complimentary about you and Katie. He also mentioned that Rachel Hanson had nothing but nice things to say about you."

I wanted to ask: *what else did he say??*

But I played it cool.

"Yeah, Rachel was lovely."

"I bet she was! Anyway, just rang to check in. See you when you're back in the office next week."

"Thanks, Sebastian. See you then."

Next up: the missed call and text from Katie. I was about to call her back but I stopped.

Better to text instead, I thought:

Sorry for the late reply. Busy day! I'm tied up tonight. But I'll call you tomorrow. X

The next two hours sped by.

I got home. Whacked on my date night playlist. Shaved. Showered. Moisturised. Did my hair. Put on my newly purchased designer gear and headed back out to the car.

I ran my hand over its sleek, muscular contours. I smiled. It really felt like my car. My Porsche. I jumped in. I put on my aviator sunglasses, tapped the leather steering wheel twice for good luck and turned on the ignition.

The twin-turbo six-cylinder engine revved eagerly. It summed up my mood.

I was raring to go.

I was ready to meet Rachel Hanson for the second time in as many days.

42

"Do you think we've known each other before?"

All eyes on me.

That's how it felt. The windows were down. Music blaring out from the speakers. This car certainly attracted a lot of attention.

Worth every penny, I told myself, as I pulled into The Grosvenor.

I revved the engine, loudly, one last time before turning it off. Heads turned my way. I jumped out, locked the doors, and surveyed the car one last time before walking over to the concierge on duty. It was the same gentleman who had opened the door to me at 12.01am last night.

"Hi. I'm meeting Rachel Hanson here at 7pm. Could you kindly let her know that Vee is waiting for her outside?"

"Certainly, sir. Would you like me to park your car for you?"

I turned around, looked at the Porsche and smiled.

"No, thank you. We'll be heading out for a drive."

"As you please, sir."

He made a call to the front desk, who made a call to Rachel's suite.

Five minutes later, she appeared.

I leant back against the 911 as the concierge held the door open for her. She walked towards me, as if in slow motion, looking every inch the movie star. Her outfit sent my pulse racing. Dark shades, a black leather jacket, tight blue jeans, and knee-high boots.

"Wow. You look stunning," I said, kissing her on both cheeks.

She brushed aside the compliment and took off her sunglasses.

"Is this your car, Vee?" she said, stroking the bonnet.

"For the time being," I replied, not giving the truth away.

She flashed her eyebrows, by way of approval.

I walked around the car, opened her door and helped her in. Eagerly, I then practically slid across the bonnet and jumped in the other side.

"So, where are we going nice?" she asked, turning her beautiful brown eyes on me.

"It's a surprise."

I started the car, freely revving the engine. I couldn't help it. It was a treat for the ears. I noticed again how passers-by looked in my direction. The attention was intoxicating.

"Sounds like there's a lot of power under that bonnet," she said, patting my leg.

"Yeah. The car's not bad either."

She laughed out loud. I loved that I could make her react this way. I was beginning to feel right at home with this alluring A-list celebrity.

On the drive to our secret destination, the banter between us was on point. The vibe, just like last night. The conversation flowed effortlessly from this to that, without any unwanted awkward pauses.

"Hey, I want to ask you something," I said interrupting her, at one point.

She was midway through telling me about life in L.A.

"Go on," she replied.

"Why did you think the premiere last night was dull?"

She rolled her eyes. "They're all the same, Vee. Pretentious. Pompous. Everybody wants to stand out, everybody wants to be noticed…"

"Everybody wants their ego stroked?" I chipped in.

"Yeah. Sometimes more than their ego."

"Oh. Can it get a bit sleazy?"

"Sometimes."

"But Albert Stines is not like that, is he? You seem to enjoy his company."

"No, Al is a wonderful human being, on every level. He really helped me out when I moved from London to L.A. He's deep too."

"Deep?"

"Spiritually."

"Oh, really?"

She nodded. "You remind me a bit of him."

"Do I?" I asked, loving the comparison.

She nodded back and smiled. "I love all that spiritual stuff too. Hey, have you read…"

She mentioned the name of a spiritual classic.

"Read it," I replied.

"What about…"

She mentioned the name of another.

"Read that too."

She laughed.

Next, it was my turn. I reeled off the names of a couple of books.

"Ha! Ha! Read them both too," she replied.

"Two peas in a pod, you and me."

"Seems that way, Vee."

Our eyes locked once more. The spark between us was undeniable. Palpable. Electric.

"Strange question, but do you think we've met before?" she asked.

"What? Like in another life?"

She nodded. "I've been reading this book a crew member on set gave me."

"What's it about?"

"Two soul mates, who have loved and lost each other in many lifetimes but who find each other again in…."

I didn't catch the end of her sentence.

My mind shot back to my conversations with Sophia. About how we'd allegedly known each other many times before. That, I was once a Greek statesman who had it all but lost his way. And she, the hetaira – the sophisticated courtesan – who was unable to save me from my eventual ruin.

As I sat there with this beautiful actress by my side, driving this gorgeous Porsche, living what felt like my 'best life', all those conversations with Sophia suddenly felt alien to me.

All her warnings about what I should and shouldn't do, felt far removed from the glitz and glamour of this Hollywood moment I was experiencing.

"Hey," Rachel said, prodding my arm. "*So,* what do you think?"

"About?"

"Whether we've met before."

"It's possible."

I was tempted to tell her about Sophia and our past life conversations. But I decided against it. As interesting as they were, they hardly painted a flattering picture of me.

"I think we've definitely known each other before," Rachel said, convincing herself of it.

"Then we must have," I smiled back. "If that is the case, I'm looking forward to getting to know you all over again."

Sophia looked across at me with a raised eyebrow and a seductive smile. "Are you now?"

I nodded back, my eyes giving away the thoughts of desire that had hijacked my mind.

"You've just reminded me of something," she said.

"What?"

"I need to prove something to you."

"You do?"

"Yes, remember? That I'm the *real* Rachel Hanson."

Rachel circled a spot on her inner right thigh with two of her slender fingers.

"Oh, the tattoo," I replied, with a devilish smile. "Yes, I'm looking forward to… verifying you."

"I bet you are," she laughed, leaning across and caressing my thigh.

"Why the butterfly by the way?"

"I love what they symbolise. Transformation. Change. Freedom. I'm just a little butterfly at heart, Vee," she said, fluttering her arms like wings.

"Let's hope you don't sting."

"Sting?" she replied, cocking her head to one side.

"Like a bee," I laughed back, feeling prouder than I should have of my clichéd humour. "So, do you have tattoos in other places you'd like to show me?"

"Maybe."

She winked seductively, sending my hormones wild. I felt so alive next to her.

Just then, we pulled into the grounds of a beautiful stately home, recently converted into a luxurious five-star hotel.

"Wow, Vee. This is amazing."

"Wait until you get inside."

As we drove up the long gravelly drive leading to this large three-story Victorian mansion, I noted the cars parked outside. Bentley. Aston Martin. Ferrari. A Mercedes limousine. Three Range Rovers.

I pulled in between the Aston and the Ferrari. The perfect spot for the Porsche.

The hotel concierge walked over and opened Rachel's door.

"Good evening. May I help you out of the car madam?"

"That would be lovely. Thank you," Rachel replied, taking the concierge's hand, who gently helped her out of the Porsche.

"I hope you enjoy your stay with us," he said after I'd tipped him generously.

"I'm sure we will," Rachel replied, flashing a telling smile in my direction.

43

"You've made the press."

With a hint of fanfare, we strode into the hotel lobby.

Rachel was a real head-turner. Some looked on in admiration. Others cast more envious glances. I wondered whether they recognised her. Or did she just have that kind of aura that made others take notice?

Rachel just took it all in her stride as we made our way through to an opulent dining room. The smiling waitress on duty showed us to our table, perfectly positioned next to a large south-facing window. I stood before it, looking out at the hotel's ornately landscaped gardens. They backed onto the countryside and the River Thames in the distance. The sun was setting over to the west, bathing the scene in an enchanting light.

"Quite the view," I said, turning to Rachel as I took my seat.

"Out there? Or here?" she said, playfully pointing to herself.

"Both," I replied, holding her gaze.

Our feet touched under the table. Rachel's foot lightly caressed the inside of my leg.

The waitress returned with an even wider smile and handed us a menu each. She then told us, jauntily in exquisite detail, what the specials were that evening.

We placed our order.

"Would you like the wine list?" she then asked, raising her eyebrows as if to tempt us.

"No thank you," I replied. "But we will have a bottle of your finest champagne."

Cliché, I know. But I'd always wanted to use the line for the perfect occasion. What was more perfect than this?

Rachel laughed. "Vee, stop trying so hard."

I blushed. "I just want everything to be perfect for you."

"Well in that case," she said, turning to the waitress. "Have you got a bottle of…"

She mentioned the name of a Chilean Sauvignon Blanc, the coastal valley it originated from; how the climate provided the perfect ripening conditions for the grapes.

"Sounds exquisite," I said. "Like you."

"Oh please, Vee, do stop it. You'll make me blush."

As the waitress went in search of the wine, hearing Rachel speak of it with such refinement gave birth to a new desire within me: one of sophistication. If I was going to keep pace with Rachel, I needed to be more discerning; a connoisseur of the finer things in life.

It turned out they did have the wine.

Its delicate flavour provided the most delicious kind of intoxication. Everything felt top drawer. The food. The surroundings. The conversation. The humour. The flirtation. The chemistry. *Especially*, the chemistry. We couldn't get enough of each other.

At 10.15pm and one and a half bottles of Chilean Sauvignon Blanc later, Rachel looked down at her diamond-encrusted watch.

"I think we've had a little too much vino. You're not going to be able to drive us back in that gorgeous little Porsche of yours," she said, measuring out the remaining wine between us.

"The only thing I'm planning on driving now is… you… wild with desire."

She flashed her eyebrows at me and laughed. "Promises. Promises. So, shall we call a taxi then?"

"No need. I've gone one better."

"Have you?"

I nodded, with all the assurance of a man with a plan. "I didn't want to be too presumptuous but…I've booked us a suite for the night."

"You have?"

I nodded back, finishing the last of my wine.

She looked at me seductively with those sultry brown eyes.

"Well, in that case, let's go," she said. "It's about time you saw my little butterfly."

An elderly couple on the table next to us smiled at Rachel's apparent euphuism. Evidently, they were rather enjoying our racy innuendos.

I stood up and held out my hand. "This way my lady."

Rachel took my hand as regally as she could, after four glasses of wine.

As we walked out, giggling as we went, I asked the smiling waitress to charge the bill to my room. We then made our way across the lobby to the hotel reception to pick up the keys to the suite.

After the check-in formalities were complete and we were about to head to our room, the receptionist asked if we'd like a wakeup call.

"Most definitely not," I smiled back, giving Rachel a wink.

"Would you like a newspaper in the morning?" the receptionist then asked.

"Sure… yeah… fine," I replied eager to get away, as Rachel tugged playfully on my arm.

"Any particular paper?" the receptionist asked.

Out of politeness, I was about to ask which papers they had when Rachel interrupted.

"Just send a selection," she said impatiently. "You can leave them outside the door."

"Someone's eager," I said, as she pulled me away to an elevator nearby.

I pressed the up button to summon the lift. The doors opened immediately, as if sensing our carnal urgency. We stepped inside and were alone, at last. Rachel threw her arms around my neck and kissed me. Softly. Tenderly. Then, passionately.

"It's time," she said.

"For?"

"That night you'll never forget."

My pulse went through the roof. In every way imaginable, the night proved unforgettable.

It was the following morning.

I awoke before the Hollywood actress by my side. I looked across as she slept next to me on the four-poster bed. A smile spread across my face.

Rachel Hanson! My mates would never believe me if I told them.

As I gently flicked back a strand of hair that had fallen across her face, she stirred slightly.

"Morning," she said, stretching out one arm, covering her face with the other.

"Good morning sleepyhead," I whispered softly, letting my lips caress her ear lobe. "I'm just going to take a shower."

She nodded and pulled the duvet over her head.

For ten minutes, I stood under a hot shower, letting my head slowly roll left and right. Everything felt like a delightful dream. The kind you hope will never end.

The bathroom door then opened. Rachel walked in holding the morning papers.

"You've made the press," she said.

I stuck my head out the shower. "Sorry? I didn't quite catch that."

"I said, you've made the press," she replied, casually.

"What?"

I turned off the shower. I grabbed my towel, wrapped it around my waist and jumped out dripping wet.

Rachel held up page 2 of a tabloid newspaper. I read the headline:

Hanson's New Mystery Man

Below it was a photo of Rachel and I kissing outside that private member's club in Mayfair, on the night of the premiere.

Rachel tossed the paper into the waste basket.

"Hang on," I said, scooping it back out like it was gold dust. "Don't you want to read it?"

"Not particularly."

Rachel slipped out of her bathrobe, turned on the shower and walked in. She looked delectable but I was more interested in the newspaper.

I moved into the bedroom and sat on the chaise longue at the foot of the bed. I began reading the article but got distracted. My phone started vibrating incessantly. Within seconds there were four text messages.

The first was from Sebastian:

You've made the press! Don't expect a pay rise for this. But if you get RH to sign for Elevate, there's a big bonus waiting for you.

I smiled as I read it. The second was from Trev:

I hate you! Rachel Hanson! Is she into double dating?? Call me, NOW!

I laughed as I read it. The third was from Sophia:

Are you ok? I'm worried about you, Vee. Call me.

I frowned as I read it. The fourth was from Katie:

Well, you didn't lie. It seems you were "working" early next morning. Working your way into Rachel Hanson's pants by the looks of it. Hope it was all worth it, Vee.

I felt guilty as I read it.

I put my phone to one side as it continued to buzz away. I held my head in my hands and lightly rubbed my temples.

Half of me was ecstatic. I'd made the press. I'd been photographed kissing Rachel Hanson. What an ego boost. That photo would do no harm at all to my street cred and career prospects.

The other half was concerned. What was Sophia's text all about? And how on earth was I going to make up with Katie?

A conflict was brewing within, between the quiet voice of my conscience and the booming self-interested voice of my ego.

But still, my ego pressed on, more powerful than ever. Intent on gratifying nothing but its own desires.

44

Be careful what you wish for

"There she is," I said, smiling.

The Porsche's black paintwork gleamed in the morning sun, accentuated by the green of the Aston Martin and the red of the Ferrari – its luxurious car park companions.

"Boys and their toys," Rachel said, walking alongside me to the car.

"You have to admit, she is a stunner."

Rachel stood between me and the car.

"Ok, choose. Me or the Porsche?"

"Oh, come on. That's a horrible position to put me in."

She punched my arm.

"Oww! If you're going to get all violent about it, I choose the car."

"I think we both know who you'd really choose," she said, putting her lips tantalisingly close to mine.

She pulled away just as I was about to lean in for a kiss.

We got into the car.

Rachel asked if I'd drop her back at The Grosvenor. She still had a round of interviews to do on the movie release.

The drive back gave us more time to talk.

"I can't believe how life has brought us together," I said to her, as we drove away from the country hotel.

I explained how I'd left my grad job to do acting. How I left acting to do a sales job. How I walked out of that sales job with nothing else lined up. How I then met a lady in a taxi queue who got me an interview at Elevate. How I got the job and met Albert Stines there. How he noticed me when I noticed him at the premiere and so on.

"If *all* that didn't happen," I said, "you and I would never have met."

"You would have found another way to make it happen."

"Do you reckon?"

She nodded. "You're that kind of guy, Vee."

"What kind?"

"The kind that can manifest anything he desires. I'm that kind of girl too."

She started humming along to some 90s pop song on the radio.

"Do you really think we can?"

She nodded back like it was no big deal.

"I've manifested everything good in my life," she said, with a certainty I envied.

"Like what?"

"My acting career. The lucky breaks I needed. Getting the roles I wanted. The move to L.A. Breaking into Hollywood."

"Meeting me?"

"Yes, Vee. Meeting lots of attractive guys like you."

"Guys?" I asked, raising a disapproving eyebrow.

Rachel flashed a devilish smile in my direction and started humming again.

"Do you like all this fame you've manifested, then?" I asked.

"Not sure," she replied. "Sometimes it's great. Sometimes it's fucking scary."

"Scary?"

"Like when a stalker develops an unhealthy infatuation with you."

"Oh. That can't be very nice."

"No. It isn't."

I thought back to something Sophia had said in one of our meetings.

"Maybe we need to be careful what we wish for," I remarked. "That's what a spiritual friend of mine told me."

"God, he sounds dull."

"She," I corrected.

"Well, *she* sounds dull. I'm more of a go-get-what-you-want kind of girl."

"But what if…"

I was going to say: what if the things we desire are not good for us? But my phone started buzzing in my jean pocket. Keeping one hand on the wheel, I pulled out the phone with the other.

"Who's calling?" Rachel asked. "Not your lady friend from the other night, is it?"

"Lady friend?"

"The girl you took to the premiere."

It's the first time she'd mentioned Katie.

"No, it's not her," I replied, glancing down at the phone. I didn't recognise the number.

"Is she ok with us meeting up by the way? I didn't ask before because I figured… if she meant more to you, you wouldn't be here with me."

The brutal frankness of her remark caused a wave of guilt to cascade through me.

"She'll be fine about it," I replied. "We're just…um…friends."

"With *benefits* –" Rachel laughed.

"Um."

"It's ok. No need to confirm what I already know."

I wondered how I should respond when Rachel shrieked.

"Oh, I love this!" she said excitedly, turning up the radio.

The presenter of the morning show was playing a game. A couple had to answer a quick-fire round of questions, which pitted them against each other.

Rachel and I hijacked the game and played our own version of it.

Rachel called out the questions:

Who is the sexiest? The brightest? The hottest? The funniest?

Unsurprisingly, to every question we both cried out: "Me!"

Mixing it up, I then asked: "So, who's into who more?"

As quick as a flash, we pointed at each other.

We couldn't stop laughing.

Bantering all the way back, we pulled up at The Grosvenor, thirty minutes later.

I really didn't want her to leave.

"It's been special," I said, greedily looking into her big brown eyes one last time.

"It has," she replied, leaning her head to one side and holding my gaze.

The captivating beauty of her face was something else.

I didn't know whether this was a one-time thing or whether we'd see each other again. But I had to ask the question.

"Would you care to meet up again?"

God, that's very formal, Vee.

I tried to be all cool and casual about the whole affair.

She paused and bit her lip.

My heart sank.

She laughed. "I'd love to! I'm meeting a few friends for a dinner party in Chelsea on Saturday night. Why don't you come?"

"Saturday night, as in tomorrow night?"

"Yes. Sorry, I'm losing track of the days."

"Yeah, I'd love to come."

"Great. I'll text you the address."

She kissed me one last time and got out of the car. I watched as she walked away.

Shit!

I quickly jumped out of the car.

"We haven't got each other's numbers!" I said, calling out to her.

She turned around, smiled and walked back towards me.

"Pass me your phone," she said.

I handed it to her. She punched her number in and gave it back to me.

"See you tomorrow, Vee."

She ruffled my hair as she left.

I leaned back against the Porsche, my eyes following her as far as they could. My imagination took over from there, creating a stream of future memories: Rachel and I happily passing away the time, doing this, that and the other. The thought of it all made me smile, satisfaction and anticipation mingled together.

"Was it a good night, sir?" said a voice, disturbing my thoughts.

It was the concierge from last night.

"The best," I replied.

I got back in the car and gripped the steering wheel with both hands.

Where to next then, Vee?

It was Friday morning. My last day off from work and I had this beautiful Porsche at my disposal.

A plan formed in my mind, with lightning speed.

Next stop: The office.

45

"Is there nothing you can't do?"

Perfect timing.

There was a space right outside the office. I parked the Porsche, revving the engine before turning it off – secretly hoping that would announce my arrival.

As I got out of the car, Ken and Manny, a couple of guys from the accounts department were just leaving the office. They walked over to me. Usually, they would fake smile at me; smiles that were really sneers.

But not today.

"Are you the same Vee?" asked Ken.

"What do you mean?" I replied.

"Are you the same Vee who was working here last week…who wasn't driving a 911 and who was definitely not dating Rachel Hanson?"

"Ha! Ha!"

"So, what's your secret, Vee?" asked Manny, eyeing up the Porsche.

"Got to be in the right place at the right time boys," I replied, espousing another cliché, as I leaned back against the Porsche's curvy rear end.

I was beginning to feel like the star of my own movie:

Vee's Week Off

That's what I'd call it. An ode to one of my favourite childhood movies. About a smart-ass kid called Ferris, who skips school, dodges the high school principal at every turn and who has the most amazing day off school he could ever imagine.

My spectacular week off work felt even more epic. If someone had told me at the start of the week what would happen by the end, I'd never have believed them.

Just then, a tall imposing figure appeared in the glass-fronted reception of the office. It was Sebastian. He was on a call but he noticed me. He gestured with his hand for me to remain where I was.

Seconds later, he walked outside. Ken and Manny abruptly left. They always got tongue-tied in Sebastian's presence.

"Is this yours?" Sebastian asked, pointing to the Porsche.

"No, no. Just borrowing it for a couple of weeks."

"Good. For a second, I thought I was paying you too much. So, what brings you this way? I thought you were off all week."

"I am. I just dropped Rachel off at The Grosvenor and…"

"*Rachel?* Rachel Hanson?"

I nodded back, suppressing a smile.

"You never stop surprising me, Vee. Is there nothing you can't do?" he joked, shaking my hand.

I blushed but boy did I love the praise. Especially coming from Sebastian.

He asked me a few light-hearted questions about the premiere. I suddenly felt like we were more friends, than boss and young apprentice.

"So, are you coming in?" he asked, turning back towards the office.

"Yep. Just here to pick up my spare phone charger," I said, following him in.

It was a lie.

I didn't need the charger. I just wanted to be in the office that day. I knew I'd be the topic of conversation on everyone's lips.

I felt like a celebrity in my own right walking in.

All heads turned my way. A little ripple of applause, led by Sebastian, broke out on the office floor. Followed by whistles and hollering. I played along and bowed (before what I imagined to be an adoring audience) soaking up the attention as I strolled across to my desk.

Sonia walked over holding the tabloid newspaper that had carried the story that morning.

"Thought you might want to keep this," she said handing it to me. "A little memento of your evening."

"Thank you," I replied, seating myself down on the edge of my desk.

I flicked open the paper to page two.

"You look good together," Sonia decided, after considering the photo for a few seconds.

"Aww, thanks."

"*So*, what's she like?"

"Like a dream."

Sonia smiled.

Just then, Sebastian called out from his office.

Sonia turned to me. "I've got to go. I have some interviews to arrange for next week. But when you're back in on Monday, I want all the details. And I mean *all* the details."

I promised I would tell her everything. I could trust Sonia to keep things to herself – even the most delicate or delectable secrets.

As Sonia left, a handful of colleagues crowded around me. The questions started flying my way in rapid succession:

"What is she like?"

"Where did you meet?"

"How did *you* manage to pull *her*?"

"Are you dating?"

I didn't mind everyone prying into my business. It felt good being the centre of attention.

When the questions subsided, I looked down at my phone. The text messages and calls had continued since the morning.

I went back and re-read Katie's message. I felt *so* bad inside.

I called her but there was no answer. I tried again but still, she didn't pick up. So, I texted instead:

I'm sorry Katie. Didn't mean to hurt you. Are you free this evening? I'll explain what happened x

I hit send.

Then, I started scrolling through the other messages. I was looking for one in particular: Sophia's.

I felt a feeling of foreboding when I re-read it. It was unusual that she'd texted me. I'd only seen her days before. And usually, I was the one who texted her. Not the other way around.

Why is she so worried about me?

I called her. She answered.

"Hey Vee, are you ok?"

She sounded concerned.

"Yeah, why?"

"Just needed to make sure. What are you doing right now?"

"Nothing much. Got the day off."

"Shall we meet?"

"Um, ok," I replied, feeling a touch concerned myself. "Is something wrong Sophia?"

"I'll explain when you get here. Same place? 1pm?"

"Yeah, ok. I'll head over now."

I was about to leave the office when Ralph and Dwayne, Elevate's two Talent Directors (and Sebastian's most senior lieutenants) appeared at my desk.

"Here he is," said Ralph, patting me on the back. "The man of the moment."

I smiled back.

"So, you and Rachel Hanson, hey," said Dwayne, nodding his head by way of approval.

"Yep," I nodded back.

"We always knew there was something special about you," Ralph said. "Crème always rises to the top. That's why we think you might be ready."

"Ready? For what?"

Where are they going with this?

Ralph and Dwayne exchanged glances.

"Has Sebastian said anything to you?" Ralph replied, lowering his voice.

"About what?"

"A role he's recruiting for," said Dwayne, almost whispering.

I shook my head. I hadn't heard anything.

"Well, he's recruiting a third Talent Director," said Ralph.

"He's looking external," said Dwayne following up. "But we think *you* can do that role."

"Me! Really?" I asked, genuinely taken aback. "But I've got no leadership experience. And I've only been here a year. I don't think Sebastian will go for it."

"No, that's where you're wrong," said Ralph. "Look, let's talk next week. When you're back in the office."

Both of them shook my hand and left me to it.

I quickly grabbed the paper. And my phone charger. Just to make sure my reason for stopping by appeared genuine.

Then, I strode confidently out the office, got back in the car and turned on the engine.

I revved it hard and glanced around to see who was looking my way. My mind then turned back to Ralph and Dwayne.

Talent Director, hey?

I liked the thought of that.

I put on my aviator shades. Turned on my music. Dropped the windows and headed across town to meet Sophia.

46

"A disturbance in your auric field."

It was 1.05pm when I arrived.

I smiled. There were no free car parking spots on the street, except one right outside the café.

A Godsend.

It felt like life was attending to my every need. The universe catering for my every desire. It all added to the growing feeling within me that I was favoured in some way – a golden child.

As I reversed into the empty space, I happen to notice Sophia sat by the window, inside the café. She was staring right at me with her rapier-like gaze. I felt unnerved. A sense of foreboding gripped me again.

I parked up carefully. This time I didn't rev the engine loudly before switching it off. I just got out of the car without any fanfare. Sophia's eyes followed my every step into the café.

She can be so intense sometimes.

She didn't smile as I approached. She had that concerned look on her face again. The one she usually had when she was about to dispense some stark spiritual warning.

"Two meetings in one week," I said, taking a seat beside her. "You must be missing me."

I was purposely tongue-in-cheek. I wanted to gauge her mood. Sophia didn't acknowledge the comment.

"A bit flash," she said, pointing through the window at the Porsche.

"Oh, it's not mine. Just hired it for a couple of weeks to knock around in."

"I see."

There was an uncomfortable pause.

"So, about your text this morning," I said, moving the conversation along. "You said you were worried."

Sophia nodded, with concern. "I sensed something was wrong."

"Like what?"

"A disturbance in your auric field."

"Auric field?"

"Your aura, Vee."

"What? You can pick up on that?" I asked, dismissively.

She nodded back. "We've got a connection. Like I told you before, we've known each other many times."

So you keep telling me.

"So, what's this disturbance then?"

"That's what I wanted to ask you. Has something happened?"

My eyebrows knotted.

"Like what?"

"Has anything deeply upset you?"

I felt annoyed. I was having the week of my life. I felt like a movie star and here she was thinking that something bad had happened.

I tried to not show my irritation. "*Nothing* is wrong. Quite the reverse in fact. I'm having a good week. In fact, I'm having a bloody excellent week."

"Oh," she replied.

Her eyes darted left and right. She looked a little confused. Like her usually infallible radar was off or something.

"Just wait one second," I said, getting up. "There's something I want to show you."

I went back to the car and picked up the tabloid newspaper Sonia had given me. It was lying on the front seat. When I returned, I confidently flicked it open to page two and placed the paper on the coffee table. Sophia leaned across and read the article.

She looked unsure of how to respond.

"I wasn't lying to you before, Vee," she said, leaning back in her chair.

"What about?"

"About *being careful*. Those stormy waters might be upon you sooner than you think."

I reclined back in my chair and groaned, purposely making my frustration evident.

"I know sometimes you might feel a certain animosity towards me," Sophia said, staying utterly composed.

I just stared back at her, with flinty eyes, neither confirming nor denying her speculation.

"You might be thinking, what's her angle? Why is she saying this? But you have to believe me. I've only got your best interests at heart. It's just …"

"Just what?" I snapped back.

Sophia sighed. "If I don't tell you how it is, I'm not sure who will."

"I know but I'm getting sick of all these warnings," I said, leaning forward. But that felt too confrontational, so I leaned back again in my chair.

"I'm only trying to look out for you, Vee."

"Ok, I get that. But what possible danger is there in me dating Rachel Hanson? We get on like a house on fire. We're *so* similar. She's spiritual as well you know."

I told Sophia about the conversations Rachel and I'd had. How we talked the same language. Shared the same wavelength. Read the same books. Used the same words. Finished off each other's sentences.

We're practically made for each other.

Sophia looked unmoved. "Vee, I hate to be the one to break this to you—"

"What?"

"I don't think Rachel is going to be a permanent fixture in your life."

"Oh, so you don't think it will last?"

I felt more annoyed.

She shook her head. "I think she's here for one purpose."

"And what's that?" I asked, sarcastically.

"To reflect back to you what *you're* like."

"What do you mean?"

"You know, someone who looks pretty on the outside but with no real substance - yet - on the inside. Someone who says stuff that sounds good but has no real depth of understanding."

"You're being unfair. She's deeper than you think," I hit back.

I'm deeper than you think, I thought angrily.

I shook my head to make the point more vehemently.

"Talk is empty, Vee. Real wisdom comes through what we've experienced. Not from how many spiritual books we've skimmed over."

I huffed out loud but Sophia continued to press home her point.

"Rachel Hanson is young, attractive and privileged. *Like you.* She hasn't experienced any real hardship. Like you. She's living in a Hollywood bubble. Like you."

Oh, stop patronising me.

I looked out the window at the Porsche. I felt like getting up and driving away.

Sophia turned around to see what I was looking at. "In some ways that car is a symbol, Vee."

"Of what? It's *just* a car."

I really wasn't disguising my annoyance now.

"It's not just any car. It's special. It stands out and you know it. It's an outward symbol of the attention you crave – of the constant affirmation you always need."

"Affirmation of what?"

"That you're special in some way. That you're better than the rest."

I didn't acknowledge her comment.

"That's why you need all this glamour to prove it," she said.

"So what? What's wrong with wanting to feel good about yourself?"

"Nothing, except when–"

"What?"

Sophia hesitated. "Except when the only person you think about is yourself."

I shook my head, indignantly. "You always point out the worst in me. You *never* give me any credit."

I stared back out the window in defiance.

"That's not true, Vee. I've told you before about the wonderful attributes you possess. A compassionate heart. A creative mind. One day, if you get over your self-preoccupation, you may go on and touch many lives, in the most wonderful way."

I shook my head. All I heard was:

Get over your self-preoccupation!

"Vee, you're an advanced soul. A light worker. I know there is a strong latent desire in you to help others. But your ego has a strong pull on you too. It's dragging you in the opposite direction. It poses a real danger to you. It's derailed you many times before. However –"

She paused, checking if she had my full attention. I glared back at her to show I was listening.

"… you can make great spiritual progress in this lifetime *if* you overcome your ego."

She paused to allow me to respond. But I said nothing.

"When you're ready to pursue some greater purpose, the stars will align for you. But there is no guarantee that will happen. Unless you decide."

"Decide what?"

"Are you here to serve yourself? Or are you here to help others? Everything hinges on this."

I sat back in my seat and looked out the window again.

All I wanted to do at that moment was cut the conversation short.

I turned back towards her. "Sophia, I appreciate your concern. I really do. But unfortunately, I've got to go."

"Just one last thing, Vee," she replied, holding out her hand.

I rolled my eyes. Instantly, I felt bad for doing it.

But Sophia spoke on, undeterred.

"At the moment, there's a mismatch between what you're projecting to the world outside and who you really are within. Are you listening, Vee?"

I was looking out the window again.

"*Yes*, I'm listening."

"Good, because *you* have to resolve this conflict. Your ego is obsessed with building a self-image that impresses others. Your soul wants you to be the best you can be…to help others."

All this talk of egos and souls started to bother me. "So, who am I then, really? My soul or my ego."

"You must discover that for yourself. Are you the kind of man who dates actresses and hires fancy cars to impress others? Or is there something more to you, Vee? You decide."

I tutted and shrugged my shoulders.

Sophia realised she wasn't getting anywhere with me. Calmly, she put on her coat and collected her things.

"Let's talk some other time, hey," she said.

I felt really bad but I didn't respond. I didn't even make eye contact. At once, I felt childish and insolent.

Sophia walked away and left me stewing in my own thoughts.

I sat there for a while. Looking at the Porsche, reflecting on what she'd said about the car and what the car said about me.

But her words, as wise and true as they were, didn't hit home. Their wisdom eluded me. The message they conveyed just aroused greater resentment in my over-inflated ego.

The ego, which was now firmly in charge and showed no signs of ceding control.

47

"I hate you. Do you know that?"

Trev will want to see the car.

That was my first thought when waking the next morning. I was seeing Rachel later at that Chelsea dinner party but I had a few hours to kill in between.

I called Trev. I told him I'd be at his for 12.30pm.

"Got a surprise for you," I added.

For some reason, Trev sounded beside himself with excitement.

First stop, however, was the car wash. Not that the Porsche needed cleaning. I just wanted it to look as polished as possible for the day ahead.

I arrived at Trev's a few minutes early. I parked up, walked to his front door and knocked twice.

"I am coming," he said, almost singing the words.

He opened the door wearing a suit. His hair was immaculately swept to one side. Judging from the strong scent of orange blossom and ginger wafting up into my nostrils, he'd obviously caked himself in perfume.

"So, where is she then?" he said, looking past me.

"Who?"

"Rachel bloody Hanson, that's who!"

I chuckled.

"Oh, when I said there was a surprise…"

"Yes…."

"That wasn't it."

"Oh! You fucker! I've spent the whole morning getting ready."

"Mate, the last time I checked, *I* was the one dating her, not you."

"That's very true. I give you that. *But* she might just hook me up with one of her celebrity friends."

Trev looked dead serious about it.

I shook my head and laughed.

"So, what's this bloody surprise then?"

"Follow me."

I walked to the Porsche and leaned against it.

Trev gasped. "No way! A 911?"

"Yes, and it's fully loaded."

"Is it yours?"

"No. I'm just borrowing it."

"Borrowing it?"

"Well, technically I've hired it."

"For how long?"

"Two weeks."

Trev rubbed his hands.

"Give me the keys then," he said, making a move towards the car.

"Sorry, my man. I'm the only one insured to drive it."

"You really are a fucker, aren't you!"

I smiled back, holding my hands up apologetically.

"Well, now that I'm all suited and booted, the least you can do is take me for a spin… and buy me some lunch."

"Deal. Let's go."

We stopped off for lunch first.

We hit a small café nearby. The weather was good, so we opted to sit outside. We could admire the aesthetic beauty of the Porsche that way, which naturally I'd parked right out front. Not that we spoke much about the car.

Over lunch, the Porsche played second fiddle to Rachel Hanson. I spent most of the time answering every imaginable (and inappropriate) question Trev could ask about her.

"No," I told him at one point. "I'm not going to share my 'salacious secrets' with you."

Trev laughed. "Can't blame a guy for asking!"

After the interrogation was over, Trev decided something.

"You know, I've given this a lot of thought now and I've decided, you're not just a fucker. You're a *lucky* fucker. Do you know that?"

I just laughed. He always had me in stitches.

After lunch, as we were about to leave, two young attractive women came across to our table. One was holding a weekend magazine.

"Excuse me," she said, clearly the more forward of the two. "Is this you in this magazine?"

I looked at the page she'd opened. It was the same photo the tabloid newspaper had used yesterday of Rachel and I kissing outside the private member's club in Mayfair.

"I can't deny it," I replied, holding my hands up. "That's me."

"See, I told you," said the girl, to her shyer accomplice.

She took out her pen. Wrote her name and number down on another page of the magazine, ripped it out and handed it to me.

"Well," she said, lightly running her finger over my hand. "If things don't work out with Rachel Hanson, call me."

"Thank you. I certainly will," I replied, smiling from ear to ear.

As the girls walked off, Trev turned to me, with a look of exasperation. "*I hate you*. Do you know that?"

We both laughed, as we got up and made our way to the car. I must confess, I really was enjoying my little slice of fame. It felt good to be recognised. The attention felt irresistibly pleasing.

"So, shall I show you what this baby can do?" I said, tapping the roof of the Porsche.

"Let's do it," said Trev.

As I was about to drive off, I noticed the two women from before looking in our direction. *My* direction. I gave them both a little finger wave as I drove past them. They returned the compliment and giggled. All these little exchanges, all this attention, was feeding my ego's ever-growing appetite.

I love being me.

And I was falling more and more in love with myself. Unaware, that narcissism was taking root within me like a fast-growing weed.

As we sped away, I headed out to a country road. I wanted to show Trev how well the car handled and how blisteringly fast it moved.

We were winding left and right through a country lane when I saw an open stretch of road ahead. I floored the accelerator. Instantly, we were snapped back in our seats. The back end of the Porsche kicked out. I just managed to get hold of it before I was about to lose control.

"Woah, easy tiger!" Trev said, one hand on the dash, the other gripping an armrest. "Don't write off the car! Not with me in it!"

We both laughed. Nervously.

I decided to drive at a more leisurely pace for the rest of the journey.

After dropping Trev off, I still had two hours to kill.

Who else might want to see the car?

Normally, I would have thought of Katie. But that was a no-go. She hadn't replied to any of my calls or texts in the past twenty-four hours.

Grandad.

He was the next person that sprung to mind. He always took great delight in any progressive new developments in my life.

He'll love seeing me in the Porsche.

I was wrong.

He was out for a walk when I caught up with him. I noticed he was moving a little slower than usual. I pulled up alongside him and revved the engine. It roared. But he didn't hear. I then beeped the horn. Finally, he looked across.

I dropped the passenger side window. He peered in but couldn't seem to make me out.

"Papa, it's me."

"Viryam?"

"Yes."

He looked disorientated. Distressed.

I parked the car, got out and embraced him with a hug. He had tears in his eyes.

"I'm glad it's you," he said. He was shaking.

"Papa, are you ok?"

He slowly shook his head. "My body is feeling a bit weak. I wasn't sure how I was going to make it home."

My heart melted. Tears came to my eyes.

"I'm here now, Papa. You don't need to worry."

I helped him into the car. He struggled, given the Porsche was so low off the ground.

As we drove away, he turned towards me. "Is this your new car?"

"No, I've just hired it."

"But you have a car," he said, breathlessly. His voice shaky.

"I just wanted to know what a real sports car feels like."

I mentioned nothing about Rachel. He never spoke very highly of the acting profession.

Grandad looked thoughtful. We drove along for a few minutes in silence.

Dark clouds above had replaced the earlier sunshine. They looked ready to burst. A few sporadic raindrops hit the windscreen. Then, the heavens opened. The rain was torrential.

I struggled to find the windscreen wiper lever. As I searched for it clumsily, pressing the horn by mistake, grandad reached across and lightly touched my arm.

"Viryam, be careful in this car," he said, tiredly. "You're not used to this kind of power."

I thought back to the little scare Trev and I had just had.

"I will," I promised, finally switching on the wipers.

Grandad signalled his approval with a slow nod of the head.

Again, he looked thoughtful.

"Listen to me, Viryam. There's one thing I don't want you to become," he said.

"What's that Papa?"

"A young man in a hurry. Don't make that mistake. It's a dangerous road."

I hit my head back against the headrest and sighed inwardly.

I was surprised by grandad's comments. Normally, he was the one urging me on. Not the one telling me to slow down.

We sat in silence for the rest of the journey. Nothing but the sound of rain hitting the roof of the Porsche for company. Grandad looked too tired to talk. I needed the quiet time to reflect.

We pulled up outside the family home just as the rain stopped. I was about to step out of the car to help grandad get out, but he reached over with his hand and stopped me.

"Remember what I'm about to say, Viryam," he said, summoning up the strength to speak. "If you ever get the urge to do something reckless –"

"Yes –"

"Don't. Do you hear me?"

I nodded back.

But I was surprised by this forewarning. It sounded a little extreme. Scary even. But I didn't tell grandad that. I just helped him back into the house, made sure he was comfortable and left him in mother's capable care.

My mind then switched gears. Next stop was my apartment. Then, *Chelsea*. There was only one thought on my mind now.

The dinner party.

I needed to make a big impression.

48

The dinner party

I rang the bell.

There was no answer. I checked the address Rachel had given. It was definitely the right house. It was an elegant three-story Georgian terrace. Its imposing front door had a perfectly trimmed ornamental box hedge to either side.

I rang the bell again. Finally, there was the clamour of footsteps coming towards the door.

It opened and there stood Godfrey Brookes. One of the most established and well-respected actors in British film and TV. He was larger than life in all respects.

"Here he is! Our final guest for the evening," he said, embracing me with a full-on inescapable hug. "You must be, Vee. Rachel was right. You are a handsome devil."

I blushed.

"Sorry I'm late."

"No bother at all my good man. Arriving late to a party is the only way to make an entrance! Please come in. Everyone is in the garden."

I wondered who 'everyone' was as I followed Godfrey into a large drawing room. Two French doors at its rear opened out onto a stylish garden terrace.

I counted six people there, including me.

Rachel stepped forward and kissed me on either cheek.

"Everyone, this is Vee," she said, parading me before the group.

My heart beat faster as everyone looked my way.

"Hi," I said, disguising my nerves behind an awkward smile.

"So, you've met Godfrey," Rachel said, grabbing my arm. "This is Peter. A rising star of the West End."

Peter had a raffish air about him that contrasted sharply with all the designer labels I was wearing. I was about to shake his hand, but Peter offered nothing more than an unsmiling, almost imperceptible, nod of the head.

"This is Simmy, an old Uni friend and this is Ella, Peter's rather sexy love interest."

They were both stood to Peter's right.

Ella, who was smoking a joint, removed it from her lips and kissed me on both cheeks. Simmy followed suit.

Ella then took another puff of the joint and handed it to Peter who did likewise.

"Sorry, where are my manners? Fancy a little puff?" Peter said, half holding out the joint to me.

"No. I'm ok, thank you."

Drugs of any description were not my thing.

Peter seemed to scoff at my response.

What's his problem?

In the infinitesimal time we'd known each other it seemed he'd decided: he did not like me. Why, I don't know.

For a second, there was an awkward silence, but Godfrey skilfully jumped in and kickstarted the conversation.

"Vee, we were just talking about my dastardly neighbour," he said, lowering his voice a tad. "He's just bought a Ferrari."

"Oh nice," I replied.

"Yes," said Godfrey, nodding his head expressively. "Except, he wakes up the whole bloody street when he turns the beastly thing on every morning."

"You look like a car man, Vee," said Peter, with a sideward glance in my direction. "What do you drive?"

"A brand-new Porsche 911," said Rachel, before I even had chance to reply.

"Blimey. Business must be good," said Simmy. "What do you do?"

"I work in Talent Management," I replied, chewing my lip.

"Ah, I see we have a corporate prodigy in our midst," said Godfrey.

"Do you always see yourself working in corporate?" asked Simmy, following up on her first question.

I turned my head her way. "Not if I can help it. If I stay there too long, I'll feel like Sisyphus. Forever rolling his giant stone up a hill."

"The man quotes Sisyphus," said Godfrey triumphantly. "I love him already. I take it you've read the Iliad?"

"Not yet," I replied, as though I had every intention of doing so.

I'd only used the quip about Sisyphus because I'd heard Sebastian use it once.

"Vee, you simply must read it," said Godfrey placing his hand on my shoulder. "How else will you ever know about the heroism of Achilles, the bravery of Ajax or the downright cunningness of Odysseus?"

"It's next on the reading list," I replied.

"Good man!" Godfrey said, patting me on the back, almost knocking me off my feet.

Then, feeling some absurd need to gain back some intellectual ground, I said: "But to be honest, I think I prefer Greek philosophy to mythology."

The comment surprised even me. I was getting quite ahead of myself.

"I studied philosophy at Uni," said Simmy.

"…and she came out with a first," added Rachel, her eyebrows rising up, for added emphasis.

Uh oh!

"So, come on then. Who's your favourite philosopher?" asked Simmy, nudging me with her elbow.

"Um… Socrates," I replied, as though I'd given the matter a great deal of consideration.

"Why Socrates?" asked Simmy, frowning.

"It's his take on things…it just resonates with me. You know…that the unexamined life is not worth living."

It's the only Socrates quote I knew.

Simmy, whose turn it was to take another puff of the joint, did so and looked thoughtfully into the air, cocking her head one way, then the other.

"I'm more of an Aristotle fan," she professed. "I like Plato too, but he might be too much of an idealist for me."

I nodded back, as though I could fully appreciate the finer details of her preference for one philosopher over the other.

"Hey, have you read…" she mentioned the name of a book that according to her was *the* authority on the history of Western philosophy.

"No," I confessed, feeling increasingly out of my depth. "*Another one* for the reading list."

They all laughed, probably more on account of the joint than my humour.

Speaking of the joint, I was offered another puff. By Simmy this time.

I shook my head. "Not really my thing."

"You're not a shroomer, are you?" Godfrey joked, poking me playfully in the ribs.

"A shroomer?" I asked. I'd never heard the term.

"Someone, who enjoys tripping on magic mushrooms," Rachel clarified, as she received the joint off Simmy.

"Magic mushrooms?" I asked, nonplussed.

"It's a psychedelic," added Peter, as though it was obvious.

"Oh," I replied, feeling wet behind the ears.

Come on, Vee. Raise your game.

Something clever then came to mind.

"Do you know where the term psychedelic comes from?" I asked the guys and Peter in particular.

They all shook their heads.

"Hang on," Simmy said. "I know psyche comes from the Greek word for soul."

"That's right," I said. "And Delos is the Greek word for reveal. So, psyche and delos…together make the word psychedelic … something that reveals your soul."

"My word," said Godfrey, "The man is clever as well as obscenely attractive."

I blushed but enjoyed the compliment.

"And have you ever got tempted to take a substance that might *reveal your soul*?" asked Peter sarcastically, two fingers on each hand forming quotation marks in the air.

"No," I replied. "I think if your soul wants to reveal something to you, it will do so itself when the time is right."

"How?" challenged Peter, putting me on the spot.

"Through a dream or a premonition. Or maybe through some direct revelation. It's only our egos that stand in the way. When we let go of the ego, our spirituality flourishes."

I sounded like Sophia.

The irony of my remark, however, was lost on me at the time. Here was me, talking about relinquishing the ego when mine had me in a tight bind; my arm firmly locked behind my back.

"Hey! Vee's writing a book on this stuff," said Rachel, smoking the joint.

"Is he?" said Godfrey, as though it was the most astounding news ever.

I nodded back.

"Are you really?" asked Peter, as though the very thought pained him.

"Yep," I replied, saying nothing more.

"What's it about?" asked Simmy, nudging my arm once again.

I hesitated.

I'd only mentioned that damn book to Rachel the other night because I was pissed and wanted to impress her.

God, what do I tell them?

I had to make the book sound more compelling than it was.

"Um…" I said, looking up into the air and rubbing the side of my face, "It's about the spiritual experiences we have… the ones we never really talk about."

Hah! No, it's not. It's about how self-indulgent Vee is!

That's what I imagined Sophia would say if she were stood there in the garden with us.

I shook off the thought, as Godfrey turned to me and said: "How very intriguing."

"Vee, tell them about that tree in Barbados," said Rachel, teeing me up again. "That story still gives me goosebumps."

I felt myself perspiring under my jumper. I casually glanced down to see if there were any visible sweat patches – not a good look at the best of times.

Phew.

I was ok for the time being.

As everyone looked on, I turned my attention to 'the tree story'.

"Hmmm. Where shall I start?" I said, cocking my head to one side. "Ok, what I'm about to reveal happened when I was going through a spell of lucid dreaming and having the odd out-of-body experience."

"You've had an out-of-body experience?" said Ella, joining the conversation for the first time.

I nodded back.

"Really?" asked Simmy, grabbing my arm.

I nodded again.

"How ridiculously cool is that!" Ella said, turning to Peter, jabbing him with her elbow.

Peter just shrugged but the others looked intrigued. My confidence began to rise.

"So, about this tree…" I said, holding my hands out.

I told them the story. They were spellbound. From that moment on, spirituality became *the* topic of conversation.

As I held court in Godfrey's garden terrace, Rachel shot amorous glances in my direction. Godfrey lavished praise effusively on my shoulders. Simmy and Ella hung on my every word. Only Peter responded with disinterest.

But I'd achieved my objective.

I was no longer an interloper. I'd cemented my place in the group. I hoped I'd done the same in Rachel's heart.

As the evening drew to a close, I asked Rachel if she wanted a lift back to The Grosvenor, hoping another intimate night of lovemaking was on the cards.

"Oh, I'm having a little girly sleepover at Simmy's tonight," she replied.

"Sorry," said Simmy, shooting a pitying look in my direction.

I pretended to be devastated.

"But tomorrow*,"* Rachel whispered, coming in close and letting her lips caress my neck. "I'm all yours."

The following day and night, we spent every minute together. If only each second could have lasted a day. I was head over heels in love. It felt like Rachel and I were playing the lead roles in our very own Hollywood rom-com.

Every moment spent by her side I wanted her more.

49

Junior talent director

£35!

That was the cost of parking the Porsche in a secure spot for work the next day.

But spending the money felt like nothing. I was riding high. Nothing could wipe the smile off my face. Anything felt possible.

I entertained myself with all sorts of pleasing fantasies as I walked the short distance from the car to the office. Like signing Rachel and her most illustrious friends to Elevate's roster of talent. Living in London *and* L.A. Mixing in all the right circles. Meeting all the right people. Doors opening to who knows what, leading to who knows where.

Nothing is off-limits.

It's all the rage now to talk about 'multiverses', but back then with Rachel by my side, the possibilities seemed endless. New worlds, options, choices etherealising before me. Waiting to be grasped. And I was in the mood to seize them.

I walked into the office with extra pep in my step. I knew my now very public relationship with Rachel would do nothing but enhance my kudos. It felt that way. My colleagues seemed to look at me through different eyes.

Finally, I felt like that someone I'd always wanted to be. A man on the rise. A star in the making. *Somebody special.*

"Morning, Vee," said Sonia, as I settled down at my desk.

"Morning."

"Ralph and Dwayne were looking for you earlier."

"What did they want?"

"Something about taking you out for a champagne brunch."

"That's nice of them."

"Yes," said Sonia, with a dubious look on her face. "No doubt they want the gossip on Rachel or some other juicy titbit they can extract from you."

"I'm sure the champagne brunch will more than compensate for it," I said, turning on my computer. "Why don't you join us?"

"I did float the idea."

"And?"

"They seem intent on it just being the three of you. I guess four's a crowd."

On cue, Ralph and Dwayne appeared, as they so often did, together.

"Vee, cancel your plans," said Ralph. "We're taking you out."

"Where?" I asked, pretending to be oblivious.

"For a celebratory brunch!" said Dwayne.

"What are we celebrating?"

"You, of course," said Ralph.

"…and Rachel Hanson," smiled Dwayne.

Shortly afterwards, we were sat in Ralph and Dwayne's favourite little eatery. The place they liked to go when they needed to 'chew the fat' or 'put their heads together'.

Three glasses of champagne fizzed on the table before us. As I sipped mine slowly, they praised me no end. Words like 'superstar', 'high flyer' and 'legend' were bandied around freely. A more sceptical mind would have asked: *what are they after?*

But feeling punch drunk on all the praise, I didn't question their motives. I was too absorbed with the heady delights of being somebody special – a man in demand.

After the compliment-giving had ceased, they asked some rather intimate questions about Rachel. I was very cautious about what I revealed, which was nothing. I wanted to protect Rachel's privacy. Ralph and Dwayne were well known for peddling more than their fair share of office gossip.

Then, finally, we got down to it.

"We think you are talent director material," said Ralph, who nearly always took the lead in steering the conversation where they wanted it to go. "I think you'd work perfectly alongside me and Dwayne."

"Naturally, we'd be the senior directors," said Dwayne, chipping in. "But you could be… a junior talent director."

I cast a doubtful look back at Dwayne.

Junior talent director?

That didn't sound very flattering.

"Naturally, we wouldn't call you that," said Ralph, intervening as though hearing my thoughts.

I looked back at them both, glancing from one to the other thoughtfully. "Do you really think Sebastian will go for it?"

They both exchanged glances. Some secret passing between them.

Ralph answered: "We think he will *if* it comes from you."

"You've just got to pitch it the right way," added Dwayne.

"But you said, he's looking external. And I'm sure Sonia mentioned she was arranging some interviews."

"What did she say?" asked Ralph, seizing on my comment. "Did she tell you who they are interviewing?"

Both stared at me, intently.

"No, I don't even know if they're interviewing for this role."

Ralph and Dwayne again exchanged looks.

"Well, let us know if you hear anything else," said Ralph. "But I don't think it will matter once you convince Sebastian you're right for this role."

"Do you really think I should throw my hat in the ring?"

"Yes," they both replied, in unison.

"The timing is perfect," said Ralph. "You've had a stellar first year here. You're exceeding expectations. You know how highly Sebastian thinks of you."

"And your stock is running high at the moment," added Dwayne. "Who else here is dating a Hollywood actress who could introduce the firm to the crème de la crème of acting talent."

They continued to sell the idea to me like a pair of pied pipers.

The more they pitched, the more I was sold.

I imagined what it would be like to have my own office. To be one of the senior guys in the business. To have raced my way up the corporate ladder in no time at all. To have my salary doubled. Or would it be tripled? After this past week, nothing seemed out of the question.

When I got back into the office, I headed over to Sonia's desk.

"Hey," I said, pulling up an empty chair next to her. "Is Sebastian recruiting for a new role?"

"Oh yeah, I forgot to mention it. He wants to bring in a third talent director."

"Is he considering anyone internal?" I asked, with a casual air of indifference.

"No. He's definitely looking external. He said he wants to shake things up a bit."

"Oh," I replied, rubbing my hands together.

"How come you're asking?"

"Oh, just something Ralph and Dwayne mentioned."

"What did they say?" asked Sonia, with negative expectation.

"That... I... could perhaps do that role. In a junior capacity, of course."

"Hmmm," replied Sonia. "But you know Sebastian. If he wanted you in that role, he would have told you."

"Yeah, possibly. But maybe..." I said, catching wind of an idea. "Maybe I need to pitch him the idea first. Show him I've got that ambition."

Sonia scrunched up her face.

"I'm not sure, Vee," she said, resting her chin lightly on the tips of her fingers. "But then again, you are the guy we recruited from a taxi queue."

That was all the encouragement I needed.

Sebastian was away on business for a few days. He would be back on Friday. That gave me enough time to work on my pitch.

Just then, my phone beeped. It was a text from Rachel:

Heading to Wales tomorrow. On location there for a month. Tonight is my last night at The Grosvenor. Shall we hook up? xx

50

Hooking up

It was 7.30pm by the time I got across.

Pulling up at The Grosvenor, I had mixed emotions. One more night of intimacy with Rachel lay ahead but would it be the last, for a while at least?

As I got out of the car, the concierge who I had become quite familiar with, walked across to greet me.

"Back again, sir?"

I smiled. "I just can't stay away."

"And with good reason. You've landed a real stunner."

"I really have," I replied, at once understanding his meaning.

"Would you like me to park the car for you, sir?"

"Yes, that would be very kind," I replied, handing over the key to the Porsche.

I made my way across to Rachel's suite. I checked myself over before knocking the door.

She opened it, her smile even more seductive than I last remembered. She was wearing a white bathrobe. It was untied. Her smooth, tanned physique clearly on show.

"Just in time," she said, tilting her head to one side.

"What for?"

She playfully pulled me through the door and kissed me.

"Room service has just delivered a chilled bottle of my favourite vino," she replied. "And I've just run a steamy hot bath for two."

"That *is* good timing."

Rachel nodded, as she proceeded to undress me, kiss me and lead me all at the same time to the bathroom.

Minutes later, we were lying head to toe in a spacious freestanding bath, surrounded by opulent amounts of white marble.

It still felt so surreal.

Me, lying there with this Hollywood actress. Our bodies emersed in a profusion of delicate bubbles and soapy water.

As I sipped the chilled wine and caressed her soft skin, Rachel began telling me about her upcoming film shoot. A big-ticket fantasy adventure. Wales and its most dramatic landscapes serving as the stunning backdrop to the film.

She told me about the A-list cast. Who she was looking forward to working with. Who she couldn't stand. How demanding the director was. How big the production budget would be. How much she was getting paid. How much training she'd have to do for her role. How long and intensive the days would be.

When she finally paused, I got chance to share some of my own news.

"I've got something to tell you too…"

"Hold that thought," she said, reaching over the side of the bath and grabbing what appeared to be some kind of hotel brochure.

"This is where I'll be staying for the next month."

She handed me the brochure.

"Looks stunning," I replied.

"It does, doesn't it?"

"Like heaven itself," I said, handing her back the brochure. "So, about my news…"

"Oh yeah," said Rachel, dropping the brochure over the side of the bath.

She closed her eyes and relaxed her head back on a bath pillow.

"Well… it looks like I'm going to get… promoted!"

"Oh, that's nice," she replied, her eyes still closed.

"I'll be the youngest director in the business," I added, for good measure.

"Oh, that's lovely," she said, getting even more relaxed. "You wouldn't mind massaging my feet, would you? I've been on them all day."

I complied with her request. But I felt pissed off. She hadn't paid any attention to what I'd said.

And to think, I've spent the last twenty minutes listening to you.

But I kept that thought to myself.

"Do you know what we should do?" she said, opening her eyes.

Celebrate my promotion? I thought, sarcastically.

"Why don't I jump out. Dry off. You can give me a full body massage with the luxury lavender and sweet orange oil I bought today and then…"

She flashed her eyebrows at me to convey her intentions.

In an instant, my mind moved on from thoughts of promotions at work to things of more immediate interest. Rachel's bodily charms were just too hard to resist.

It was the next morning.

We were both up early on account of work. Rachel had to pack what was quite a considerable wardrobe. I needed to do some prep for a couple of meetings later that day.

I was ready to leave first.

I grabbed my things and headed to the door. Rachel pulled me back into her arms.

"I'll text you the address of the hotel, once I've had a chance to settle in."

"Promise?"

"Of course. It'll be nice to hook up again," she said, kissing me as I made my way to the door.

"It will," I replied.

The prospect of seeing her again excited me. But her last comment concerned me.

Were we just 'hooking up'?

Is that what this is?

I decided not to ask. I didn't want to come off a little too serious, too soon. I didn't want anything to jeopardise whatever this was with Rachel.

Walking out the hotel I was immediately confronted by a small group of paparazzi. Evidently, they recognised who I was. I guessed they'd been tipped off that this was Rachel's last night at the hotel.

The camera flashes and questions began simultaneously.

"Is Rachel on her way?"

"No comment."

"Are you and Rachel an item?"

"No comment."

"Are you serious about Rachel?"

Getting bored of saying *no comment,* I facetiously replied: "Who wouldn't be serious about Rachel Hanson?"

"Is Rachel having it away with someone else, as well as you?"

"What?"

I turned around and faced the reporter who'd had the temerity to ask that question.

"Wouldn't be the first time," he replied nonchalantly, with a dismissive shrug of his shoulders.

"Watch your mouth," I hit back, drawing closer to him with clenched fists.

"Or what?" he replied.

Or what?

That was a good question. I was hardly going to knock him out and give the rest of these paparazzi piranhas an unexpected feeding frenzy.

So, we just stared each other out. Eyeball to eyeball. Nose to nose. But that was it. I had enough self-control to not do anything stupid. I wasn't going to throw away what I had with Rachel for one lousy untruthful comment. Especially coming from the mouth of some schmuck reporter.

I turned away and walked across to the Porsche. The concierge had parked it right outside the hotel. I jumped in but paused before hitting the ignition.

What exactly have I got with Rachel?

Were we an item? Were we serious? Not knowing where I stood, bothered me.

But I shook off the thought, thinking instead of the big things that lay ahead. I switched on the engine and revved it freely. The sound roused my spirits. It was like a drug. The paparazzi's cameras flashed as I put the car into gear. A few bystanders peered into the Porsche, looking in to see if I was someone famous.

I felt famous, as I looked back out in their direction.

God, I love this car.

I loved the effect it had on others, attracting attention and admiring glances wherever it went. But then I remembered: I had to hand the Porsche back in a week. For a split second, the prospect depressed me. But I pushed that thought to the back of my mind too. I didn't want anything to upset my flow.

I pulled away from the hotel. I gave the accelerator a little tap. The Porsche responded instantly. But something – *someone* – made me hit the brakes.

It was Katie.

51

"I'm sorry, Katie."

It felt like a lifetime ago that I'd seen her.

It had in reality been less than a week. But in that passage of time life felt considerably different. I was living in a new world now. Moving in different circles – with glamourous new connections.

I pulled over to the roadside. Katie was gliding along the pavement just ahead of me. She seemed in a hurry.

Say hello? I wondered, tapping my finger on the steering wheel.

I edged the car forward slowly. I pulled up alongside her and lowered the passenger window.

"Katie," I called out.

She looked across at me, rolled her eyes and continued walking, at an even brisker pace.

I pulled up alongside her again.

"Katie, it's me, Vee."

She stopped where she was and turned towards me, angrily.

"I don't recognise who *this* Vee is," she said coldly, looking at me, then the Porsche and then back at me again.

"Don't be like that," I pleaded. "I'm the same Vee as before."

"But you're not," scoffed Katie. "The old Vee would never have treated me like you did, last week."

"I'm sorry. Rachel wanted to meet after the premiere and one thing led to another."

"I don't care whether you and Rachel Hanson hooked up!"

Hooked up?

There was that bloody phrase again.

"I'm just disappointed you lied, Vee. You didn't have to get me out the way, so you could sneak off with her. You should have just been honest."

"It wasn't like that."

But we both knew: it was just like that.

"She was so rude to me as well, Vee. She didn't acknowledge me once. I reckon she could be a real bitch if she wants to."

"She's not like that."

"Oh, come on, Vee!" Katie shouted, slapping her forehead. "Stop being so bloody naïve. You've only known her a week."

I shook my head, swearing under my breath.

"I'm sorry Katie. I really don't know what else to say."

"That's because there is nothing to say."

I stared back at her forlornly.

Katie glanced down at her watch. "I've got to go, Vee."

She turned to walk away.

"Wait. Can I at least give you a lift somewhere?"

Katie turned back my way, with a look of disgust.

"*What?* So you can impress me with your fancy new Porsche?"

I was about to tell her it was a hire car. But I didn't want her estimation of me to sink any lower.

"You just seem in a rush, that's all," I replied, in my defence.

But I don't think she heard me.

She began walking away but then stopped all of a sudden.

"Do you remember when you asked me that question?" she said, turning around.

"What question?"

"Katie, am I self-absorbed?" she said, mocking my voice. "Well, I was wrong. The answer is *yes*. You are so *fucking* self-absorbed, it's a joke."

Ouch. That hurt. Especially coming from Katie. Nicest-person-in-the-world-Katie. Wouldn't-hurt-a-fly-Katie. Never-say-boo-to-a-goose-Katie.

She turned around and walked away.

I felt embarrassed. But a little heated too; my run-in with that crass journalist moments earlier didn't help. The anger kicked in. My nostrils flared. I floored the accelerator. The

Porsche shot off like a rocket. Katie shook her head as I roared past her.

Oh, whatever!

I acted like I didn't give a shit.

But I did.

Five minutes later, I parked up the car. I had to get things straight in my own head.

Immediately, two opposing voices took up the case:

FORGET ABOUT IT, VEE. SHE'S JUST JEALOUS.

But she's got a point. You were, *you are*, self-absorbed.

HOW?

You completely disregarded her feelings. You thought only of yourself.

YEAH, BUT HOW MANY TIMES IN YOUR LIFE ARE YOU GOING TO GET A CHANCE WITH SOMEONE LIKE RACHEL HANSON? YOU JUST SEIZED YOUR MOMENT, VEE. CARPE DIEM.

You did but you literally pushed Katie aside to do it. You didn't give her a second thought.

OKAY, SO YOU FEEL A LITTLE BAD. YOU'RE JUST HUMAN LIKE EVERYONE ELSE.

But you're better than that, Vee.

LOOK VEE, YOU DID WHAT YOU HAD TO DO. IF YOU DON'T TAKE CARE OF NUMBER ONE, WHO WILL?

Even if that means selfishly pushing others aside?

KATIE WILL BE FINE. IT'S NOT LIKE YOU WERE DATING. NOT REALLY.

That's not the point. You lied to her. You disregarded her. You acted like your relationship meant nothing.

YEAH, YOU PUT YOURSELF FIRST FOR A CHANGE. AND NOW YOU'RE DATING RACHEL HANSON AND YOU'RE ABOUT TO GET PROMOTED AT WORK. TELL ME WHERE THE PROBLEM IS.

That last comment hit home. It won the argument. For now, the loud self-serving voice in my head had won the battle within. Little did I know it was a pyrrhic victory.

I turned the engine back on. I hit the accelerator hard as my ego pushed on, pursuing its own relentless course.

But, payback was on the way.

52

Not ready yet

Friday. At last!

Sebastian was back in the office.

Finally, I'd get the chance to pitch my idea to him. Well, Ralph and Dwayne's brainchild.

I'm getting promoted!

Nothing else (except Rachel) occupied my thoughts. But she hadn't been in touch after leaving for Wales. So, the prospect of promotion took centre stage in my mind: there was no thought of *if* only *when*.

Feeling confident, I penned a list of goals – "future happenings" – in my journal:

When I'm PROMOTED, I am going to…

Buy my own Porsche :)

Have it washed every day.

Buy a bigger place.

Buy a new wardrobe.

Add to my watch collection.

Buy Rachel something nice.

Take her somewhere special, that only money can buy.

Go to L.A.

Set up an office there.

Break into all the right circles.

Spend time between London and L.A.

Travel first class whenever I go.

Make a lot of money. £££

Be rich.

Live life on my terms :)

These intoxicating thoughts gripped my mind. They spoke of the greater riches I was convinced were heading my way. It all seemed in touching distance now.

At last – an ironic thought to think, given I'd hardly been working for this life-defining moment all that long.

There was just the formality of speaking to Sebastian. I told Ralph and Dwayne that today was the day. Both gave me their seal of approval.

I told Sonia of my intentions too.

"I wouldn't today," she replied. "Sebastian's got a lot on his plate right now."

But I disregarded her advice. With the perfect life within my grasp, I told myself today was the day.

At 3.30pm, I convinced myself now was the time. Sebastian and I were wrapping up our usual end-of-week meeting.

"If there's no other business, you might as well knock off, Vee," he said, leaning back in his chair, his head falling back on the headrest.

He looked tired. But I pressed on with my plan.

Do it now, Vee.

"Just got one other thing to discuss Sebastian."

He leaned forward towards me. "I thought we'd covered everything."

I hesitated.

All of a sudden, pitching him the idea I'd been salivating about all week felt awkward.

"Um. You know that talent director job…"

"What about it?"

Sebastian's face hardened. My nerves kicked in. My palms became sweaty. The next line felt so hard to say. I felt stupid saying it.

"Do you think…perhaps…maybe…I…could do that job?"

There was a very long, very uncomfortable pause.

Sebastian stared at me with a look of pure incredulity. Immediately, I knew: I'd overstepped.

"What on earth makes you think you can do that job?" he asked.

He looked vexed.

I shrugged my shoulders and bit my lip.

"You're not ready for that role, Vee. Not even close."

I felt more stupid. I'd completely misjudged the situation.

"I know I'm not ready *yet*," I replied, trying to claw back some ground. "I just thought I might be able to do the job in some junior capacity."

Sebastian's eyes narrowed. His upper eyelids disappeared. His nostrils flared.

"*Junior capacity*? What kind of business do you think I'm running here?"

Again, no reply came forth from my trembling lips.

"Who put you up to this?" he asked, angrily.

"Um…"

I didn't want to say. It felt unfair to bring them into it.

"Go on, tell me. Let me guess. Ralph and Dwayne?"

My head dropped. I looked down to the ground. My body language immediately confirmed Sebastian's suspicions.

"I'm *fucking* pissed off," he shouted, banging a fist on his desk.

I recoiled back in my chair. Sebastian hardly ever swore or lost his temper.

"I'm sorry," I uttered, my mouth dry with nerves.

"I'm not pissed off with you. I'm pissed off with *them*," he growled. "They've just used you."

"I don't understand. How?"

"To get information from me. They're afraid—"

"Of what?"

"That I might bring someone more capable than them into the business."

The penny dropped.

My cheeks flushed red with embarrassment. I couldn't believe how stupid, how over-ambitious I had been.

How could I not have cottoned on to Ralph and Dwayne's real intentions? Their ulterior motive was obvious now.

I felt myself shrinking in Sebastian's presence. I put my hand on my forehead to hide my shame. I shook my head. I had been played, good and proper.

"Listen, Vee," Sebastian said, his tone a little softer. "Don't get ahead of yourself. Ok?"

I nodded back, my face solemn and serious.

"You've had a great week. You've done exceptionally well this past year. But you need to know the stretch in a job before you ever put yourself forward for it. And the stretch here is *so* big Vee, I'm surprised you even had the temerity to ask me about it."

"I'm sorry. Ambition got the better of me."

"Don't worry. You're not the first. You won't be the last."

I nodded back, failing to hide the mortification that had hijacked my face.

"But stop being in such a hurry, ok? Otherwise, your ambition may be your undoing."

Sebastian motioned with his hand that I was free to leave.

I got up, picked up my notebook and laptop and headed to the door.

"Just one last thing," Sebastian said.

"Yes?" I replied, turning around.

"Send those two schemers into my office."

I walked out. Headed straight to Ralph's desk. He was perched behind it. Dwayne on the edge of it. They were yapping away. No doubt hatching some plan or peddling some new titbit of gossip.

Their voices hushed as I approached.

"Sebastian wants to see you both," I said, my face a mixture of anger and anguish. "Now."

"What about?" asked Ralph, at once springing to his feet, his partner in crime doing likewise.

I shrugged and said nothing more.

I really wanted to give this duplicitous duo a piece of my mind. But – feeling fragile – I walked straight back to my desk and grabbed my things.

"What's wrong, Vee?" asked Sonia, walking over to me. "You look really upset."

"Can we just talk on Monday?"

My voice quivered.

"Yes, of course. But are you sure you're ok, Vee?"

I nodded back. I couldn't bring myself to say anything more.

I averted my eyes away from Sonia's. I didn't want her to see the shame in my eyes. My reputation felt tarnished. My inflated ego, bruised. I now felt like a man much lesser in stature than the one I had believed myself to be.

I put on my coat, kept my head down and left the office.

When I got back to the car, I opened the door, slumped into the driver seat and then slammed the door closed again.

I wanted to shut myself away and process what had happened. I felt like I'd just slammed the door closed on the future I desperately wanted.

How could I have been so stupid?

53

Narberth

I thrust my head back against the Porsche's headrest.

Sitting here in this car – my constant companion this past week – felt different now. Insipid, not exciting.

I felt so many emotions all at once.

Anger. At Ralph and Dwayne for selfishly using me as a pawn in their game.

Annoyance. At myself for letting my jumped-up pride blindside me.

Embarrassment. For playing the over-ambitious fool in front of Sebastian.

I felt like getting away; somewhere far.

But where?

At once, the appealing thought of seeing Rachel flashed into my mind. But I felt conflicted. I wanted to see her. Her beautiful brown eyes would soothe away my pain. Her playfulness would ease my troubles. But I didn't want her to know that I'd come up short. That the promotion I thought was in the bag, was never really on the cards.

I just won't tell her.

But then, it occurred to me. She hadn't texted me her address. In fact, she hadn't been in touch at all since we'd parted.

Then, I remembered: the brochure. The one she had shown me. The hotel she was staying at was in *Narberth*. A picturesque Welsh town, on the fringes of Pembrokeshire Coast National Park. I only vaguely recalled the name of the hotel. But it didn't matter. I had enough to go on. I punched Narberth into the sat nav.

It was a five-hour drive away.

You've got to be kidding me.

It was further than I hoped. But seeing Rachel would be worth it.

Love has no limits.

First, however, I needed fuel. The Porsche – like my self-esteem – was running on empty.

I pulled up at the first petrol station I saw. When filling up the tank, a happy chappy at the pump behind called out to me.

"Hey, fancy swapping?" he said, pretending to throw across the keys to his white van.

I half-smiled back.

"Business must be good," he said, eying up the Porsche. "I'd need to clean a lot of windows to get my hands on a car like that. One day, hey."

I felt like a fraud. Imposter syndrome took hold. All my life I felt the need to be someone. To be that stand-out guy in a crowd. But in that moment, all I felt like was a *phoney*. If only this smiley van driver knew the truth: the car wasn't mine. This image wasn't me. I was about to tell him, but it seemed like too much effort.

"Well cheerio," he said, when ready to leave.

I nodded back, barely able to smile.

I felt like a miserable sod. His upbeat nature contrasted sharply with my darker mood. But try as I might, I couldn't stop thinking about how I'd just screwed everything up at work.

Deep down I knew I wasn't ready for that job. I wasn't director material yet. So why the hell had I entertained the scheme? Why was I such a young man in a hurry?

I took up the thought as I began the long drive to Wales.

Sebastian had told me not to be in a hurry. Grandad had said the same. Sophia too had told me to stop rushing – multiple times. But I'd ignored them all. Now, I berated myself for it.

My mind then took up another depressing line of thought: how I'd unhappily crossed paths with Katie again, earlier that week.

I could still hear her words:

"You are so fucking self-absorbed, it's a joke."

Days later, they still stung.

They reminded me of all of Sophia's warnings. About me and my self-indulgent ego. How it had derailed me many times in the past. How, because of it, I might be sailing my ship into stormy waters.

The first two hours of my journey passed by with these unhappy reflections. The minutes and the miles ticking by laboriously. Painfully.

The weather didn't help. Like a cliché scene from some apocalyptic movie, the skies grew a darker shade of grey. Every now and then, the heavens would open. The rain would lash down and the fastest wiper setting on the Porsche would struggle to keep up. It made it difficult to see clearly. Impossible to drive quickly. It was exhausting.

As I struggled with the conditions, a call came through on my phone.

It was dad.

"Where are you, Vee?" he asked, getting straight to it.

"I'm… just heading out somewhere."

"Where?"

I hesitated.

"Um, Wales. *Why?*"

"Your grandad's not feeling well. He looks very poorly. He's asked if you'll come and see him."

Immediately, the dilemma this presented weighed heavily on my mind.

Turn back and head home?

There was a turning off the motorway just up ahead.

I loved grandad. I took every opportunity to make him happy. I'd do anything for him. But…I *really* wanted to see Rachel.

"How bad is he?" I asked.

"I think he'll be ok but could you pop by? He always feels better for seeing you."

"No problem, dad. I'll come by, as soon as I've finished my meeting."

"Ok, Vee," dad replied, not pressing me any further.

After I'd hung up, I thought back to when I saw grandad last. He didn't look well then, walking and talking a little slower than usual.

I passed the motorway junction where I could have turned back. Immediately, I felt bad for not doing so. But I promised myself, I wouldn't stay the night with Rachel. I'd head back once we'd spent a little time together.

Ah, Rachel.

I smiled at the thought of her. I imagined what her reaction would be when opening her hotel room door and seeing me standing there. I fantasised about what would happen next. How we might gratify each other greedily again.

9.15pm. Finally, I arrived.

I thought I'd have to drive around Narberth to find the hotel. Or, ask a local where it was. But by chance, I came across a road sign directing me to some upmarket-sounding hotel.

Surely, it's the one, I figured.

It was. I recognised the hotel immediately from the brochure Rachel had shown me.

It was still raining heavily when I arrived. I sat in the car for a minute or two, hoping the downpour would subside. It didn't.

I braced myself. I opened the door, jumped out and made a mad dash to the hotel reception. It was a few hundred yards away from the car park.

I got absolutely drenched. My hair and clothes were soaking. I needed to dry off, but I had a more pressing concern: how to covertly obtain Rachel's room number, without her knowing I was there.

I wanted it to be a big surprise.

It was.

But not at all the way I expected.

54

Surprise!

No one noticed me walk in.

The staff on reception were preoccupied with guests checking in and out.

As I watched the comings and goings before me, I still had no idea how to locate Rachel's room. Short-sightedly, I hadn't given it any thought on my five-hour journey here.

With no plan in mind and with the reception desk busy with guests, I headed straight to the men's toilets to dry off. I didn't want Rachel to see me looking like a drowned rat that had been plucked from a puddle.

But chance intervened.

I was about to push open the door to the toilets when a man from housekeeping called out to a girl on reception.

"I've got those extra towels for Miss Hanson."

"Take them straight up please," came the reply.

He nodded and bolted up a double-width wooden staircase, leading off the hotel lobby. I followed, in stealthy pursuit. Surely, he was heading to Rachel's room. How many other Miss Hansons could be staying there?

Adroitly, he flew up two flights of steps; taking them two at a time. He then pushed through a fire door and strolled down a long corridor that had been luxuriously carpeted.

Halfway down, he halted outside one of the hotel rooms. From my reconnaissance position, I couldn't make out the room number but I got an exact eye on the location.

He knocked twice.

"Housekeeping," he said, balancing three white towels on one hand, whilst straightening his black tie with the other.

I could do with one of those towels, I thought distractedly. I was still dripping wet.

The door opened.

The hotel employee half-stepped in and handed over the towels. Seconds later, he stepped back out as the door closed behind him. He emerged holding a ten-pound note.

Blimey, she tips well.

The man from housekeeping then briskly headed back my way. I pretended to search my pockets for a room key. But he was consumed by the note in his hand; he paid scant attention to me.

After he'd walked by, I thought about heading back down to the toilets to dry myself off. But I didn't want to waste any more time. Besides, I thought:

How romantic is this? Me standing here all rain soaked, all dripping wet, because I just couldn't wait to see the woman I've fallen for so bad.

Eagerly, I strode to her door. I knocked on it playfully, with a rat-a-tat-tat.

I smiled and flicked my wet hair to one side. I was all set to shout '*surprise*' but when the door opened, it was a man that answered. An instantly recognisable man. Dylan Johnson. A Hollywood movie star.

"Yes, can I help you?" he said, standing there imperiously in nothing but his boxer shorts.

Immediately, I felt inadequate. I looked far from my best whilst he stood there like a colossal Greek god, with all his glory on show.

He leaned with one hand against the door and looked me up and down; with a certain disdain. I stood there, stupefied as raindrops fell from my hair and trickled down my face.

"Is…is…" I stammered.

"Is, what?" he asked, impatiently.

"Is… Rachel, here?"

"*Why*? Who wants to know?"

I was about to answer when Rachel appeared at the door – wearing nothing but a towel wrapped around her midsection.

"Oh," she said, seeing me.

"Yeah. Oh!" I replied back, sarcastically.

Dylan smirked, shook his head and said, "I'm gonna leave you two, to whatever this is."

I watched him stroll back into the room all nonchalant and triumphant. I felt like punching his perfectly chiselled jaw. I glared back angrily at Rachel, with a look that screamed: *what the fuck!?*

"I would say this isn't what it looks like," she said, biting her lip and rubbing the back of her neck. "But, it kind of is."

Her tone was soft and apologetic. She clearly didn't mean to cut me with her words. But they wounded me deeply.

"So now I know why you haven't been in touch. You've been shagging Dylan fucking Johnson all week."

"I'm sorry, Vee."

"I thought we had something special," I said, feeling every bit the victim.

"Yeah, there's something there but…"

"But what?" I demanded.

"I don't do exclusive relationships, Vee. They make me feel…trapped. You wouldn't want me to feel trapped, would you?"

I couldn't believe what I was hearing.

Trapped?

"Well, I'm sorry if I ever made you feel that way," I replied, with all the sarcasm intended.

"Don't be silly. You haven't, Vee," she said tilting her head to one side, looking back at me with pity through those beautiful deceitful brown eyes.

There are so many things I could have said to her next, like:

How could you do this to me?

How could you be so dismissive of what we had?

How could you just sack me off without a second thought?

But I said nothing. I shook my head, turned around and walked away.

My vanity, wounded. My ego, bruised. My pride, shattered.

"Vee…*Vee*…" she said, imploring me to turn around.

But there was no chance of that. I was angry. Hurt. Humiliated. I never wanted to see her again.

"Oh Vee, don't be so bloody dramatic…" she shouted out, dramatically; every bit the actress.

That was the last I caught of what she was saying. Her voice trailing off long before I bolted down the wooden staircase, into the foyer and out of the hotel.

It had taken me five hours to get there. I was leaving in less than five minutes.

A wasted journey of epic proportions.

The rain was still lashing down hard. But I didn't quicken my step. I didn't make a mad dash to the car. Like a sucker for punishment, I walked slowly in the rain, getting wetter and colder. Feeling numb and depressed.

I felt twice the fool today. First, I'd misjudged where I stood at work. Now, I'd misjudged where I stood with Rachel.

By the time I got back in the Porsche, I was thoroughly soaked. For several seconds – an agonising eternity – I sat there motionless, staring dead straight ahead, watching and listening to the rain batter the windscreen.

Then, a fiery rage erupted within me.

"You fucker!!!" I screamed, not sure whether I was referring to Rachel, Dylan or myself.

I punched the steering wheel hard, twice. It should have hurt but I was numb to the pain.

What a completely shit day this had turned out to be. It had begun with such high hopes. I should have been promoted by now; my career propelled into the stratosphere. But my head was in the clouds. Like Icarus, I flew too close to the sun. Now, life had clipped my wings and killed my pride. Humbled, I had come crashing back down to earth.

I felt embarrassed. Diminished. Foolish. Humiliated. Angry.

The cocktail of toxic emotions began to take effect. My rage consumed me even more.

I turned on the Porsche's ignition. I aggressively put the car into gear. I floored the accelerator. The wheels spun. The engine roared. The Porsche – this beast of a car – skidded away furiously. Within seconds, I was hurtling down a dark, wet, country lane.

I was out of control.

55

It's your grandad.

I didn't glance down to check my speed.

I knew I was driving fast. Stupidly so. But anger urged me on. The deafening roar of the engine drowned out any thoughts of reason.

The rain was still hammering down. Visibility was compromised. But I raced on, undaunted. Not through fearlessness. But recklessness.

As I ate up the road, I saw the rear lights of another vehicle not far ahead. It should have been a signal to slow down. But I sped up. I came dangerously close to its rear end, impatient to overtake it.

I flashed my headlights, urging the car to move to one side but the driver wouldn't budge.

Get out of my way!

I honked the horn. Still, the driver refused to yield. I felt infuriated.

I took matters into my own hands. I pulled to the outside of the car. There was hardly any space to overtake but I went for it.

The driver horned as I flashed by, our cars just millimetres away.

"Oh, piss off!" I screamed, looking back in my rear-view mirror.

I should have been looking the other way. I panicked when I did. A road sign ahead depicted a sharp left turn. Quickly, I hit the brakes. I tried to guide the Porsche through the corner but I was going too fast. The backend kicked out uncontrollably.

Everything happened in slow motion.

The car spun round. I'm not sure how many times. I thought it was going to flip over and hit a tree. The moment felt fatal. Like this was it. This was where it was all going to end. In Narberth of all places. In some obscure, dark, wet, country lane. I waited for my life to flash before my eyes.

But it didn't. Miraculously, I hit nothing.

The Porsche came to a sudden halt. The back end was resting up on a grassy verge. The front protruding out onto the road facing the wrong direction.

Suddenly, I saw two headlights coming towards me from the right. A horn sounded loudly, followed by the piercing sound of screeching brakes. I closed my eyes, braced myself for a violent impact and prayed. Surely, this was it. In the milliseconds that followed, I wondered what others might make of the short life I'd lived. The short life I'd wasted.

But again, nothing.

No deafening collision. No horrific sound of metal crashing into metal.

Tentatively, I opened my eyes. I saw a car halfway up the grass verge on the other side of the road. A man stepped out of the vehicle. He came towards me. I couldn't really hear what he was saying.

But all became clear when he drew close.

"You fucking twat!" he screamed.

He kicked the side of the Porsche and punched my window. Surprisingly, it didn't break.

"You could have fucking killed us all!"

I held my hand up, weakly. Not a fitting apology. The man kicked my door again.

"I've got young kids in the car. You irresponsible shit!"

Now, I felt really bad. I thought I could hear the sound of children crying.

I was going to step outside and give the man a heartfelt apology but he kicked the side of the Porsche again.

Then, I heard another voice. That of a woman.

"Leave it, Gary," she pleaded. "*Please* just come back in the car. The kids are getting scared."

He looked at me with evil intent. Oblivious to the rain lashing down on his face. Pure aggression contorted his features. He clearly wanted to do me harm. The harm that I so nearly caused him and his family.

He stood there looking in. I sat there looking out. I wondered what he might do next.

He turned away, then turned back and kicked the Porsche one last time.

Finally, he stomped away. He got back in his car and reversed it off the grass verge. Miraculously, it had sustained no damage. Before leaving, he pulled up alongside the Porsche, wound down his window and stuck two fingers up at me; his partner covered her face.

My head dropped in shame, especially when I saw two young kids crying in the back. One of them looked my way; scared tears rolling down his red cheeks.

You idiot, Vee.

I was relieved to see them drive away. Thankful they hadn't been hurt. I would never, *ever*, have forgiven myself if they had.

I looked left, then right. There was no one else on the road. I had to get the car facing the right way. It was no easy task. Other than the beam of light coming from the Porsche's headlights, it was pitch black. My legs were shaking. My hands, trembling. My heart, racing.

I put the car into gear. I moved it back and forth until I was on the right side of the road. I set off again but I'd barely driven five hundred yards when I pulled up into the nearest layby.

I jumped out and stepped away from the car. The engine was still running. The headlights were still on. I looked back at the Porsche's muscular body under the light of one solitary street lamp. It looked completely different to me now. Before it was stylish and sleek. Now, demonic and fearsome.

All of a sudden, this car – my pride and joy which wasn't even mine to own – terrified me. I didn't want to drive it. I wished I'd never hired it. It was just another stupid vain thing my ego had convinced me to do.

As I stood there, getting soaked, my conscience spoke loud enough for me to hear:

You could have killed yourself.

You could have killed that young family.

You could have caused so much pain to so many people.

And for what? Because you lost face at work? Because you lost out in love?

The only thing that's lost, is you.

Wake up, Vee.

Wake up.

I started breathing anxiously.

It was not like me. My chest tightened. I felt like I was struggling for air. Just then, my phone rang. It was dad. As I answered, an instinctive feeling of foreboding overtook me. Something was wrong. I could hear sobbing in the background.

"Dad…dad…what is it?"

"It's your grandad."

"What's happened? Is he ok?"

"Vee... he's…"

"He's what dad?"

Silence.

"Dad, come on. What's wrong with grandad?"

"He's… just… passed away."

My legs gave way. I fell to my knees. Tears began streaming down my face, intermingling with the rain that was relentless. Merciless.

I wanted to scream out in anguish. But no sound came forth.

The silence, the darkness, the cold, the rain, all closed in on me.

"Vee…Vee? Are you still there?"

I tried to say something. But the pain in my heart, the lump in my throat, the distress in my soul made it impossible to speak.

"Why…why… did it have to be like this?" was all I heard myself say.

I knew grandad was old. It was only a matter of time before he left this world. I knew that. But the fact that I was not there, when he asked me to be by his side, killed me.

56

Lost

The drive back was beyond hard.

Regret weighed heavily on my mind. I had decided that seeing Rachel was more important. I had continued en route to Wales when grandad, close to death's door, had asked to see me. I didn't know he was dying. But that didn't make me feel any better. The profound sense of loss was tearing through me.

I was never going to see him again. Talk to him again. Receive his wisdom again. Hear him laugh again. Or just sit and be with him again. As the rain hammered down, battering the roof of the Porsche, I thought back to what he'd said in our last conversation:

"Be careful in the Porsche.
Don't be a young man in a hurry.
If you have the urge to do something reckless, don't."

His warnings were clear. But I had not heeded them. I coveted a job I was not ready for. I became the young man in a hurry he warned me not to become. On every front, I'd got ahead of myself.

As for the Porsche – this damn Porsche – I had not been careful at all. I'd mishandled its power. Driven it recklessly. Angrily. I almost paid a terrible price. I'd nearly killed myself and an innocent young family.

I shook my head. More tears rolled down my cheeks.

The feeling of shame mingled with sadness hung heavy around me; an oppressive presence, refusing to leave.

I should have been with Grandad. Not Rachel.

As I berated myself something occurred to me. Grandad seemed to know *in advance* something bad might happen. Why else would he have given me those warnings?

Sophia did too.

She had contacted me a week before, when the story of Rachel and I first broke in the papers. She said she'd felt an emotional disturbance in my aura. She told me:

"You might be sailing your ship into stormy waters.

Be wary of your ego. It poses a real danger."

I'd just brushed aside what she'd said. But now, her words rang true. My whole being felt disturbed. Stupidly, having blindly followed my ego's selfish dictates, I'd now suffered the painful consequences.

Bad luck comes in threes.

I thought that was just superstition. But now I'd experienced my own tragic trilogy of misfortune. My work life, love life and personal life all lay in ruins.

Other hard-hitting words Sophia had spoken then came back to haunt me:

"Are you the kind of man who dates actresses and hires fancy cars to impress others? Or is there something more to you, Vee?"

Was I really that shallow? That superficial? Was the sole purpose of my existence just to impress others? Was there nothing more to me? Was I really that bloody obvious?

In my despair, my mind took another turn.

Ok. So maybe I do have an ego.

But there was something I was struggling to understand. If I had killed myself in the Porsche, if I had killed that innocent family too, why would I have paid such a heavy price? The punishment did not fit the crime.

And it's not like I was a bad person. I wasn't the only human being with an ego. The world, as I saw it, was full of self-absorption. Full of people who defined themselves by the objects they possessed, the money they earned or the talents that set them apart. Full of egotistical people driven by nothing more than their own vain desires and selfish interests. So, why then would I have been punished so severely?

Suddenly, my thoughts circled back to the pain in my heart.

Grandad's dead.

I hadn't escaped punishment. The regret, the timing, the anguish of his death was punishment enough.

A car horn sounded. I realised I'd just veered across into the wrong lane. I shook my head with self-loathing. Grandad had just died and here I was *still* thinking about myself. It seemed my self-absorption had become a full-time preoccupation. My self-centredness made me feel even more wretched.

I tried to think about mum and dad.

How must they be feeling?

They were close to grandad, too. Really close. Everyone had a strong bond with him. He was that kind of man. One of life's genuinely uplifting souls. Always connecting to others with ease. Always being welcomed with open arms wherever he went.

He's gone. Forever.

I couldn't imagine life without him.

This was the thought that afflicted me most on my lonely journey back. This, the feeling that troubled my heart as the minutes and hours ticked by slowly on that endless drive back, to a destination I was reluctant to reach.

Finally, I arrived at the hospital.

My father was waiting for me. All other family members had gone. Silently, he led me to the ward and bed where my grandad lay. Slowly, he pulled back the curtain.

I felt utterly distraught when I saw grandad's face. He lay there, as if asleep, on the hospital bed. I took up a seat by his side. I took hold of his hand. It still felt warm. I let my forehead rest softly on his chest. Then, I cried. Unceasingly. I felt the tears would never end. I felt the lump in my throat would never subside. I thought my broken heart would never mend.

The loss was too much to bear.

As I grieved, some distant part of my mind counted up all the losses I'd suffered in such a short space of time:

I'd lost my grandad.

I'd lost my relationship with Rachel.

I'd lost my connection with Katie.

I'd lost face at work.

I'd lost a future that was never mine to possess.

I'd lost connection to the spiritual path.

I'd lost sight of Sophia's warnings.

I'd lost respect in Sebastian's eyes.

I'd lost respect in Katie's eyes.

I'd lost respect for myself.

I recollected my thoughts and silently chastised myself. Again, I'd lost myself in self-absorption. This time intermingled with a large dose of self-pity.

What is wrong with me?

I reminded myself, that grandad – the anchor of my life – was no longer here.

I felt cut a drift.

I don't know how long I stayed there, with my head on his chest. Eventually dad, who had hardly spoken a word, gently tried to pull me away.

"Come on, Vee. Let's go home."

I held up my hand to him.

"Just a few more minutes," I replied, battling through more tears.

"Ok."

He walked away, leaving me alone with grandad. I lifted my head and looked at his face. Even in death, his countenance was serene. I wiped away my tears with the sleeve of my jumper and tried to get hold of my emotions.

"I'm sorry grandad," I said inaudibly, leaning in towards him. "I should have been here with you. Not there with…"

I couldn't complete the sentence. I felt ashamed.

As I gazed upon his face through tearful eyes, a stream of recollections flooded my mind of times we'd spent together.

Two in particular dominated my thoughts:

1986 – the first recollection:

I am nine years old. I'm in India on holiday. Grandad and I are having a conversation, alone.

"You and I already know each other well," he says, even though I've only just met him in person for the first time.

"How?" I ask, innocently.

"Our relationship runs very deep. We've met each other before."

I just smile back, affectionately.

I don't know what grandad means. But it seems like he's telling me something important. I feel like I've known my grandad forever. The thought makes me feel warm inside.

Thinking back, it was clear to me now. He must have been talking about *past lives*. How else could we have known each other like he claimed?

It's strange. He never mentioned it again. I, for my part, never asked him about it either. I just assumed we had a close bond and that he was speaking symbolically. Now, in this moment, I felt he was speaking literally.

1986 – the second recollection:

I am still in India.

I'm sat on the back of my grandad's bicycle. We are cycling to see the village holy man. Grandad says he has asked to see me. When we arrive at his ashram, grandad asks one of the holy man's disciples to take us to him.

He refuses. "Guru ji is meditating."

"But he's asked to see us. To see my grandson," says grandad.

"I can't disturb him. I won't disturb him," replies the stone-faced disciple. "Come back another time."

"Will you at least tell him we are here?" implores grandad.

The disciple shakes his head. He looks angry. I think we should turn back and go home.

But grandad stands his ground. "Just tell him we are."

The disciple tuts and walks off in a huff. But he returns minutes later. His whole disposition has changed. He's smiling. "Please, please, come this way."

We are taken to the holy man's private quarters. He receives us warmly. He sits me down next to him and wraps his blanket around me. I feel snug, safe, and secure in his presence.

He begins speaking – his voice calm and uplifting – sharing prophetic words about my future.

Years later, they were words grandad never let me forget. Words that set the aspirational tone for my life. The words that one day I would realise my full potential.

Other recollections came and went fleetingly, but these two remained, succouring me in my time of distress. They lifted my sad and weary mind. They brought a touch of peace to my troubled heart. But more than that, they inspired a new aspiration in my soul.

I was sick of being self-absorbed.

Clenching grandad's hand tightly, I decided:

I am going to be like you.

Strong. Serene. Spiritual.

All the wisdom he'd shared with me would not be in vain. I was going to change. I was going to walk the spiritual path. Nothing was going to pull me away from it.

From now on, I was going to listen to the spiritual voice within. Not that of my self-serving ego.

From now on, the wisest voice in my mind would be my ultimate counsel. When this voice spoke, I vowed to listen.

Three days later it did.

57

The leaves

Three days passed by.

The funeral had been arranged for a week on Monday. But as is the custom in Indian households in mourning, we expected a flood of guests at the house.

The night before had been no different. Friends and family turned up in swathes, keen to pay their respects to a man they all revered.

But it was morning now and quiet in the house. I was sat alone in grandad's room – reminiscing one moment about the times we'd spent together, feeling guilty the next about that one time I should have been by his side. The *last* time this would ever have been possible.

As I hung my head in sadness and shame, my eyes took in the familiar details of his room. The single bed he slept on. The little walnut coffee table to its side that had never had a coffee cup placed on it. Only tea. Only Indian tea at that, with all the extra taste of fennel seeds, cardamom and ginger.

To the right of that was a simple cream armchair, where grandad sat to meditate or listen to prayers that played out on an old cassette player.

Downloading and streaming music was yet to be invented. It was CD players that were all the rage back then. But grandad preferred his tried and tested cassette player. And his prayer tape. Side A was the morning Sikh prayer. Side B, its evening counterpart. He listened to them – he *used* to listen to them – each day without fail.

I should say there were no books anywhere in grandad's room. Surprising you may think for a man considered to be the wisest of men, by those who knew him best.

But grandad was illiterate. His dogged fight with poverty in the early years of his life cruelly robbed him of any formal education. It never held him back mind you. Grandad graduated from the school of life, with honours.

The final piece of furniture was a cream cupboard, housing his modest collection of clothes. I got up and walked across to it. Opening it, I smiled. Then, I laughed. That's when dad walked into the room.

"Dad, do you remember when you bought Papa that pair of trousers for his birthday?"

"How can I forget?" Dad replied, with the faintest of smiles.

"I've already got two pairs of trousers!" I said, mimicking grandad's voice. "What am I going to do with this new pair? Take them back. I don't want them!"

Dad's smile broke into a little laugh, as tears formed in his eyes. He missed his dad. I missed my grandad.

We stood there silently for a moment, each of us remembering him in our own way.

"I need your help, son," dad then said, wiping away his tears of sorrow.

"With what dad?"

"The leaves."

I sighed.

I knew what that meant. It was a massive job. My parents lived off a long private drive lined with a generous helping of oak trees. Being a private drive, no one from the local council ever came to collect the heavy blanket of leaves these majestic oak trees shed every autumn. We had to pick them up each year ourselves. It was a good two to three-hour job. Back-breaking work.

"Can we do it later, dad?"

I was just not in the mood to do it there and then.

Dad looked at me impatiently. "When later?"

"Just later dad. I promise I'll do it. Just don't feel up to it right now."

"Ok."

He left the room and closed the door behind him.

I sat back down on grandad's bed. I tried to recall what I was reminiscing about before dad had come in. That's when a voice spoke within me.

A clear, decisive and yet quiet voice.

"Do it *now*," it said.

Intuitively, I knew what it was referring to: the leaves.

Immediately, I felt the urge to comply with the command. This voice, as quiet as it was, was compelling and persuasive. It spoke with an authority I willingly accepted. With a knowingness, I instinctively trusted.

I rushed out of the room.

"Dad, dad?" I called out.

"I'm in the living room," came the reply.

I bounded down the staircase, slid across the tiled hallway, and rushed into the living room.

"Let's do it now," I said, breathlessly.

"Do what now?" said dad.

"The leaves. Let's pick them up now."

"But I thought you said…"

"I know, I know," I replied cutting him off. "But let's just do it now."

Dad must have wondered what the sudden urgency was.

But he shrugged and said: "Ok, let's do it now then."

So, we did.

Three and a half hours later, we had collected seventeen black bags of heavy wet leaves.

As I tied a knot in the last bag, dad turned to me.

"What shall we do with them?" he said.

I looked at the bags. There were so many.

"Wouldn't it be funny if the bin men suddenly pulled up outside our drive," I said, smiling tiredly.

"Chance would be a fine thing," replied dad, with a sigh.

I noticed how cold and exhausted he looked.

Just then, I heard a truck coming towards us. You might find this hard to believe but who should pull up *right outside* our drive? None other than Garden Waste Collection Services.

I looked at dad wide-eyed.

Dad looked back at me in disbelief. I sensed what he was thinking – that these crazy coincidences only ever happened in my world. Not in the logical, rational, practical world he lived in.

I seized the moment. I went up to the truck, reached up and knocked on the driver's window. The window dropped. A cheerful-looking man smiled down at me.

"Can I help you, mate?" he said.

"Maybe," I replied. "I know you don't normally collect from our drive, but my grandad's funeral is in a few days, and me and my dad have just collected all these bags of leaves."

The driver looked across at the bags. "Blimey! You two have been busy."

I nodded back.

"So, could I ask a really big favour?" I said, bringing the palms of my hands together. "Would you mind if I lugged the bags onto the back of your lorry?"

"Not at all," replied the man, warmly.

"Ah, thank you *so* much."

I picked up the first of the black bags.

"Wait," said the driver, jumping out of the truck. "We'll do it.'

Three other men jumped out with him.

Dad looked on, amazed, as these four men – like angels sent from heaven – gathered up all the bags and threw them onto the truck.

"Honestly, I can't thank you enough," I replied, when they'd finished.

I felt close to tears. I just about managed to hold them back.

"Our pleasure," said the driver, getting back in the truck. "Hope the funeral goes as well as can be expected. God bless."

With that, they were gone.

Dad and I walked back to the house. We were both shivering. Dad with the cold. Me, with excitement.

"Isn't that amazing dad? I told you; these kinds of things *do* happen."

Dad replied with a slight nod of the head.

"How does life even orchestrate this stuff?" I asked, shaking my head.

Dad shrugged. "It's just coincidence, Vee."

I didn't bother to argue the case. We'd had so many of these conversations before. Nothing I said or experienced ever seemed to shift his worldview. He said he believed in God – "some natural system" – but not in miracles. His was a very grounded philosophy.

It didn't matter. I *knew* it was more than a coincidence. I'd listened to my intuition. Followed my inner conviction. Acted decisively. And it had paid off.

It was a sign. That I was on the right path. That listening to the spiritual voice within was the way to go. My faith felt boosted. My mind revived.

A week later, after the funeral had come and gone and many tears had been shed, I cried again when I was alone. But this time, I cried for a different reason than grief. I cried when I thought back to the incident of the leaves.

By listening to the voice of my intuition, I had taken one step back towards the spiritual path. The spiritual had taken a thousand steps towards me.

It uplifted me in a moment of profound sadness. It restored my faith when all felt lost. It embraced me after my own self-absorption had pulled me away. It invited me back into the fold after I had egotistically turned the other way.

Now, feeling redeemed and less ashamed, there was someone I needed to see.

58

Akashic records

Sophia and I were sat opposite each other again.

First things first – I apologised for how I acted the last time we met.

"It was unacceptable," I said.

She brushed aside my comment and smiled.

Next, I told her about everything that had happened since. About grandad, Rachel, Katie, my near fatal accident and for overreaching at work.

Sophia looked on compassionately as I revealed all my misfortunes – vicariously living my journey through the heartfelt words I spoke. When I became teary-eyed, she did too.

"I feel for you, Vee," she said, placing her hand on mine. "Really, I do."

"Thank you. I know at times it may not seem it, but I do appreciate all your help."

Sophia waved away my gratitude. "You don't have to thank me. You're like family."

I felt overcome with emotion. We sat in silence for a while. Sophia waited patiently until I was ready to speak again.

"You were right," I said.

"About?"

"My ego."

Sophia again waved away my comment. "I know the danger your ego poses because I'm still battling mine."

"It's hard though," I said, sighing, "this battle against it. My ego has seemed stronger than me at times."

"It's a force of nature, Vee. But we can bring it under our control," Sophia replied, her eyes conveying the conviction of her words. "It's one of the first challenges light workers must overcome…to prove they're ready."

"Ready?"

"To handle greater spiritual power," she replied with emphasis. "With that power, you can make a bigger difference to those in need; become a brighter beacon of light to those lost in the dark."

But first, she said, we needed to prove ourselves worthy of handling that extra power. Prove, that we can be trusted to wield it for the greater good. Not for selfish gain.

"That's why," she continued, "all the great spiritual traditions emphasise the importance of love before there is any talk of enhancing one's spiritual power. It's only those who love deeply, that can be trusted to act most wisely."

I nodded back. Her words made sense.

"But there's just one thing I'm struggling to understand," I replied.

"Go on."

"If I had killed myself in the Porsche and God forbid that young family too, why would I have paid such a high price for my ego?"

"It was just a warning, Vee. Nothing more, nothing less."

"A warning?"

"Yes, sometimes a good scare is more valuable than good advice. Now you know that you must not let your ego hijack your life. You must take control of your ego. Which reminds me –"

Sophia sat up straighter in her chair, causing me to do likewise.

"I've seen your Akashic records," she said, mysteriously.

"Sorry, what?"

"Akashic records. It's the indelible memory of nature. It contains a history of everyone's past lives, of *all* past events."

"Really?"

I sounded sceptical.

Sophia nodded. "It was your higher self that gave me a glimpse of yours."

I looked back at her perplexed. Just like in the past, Sophia had shifted the conversation to an esoteric level that defied belief.

"So, what did my record reveal?" I asked, trying to stay open-minded.

"Something I knew and something I didn't."

"Go on," I replied leaning forward on my chair.

"I knew already that your ego has called the shots in many of your past lives."

"And the bit you didn't know?"

"That this life has special relevance to you."

Sophia's eyes widened to make the point further.

"How?" I asked.

"All the conditions and circumstances are in place for you to make a real spiritual shift."

"What kind of shift?"

"Towards your soul. One that will finally see you break free from the vice-like hold of your ego."

I stared back at Sophia, as we sat there in the normality of the busy coffee shop that had been party to so many of our unconventional discussions.

Could all this talk of past lives, Akashic records, higher selves, souls and egos really be true?

Sophia broke into my mental speculations. "I think that's why the warning you received was so clear," she added.

"In what way?"

"Your soul – your higher self – may not be as tolerant of your ego as it has been in the past."

"But why?" I asked, trying to keep up with her esoteric reasoning.

"Because the potential spiritual gain in this lifetime is so high, as will be the cost, *if* it's something you forsake."

It sounded like a game of spiritual snakes and ladders. A square with a ladder leading to heaven, next to a snake leading back, way back, to a place I did not want to go.

I sat back and listened as Sophia extrapolated on the matter. Sometimes looking at her. Sometimes looking away into the distance.

As she finished speaking, a long-forgotten memory flashed into my mind. It made me smile.

"What is it?" she asked, noting my change of expression.

"I just remembered something from my childhood."

"Go on."

"It's a bit bizarre. Not sure if it's profound or stupid."

"Well, let's hear it," she said, leaning in towards me, intrigued.

"I was four or five years old. I was playing outside with some kids. I fell in some mud so I came inside to wash my hands. That's when it dawned on me. I thought – if I'm not outside there with them… I'm inside here, alone…that means …*I'm separate* from them. I'm an individual. Does that sound stupid?"

"No. I think you're on to something. Carry on."

"I suddenly realised I was something distinct from the world around me. It was like I'd just witnessed the birth of my own ego."

"How did you feel before that moment?"

"Like I was just a part of everything else."

"And after?" asked Sophia, absorbed by my tale.

"I became very self-conscious. Painfully shy."

"It's that whole imaginary audience thing," she commented.

"Oh, what's that?" I asked.

I'd never heard the term before.

"It's that adolescent belief we have that the whole world is watching us."

"Yeah, that was it exactly," I replied, pointing my finger at what she'd just said. "And I hated being the centre of attention."

"How come?"

"Perhaps because I became aware of what others thought of me."

"Which was?"

"It's not very flattering," I laughed, rubbing the back of my neck.

"Tell me anyway."

"Lazy, weak and slow," I said. "That was the general consensus."

I could have added *fearful* to the list.

Sophia smiled. "Well, you've turned out pretty well."

All things considered, I guess I had.

"Hey, do you know what?" I said, shifting to the edge of my seat. "I think it's because I was written off as a kid that I am the way that I am now."

"How so?"

"I decided, I wasn't going to be that kid that got left behind, the one who was always last to get picked."

"What did you decide to become instead?"

I looked back at her with the same fierce determination I had as a child who'd been pushed aside one too many times.

"I wanted to be special. Someone who would lead the pack. Not prop up the rear."

"I see," Sophia replied.

"But that's when the pressure started too. To make it big. And the fear, that I might not make it at all."

"I think that pressure and fear are still driving you now," Sophia replied.

I nodded. "I think it is. I think deep down I fear I might not become the man I feel I should be. That undisputed, unmitigated success in the eyes of the world."

Sophia looked back at me compassionately.

"Anyway, something else happened as well back then in my childhood."

"Go on."

"I went to India for the first time and came back different."

"How?"

"Something switched on in me over there. I came back sharper, brighter, stronger in every sense."

"That must have felt good."

"It was a real buzz. For so long, I'd been overlooked. But now, *I* was the one catching the eye. I loved it."

"I picked that up about you, from your Akashic records," Sophia commented.

"What, that I love attention?" I laughed.

Sophia smiled. "No. That you're a late developer. The ugly duckling that becomes the beautiful swan."

"Interesting."

"There was just one problem with you."

"What?"

"Like Narcissus, you fell in love with your own reflection."

We both laughed.

"Joking aside, I think it's why you were born with that face," she added.

"Why?"

"It's one of your ego fixations. You love being told how attractive you are."

She mentioned how the ego can never get enough validation. Always seeking more praise, recognition or affirmation of its own specialness.

I sighed. "But I don't want to be like that anymore."

Sophia looked on compassionately. She knew I was being sincere. "Do you really want to change?"

"Yes."

"Then there is something you must do."

"What?"

"There's someone you must face."

"Who?"

"*Yourself.*"

59

The mirror test

I remembered a scene from a movie:

A caped superhero is caught in a violent struggle with his shadowy alter ego. The battle is fierce. It is unclear who will win. But the shadow self gets the upper hand. The superhero is almost crushed into oblivion. He looks done for. But he fights back and strangles his villainous self. His alter ego can't breathe. But the superhero knows it's a fight to the death. He tightens his grip. His inner nemesis disappears right before his eyes.

But I wasn't a superhero. My life wasn't a movie. Real life was more challenging. My alter ego, more elusive.

"How do I face myself?" I asked Sophia.

She was clear about what needed to be done.

"Look in the mirror. Take a good, long look at your own reflection," she said, locking eyes with mine.

"And then?"

"Courageously see yourself as you are. The whole truth. The good and bad. The positive and negative. The appealing and unappealing."

"But how?" I asked.

"After taking a good hard look in the mirror, complete the following sentence with complete honesty…

This is the face of someone who …"

After it, Sophia suggested I use words such as: *is, has, does* or *thinks*.

"*This is the face of someone who* is…*the face of someone who* does… *the face of someone who* thinks ..."

"Ok."

"But do the exercise without any defensiveness or self-judgement" she instructed. "Do it with compassion and understanding."

I nodded.

"And, Vee…"

"Yes?"

"If you see something in the mirror of truth you don't like, don't shrink away from your reflection. Have the courage to confront the truth of who you are, within the sacred space of your own heart and mind."

I promised I wouldn't shrink away. I promised I'd give the mirror test a go.

One week later, we met again.

The mirror test was our first topic of conversation.

"So?" Sophia asked. "Did you do it?"

I nodded.

"Did you find it hard or easy?"

"Both," I replied, earnestly.

"How so?"

"It was easy to dwell on the positives. But hard to admit the negatives."

"Yes, it's hard facing up to the unlikable elements of yourself."

I puffed out my cheeks and nodded.

"Do you know, for some it's the other way around," Sophia said.

"Really?"

She nodded. "If you're self-critical you'll find no end of negatives, but struggle to find any positives."

"Makes sense. But for me, it was harder to confront my negative side."

"Wait until you have to face your shadow self for real on the inner planes," Sophia said, widening her eyes. "*That's hard.*"

"Does that really happen?"

She nodded. Her expression dead serious. "But that's a conversation for another time. So, tell me. What did you see in the mirror?"

I started with the positives.

"I saw the face of a light-hearted and fun-loving soul. Someone with honesty and integrity who seeks to do no harm to others."

I looked up thoughtfully, trying to remember what else my reflection revealed.

"I saw the face of someone who believes he can do anything. The face of someone strong and positive. Someone who, when push comes to shove, will stand his ground and stand up for others."

I paused.

"Go on," Sophia said.

"I saw the face of someone with love and compassion for all people. Who feels a deep empathy with others. Who can cry when others cry, laugh when others laugh. Who feels the joy that others feel."

Sophia smiled.

"And the negatives?"

I took a deep breath in. This was the hard bit.

"I saw the face of someone who can be selfish. Someone who can put his needs, desires and ambitions before those of others. Not in a malicious way though."

"Of course not," Sophia agreed, her tone putting me at ease.

"Like I said, I'd never harm anyone," I clarified. "But I did see the face of someone who can influence others to do his bidding. Who can subtly manipulate others to get what he wants."

I paused there for a second. It felt uncomfortable admitting my flaws so openly.

"Keep going," Sophia said, with an encouraging look.

The rest of the negatives came flooding out.

"I saw the face of someone who loves attention," I continued. "Someone who desires wealth, power and status for the external recognition it will bring. Someone who is desperate to stand out so others will take notice. Someone who, at times, thinks he is perfect. Someone who loves giving others advice because it's a way of showing others how clever he is. Someone who is impatient for success. Someone who is always looking for the quickest and easiest route in life."

"Yes. Why is that, Vee?"

I looked upwards and sighed. "Maybe I'm not prepared to work hard enough. Or sacrifice everything to achieve what I desire. Maybe you called it right when we first met."

"In what way?" asked Sophia.

"Maybe I *do* lack courage. I do give in easily. I do back out when things get tough. I do succumb to doubt when conviction is needed most."

I sat back and sighed. It felt cathartic to bare my soul. But, exhausting too. I rubbed my face with both hands. Was it to hide my discomfort? Or an attempt to re-energise myself? Maybe it was both.

Sophia touched my hand and gave me a reassuring smile. "Well done. You really didn't pull any punches, Vee. Admitting the hard truth to yourself is never easy."

"Thanks. Looks like your tough love is paying off."

Sophia laughed.

"But can I be honest with you…" I said.

"Yes, of course."

"Now I'm more aware of my ego, I'm feeling a bit lost. I know I don't want to dance to its tune or let it pull me in the wrong direction. But I'm afraid to walk the other way too."

"The other way?" she asked, seeking clarification.

"Down the spiritual path."

I paused to recollect my thoughts.

"I want to believe there is something more," I said. "That, there *is* a divine plan. That life is not random. That everything *is* happening for a reason. That *I'm* here for a purpose."

Sophia seized on my last comment. "After everything that has happened, what do you think *is* your purpose?"

I turned my eyes up to heaven. "That's just it. *I still don't know.*"

Sophia was thoughtful.

I tracked her eyes as they looked left, right, at me and then into the distance. She was about to say something then paused.

After thinking something over, she spoke again. "Let's leave things here for the time being, Vee."

"Oh, ok."

"You've made great strides this past week. Let's meet again, in one month. Tell me then, what you think your purpose might be."

60

"What's your fucking purpose?"

My purpose?

One month on, I *still* didn't know.

But I didn't want to tell Sophia that as we were sat opposite each other again, in our favourite coffee shop.

Just wing it.

Thankfully, the conversation kicked off on a light-hearted note.

"I've noticed that's something you don't do any more," Sophia said.

"What's that?"

"Check other women out when you're talking to me."

Sophia laughed.

I blushed, then smiled. "I'm too scared now to even try."

"Oh, come on! I'm not that bad."

She was about to flick her hair to one side. I jokingly ducked out the way, as though evading a punch.

"Ha, ha!" she laughed. "Am I *really* that bad?"

I nodded vehemently. "You're the queen of tough love."

"Speaking of tough love," she said, feigning seriousness. "Has Katie called you yet?"

I shook my head.

"Can't blame the poor girl. You did make her feel a tad inadequate. I'm not sure how secure any woman would feel by your side with that roving eye of yours."

I covered my face with both hands. "God, don't make me feel worse."

Sophia laughed. "Don't worry, she'll come around. Just give her time."

"Do you really think so?"

Sophia nodded back.

"Is that your clairvoyance talking?" I asked.

"No, just a woman's intuition."

"Oh."

"Anyway. Let's get down to it."

"To what?"

"Your purpose. You've had a whole month to think about it."

"You don't forget a thing, do you?"

"No," she said, sitting herself more comfortably, tucking a stray hair behind her ear. "So, what is it?"

I shuffled around in my seat and rolled my head from side to side. "Well, I've been thinking about the whole meaning of life thing."

Have you?

"And?" asked Sophia.

"And… I think it's about becoming enlightened."

"Ok. How?"

"Through self-realisation."

"Which is?"

"Um…the process of knowing the truth of who you really are."

"Which is?" asked Sophia, interrupting.

"Infinite spirit."

I really was winging it now.

"And what is infinite spirit?"

"An energy."

"What kind of energy?" she asked, testing me.

"An unlimited all-powerful one."

"And when you know yourself to be unlimited and all-powerful, then what?"

"Then…you seek to become all that you can conceive and believe in your mind."

"And next you're going to tell me that what you can conceive and believe, you can achieve."

"Yes!" I replied, not realising how clichéd I sounded.

"Ok, Vee. Let's start again. What is your purpose?"

"Like I just said," I replied, not really believing what I was saying.

Sophia sighed and shook her head.

"Vee, I want to know what your purpose is. Not God's, not the Universe's, not something clever you have read in a book or what some guru has told you. What is *your* purpose?"

"To be all that I can become," I replied, visibly frustrated.

"Oh, come on, Vee!" Sophia fired back. "Drop all these bloody catchphrases. You can do better than that. Stop giving me generic answers. In less than ten words, tell me what *your* purpose is?"

I scratched the top of my head. "To live a meaningful life. To do something fulfilling in this world."

Sophia tutted.

She was really starting to annoy me.

"Come on, Vee. Think harder. What's your *fucking* purpose?"

Her choice of words shocked me. They triggered an angry response.

"I don't *fucking* know!" I shouted back, with a profanity of my own.

"There it is," Sophia replied, sitting back calmly in her chair. "You don't know. Why didn't you just say?"

I shrugged.

"You do know that's why you're confused all the time?"

"What do you mean?"

"You fundamentally don't know *why* you are here or *what* you are here to do."

I shrugged again.

"And you hate the feeling of not knowing. You like to be the one *in* the know. The one with all the answers."

There was a pause.

Sophia then started to giggle. "It's quite funny really."

"What is?" I asked, not seeing the funny side.

"You like to be the one in the know. But you don't have answers to the big questions concerning your own life."

I glared back at her. *Is she belittling me?*

"Just telling you the truth, Vee. Only the truth can set you free. But you're still bound by your old thinking."

"What do you mean?"

"All your life you have been seeking validation from others, about how wonderful, wise and attractive you are. It's that whole *look at me, aren't I pretty* routine that you do."

She fluttered her eyelashes to drill home the point.

"You don't have to mock me. I do know my own flaws by now," I bit back, feeling even more triggered.

"Maybe. But you don't know how to break free from them. Do you?"

I didn't reply.

"Especially the never-ending concern about what others think of you," she said. "Your self-worth is all wrapped up in it."

"So, what?" I hit back. "Everybody likes praise. Everybody craves recognition. *I'm* no different."

"That's true. But what does it say in that book you like preaching from so much?"

Preaching!

"Which one?" I asked, incensed.

"The Tao Te Ching. How does that line go? If you seek other people's approval too much…"

"… you become their prisoner," I replied, finishing off the sentence.

"Exactly," replied Sophia, getting to the edge of her seat. "You'll never be free if you care too much what other people think."

I sat there silently, listening to Sophia speak the truth. About how it takes courage to be yourself, especially if others judge, condemn or disagree with you.

Some of Sophia's methods really jarred on me. But I couldn't deny the honesty with which she spoke.

When she finished saying her piece, she looked thoughtfully into the air. She nodded to herself a couple of times.

"Yes, let's go there," she replied, doing that thing she did of outwardly consulting her inner guide.

"I have a question for you, Vee."

"Go on."

"If you had all the money in the world and you had satisfied all your personal desires, what would you do then?"

"I'd help people."

"Good. How?"

"With all the money I have, of course."

"But aren't you also in a position now to help them with something more than money?"

"More than money? Like what?" I asked, glibly.

"Like time."

"*Time?*"

"Yes. If you could give others your time, your talent, your knowledge, your energy, what would you do?"

I shook my head. I'd reached that dead end again.

"That's just it, Sophia, *I don't know*. If I knew I'd tell you."

I slid my cup of coffee away from me, then back, as if that might stir up an answer.

"If I could tell you what your calling is, would you want to know?" asked Sophia.

I looked up. "Yes."

"Are you sure?"

"*Yes.*"

"Would you commit your whole life to it if you knew what it was?"

I hesitated. "Yes."

"Then, there's something you need to do."

61

The pledge

"Leave everything to God."

"*What?*" I replied.

"Let go and let God," Sophia said, as though it was simple.

I looked nonplussed. "I don't understand."

"Put your trust in God, Vee."

"How?"

"Have faith He will guide you to your calling."

"Ok."

"No matter how long that takes."

"Ok," I replied, not feeling ok at all.

"And then…"

And then?

"…make your pledge," she said, looking me in the eye.

"My pledge?"

"Yes – a promise to God."

"What promise?" I asked, shuffling uneasily in my seat.

"That you'll dedicate your life to your calling, *whatever* it might be, *wherever* it might take you. Can you do that, Vee?"

I was at a loss for words.

This pledge sounded extreme. An unfair request. Surely, it was too much to ask of anyone?

How could I commit myself to a calling I knew nothing about? How could I follow God blindly on a path I couldn't see?

My face was riddled with doubt. But Sophia pressed on regardless.

"The choice for every light worker is clear, Vee," she said, smoothing out a crease in her jumper. "Either you're here to serve your calling. Or…"

"Or what?"

"Or you're here to serve yourself. What is it, Vee?"

She looked at me for some definite response. I remained silent.

Sophia was thoughtful, as if considering her next line of questioning.

"Vee, do you think of yourself as being spiritual?" she asked, changing tack.

"Yes."

It was the one thing I was most passionate about.

"Ok. Then, are you prepared to put your money where your mouth is?"

I rolled my head from side to side. "Like how?"

"By putting your complete faith in God."

I sighed. So easy to say, so hard to do.

"I'm not sure," I replied, honestly.

"After everything you've experienced this past year, don't you believe God, life, or something higher is guiding you? That life knows the way? That life has a plan?"

"I do."

Those two words came instinctively. Not convincingly.

"Then if you believe, *really believe*. Stop being half in half out," she said, banging her fist on the coffee table.

It startled me.

"But how?" I asked, as if it was a bridge too far.

"Embrace the uncertainty that lies ahead. Let go of the outcome. Have faith that life will point the way. That God will show you what you're here to do."

"Hmmm."

I was besieged by doubts; my mind a wavering mess.

Sophia sighed. "Just admit it, Vee."

"Admit what?"

"You're scared."

"*Scared?* Of what?"

My face hardened.

"You're scared to take the plunge. Scared to make your pledge. You're afraid of what it would mean. Afraid of the upheaval it would cause."

She was right, but I was unwilling to admit it.

"You like being you," she continued. "You like the way you look. You like the way you are and all the attention you get. You're not willing to give all that up. Just admit it."

I shook my head. She was really pressing my buttons. Really pissing me off.

"That's why you don't know your calling. You're not ready for it yet."

I glared back at her.

"I know you think I'm picking away at you," she added.

"No, I don't," I snapped back, lying of course.

"Oh, come on, Vee! Admit it. I know these things I say annoy you. But I'm prepared to take that risk because I need you to understand something."

"What?" I huffed.

"That your ego is *still* pulling the strings. Still calling all the shots. It's still wrapped up in itself and the attention and adulation it craves. Just admit it."

I remained silent, outwardly refusing to admit anything. Inwardly knowing it was the truth.

"Look, can I make a simple, humble suggestion that might unlock something for you?"

I nodded back, hoping she might reveal some life-changing advice.

"I want you to do something."

"Do what?"

"Help others in whatever way you can," she said.

Is that it?

I felt underwhelmed. I found nothing enticing in her suggestion.

"Make a difference somewhere, to someone," she continued. "But seek no recognition for yourself."

"I don't understand."

"Tell no one of your good deeds," she said, spelling it out.

What?

Where was the thrill in that? Recognition, attention, admiring glances, respect and praise were the delicacies my ego fed upon.

Just then, we were interrupted. The barista on duty came and stood by our table.

"Sorry," he said, holding his hands up. "I know you're engrossed in conversation. But can I get you anything?"

I declined but Sophia asked for some tap water.

"Coming right up," he smiled.

He returned moments later with two cups of water. He placed one cup carefully in front of Sophia.

"Just thought you might want one too," he then said, placing the other in front of me.

I smiled back at him, appreciatively. I was actually feeling quite parched, now the water was there in front of me.

"He has a lovely way about him," Sophia said, as the barista walked away. "The way he is, is what *the being in the doing* is all about."

"How?" I asked, sipping the cold water the barista had kindly provided.

She'd mentioned something along those lines before.

"Spirituality is about expressing who you are, through what you do. All he did was bring you water. But he did it with a real touch of consideration. He was *being* kind whilst *doing* his job."

I shrugged, like it was no big deal.

Sophia responded with a quote by Martin Luther King. "If it falls to your lot to be a street sweeper, sweep streets like Michelangelo painted pictures, sweep streets like Beethoven composed music … Sweep streets like Shakespeare wrote poetry. Sweep streets so well that all the hosts of heaven and earth will have to pause and say: Here lived a great street sweeper who swept his job well."

"Nice quote."

She nodded. "Except most people never think about *the way* they do what they do. Only *what* they do. You're like that."

"Am I?"

She nodded. "You're still obsessed by what you *do* and the status it implies. Admit it."

I shrugged.

"Spirituality is not about success or glory in the eyes of others, Vee. It's a state of *being*. A way of life. An authentic expression of who you really are."

My eyebrows knotted together. I scratched the back of my neck. "I'm confused. You talk a lot about who I *really* am. So, who am I then, really?"

"Don't you see? This has been your central quest this past year – a voyage of self-discovery to work out who you are."

"I don't see how."

"You wouldn't. You've been too caught up in the journey. Too caught up in yourself. But you have been shown the truth of what your ego is like."

I scoffed. "Yeah, and it's not very flattering."

"But," Sophia said, one hand in the air, halting that discouraging thought of mine. "You've also been given glimpses of who you are under the mask of your persona. Who you *really* are, beyond your ego."

I looked back at her, confused. "I don't get it. So, who am I then? *Really?*"

This was the burning question on my mind. The one I wanted the answer to the most.

62

The bridge

"Your soul."

"My soul?"

Sophia nodded. "That's who you really are."

"But what is the soul?" I asked.

"Do you really want to know?"

"Yes."

"Then go and help those in real need. Those who have lost their way. The prostitutes, drug addicts or alcoholics of this world. The homeless, the poor, the destitute."

Sophia's words came across as a direct challenge. Heavy going. Burdensome. Unappealing. I wasn't sure if I was up to the task.

"But seek no recognition for any help you give," Sophia continued. "Do it simply because it is needed. Do it and tell no one about it. That's when you'll know."

"Know what?"

"That your soul is nothing but pure love – a love that is limitless, wise, powerful, selfless, relentless."

Sophia looked at me searchingly as I reflected on her words.

"I'm not sure if I'm cut out for the spiritual path," I said, feeling daunted.

Sophia reached across and placed her hand on my arm. "Vee, trust me. You have all the qualities for the path. You have all the gifts a light worker needs. More than most."

I shook my head.

"I'm not sure I am that light worker you think I am."

Sophia smiled, reassuringly. "I don't think it. I know it. But you don't see it. Not yet. But have faith. God has a wonderful plan for your life, beyond anything you can imagine."

Sounds too good to be true.

"But what is that plan?" I sighed. "Why don't I know my purpose?"

It felt like we were going around in circles.

"Because, at the moment, you talk about finding *your* calling. Knowing *your* purpose. It's all about *you*. Not about the people you're here to help."

A sigh of frustration escaped my lips. It didn't stop Sophia from drilling home her point.

"You haven't felt that *real love* yet in your heart, when you feel deeply moved by the suffering of others. When you feel compelled to help those in need."

She was right, I hadn't. The painful plight of others did touch my heart but I hadn't yet felt that all-encompassing love of which she spoke.

She gave me a moment of silent reflection before continuing.

"If only you could see it, Vee, you are a divine being, full of love and light. That's who you really are. Who we all are. But you don't know this yet. You haven't experienced this divinity – this love – within you, other than as a brief glimpse from time to time. If you had, it would give you the unshakeable belief and faith you need to walk the spiritual path with confidence."

My head dropped. My heart sank. We both knew we had come to the core of my problem. The crux of my issues.

I wanted to walk the spiritual path. But I lacked the faith and courage needed.

Sophia paused to rest. She had clearly expended a great deal of energy conveying her thoughts.

She took a couple of sips of water and sighed. The kind of sigh we make after a hard day's graft, when we're not quite sure how much progress we've made despite all the work we've put in.

"Vee, can I make a heartfelt plea?"

I nodded back.

"Just walk across to the other side of the bridge," she implored, bringing the palms of her hands together.

"What bridge?"

"The bridge to your spiritual self. To the spiritual life. At the moment, you're stuck halfway. In the wilderness. Between your ego on one side and your soul on the other."

I don't know why or what it was that Sophia had said, but tears began to stream down my face. My head dropped. A deep sadness descended on my heart.

Sophia reached across and placed her hand on mine.

"Vee, think about it. You have lived a privileged existence. You have been blessed with intelligence, looks, money and so much more. But you must recognise from these tears you're shedding, that you're *still* unhappy. That something is still missing. That, there is something more you're still searching for."

"Yes, I know. But am I *ever* going to find it?" I asked, looking away from her as I battled through the tears.

"Yes. One day you will."

"But *when*?"

Sophia shrugged. "I don't know, Vee. We've reached this point many times before. In many of your past lives."

"And?"

"You've always given in to your ego. Unfortunately, you've always then paid the price."

I just sat there. Thoughtful. Tearful. Emotional.

"And what about this life?" I asked, concerned. "Will my ego ruin me again?"

"Only you can decide that."

I covered my face with both hands. I wanted to hide away my pain. My vulnerability. I didn't want Sophia to see more of my tears. But she gently pulled away my hands. I noticed she had tears in her eyes too.

"I think the time has come," she said, with tenderness. "For you to make your call."

I looked at her questioningly.

What she said next, upset me deeply.

"Vee, this might be the last time we meet."

I looked at her more lost than before. It felt like someone had just pulled my lifeline away. I'd already lost grandad, Katie and Rachel. Was I now going to lose Sophia too?

"Why?" I asked.

More tears streamed down my face.

"You need to be given time and space now."

"For what?"

"You must decide of your own free will, what you're going to do, with all the guidance you have been given."

"So that's it then? It all just ends here?"

I didn't mean to sound petulant. I was just hurting.

"It depends on what call you make. I'm just obeying a spiritual law. Before more knowledge can be shared, a student must first act on the knowledge that has been given."

"How can you be my spiritual teacher, if you're just going to leave me when I need you most?"

Sophia looked surprised by my comment. "Vee, *I'm* not your spiritual teacher. I hope one day you'll meet the person who is."

I wondered who she was referring to.

"But have faith," she continued. "That you have the strength within to make your call."

"I don't get it. What call are you asking me to make? What are you telling me to do?"

"I'm not telling you to do anything. I just feel the time has come for *you* to decide. Are you going to walk to the other side of the bridge or not?"

I sat there thoughtfully.

Sophia began to pack up her things. I hadn't realised how long we'd been sat there for.

"I'm going away for a few months," she said. "You won't be able to reach me whilst I'm away. I'm not sure what will happen when I'm back – whether we will meet again. But I hope you find the courage to make your call. I hope the choice you make brings you the happiness you seek."

We both stood up. We both had tears in our eyes. We hugged. Sophia left.

I was alone.

63

What if?

One month went by.

Not much happened. Work was quiet which gave me time to think.

I missed grandad. I missed our conversations. I wish now I'd spent more time with him when he was alive.

I missed Sophia. She had been a stalwart of support this past year. Always there in those critical moments when I needed her most. But now she'd gone. I wasn't sure if I'd ever see her again.

I still hadn't received a text from Katie. But two arrived from Rachel. The first said she was really sorry. The second, that she was back in London for a few days and wanted to know if we could '*hook up*'. I hated that term even more. I ignored both her messages. But it killed me. Part of me desperately wanted to go back there. Part of me said, *no way.*

In any case, I wasn't in the mood. For anything. The sadness that had descended when Sophia and I'd parted, remained. It cast a gloomy shadow on everything. Nothing felt good to do. Nothing had any joy. Everything felt flat. Pointless.

I felt hollow within.

No one really noticed this change in my bearing, bar the odd comment here or there. Sebastian told me I looked tired and needed a holiday. Trev told me I wasn't my usual self because I felt no inclination to "talk to the ladies" on nights out that I'd reluctantly been dragged along to.

I was just going through the motions, with everyone and everything.

Even Ken and Manny from accounts failed to get a rise out of me when they mocked me with their questions. They'd formed a bit of a double act.

"What's your secret to success again, Vee?" Ken would ask. "Oh yeah, I remember: got to be in the right place at the right time, boys."

"Was Dylan Johnson in the right place at the right time?" Manny would then say.

If it wasn't that, they'd mock me in some other way.

"Where's the 911?" Ken would ask.

"How's Rachel Hanson?" Manny would follow up.

You would think I would have it within me to tell them to fuck off. Or come up with some other charismatic riposte. But I just smiled back.

Grin and bear it, Vee.

Besides, what could I tell them? The truth was it felt like I'd never even met Rachel, or hired that Porsche. Life now was just a humdrum existence.

The only real stir of emotion I felt was when I saw Katie; with Rishi, her dull legal accomplice. They were ahead of me in a queue inside some bespoke sandwich bar in Soho; standing in close proximity to each other.

God, I really wanted to talk to Katie. Hear her voice again. But I couldn't bear to suffer Rishi's condescending smugness. Or the possible look of disgust that might show on Katie's face when she saw me.

So, I hid behind the person in front of me in the queue as they walked by; Katie's arm brushing mine.

So near. So far.

They were laughing and joking; sharing a moment of frivolous happiness that seemed inaccessible to me.

Life to me just felt arid. I felt a step removed from everything happening around me. I felt disconnected. Empty. Floaty. Like a boat cut adrift in the ocean. Rudderless.

I was not my regular outgoing self – actively seeking connection with or validation from the world around me. I felt no desire to talk to others, let alone impress them. I sought no attention in any way. I was getting none of my usual egotistical fixes.

My spiritual life too was languishing. I was not meditating, reflecting or reading. I was stuck. I just kept thinking about what Sophia had said. About walking across to the other side of the bridge. About doing some good in the world. But not for any recognition it might bring. If I could do that, I'd feel that divine overflowing love within me; according to her.

But within me, I felt nothing. Outside, nothing had any feeling. I was halfway across the bridge, in the wilderness.

In that insipid middle ground between two very different worlds.

I had three choices.

One: stay where I was.

Two: walk back to the side of my ego and its selfish pursuit of attention and admiration – the path of self-aggrandisement.

Three: walk the other way and live more selflessly for others – the path of spirituality.

I didn't want to walk back. I certainly didn't want to remain lost here in the wilderness. But I didn't have the courage to walk forward either.

What if, I wrote in my journal:

What if I make my pledge to God to help others but I don't enjoy it?

What if I make my pledge and I can't uphold it?

What if I end up living a life I don't want?

What if I change unrecognisably?

What if others don't like the new me?

What if I change but it's not for the best?

What if I go backwards?

What if I follow my calling but waste my potential?

At least with my ego, it was the proverbial case of 'better the devil you know'. Committing to the spiritual path felt uncertain. The likelihood of what might happen if I pledged myself to God was unclear. Surrendering myself to life felt too capricious. I couldn't just let go of the outcome like Sophia had suggested.

How could I?

I needed to retain control. Shape the direction of my life.

Sophia was different to me. She had conviction in the path. She believed in what she was doing. She had a clear sense of who she was, what she was about and what she was here to do.

I envied her. I missed her. I wanted us to talk again. The thought of never seeing her again saddened me. I reflected again on her advice:

"Help someone but tell no one about it."

I had the power to do that. But where to begin? Did I even want to? Could I spend a whole lifetime doing good for others but never seeking recognition for myself? Could I really live a quiet life of altruism and silent service?

My ego hated the idea: *you're not a monk, Vee.*

If I did anything good, my ego wanted the world to know about it. It wanted its pat on the back – its moment in the sun. That's why it didn't want me to cross to the other side of the bridge. It did its best to convince me that the spiritual path was unappealing, unexciting, unfulfilling.

But one day, late that month, a compelling thought popped inside my head: what was the harm in trying out Sophia's suggestion?

But what about that pledge? My ego hit back.

It sounded eternally binding, limiting and restrictive.

That's when I realised how ridiculous I was being. And how fear had me in its grip. Sophia was right. *I was scared.* Scared of what might happen if I walked down this path. Scared of all the changes and upheaval it would bring.

But I reasoned something out that my ego could not contend with. Surely, I would only continue walking down the spiritual path if it was fulfilling.

There was no arguing with that.

To add extra philosophical weight to the argument, I remembered something grandad had said in the past. Something I'd long since forgotten:

> *"There is no obligation on the spiritual path.*
> *Do what feels good in your own heart.*
> *Do what feels right in your own soul."*

I looked up to heaven. "*That's* what I'm going to do, Papa."

64

Three opportunities

I set forth on a new path.

Help others but tell no one about it.

Sophia was clear. This was what was needed. Three opportunities came my way to do just that. Three opportunities, which changed my life.

The first opportunity was simple enough. I was walking through Oxford Street when I noticed a middle-aged woman selling *The Big Issue*. She was being universally ignored.

"Get your Big Issue," she said feebly a couple of times.

Her attempt to extract attention and a little sympathy from each passer-by sounded like a cry for help. But no one batted an eyelid. My heart melted. I walked over to her.

"I'll take one," I said.

She looked up at me like I was some kind of angel, even though the magazine cost no more than £1.50 back then.

"Thank you," she said meekly, handing me a copy. "It's kind of you to buy one."

I placed a £10 note in her hands. She started rummaging through her pockets to find the right change.

"Keep the note," I said.

She looked back up at me. I thought she was going to cry. I thought I was going to cry!

"God bless you," she said, holding her hands up to me in prayer. "You don't know how much this means to me."

I smiled and walked away before compassionate tears fell from my eyes. I felt like I'd done something amazing. Perhaps it was that phenomenon known colloquially in scientific circles as the 'helper's high' – happy hormones released in the brain, after performing an act of kindness; holding the door open for someone, paying someone a genuine compliment or giving money or time to someone who really needs it.

But this felt more significant somehow.

I know it was only a £10 note. A sum I could easily afford to give away. But it was something I'd never done before. It felt heart-warming to do. That warmth opening my heart with more feeling. Dare I say it, more love.

Immediately, I felt like telling someone about my good deed. I was surprised by how quickly my ego craved acknowledgement. How rapidly the need for recognition came to the fore.

But I resisted the urge. I told no one. Keeping it to myself I realised how pure an act of goodness could feel in the heart when it had no tinge of ego whatsoever.

A door to a new way of life was opening within.

The second opportunity, inspired by the first, came just a week later – a homeless man I regularly walked past on the way to work. He was always sat in the same spot, just outside Tottenham Court Road station. Whenever I had some loose change I always gave it to him. But that day when I was walking towards him, I decided to do something I hadn't done before. Something my heart suggested.

Talk to him, it said.

"Good morning."

He slowly lifted his head and looked up at me.

"Morning," he replied, groggily.

"How are you?"

Immediately, I felt dumb for asking the question, given his circumstances.

"I'm ok, thank you for asking."

"Can I get you anything?" I offered. "Like breakfast or something?"

"No, I'll... be ok," he said, after a moment's hesitation.

"Ok."

I turned to walk away, but my heart wouldn't let me go.

"Are you sure I can't get you something?"

He thought again. "Actually, anything warm to eat would be nice."

I smiled. My heart leapt into action. "You got it. I'll be back in a sec."

That's how Bruce and I started talking.

Over the next month, we chatted for a few minutes each day. I got to know more about him. How he *did* have a home. But how his mum got remarried. How he fell out with his violent new stepdad. How he left home in tears and had nowhere to go. How he ended up on the streets and had been there ever since.

His story pained me. I wished there was something more I could do. Whenever I got the chance, I gave him a little extra money and a little more of my time.

Then one morning, when I walked up to him, he handed me a letter.

"Promise you won't open it until you get to work," he said.

I promised.

"Thank you," he then said. "For everything."

There was something final about the way he said these words. Like we were never going to see each other again. On the walk to work, I became worried. A horrible thought crossed my mind:

Is Bruce thinking about killing himself?

I quickened my pace. When I got to the office I rushed to my desk and ripped open the letter. This is what it said:

Dear Vee,

You may not see me again after today which is why I wanted to say thank you for everything you have done.

Whilst others have made me feel like a no one, you have made me feel like someone.

Because of our conversations, I've enrolled on a college course to study engineering and I've found a hostel to live in.

It's all down to you. Your kindness has changed my life.

Your friend,

Bruce :)

Tears came to my eyes as I looked down at the letter. I couldn't believe how much difference my conversations with Bruce had made.

What if I'd never spoken to him? What would have become of Bruce then?

As I sat there, letter in hand, contemplating these thoughts, Sonia came over to my desk.

"What's that you've got there?" she asked, pointing to the letter.

I was really tempted to tell her. I knew Bruce's letter would reflect well on me. But again, I said nothing of the good thing I'd done. Again, the pure feeling of love grew stronger in my heart.

I felt more fulfilled than I'd ever felt before.

The door within to a more uplifting way of life opened a little wider.

The third opportunity came the next month.

I was out running in Hampstead Heath. It was a wet day. Persistent light rain fell from the sky above.

I took in the sights and sounds as I jogged through the park. A couple speed-walking up ahead, furiously trying to out-waddle each other. A mother motivating her young boy to sprint up a grassy slope in his football boots.

"Nothing like hill runs," she said, positively, as I glided by.

Close by, a group of schoolboys boisterously slid down the grass bank the other way on muddy knees. They got louder and more animated as a group of schoolgirls passed by.

Braggadocios.

All the boys shouted for attention, hoping to be noticed like proverbial strutting peacocks shaking their tail feathers.

I smiled to myself at this noisy display of youthful bravado. Up until then, I too had been peacocking my way through much of my life.

As I was about to pick up the pace, I jogged past someone I knew. It was Ruchi, one of Katie's closest friends. I hadn't seen her for months.

She didn't see me go by. She was sat on a park bench, head down, knees pressed together with her hands wedged in between. I'd only caught a glimpse of her face but I was sure she was crying. I ran on for a few seconds but then stopped.

If she was upset, I couldn't just leave her there, all alone. From the first time we'd met, we'd hit it off. She felt like family.

But then, I thought about Katie. She'd probably told Ruchi about the whole Rachel fiasco. I figured Ruchi, being the loyal friend she was, probably wouldn't want to talk to me.

Sod it, I thought.

I was going to see if she was ok.

My heart insisted on it.

I'm glad I did. The consequences of not stopping could have been very distressing.

"Hi, Ruchi."

She didn't look up from the bench.

I sat down next to her and lightly tapped her arm. "Ruchi, are you ok?"

She turned towards me and slowly shook her head. Tears were streaming down her face. Her eyes, bloodshot.

"Ruchi, talk to me. What's happened?"

She looked back at me, motionless. "I just want to end it. I just want all the pain to stop."

"Has someone hurt you?" I asked, feeling her distress.

She said nothing. She stared back down at the ground.

"Ruchi?"

"I just feel like getting into my car and driving it straight into a tree," she said, clenching her fists.

I couldn't believe what I was hearing. Ruchi was always so fun-loving and gregarious.

"Do you want me to call someone?" I asked.

She shook her head and wiped away her tears with the sleeve of her coat.

We both sat there in silence. Ruchi, unwilling to talk, me, not knowing what to say.

A minute went by.

"Vee, why is God punishing me?" she asked.

More tears ran down her cheeks.

"God would never punish you."

"How do you know?"

"Everything I know in my heart tells me God is love and love would never seek to punish anyone."

"Then why am I in so much pain?" she cried out in anguish.

She began hitting herself with her clenched fists.

As gently as I could, I gripped both her arms to stop her from hurting herself.

Immediately, she relented and sat there motionless once again.

I waited again for her to speak, sensing this was the best way to help.

Another long pause followed.

"I've always been a doormat, that's my problem. That's why he treats me the way he does."

"Who?" I asked, softly.

"My boyfriend."

Everything became clear from here.

Ruchi opened up. She told me how he mistreated her, belittled her and got aggressive with her.

I felt angry but tried not to show it. I hated the thought of anyone being hurt, bullied or taken advantage of.

I'd only met her boyfriend once. *Controlling.* That's the impression I walked away with.

"I don't mean to interfere but why are you still with him, Ruchi?"

She shrugged her shoulders. "Maybe I was bad in a past life and I'm getting punished for it now. Maybe I deserve it."

I couldn't believe what I was hearing.

"God would *never* punish you," I said, with as much certainty as I could convey.

She looked across at me. "Do you really think so, Vee?"

I nodded. "But sometimes life does test us. Hard."

Just then, I thought of something.

"Can I share some words with you that have really helped me?"

She nodded.

"I turned to God when my foundations were shaking," I said, "only to realise it was God who was shaking them."

"Whose words are they?"

"An author. Charles West, I think."

"But why would God do that?" she asked, her eyes yearning for an explanation.

"So we realise we are stronger than we know. We have more courage than we think, Ruchi. We are not powerless like we sometimes lead ourselves to believe."

She looked back at me with more hope in her eyes.

"And you have so many people around you who will be your strength until you find your own," I said, putting my arm around her. "I'll be right here if you ever need me."

She reached out for my hand and gently squeezed it. "Thank you, Vee."

That night before I went to sleep, I thought back to my conversation with Ruchi.

What if I hadn't stopped? What if I hadn't seen her?

I shuddered at the thought.

I put my hands together in prayer and closed my eyes.

"God, I'm ready to make my pledge."

65

Only the beginning

I called but she didn't answer.

I left a voicemail. I told her it was important. But I said nothing more. I wanted to tell Sophia in person about the pledge I'd made, the night before.

All week I waited for a reply. But nothing came. I did, however, receive a text from Katie:

```
Thank you for speaking to Ruchi. She said it really
helped.
```

The text was short. To the point. I was relieved Ruchi was ok. I really was worried about her. I was glad too that Katie had got in touch. Maybe we could still be friends?

Over the next couple of weeks, I caught up with Ruchi a few times, just to check in with her. Make sure she was ok. Each time we met she was faring a little better. And she'd set a few things straight with her boyfriend too.

"He can take it or leave it," she said, defiantly.

I smiled at her new-found courage. "Good on you, Ruchi."

She then mentioned Katie.

"Have you spoken to her?"

I shook my head.

Ruchi sighed. "You broke her heart, Vee."

I held my hands out. "I know this is no kind of defence, but we had agreed it was nothing serious between us."

Ruchi shook her head. "You didn't break her heart in *that* way, Vee."

"How then?"

"She *believed* in you, as a person. In your integrity. Your kindness. Your goodness. But you let her down."

I looked back at Ruchi with surprise.

"All her life that poor girl has just been pushed aside, like her feelings don't matter. Like she doesn't matter."

"I feel terrible."

"She thought you were different. You made her feel different, Vee. You restored her self-worth until –"

My head dropped. My heart sank even lower. I felt tears welling up in my eyes.

"Are you crying?" Ruchi asked, surprised.

"Just something in my eye," I lied.

Ruchi's words had evoked tears. I felt like my compassion setting had been turned up to maximum. I felt pain at the pain I'd caused – from insensitively breaking Katie's heart.

As tears gathered in my eyes, they reminded me of grandad's tears. The ones that flowed freely whenever he told or heard a story that played on his heartstrings. I missed him so much.

"I never meant to hurt her," I said, picking up a napkin and wiping away my tears.

Ruchi looked back at me as if to say: *but you did.*

I looked back at her as if to say: *I know.*

I never once mentioned it to Ruchi, but I hoped an opportunity might arise to show Katie I was back to being *me* again. Maybe, a better me. If we could just have a heart-to-heart one day. Or failing that a quick tête-à-tête. I wanted to tell her: I knew I acted selfishly. I got caught up in myself. I lost sight of what was important.

But I knew I had to take things slow. Regaining Katie's trust would take time.

Another week passed by.

Still, I heard nothing from Sophia. Were we never destined to see each other again? The possibility saddened me. But it did not stop me from upholding my pledge: I promised to help those in need. Uplift those who came my way.

I made this promise to God. I made this commitment to life.

In ways small, subtle and discrete, I set about my work. Whether it was a friendly word, a helping hand or a listening ear, I offered them without reservation.

As best as I could, I tried to uplift those who felt down, give strength to those who felt weak, give guidance to those who felt lost. Don't get me wrong. I was no Mother Teresa. But I was starting to care more for others. Take a greater interest in others. Do more for others. Before, all I really thought about was myself. My needs. My wants. My desires. Now, I began thinking more of others and their needs. Their happiness.

This change imbued my life with more meaning. My pledge gave me purpose. I had no idea where it might lead. But living this way was its own reward. I felt more energised. More alive. More fulfilled. The 'helper's high' growing in intensity each day.

Sophia's *being in the doing* philosophy also started to make more sense.

She'd said:

It's *who you are* that matters. Not what you do.

For so long, it was what I did that dominated my thoughts; doing things to gain attention, admiration, recognition.

But now, my mind was in a different space. One question dominated my thoughts:

Who do I choose to be, right here, right now?

As best I could, I chose to be whatever felt good or right in my own soul; something intrinsically inspiring. Uplifting.

This is what shaped my actions. Not any recognition I might get. Not any praise I might receive. I found the need for external recognition simply fell away, whenever I focused on who *I* inwardly chose to be.

A whole month passed by.

Still no news from Sophia. But something else significant occurred. I hadn't had a lucid dream for a while. Then, two came along together in one night. Both felt symbolic.

In the first dream:

I was being projected fast across the surface of the earth. I was flying at tremendous speed. Suddenly, I arrived. I was in a green meadow. All looked tranquil but I heard a tremendous roar behind me. I turned around. Standing there was a hideous-looking beast. Half horse half dragon. Our eyes met. It moved menacingly towards me, hissing, sneering and growling.

I felt afraid. I looked for a means of escape but there was nowhere to go. Suddenly, the beast lunged towards me, violently. Evading it, I jumped out of the way. Grabbing hold of its long muscular neck, I spun myself around and landed on its back.

It jerked violently this way and that. I hung on for dear life. But no matter how hard it tried, the beast couldn't throw me off.

I sensed I was winning the battle. The creature was beginning to tire. It stopped struggling against my will. Finally, it relented. Obeying my silent command, it kneeled down on the ground. I was now in complete control.

I leaned in closer towards the creature's face, which was now transformed, looking magnificent and regal.

"I can make you fly," I whispered in its ear.

Instantly we took off. *Together*. Flying high in the sky, no journey felt too long to attempt. No distance, too great to cover. No dream, too big to manifest.

In the second dream:

I was travelling in a car with a group of people I knew. Across a field, to our left, we all saw a luminous, majestic figure in the distance. A splendid Magus dressed in white robes. The softest breeze gently ruffled his flowing white hair and beard.

We pulled up at the roadside. The Magus spoke words that I now do not remember. But instantly, every one of us *recognised* the moment. We had all seen this moment before. A déjà vu. Or perhaps a premonition?

We jumped out of the car and ran towards him like excited children. It felt like a race. I realised I could fly and be the first to reach him.

But I didn't.

I hung back and was the last to arrive.

When we embraced, the Magus congratulated me. "You were right to do what you did. Only ever use your powers when it is absolutely necessary."

He then gave me a confirmation that I was "non-negotiable" now. I felt like crying with joy knowing that I had been accepted and confirmed, whatever that meant.

Finally.

Sophia got in touch. It had been four months since we'd parted company. When we met again, she immediately sensed a change in me.

"Your voice has a completely new tone to it," she said, with a smile. "It's nice."

"Thank you."

"And your energy is different too."

"How?" I asked.

"It's more whole, grounded, complete. Like a strong heartbeat."

"I do feel different."

Sophia nodded. "So, what changed?"

I smiled. "I made my pledge."

Sophia smiled back. "I sensed that. What convinced you to walk to the other side of the bridge?"

I told her about the three opportunities that had come my way. How I'd helped The Big Issue woman, Bruce and Ruchi.

Sophia looked emotional. "So, do you believe me now?"

I cocked my head to one side. "About?"

"That you *are* a light worker."

"Maybe," I replied, reflecting back on how I'd changed.

"I'll take a *maybe*," Sophia said, clenching her fists in victory. "You were dead set against the suggestion, at first. But I was the same."

"Really?" I asked, surprised.

Sophia seemed every inch the light worker.

Sophia nodded. "It took time to tame my ego. I was a little wilder than you."

My eyes widened. "I find that hard to believe."

"It's true," she said, with a tight-lipped smile.

"Like how?"

I wondered what her backstory might be.

"A story for another day," Sophia replied.

I sensed that day was unlikely to come. I hardly knew anything of her past. Just little fragments picked up here and there:

A difficult upbringing. Hurt by those close to her. An addiction of some sort. Drugs? Or was it alcohol? Or was there even an addiction at all?

I can't be sure now. I never recorded anything personal about her in my journal – just in case it ever got into the wrong hands.

But I had no doubt. She was strong and tough because of the struggles she'd endured. Struggles, it seems, much worse than mine.

"So, what was the turning point for you?" I asked, hoping to gain a glimpse into her past.

She was about to say something but then hesitated.

"Let's just say, I too like you, took a good hard look in the mirror. I too, walked to the other side of the bridge and made my pledge to God. I became a better person for it. I found a level of happiness I never thought possible."

"It seems like being good is its own reward," I remarked.

I really believed that now.

"Yes, Vee," said Sophia, seizing upon what I'd said. "That's what the being in the doing is all about. It's the *joy* of expressing who you are *through* what you do."

"It's ironic," I said, shaking my head.

"What is?"

"All my life, I've felt the pressure to be someone outstanding. To be the best I can be, to impress others. That leading light, who dazzles others. That front runner, who races ahead of others."

"And now?"

"It sounds a bit cliché," I said, biting my lip.

"Go on," Sophia encouraged.

"Well, now I want to be the best I can be…to help others. To make a difference in this world."

"It's not cliché at all. These thoughts are from the heart, Vee."

I smiled. "I *think* I'm finally getting it now."

Sophia smiled too. "Yes. At long last, I think you are, Vee."

We both laughed.

I felt so much better. About everything. There was a new clarity in my thinking.

To be or not to be.

That's what life was about. Maybe it's why this pithy Shakespearean saying had held its own down the ages.

Anyway, I digress. Let me get back to it. Next, I told Sophia about the two dreams.

She listened attentively, as she always did. Never missing a single thing.

"You do realise what these dreams symbolise, Vee?" she remarked when I'd finished.

I shook my head.

"The first dream is symbolic of your battle within. What fought against you like a beast and then became your beautiful companion, was your *ego*. The dream was symbolic of the transformation it and you have undergone."

I leaned back and smiled. "Oh yeah, that makes sense."

It was a beautiful interpretation of the dream.

"And the second?" I asked. "What's your take on that dream?"

"That was a sign of encouragement."

"Encouragement?"

"Yes, that a master may yet take you under his wing. Spiritually, I mean."

"But I don't know a spiritual master."

"You will," she smiled, knowingly. "You have earned that right."

I wondered how and where I might meet this enlightened being; who he or she might be. But I didn't push the matter. It seems I had acquired a little more patience of late. No longer that young man in a hurry.

"I've definitely been on a journey," I said, leaning back in my chair, clasping my hands behind my head.

"You have and you've made tremendous progress. You have really mellowed, Vee. Your ego is no longer calling all the shots."

"Progress, hey?"

Sophia nodded. "And your past conditioning is loosening its hold."

"Really?"

She nodded. "Before, you acted through compulsion. Now, you are choosing who to be. Choosing what to be."

I smiled contentedly. "So, where do I go from here?"

"Keep pushing on fearlessly, Vee. You're charting a new course now. A time of great success awaits you. You deserve it for all the progress you've made."

"Thank you. But why do I sense there's another *but* coming?"

We both laughed.

After all this progress, it seems there were still more warnings for me to heed.

"But," Sophia began, "the journey ahead will also be difficult. Many challenges lie in wait. Your success will arouse much animosity. Those jealous of your achievements will try to trip you up. Those envious of your influence will seek to prize it away. I foresee many wolves in sheep's clothing coming your way. Watch out for them. And watch out for your own ego too. You will *still* be tested."

"*Still?*" I asked.

Sophia nodded.

"Why?"

"To see if you can handle worldly success without compromising who you are. Many temptations will come your way. The path stretching out ahead of you is still beset with many tests and trials. Many times, in many ways, you'll have to courageously decide who you are going to be in the face of these challenges."

I fell silent. But I felt ready too.

"But," smiled Sophia, "the journey will ultimately prove rewarding. You will grow and evolve in many wonderful ways. Everything that has happened this past year is only the beginning."

Only the beginning?

So much had happened since I first walked out on that sales job – that life-changing moment when this story began. I may not have found my calling yet (that's a whole new story) but I was content for now with how far I'd come.

We chatted, laughed and philosophised some more. But then, Sophia needed to go.

I thanked her for *everything* she'd done.

For dispelling my self-absorption. For revealing an inner capacity to love, greater than I ever expected. For revealing a door to inner fulfilment, I didn't even know existed.

I'm sure you don't need me to tell you, but I wasn't the finished article by any stretch of the imagination. Not even close. The next book will testify to that! But I did feel like a new man. I had changed for the better.

Sophia had changed my life.

As she was about to leave, I told her I'd pay it forward. I vowed to help others, the way she'd helped me.

"Do you promise?" she asked, reaching for my hand.

I nodded. "On my life."

She smiled.

We both got to our feet. I tenderly hugged her goodbye. A final gesture to convey the gratitude I felt.

As she walked away, I sat back down and looked around the coffee shop. This bustling hive of activity, which over the past year had vicariously witnessed so much of my journey. Heard so many of my hopes. Listened to so many of my fears.

I leaned back in my chair and sighed, contentedly.

Ahh.

I decided to just hang there for a while. Let everything sink in. Savour the moment, as they say.

But just seconds later, I was disturbed.

"Excuse me," said a woman, I instantly recognised. "But aren't you that guy who dated Rachel Hanson?"

I smiled. "No, I think you're mistaken."

"Are you sure? I saw you across town. I gave you my number. You were with your friend. You were driving a Porsche."

I shook my head. "No, I'm sorry. That wasn't me. That was some other guy."

I picked up my things. Put on my coat. And smiled.

For now, I'd won the battle within.

Acknowledgements

I owe a debt of gratitude to all of you who read through earlier drafts of this book: Andrea, Ayat, Chan, Dom, Ellie, Gurj, Hannah, Harj, Jakobi, Jessy, Jon, Michael, Raji, Raphaela, Sanj, Shanan, Simon, Suki, and Tirath. All the feedback you provided was immensely valuable.

I'd like to thank Hannah, for the wonderful cover illustration. You took the basic concept I had in my mind and worked it up beautifully into something better than I could have imagined.

I am forever grateful to all the mentors that life has kindly sent my way. In very different ways, you all constantly push me to be the best I can be. I hope the wisdom you have collectively provided shines through in this book and in all the work I undertake.

Finally, a massive thank you to my family for your unfailing support and constant encouragement; and specifically, to Harj and Dhyan, for your patience during the three and half years it took to write this book. I appreciate you all, deeply.